BLOOD MOON

A ROWAN GANT INVESTIGATION

An Occult/Paranormal Thriller

By

M. R. SELLARS

E.M.A. Mysteries

BLOOD MOON: A Rowan Gant Investigation

An E.M.A. Mysteries Book
E.M.A. Mysteries is an imprint of WillowTree Press

PRINTING HISTORY
First Printing - Trade Paper Edition / October 2008

For information, contact WillowTree Press on the World Wide Web: http://www.willowtreepress.com

ISBN 13: 978-0-9794533-3-5

Cover Design Copyright © 2013 – On The Edge Graphics

10   9   8   7   6   5   4   3   2

ACKNOWLEDGEMENTS

I would be sorely remiss if I didn't take a moment to thank at least a few of the individuals who were there to act as my sounding boards and as my moral support staff throughout the creation of this novel—

Sergeant Scott Ruddle, Metropolitan Saint Louis PD without whom Detective Benjamin Storm would be just another one dimensional pseudo-cop. Jacquelyn Busch Hunt, Attorney, for the legal input. Roxanne and Sharon for reading, re-reading, and then reading some more…

As the Rowan Gant series has been ongoing for more than a dozen years, the list of folks to whom I owe thanks has grown, with specific mentions for specific novels along the way. Given reprintings and revisions, if I were to include them all, the list would take up more pages than the novel itself. Therefore, in the interest of brevity—

The Usual Suspects

As for additional suspects and persons of interest…

The Breckenridge Demo Crew
Lolly and Joyce

No line bifocals, Vienna sausages™, Ramen noodles, electric pencil sharpeners, three ring binders, Mister Crane, pushpins, color coded paperclips, swizzle sticks, tape guns, Drumsticks™ (the ice cream kind—not that there is anything wrong with the chicken/turkey kind), vegetable juice cocktail, and woven wheat crackers. Oh, and also chainsaws, beer, and liniment—in that order…

As well as countless others…

And, as always, coffee…

For Denessa Smith.
I am a better person for
having known you…

The sun shall be turned into darkness, and *the moon into blood*, before the great and terrible day of the Lord come...

Joel 2:31
Holy Bible, KJV

Friday, December 16
12:53 A.M.
University Hospital
Saint Louis, Missouri

CHAPTER 1

*...THE MUFFLED REPORT OF SOMETHING THAT SOUNDED
far too much like gunshots popped loudly from the speaker of the radio
and was followed immediately by panicked screaming.*

*"Shots fired!" Agent Book's voice issued between tinny burps of
static. His distressed tone was underscored by the chaotic noise
coming from the frightened crowd.*

"Everybody move!" another voice ordered. "Now!"

*Seconds later Book's words were again hemorrhaging from the
speaker, devoid of all composure, "SHOTS FIRED! MANDALAY'S
HIT! OFFICER DOWN! OFFICER DOWN!"*

*All we could do was sit there, horrified, and listen to the distant
scene unfold. They were inside, and we were out here. Deep in my gut I
had known something would go wrong with this operation, I just
hadn't expected it to be this.*

*I glanced over at my friend, Detective Benjamin Storm. If
adrenalin hadn't been dumping into his system before this point, it
definitely was now. He came fully upright in his seat as the frantic
chatter continued to burst from the radio.*

*The device hissed for a second, then we heard Agent Book exclaim,
"JESUS CHRIST... JESUS CHRIST... ONE GOT PAST HER VEST!
SHE'S BLEEDING BAD! WE NEED PARAMEDICS RIGHT NOW!"*

I couldn't keep the horrible soundtrack from screeching through
my head. The nightmare ran in an endless loop, as clear and terrifying
as when I had originally heard it a few short hours ago. I could only
assume my subconscious was forcing me to relive the event as a by-
product of the fear that was now boring a hole in my chest; or maybe it
was the guilt that was twisting my gut into a hard knot. The way I felt,
I was willing to lay odds both of them were to blame.

However, if forced to pick one over the other I would say the guilt
was probably in the lead. Primarily because it wasn't just the ordinary
remorse one feels over being unscathed when someone else is injured.
No, this was much worse. It was the sickening sort of transgression
that came from being relieved over another's misfortune.

Special Agent Constance Mandalay was a dear friend, and I
certainly had not wished for this to happen. Not to anyone, but

especially not to her of all people. What I wanted right now was for my friend to be okay—to come out of this grinning and wondering "why all the fuss." But, in the same moment, a large part of me was grateful that it was her who was now on the verge of death, and that was the source of my guilt. I didn't want Constance to die, but if someone had to I was relieved that it was she—because the most likely alternative candidate was patently unthinkable for me.

The reason it was so inconceivable in my mind was because my wife had been the intended target. Moreover, had Felicity in all her stubbornness been allowed the choice, she actually would have been in the line of fire rather than safely distant from the scene. But, to my relief, real life bears little resemblance to melodramatic television, and the FBI wasn't about to purposely place a civilian in harm's way. Instead, Constance had taken her place. Risky as even that was, it seemed the only chance at stopping a serial killer who had escalated, was quickly decompensating, and had now set her sights on my wife and me.

Of course, before everything was over, Felicity made that step across the boundary of good sense anyway, but I couldn't really blame her. She wasn't exactly herself when it happened.

Still, when all was said and done, my wife was safe, Constance was on an operating table, and the killer had been stopped. But, her capture had come at a steep and still not fully determined cost.

We'd been told the wounded federal agent had gone into cardiac arrest during the ambulance ride, but they had managed to stabilize her quickly. All we had heard since was that she had lost a lot of blood and that she was still in surgery. The phrase "touch and go" and the word "critical" had been stressed, but other than that, nobody was saying much of anything else.

Nobody, that is, except the disembodied voices in my head.

"Book! What is your exact location?!"

"Just outside the forest exhibit! Right before the path splits! Hurry!"

"Found the gun," Agent Frye's voice blipped over the air. *"But no shooter. The area is clear. She must have dispersed with the crowd."*

"Washburn, cover southeast," a voice ordered. *"If she didn't go past Book and Frye, then she has to be heading that way. I'm on the main path coming in toward you."*

"Acknowledged."

"We're locking down the park," another voice added. "SWAT will be here in two."

The device continued to burp and hiss with various voices for a moment, all of them reporting that there was no sign of Annalise Devereaux, the serial killer at the center of this evil. There was a quick burst of silence, then one of the agents came across the speaker, "I've got something. Red wig in a trashcan outside the restrooms near the stuffed animal workshop... Be advised the subject may have changed her appearance."

"WHERE ARE THOSE PARAMEDICS?!" Book's frenzied words bled through on the heels of the announcement.

"WHERE ARE THOSE PARAMEDICS?!"

"WHERE ARE THOSE PARAMEDICS?!"

I struggled to ignore the echo of his fear-stricken voice repeating in my head. The conflicting emotions already had me on the edge of emptying my stomach with extreme prejudice. Constantly reliving the horror was only serving to make the nausea worse.

I tried to think about something else but wasn't having much luck. Out of desperation I sent my eyes searching for something on which to focus, and my gaze fell across the illuminated elevator control panel in front of me. I locked onto it and struggled to concentrate. After a moment it seemed to work as my mind shifted gears. Of course, I should have known it wouldn't last. My brain seemed intent on continuing the self-torture and wasn't about to let a little thing like switching trains of thought stop it from doing so.

With less than ten seconds respite of staring blankly at the glowing lights, my thoughts wandered right back into the darkness. My subconscious was in control, and the luminance in front of me simply triggered another morbid reminder of why we were here. Without warning I now found myself wondering about the light described by many who have come back from the brink of death. Technically, I myself had suffered clinical death on more than one occasion, but all I remembered of it was darkness. My own experience made me think perhaps the proverbial light was just a trick of the synapses. Nothing more than a hazy glare brought about by an oxygen-deprived brain being bombarded with intensely focused illumination, especially in a place like this. I hadn't been to a hospital yet that wasn't filled with harsh brilliance, and this one was no different.

Of course, since the myth of the bright light was just another thought about death rolling around in my skull, it really wasn't helping matters any. If anything, the implications of finality it brought just made the acid churn of guilt eat away at my stomach even more, especially when I found myself wondering what Constance would see if she crossed over.

I simply couldn't get away from it. No matter how hard I tried to think of something else—anything besides dying—I couldn't. I was just going to have to let the fixation play itself out. The scary thing is I wasn't so sure I was ready for the thoughts to end because as long as I feared what may be coming, that meant it hadn't happened yet. And, just as I had been afraid something would go wrong with the sting operation, another feeling was now making its way up my spine. An unearthly foreboding that made me feel painfully empty, and I couldn't shake the sensation that the loss of yet another friend was coming far too soon.

With that terrifying premonition also came a sense of panic, backed by utter helplessness. They had both started off as small eddies in the random whitewater currents of my emotions but grew exponentially on the way here, becoming violent undertows in their own right. Now, they were endeavoring to pull me down into the depths of a cold and darkened despair.

I felt something soft press against my palm. I looked away from the panel and over to see Felicity staring at me, a similar mask of fear and guilt evident across her features. I gave her hand a squeeze, trying to reassure her, but was gravely conscious of the fact that I failed in doing so. I was broadcasting my own emotions far more than I wanted to admit, and there was no way for me to soothe her when I couldn't even comfort myself.

The elevator seemed like it was taking forever to deliver us to our floor. I knew we were moving because I could feel the vibration as we poked along. Just to be sure, I broke my silent gaze away from my wife and looked up. I stared at the numbers over the door, watching them flicker to life then wink back to darkness as the next would illuminate. In my mind they were advancing nowhere near quickly enough. Of course, I'm sure the futile exercise of willing them to go faster was only contributing to my ever-increasing agitation.

Finally, after the less than one-minute upward trip folded itself into feeling like ten, the car ceased moving. An electromechanical tone was followed by the sound of the outer doors rattling as they parted in sync with the inner barriers. I stepped out of the elevator as soon as the gap was wide enough to permit. Felicity, still clinging to my hand, kept up without missing a beat. We started down the starkly illuminated hallway, following the directions we had been given by the attendant at the main desk several floors below. Agent Parker, who had brought us to the hospital from FBI headquarters, fell in close behind, but she remained mute; not that such was anything different from the established norm. The simple fact was that none of us had uttered a word for several minutes now.

A good fifty yards ahead, the corridor abruptly terminated by emptying directly into a carpeted waiting area. The softer lighting of the distant room gave it the appearance of a calm oasis, neatly tucked away from the blinding glare throughout the rest of the building; however, I knew it was anything but. Especially, right now.

We instantly picked up the pace. From the moment we were out of the vehicle downstairs, we had been traveling at a fast walk, but with our destination now in sight, we automatically broke into a jog. I realized there was no logical explanation for the urgency we felt. It was all based in pure emotion. There was nothing any of us could do, and I knew that. I was certain Felicity and Agent Parker did as well. But, knowing didn't keep us from rushing headlong toward some glimmer of hope. Whether or not it would actually be there when we arrived was another story.

Within seconds, the quick thud of our feet against the tile turned to a soft, thump, as the harder flooring gave way to the carpeted expanse of the waiting area. Entering through the wide archway, we slowed to a halt. I quickly glanced around, searching the hidden corners of the room with my eyes. Felicity and Parker were doing the same.

The lounge was devoid of anyone and anything save the furniture and dog-eared magazines resting in a haphazard pile on the center of a low coffee table. The glimmer we sought wasn't here. All was empty and still, utterly silent except for the last flat echoes of our footsteps.

"Are we on the right floor, then?" Felicity asked, becoming the first to break our collective reticence. Her pronounced Irish brogue was an audible betrayal of the fatigue we were all feeling. Normally her accent was a mild lilt, noticeable, but not terribly prominent. However, when she was tired it would thicken as it did now. The accent highlighted her words in broad strokes with each syllable she uttered. Given the uncharacteristic Southern twang that had overcome her voice during the height of this nightmare, the familiar Celtic affectation was a welcome sound.

"The seventh floor waiting area is where they said they were," Agent Parker responded. "They should be here."

I had been fumbling in my coat pocket and now had my cell phone in hand. I began dialing a number as quickly as I could. "Yeah, well they should be but they aren't," I said, eyes never leaving my thumb as it stabbed buttons on the keypad.

"Could it be they've gone for coffee or something?" Felicity offered the question with a note of uncertainty in her voice.

"Maybe," Parker replied, surety lacking in her tone as well.

Just as I was about to place the phone against my ear, a distant mechanical chime sounded from behind, prompting all three of us to turn in near unison. At the far end of the hallway, from whence we had come only moments before, a set of doors in the dual bank of elevators began to slide open with a muted rumble. As the stainless steel parted, a lumbering janitor exited, pushing in front of him a wheeled bin. Without looking up he aimed himself toward a nearby trash receptacle as if on autopilot.

The fresh expectation of hope instantly dashed, I felt myself sag right where I stood, slumping into a dejected posture that physically announced my disappointment. To be honest, at this point the only thing really keeping me upright and focused was adrenalin augmented with caffeine, but both of those were swiftly running out.

Of course, the rapid depletion of the chemicals from my bloodstream was the least of my worries. They were only keeping me awake. My emotional self-flagellation was quickly starting to get the better of me, and no amount of caffeine could fix that. I knew that if it weren't for the immediacy of the current crisis, Felicity and I probably would have already given ourselves over to the post-traumatic breakdowns we both had looming on our personal horizons. There was no doubt they were coming—the only questions that remained were how soon and which one of us was going to have the worst time of it. Something told me neither journey was going to be a cakewalk. But, one thing I knew for certain was that the level of severity for both of us was presently hinging on Constance's survival.

We had faced down far too much already, and this was just a sadistic extension of the horror we had now been living for better than a month. It was as if we were waking up only to find our fleeting relief shattered by a fresh terror in an endless cycle.

I felt someone nudge me, then a voice drifted into my ears.

"Aye, Rowan," Felicity said. "Your phone then."

I snapped out of the introspection and gave my head a tired shake, tearing my vacant stare away from the oblivious janitor. Glancing at my hand I saw the aforementioned device resting there, flipped open with my fingers wrapped around it. The small speaker on the phone was vibrating with a barely audible voice saying something I couldn't quite make out.

I immediately placed the cell against my ear and asked, "Ben?"

"Yeah, Row," Detective Benjamin Storm replied, the two words coming out slow and deliberate.

I could almost feel the exhaustion in my friend's voice. It was something I had heard coming from him countless times over the years. However, what I detected now was different in a way far worse than anything I could describe. Not only did Ben sound tired, he sounded ancient, on the verge of feeble. But beyond even that, his tone held a percussive note of unimaginable emotional pain.

I feared I knew what was causing that anguish but chose to ignore the fresh twist in my gut. There was a question I knew needed asking, but because of his tone I dreaded the answer more than anything. I simply couldn't bring myself to advance the query, so I danced around the subject as if doing so would make it magically disappear.

"We just got here, Ben," I half stammered. "We're at the seventh floor waiting room. Where are you?"

"I'm...downstairs...in the chapel," he droned out the answer, pausing randomly before falling completely silent.

I closed my eyes as the dark portent in his words crept along my spine, making me physically shiver. Ben was devoutly secular. He claimed a belief in God but in the same breath noted that he despised organized religion. For him to be in the chapel was a harbinger of the worst kind. I waited for him to continue, but after several heartbeats my chest began to tighten and I forced a single word past the lump in my throat, "Ben?"

His voice cracked as he said, "Yeah...listen Row...I've got some bad news to tell ya'..."

Tuesday, December 20
10:37 A.M.
Sacred Heart Cemetery
Saint Louis, Missouri

CHAPTER 2

THE PROCESSION FROM THE FUNERAL HOME TO THE cemetery had been long, both in its physical size and the time spent covering the distance between the two locations. Several squad cars from the county police department provided a somber escort, light bars flickering out of respect, as our pace was unhurried. Local municipalities stopped traffic at intersections along the route, waving us through as our line of vehicles slowly snaked toward the final destination. Then, even after we arrived there was a substantial delay. So many people had turned out for this solemn occasion that it took several minutes before everyone was parked and the graveside service could officially commence.

Around us now was a sea of uniforms intermixing with the suits, dresses, and overcoats, all in varying hues of grey and black. If there were any other colors, I didn't recognize them. The world had been leached to dull black-and-white halftones for me.

In my eyes, most everyone else was a faceless, nameless mannequin set apart from the others only by the subtle differences in shades of their dark clothing. While I recognized some of the officers I had worked with over the years, those few were the exceptions to the rule.

Each member of the law enforcement who was present wore a black band across his or her shield. Even though my mind was blending the crowd together in response to my grief, the overt display of respect for a fallen comrade stood out and was impossible to ignore. Another salient observation was that among them, almost any local department I could readily name appeared to be represented here by at least one officer or detective, if not more.

With abrupt sharpness, a loud crack split the cool morning air, and my wife flinched at the sound. The members of the rifle squad moved smoothly through the ceremonious steps of lowering the weapons, then on cue, placing them back against their shoulders in preparation for firing the second volley of blanks.

Felicity leaned against me. I slipped my arm around her and held her tight; her body was tense, as if she was steeling herself against what we all knew was coming next. Even so, she started as the second round and then the third sounded their reports across the cemetery grounds.

Behind us, as the echoes faded, bagpipes began filling in the void, starting as a low hum that escalated into the melancholy strains of *Amazing Grace*. Felicity was trembling now, and even without looking I knew she was no longer holding her tears at bay. I shoved my hand inside my overcoat and sent it searching for a handkerchief. Finding the one I'd stashed in an inner pocket, I pulled it out and carefully dabbed her cheeks before slipping the square of cloth into her hand. She pressed herself harder against me and allowed her head to hang, chin against her chest as she quietly expressed her grief.

The rifle squad was now standing at attention, their weapons ordered at their sides, while the honor guard carefully removed the flag from the casket and proceeded to fold it into a tight triangle. I was having trouble containing my own tears at this point, but I took a deep breath and bit them back. I would have to find time to grieve later. Right now I needed to be strong for my wife. Even though "fragile" was almost never an accurate description where she was concerned, "temporarily breakable" definitely fit the bill at the moment. Emotionally she was still floundering in the dangerous wake of her own far too recent crisis, and that left her vulnerable. One of us had to hold it together awhile longer, and it might as well be me. She had seen me through my share of moments in recent years, and I owed her.

I hugged Felicity closer and allowed her to cry as I stared past the ranks in front of us. My eyes eventually settled on the casket at the center of the crowd. I could see Ben standing off to the side of it along with the other pallbearers. Of course, being six-foot-six, and full-blooded Native American, he would have been hard to miss even if he was with the rest of the masses.

One by one, the half dozen men came forward and placed their boutonnieres atop the casket. Then each of them stepped over to the row of seated family members and offered their personal condolences before continuing on and melting into the crowd. My friend was the last of them, and he lingered silently for several moments before finally placing his flower with the rest. At this distance it was hard to tell for sure, but I thought I could see the glisten of tears welling in his dark eyes too.

"THAT WAS A NICE SERVICE," I COMMENTED, OFFERING the platitude because I wasn't really sure what else to say.

"Yeah," Ben acknowledged, nodding his head slightly as he spoke. "Yeah… it was."

We were standing on the walkway between the gravesite and the access road that ran through the cemetery. Ben's van was parked nearby along one side of the narrow, paved stretch. Since Felicity and I had been farther behind in the procession, my truck was out of sight around the corner at the back of the memorial gardens.

People were still in the process of leaving, and we had decided to give them a few minutes to clear out before we added ourselves to the crush of traffic trying to exit onto the main road. I really didn't mind the wait, especially since this was the first chance in several days that I'd had to speak with my friend at any length. Between everything that had happened only a few nights ago and him being so involved in the funeral arrangements, he had been scarce. Of course I couldn't blame it all on him. We had been doing our fair share of hiding out as well, so it hadn't been easy for him to reach us either.

There was a cold breeze blowing, and Felicity was snuggled in against me, trying to keep warm. I glanced to the side, then kissed her lightly on the forehead and hugged her close. Looking at her now, I had to admit that I was still getting used to the new hairstyle. While her loose curls had somewhat returned, and the temporary black dye was gone for the most part, it still left a dull patina, which made her normally fiery mane appear a darker auburn. And, of course, it was much shorter—now hanging only just past her shoulders instead of the longer waist length cascade it had been ever since I'd met her many years ago. The uncharacteristic coif certainly didn't keep me from thinking she was the most beautiful woman I had ever laid eyes upon, but the current picture I saw with those eyes was definitely different from the one I remembered whenever they were closed.

Of course, we had all experienced radical change in the past month, both physical and emotional—some worse than others, and some far more permanent. With time, the physical issues would heal, become accepted as the norm, or return to their original states of being. The emotional changes were the wild card because exactly how the deeper alterations to our psyches would manifest still remained to be seen. For better or worse, we would just have to ride them out.

At the moment, my wife was keeping quiet amidst the halting conversation, and a dismal air still surrounded her just as it did all of us. Her sadness, however, was a bit more obvious as she was unconsciously broadcasting it with everything from her expression to her posture. At least the flow of tears had stopped, so I knew she was coping well enough that I didn't need to worry about her too much for the moment. Still, I suspected her current state was influenced by far more than just the funeral. I knew it definitely was for me.

I turned my gaze back to my friend and said, "There were quite a few more cops here than I expected, considering."

"Yeah, I know," he grunted. "Me too. Turns out a bunch of 'em even took vacation or comp time ta' be here."

"That says a lot."

"Yeah, it does."

"Are you going to the house, then?" Felicity finally interjected, her voice soft.

"Prob'ly a little later," he said, as he looked over at her with a quick nod and then glanced at his watch. "I told Constance's parents I'd take 'em ta' lunch."

"How are they handling everything?" she asked.

"'Bout as well as can be expected under the circumstances, I guess. It's not every day a fucked up serial killer shoots your kid."

"Yeah," I agreed. "I'm sure it has to be a nightmare for them. Especially after losing their son."

"Tell me about it. Her dad keeps goin' on about how Constance was s'posed ta' be a partner in 'is law firm, not an FBI agent," Ben added. "Her mom is kinda quiet though... Just stares off inta' space a lot."

"Everyone deals with their emotions differently, Ben."

"Yeah, I know."

"So, how is Constance doing anyway?" I asked.

"Hangin' in there," he replied. "You knew they upgraded 'er from critical ta' serious, right?"

"Uh-huh." I nodded. "That's pretty much all anyone would tell us though."

"Yeah, well the docs are optimistic right now, but she's still kinda out of it. She's been conscious enough ta' talk a coupla times but nothin' that makes sense. Then she just drifts off again. Prob'ly 'cause of all the painkiller shit they got runnin' into 'er veins. I honestly dunno if she even realizes what's goin' on at this point, but I figure after lunch I'll go sit with 'er awhile anyway. That'll give 'er folks a chance ta' rest too."

"I thought they were only letting immediate family members in to see her?" I said with a questioning note in my voice.

"Yeah, that's what they said the first time I went in," he grunted. "But I got a fuckin' badge."

"I thought you were still suspended?"

"Yeah, for a few weeks yet, but the hospital doesn't know that."

"Uh-huh, I should have figured."

"Ben," Felicity asked. "Since they won't let us see her, can you keep us up to date on how she's doing?"

"Yeah, I'll do that."

I leaned to the side and looked around him at the line of cars. "Looks like they're still backed up a bit."

He cast a glance over his shoulder. "I'm not surprised. It oughta' be clear in a few though."

A thick silence settled in around us as the breeze rose and fell. Felicity shivered against the sharp wind even though she was wearing a coat, so I hugged her even closer.

"Would you be more comfortable waiting in the truck?" I asked her.

"I'm fine," she replied.

"You're sure?"

"Aye," she returned with a slight nod. "For now."

I looked back to my friend after a short silence and nodded toward the distant gravesite. "You know, Ben, that was a real good thing you did. I mean the honor guard and all."

"Wasn't just me," he objected with an animated shake of his head. "B'sides, didn't really take much. All I did was make a coupl'a phone calls."

"Something tells me there was more to it than that."

"Maybe a little, but not much really once the ball was rollin' and a few favors got called in. Shit, everyone that ever worked with Deckert loved 'im."

"He was a hell of a guy," I agreed. "I'll never forget how well he treated me even when the rest of the cops had issues with a Witch as a consultant."

"Yeah, that was Deck, for sure. Which is exactly why we couldn't let it go. Just 'cause the department doesn't do anything for retiree funerals doesn't mean the rest of us coppers ain't gonna make it happen anyway. He was one of ours. If anyone deserved it, it was him."

"Well, I'm glad you did," I said with a nod. "I'm sure his wife appreciated it too."

"Yeah, Mona's good people," he grunted as he reached up to smooth back his hair then allowed his hand to slide down and rest on his neck. He closed his eyes then gave his head a slight shake as he sighed, "Jeezus, Row... He was just sittin' there lookin' at the tube and had a goddamn heart attack. How fucked up is that?"

"Sometimes that's how it happens. He had a history. That's what forced him into retirement to begin with."

"Yeah, but it was at almost exactly the same time, Row. There's gotta be somethin' to that."

I knew exactly where he was heading with the comment, as he had mentioned it to me earlier at the funeral home, but at that point we hadn't had time for discussion.

"It was just a coincidence, Ben." I shook my head as I spoke. "There was no connection between what happened to Constance and Carl's heart attack."

"How do ya' know that?"

"Well, I guess I really don't. Not for an absolute fact, anyway." I shrugged.

"So then why are ya' bein' a skeptic all of a sudden? Deck treated Constance like she was 'is own daughter. Think about it..." He started ticking off points with the fingers of his free hand. "Damn near the same time. The ambulance brought Deck ta' the same hospital as her instead of goin' ta' one of the closer ones out in the county. When he arrived he was stable. Then it all goes south for Constance while she's on the table. The docs bring 'er back, but suddenly Deck keels over right there in the treatment room, and they can't revive 'im. Hell, you're the friggin' Witch, not me. Ain't this your kinda shit? You of all people can't tell me that doesn't seem a little *Twilight Zone*, white man. Like some kinda trade off or somethin'."

I didn't figure this was an appropriate time to argue with him over the realities of WitchCraft, or even my personal psychic abilities— something that I actually considered to be an unfortunate curse as opposed to a gift. Over the years I'd already explained to him more than a dozen times that magick didn't work quite like he sometimes wanted to think it did. Of course, I was also well aware that I probably sounded like some kind of hypocrite every time I said as much, given that he had seen me unwillingly channel murder victims on several occasions. And of course, there was our most recent brush with the ethereal, which left even me wondering just what to believe. It was hard to convince someone that the paranormal *wasn't* the everyday way of things when it seemed to rain down on you constantly the way it did with me.

Still, Ben had started out a skeptic the first time he'd enlisted my help, and he continued walking a jagged line between acceptance and doubt. At the moment, his path was obviously veering deeply into the belief side of the two, if for no other reason than to help him make sense out of tragedy. Of course, that was something we all had a tendency to do when faced with realities we weren't sure we wanted to accept.

"Did Carl even know about Constance?" I asked.

"I dunno…" he shook his head. "Prob'ly not. I didn't even know what was happenin' with him until Mona called my cell, and he was already gone by then. But that's not the point. What about some kinda divine intervention or somethin'?"

"I know that's how it might look on the surface," I told him. "Believe me, I'm not denying that at all. But we all know that looks can be deceiving. Maybe I'm wrong in this case, but not everything that happens is being influenced by some ethereal cosmic force. Sometimes a coincidence is just that, Ben. A coincidence."

"You're the last person on earth I'd expect ta' say somethin' like that, Row."

"Yeah, I know. It does sound kind of strange coming from me, doesn't it?"

"Uh-huh… Well, maybe you're right, but that don't make it any less weird-ass fucked up. Know what I mean?"

I let out my own sigh then hung my head and contemplated the asphalt surface of the pathway. "I'll give you that."

When I looked up again he was still frowning and massaging his neck. After a moment he let his hand drop then glanced at his watch again. Casting another gaze over his shoulder at the access road, he sighed, "Looks like it's startin' ta' break up a bit. Should be in good shape in a minute or two."

"Yeah," I replied with a nod.

"Rowan, why don't you go ahead and give me your keys then," Felicity said, shivering as she spoke. "I think maybe I will go warm up in the truck. Besides, I'm sure I need to fix my makeup."

"You're pretty enough just like you are," I told her but still dug around in my pocket and extracted the keys then handed them to her.

"Aye and you're blind," she returned. "I'd rather check for myself."

I could hear in her voice that the words had been delivered on automatic. They were her pat response to being told she looked just fine, and right now she was too emotionally preoccupied for anything more interactive. I envied her that, but not in a begrudging sense. I would have a chance to take my feelings off hold later. I hoped.

In reality, her desire to wait in the truck was serendipitous. I still had a question for Ben, but it was something I didn't want to ask with Felicity around. It had been starting to look as though it was going to have to wait, but now a fresh opportunity was emerging. Of course, given the nature of the question and the fact that I had just poked holes in the thin fabric of my friend's already tenuous belief in the paranormal, I wasn't sure he would take me seriously. At the very least, I knew I was once again going to be playing the hypocrite in his eyes.

"You take care of yourself, Felicity," Ben told her. "Do me a favor and tell Mona I'll be by later, okay?"

"I will," she answered, detaching from me and stepping forward to give him a hug. "I'm sure she would appreciate that. You'll give Constance our love, then?"

"Yeah, will do." He gave her a squeeze in return while saying. "You gonna be okay?"

"Aye," she said. "Eventually."

"Ya'know she was doin' 'er job, right? Constance doesn't blame you for what happened."

"You can't know that, Ben."

"Yeah, I can. Trust me, it's a cop thing."

"Maybe so," my wife replied as she pulled away, tears starting to well in her eyes again. "But that doesn't…"

"I'm tellin' ya' don't go there…" he returned, cutting her off as he reached out and gave her shoulder a squeeze. "She may be a Feeb, but she's still a badge. She was doin' 'er job. B'sides, she's gonna be fine." He let out a nervous chuckle that sounded as if he was trying to reassure himself as much as her, then added, "Ya' don't really think she's gonna let me off the hook that easy, do ya'?"

I caught a glimpse of a forced smile pulling at the corner of her mouth as she tried to respond to his attempt at cheering her up and then watched as her lips quickly turned back into a frown. She shot a glance toward me, and I could see in her expression that she was wrestling with a different guilt entirely. I had a feeling I knew the source of the anguish all too well because I was feeling it too. And I suspected the two of us weren't the only ones fending off the pain it brought. Ben probably was as well but when it came right down to it, none of us wanted to be the first to confess the sin.

She looked back at him and said, "Thank you," before turning fully to face me and adding, "Don't be long?"

Her voice was soft, yet held the benign note of insistence that was so often exchanged between husbands and wives, telling me she wanted to be on the way soon. When I looked into her eyes, however, a "demand" wasn't what I saw.

If anything, she wore an expression that was no less than a pleading question mark.

CHAPTER 3

BEN AND I BOTH WATCHED AFTER FELICITY AS SHE walked down the path and started along the edge of the access road rather than chance crossing the soft ground in heels. The hard sound of her shoe soles against the asphalt dulled with each step she took, but I continued to gaze in her direction until she disappeared behind the end of a small hedgerow.

Certain she was out of earshot, my friend turned to me and asked, "Whaddaya think? She really gonna be okay?"

"Yeah, she'll be fine. Like she said, it's just going to take some time," I replied, nodding my head. "She hasn't really had the opportunity to decompress yet, obviously. Neither of us has. There are just things we both still have to come to terms with."

I left it at that. I wasn't about to get into a deep explanation. Not here, and not now. There was something sacrosanct about the moment and location that made me feel like doing so would be blasphemous, even in a secular sense. Besides, in my mind at least I had something more important that needed to be addressed. Unfortunately, right now my friend was intent on being just that, a friend, so he continued to probe out of concern.

"So what about you, Row? You holdin' on?"

"I have to—for now anyway. We can't have both of us turning into basket cases simultaneously."

"Why not? If ya ask me ya' both deserve it after what you've been through."

"I won't argue with you there." I shrugged. "But, my time will come later. Right now she needs it more."

"Yeah, I know what ya' mean... So have ya' been talkin' ta' Helen at least?" he asked, referring to his sister, who was not only a friend but a therapist who had helped all of us cope with some of the horrors we had faced over the years.

"Not yet, but we will."

"Good. Make it soon, 'kay?"

"Yeah," I nodded. "Soon."

He huffed out a sigh and looked back toward the dispersing traffic once again. "So, listen, I hate ta' run, but you need ta' get back ta'

Firehair, and I really should go ahead and get movin'. I'll catch up with you two and let ya' know how Constance is doin', okay?"

He reached to shake hands, so I extended my own out of reflex. A moment later he was turning to leave, and I realized I was completely sidetracked. I had allowed his concern for Felicity and me to dominate the remainder of our conversation, and now my unexpected opportunity was about to escape.

"Hey, Ben," I blurted, just as he was about to take a step. "Before you go can I ask you something?"

"Yeah, what's up?" he said, stopping and turning back to face me.

The question I had for him was one I wasn't so sure he was going to want to answer—for several reasons, not the least of which could be where it might lead. I started to ask it anyway, but then hesitated as my mind flashed on the still fresh memories of the recent investigation—in particular, a victim Annalise Devereaux had literally trampled to death, using his prurient fetish as a vehicle for his demise and in the process, her own twisted gratification. My query was directly related to something she had done with that victim's blood, and it was weighing on me heavily. In fact, it had been ever since I'd seen it.

Obviously, my pause was longer than I imagined because Ben furrowed his brow and looked at me with worry in his eyes as he gave me a verbal nudge. "What's wrong, Row?"

"Sorry..." I told him, then let out a heavy sigh and asked, "Remember when we were at the scene of the Lewis homicide?"

"Yeah, I may be on the downhill slide ta' fifty but I ain't senile yet. That was just a few days ago, white man."

"So then I'm sure you remember the piece of spellwork Annalise did in the kitchen with the blood and the cloves, right?"

"Well yeah... It was the reason I took ya' there ta' begin with."

"Exactly. Do you know if anyone ever found the bottle or jar that she used?"

"No." He shook his head. "Not that I've heard. But I'm on suspension, so I don't exactly get daily reports. Why?"

"Dammit," I muttered. I had been afraid that was going to be the case, and I knew it meant I would have to ask a different question he wouldn't be nearly as quick to answer. I sucked in a breath and blurted it out anyway. "Okay, then is there any chance you can tell me where Annalise is right now?"

"Yeah, in an eight-by-twelve cussin' the fact that bright orange ain't 'er color. Don't worry, she's not gettin' out."

"I'm not worried. About that anyway. But I do need to know where she is specifically. Saint Louis? Somewhere else?"

"Ain't important, white man," he returned with a hard, dismissive tone underscoring the words. Even with that, at least his overall reaction was calmer than I had expected it might be.

"Do you even know where she's being held, Ben?"

"Yeah. She's in an eight-by-twelve, just like I said."

"Dammit, you know what I mean."

"Yeah, well actually I do know where she is. But I'm tellin' ya' to leave it alone, Row."

"I can't."

"Yes, you can."

"No, seriously, Ben. I can't."

"Okay, I'll play. Ya' wanna give me a good reason why?"

"Maybe I'm wrong, but I've got a bad feeling this isn't over yet."

"What isn't over?"

"Miranda."

"What? How the hell can it *not* be over?" he almost barked the question. "The bitch is in custody. There's enough hard evidence ta' get 'er the needle. It's a slam-dunk. Once the Feebs are done with her, she's gonna be puttin' in her order for a last meal. It's done. Finished."

"You're talking about Annalise," I told him, nodding my head in agreement. "But I'm talking about Miranda. The *Lwa* that was using her as a horse."

He shook his head. "Horse. Jeez, that gets me every time I hear it."

"It's just Vodoun terminology for the body a spirit possesses, Ben."

"Yeah, I know, you told me. Still sounds weird though." He threw up his hands and shook his head. "Either way, white man, it doesn't matter. Like you said, Miranda's a ghost."

"Actually she's a *Vodoun* ancestral spirit."

"Say it however ya' want. Horse, Spirit, Low-ahh, Miranda, I don't care—you're still talkin' about a friggin' ghost."

"If that's what you insist on calling her, fine. But the fact remains, she's still out there."

"Row, she ain't real."

"Yes, she is. You've seen way too…"

"Gimme a break, you know what I meant," he interrupted. "How many times do I hafta tell you I can't help ya' there? I can't arrest somethin' I can't even see."

"I'm not asking you to."

"Then would ya' like to explain exactly what it is you're wantin'?"

"Access to Annalise."

He snorted out a sarcastic chuckle. "Yeah, like that's gonna happen. Get real. Why don't we go back ta' me arrestin' the ghost, it'd prob'ly be easier."

"It's my only recourse at this point," I replied.

"What's seein' her got ta' do with Miranda?"

"Maybe everything."

"Well, ya' might as well forget it. Even if I wasn't suspended, there ain't enough strings on the planet I could pull ta' get you access ta' her. Not that I would if I could."

"Well I need to find some way to make it happen, so if you won't help me I'll have to find someone who will."

"Yeah, well good luck. C'mon, Row. Seriously. Whaddaya need ta' see 'er for?"

"To find out what she did with that spell."

"Okay, so we're back around to the missin' bottle-jar thing."

"It's more than just a bottle, Ben," I replied. "You know that."

"Uh-huh. All I know is what you said, and the way I remember it, you didn't know exactly what it was yourself."

"At the time I didn't, but now I've got a theory."

"Why am I not surprised?"

"So are you suddenly doubting me?" I asked.

"I didn't say that…" He shook his head and huffed out a resigned breath. "Okay, fine, so you wanna share this theory or is it top secret?"

"I think the spellwork she did might have something to do with bonding Felicity to the *Lwa*."

"So you think the jar thing is why Firehair flipped out again and went all psycho bitch even though you did a bunch of hocus-pocus to keep it from happenin'."

"That's pretty much it."

"Why?"

"I just do."

"Are ya' sure?"

"Like I said, it's a theory."

He shook his head. "Don't tell me… Ya' got a feelin'…"

"Yes."

"Friggin' wunnerful," he huffed. "So five minutes ago ya' stood here and told me I was wrong about Deck and Constance, but now you got a feelin', and I'm s'posed ta' just accept it without question?"

"Yeah, Ben, I know how that sounds… But, that's usually how this works. You said it yourself. I'm the Witch, not you."

"Uh-huh, well you oughta be glad you don't really ride a broom 'cause I'd shove it up your ass right about now if ya' did…" He paused, and looked at me for a moment then finally said, "Jeezus… Okay… So just how bad is this feelin' anyway?"

"Bad enough."

"Lovely," he muttered. "Does Felicity know?"

"I haven't mentioned it just yet. I don't really want to worry her with this right now."

"Crap, Row… Isn't she the whole reason you're…"

I cut him off. "Don't worry, I plan to tell her. I just didn't want to drop it on her just yet. She's still coming to terms with the fact that Miranda possessed her to begin with. Not to mention finding out that Annalise is actually her half sister. It's like a damned soap opera, and she's got a lot to digest. Not to mention that everything else that's happened the past few days isn't making it any easier."

"Yeah… I know… I'm just sayin' don't wait too long on that, or she'll be the one gettin' hold of ya' with the broom when she finds out… Hell, I know how she is, and I ain't even the one married to 'er…"

"I know, Ben. Believe me, I know. And I'll tell her."

He fell silent for a moment then shook his head. "So… 'Bad enough'. Just exactly how bad is that? And gimme somethin' specific. Like, is Miranda gonna climb inside Firehair's head again or what?"

"Well, we know for a fact she'd like to. And if I'm right, that's what the spell meant to facilitate. But I don't plan on letting it happen."

"Seems ta' me you weren't too successful at stoppin' it this last go 'round."

"I know, but let's just say this time I'm holding an ace," I replied.

"What kinda ace?"

"A necklace."

"A necklace?"

"Long story. Just trust me."

"Yeah. Trust you," he harrumphed. "Famous last words. Okay, so if you got this necklace, then why do ya' hafta find this bottle so bad?"

"Because I don't like loose ends. Especially this kind. Besides, if I'm right, the necklace and whatever is in that bottle are connected, so it's really the key to ending all of this."

He stared at me for a second then looked at his watch. "Look, I really gotta get movin'. So is this just a Witch thing, or do I need to be worried at my end?"

"It's definitely a Witch thing," I said. "Like I said, it's not a good idea to leave magick like that to its own devices. It can have a tendency to take on a life of its own."

"Yeah, yeah, okay, but cut ta' the chase. Are ya' tellin' me this is just you bein' anal, and it ain't an emergency, or is it somethin' else?"

"Could be all of the above or maybe none of the above. I don't know for sure."

"Jeezus, Row. Do you ever give straight answers?" He huffed out the question in a disgusted tone and didn't wait for my reply. "Just tell me straight—are there gonna be more bodies turnin' up because of this?"

"I'd like to say no, but I can't for sure."

"Dammit, Row..."

"Honestly, I don't know, Ben," I appealed. "I certainly hope not. But, we know Miranda wants to use Felicity as a horse just like she did with Annalise, and she's proven she'll do anything to get to her... If I don't sever the connection and finish this for good... Well... It's hard to know what she'll do. I will say this though—it's a good bet that if you do end up with more bodies, mine will probably be the first."

"Jeezus, white man... Ain't that a bit morbid, especially today?"

"You wanted the truth." I gave him a resigned shrug before continuing, "I don't think it will happen. Everything is a stalemate at this point, and if that status quo is maintained, everything should be fine. At least that's my hope. But, let's face it, Ben—this is a Pandora's box scenario. Annalise more or less let Miranda loose on the world, and we know how that turned out. Then I screwed up and fostered a connection to my wife without even realizing it."

"But you fixed that, didn't ya'?"

"Yes, but by that point the damage was done. The *Lwa* has fixated on Felicity, and she's obviously looking for new meat, which is why I think the spellwork connects her to my wife. Think about it. Miranda used Felicity's body to try killing me twice before. I'm an even bigger obstacle now than I was then. With me out of the way, she could assume control. And if she does that, the cycle will just start over again. Different physical body, but for all intents and purposes, the same killer."

"But if you got a stalemate, like you said, everything is fine. Right?"

"Unless she tries an end run and uses someone else as a horse."

He closed his eyes and shook his head. "Fuck me... Ya'know, this shit just gives me a headache."

"Yeah, I know. Me too. Literally," I agreed. "Fortunately, I think that last option is less than likely. She would need a connection to the person, so unless someone else is using Miranda as a personal *Lwa*, then we should be relatively safe."

"Relatively?"

"Annalise is still alive and connected."

"Yeah, and locked up."

"As long as she stays that way, then we should be fine. Either way, that's where I have to trust *you*."

"Not me. More like the Feebs and the penal system."

"Okay. But in any event it's not something I have control over, so I'm left trusting someone else to keep that factor from changing."

"Uh-huh... Okay... Tell ya' what, I'll make a coupl'a calls. Lemme see what I can find out, but I'm not makin' any promises. What you're askin' is pretty much impossible."

"I appreciate it."

"Yeah. I'll add it to your friggin' tab," he said as he turned to go. He hesitated then turned back and asked, "So what makes ya' think Devereaux would tell ya' what you wanna know anyway?"

"Revenge. I think Miranda forced her to do that spellwork. I don't believe for a minute she would have done it of her own free will."

"Why not?"

"Easy. She's addicted. She'll do anything to keep from giving up Miranda to another horse, so why would she work magick to create a connection to one? That's why Constance is in the hospital right now. Annalise wanted Felicity dead, so Miranda would be hers and hers alone."

"Yeah," he grunted. "Well do us all a favor and go do some more hocus-pocus or whatever and stop havin' bad feelin's. I got enough on my plate right now."

"I'm right there with you."

"Okay, last question—what if you can't get the low down on this... What then?"

"We hope like hell I'm right about the status quo keeping everything in check."

"But if you're wrong and Miranda gets back into Firehair, she goes off the deep end and this shit could start all over again?"

"Yeah… Pretty much."

"That's fucked up, Row."

"You won't get any argument from me there."

WHEN I FINALLY ARRIVED BACK AT THE TRUCK, I HAD already blown well past the outer marker of "don't be long." However, I knew that if Felicity had been in a real hurry, she would have simply taken the wheel and driven around into sight as a cue for me to get moving. She hadn't, so I wasn't too concerned. I approached from the front, and I could see my wife through the windshield, seated on the passenger side, but her attentions were obviously focused elsewhere.

I stepped off the roadway onto the dormant grass then carefully slid between the idling vehicle and a small hedge so that I could open the door and climb in. The interior was already considerably warmer than the outside temperature; of course, I'm sure some of that had to do with the fact that my tardiness gave it even more time to heat up. At any rate, it was too warm for me, so as I settled in I reached over to the dash and adjusted the driver's side climate controls.

"Sorry," Felicity said absently, giving me a quick glance. "I meant to do that earlier."

She hadn't acted startled when I opened the door, so apparently she had seen me coming after all. She quickly returned her gaze to the mirror on the back of the sun visor and continued half-heartedly fussing with her makeup. A bottle of eye drops and a handful of cosmetics were lined up across the dash in front of her, but it didn't appear that she had attempted any major resurfacing where the latter was concerned. It wasn't as if she really wore that much makeup anyway, and as I'd told her, she really did look just fine.

"No problem," I replied. "Sorry I took so long."

"I was beginning to wonder what happened to you then."

"Just lost track for a few minutes."

The radio was tuned to the local classical music station and set to low volume. In the background, just above the hiss of the air vents, an unnamed orchestra was ringing its way through *Carol of the Bells*.

"What were you two talking about?" Felicity asked after a moment.

"Nothing important."

"*Thug tú d'éitheach,*" she returned, calling me a liar. Even though her tone held no anger, I knew she was somewhat serious because she had resorted to Gaelic.

"Okay, how about nothing for you to worry about."

"Aye, do you really want me to say it again?"

"Not really."

"Then tell the truth."

I fell quiet for a moment then attempted to redirect the conversation. "Are you about ready to go?"

"Just a minute, I'm almost finished," she told me then paused for a moment herself. I really should have known better than to think I could get away with diverting the topic, and she proved that when she asked, "You were talking about her, weren't you? Miranda."

"She came up," I replied.

"And?"

"And what?"

"And what about her?"

"We decided not to invite her to the Christmas party," I said, unsuccessfully trying to lighten the tense mood.

"Be serious."

I shrugged in surrender. "Honestly, I'm not sure what you want me to say, sweetheart."

"I'm not sure either," she sighed, then her voice took on a hint of fear as she added, "She's still out there."

"I know," I said, trying to sound soothing. "And, yes, that's what we talked about."

"So what do we do about it?"

"I'm working on it. We have the necklace put away."

"Aye. Do you plan to explain that at some point?"

"Eventually, once I'm sure about some things. But, for right now though, as long as it stays in that jar of salt and you don't come into contact with it, we should be fine."

"And what if it isn't?"

"That isn't an option."

"But…"

"No… No but's…" I calmly interrupted her. "Listen to me, honey, it's only been a few days. Everything is way too fresh right now. Just give yourself a little time to deal with all this, okay?"

She didn't respond. Instead she glanced down and began carefully tucking the tubes and compact into her purse. "I just need to touch up my lipstick," she finally said, her tone flat and words terse. "But I'll do that when we get there. I suppose we should get moving."

"So, are you mad at me now?" I asked.

"No." She shook her head as she looked over at me. "No... I'm sorry... I'm just..." She let out a frustrated breath and shook her head again. "I'm just trying to cope with... with..."

"The guilt?" I offered.

"Yes, but it's not what you think... I mean, it is, but it's something else too... It isn't just... It's... It's just something you wouldn't... It's..."

"I know, honey," I cut her off. It was obvious that the time had come for confession whether I wanted it to or not. At least it had for Felicity and me. I held up my hand to stop her from stammering on further then said, "Believe me, I know exactly what you are feeling..."

"You can't possibly..." she began.

I rushed to interrupt her again. "You feel guilty because as sad as you are that Carl died, you're glad it was him we put in the ground today instead of Constance."

She gave me a startled look then slowly nodded as she placed her hand to her mouth and closed her eyes. After a moment she let out a long, low sigh and with a slight tremble in her voice, asked, "What did Miranda do to me, Row? What did that *saigh* change inside of me that I can even think such a horrid thing?"

"Nothing," I said, reaching over and brushing the hair away from her face. "Nothing at all... Because, Gods help me, I've been thinking the exact same thing."

Sunday, March 12
8:22 A.M.
Saint Louis, Missouri

CHAPTER 4

"YOU LOOK LIKE HELL," I SAID, VOICING MY MATTER-OF-fact observation in as jovial a tone as I could muster.

"Yeah, fuck you too," Detective Benjamin Storm grunted as he fixed me with a bleary-eyed gaze then shook his head and let out a heavy sigh.

He was sitting across the table from me, where I had just joined him in a booth at Charlie's Eats, a small diner that occupied a piece of corner real estate at Seventh and Chouteau, not terribly far from city police headquarters downtown. It was a favorite hangout of cops for meal breaks since they could get something more than just a sandwich. On top of that, the service was fast, the prices were reasonable, and its close proximity to the station didn't hurt either.

I was actually no stranger to Chuck's, as the greasy spoon was affectionately called, though at times I felt like the only civilian in the place—with the exception of the staff of course. However, with life having been in such turmoil over the past several months, it had been quite some time since my last visit. Still, I wasn't surprised in the least to see that little, if anything, had changed. Even the age-yellowed, multi-generational photocopy boasting that these premises were protected by Smith and Wesson still occupied its conspicuously prominent place on the back of the cash register for everyone to see. Of course, given that standard issue for city police officers was the Beretta nine-millimeter, someone had used a marker and added that fact underneath as well.

"Rough night or something?" I asked my friend as I settled in and folded my jacket in the seat next to me.

"Yeah, I guess ya' could say that," he grunted again. "Got called out on a body in a dumpster at around one this mornin', haven't stopped since."

"Never seems to end, does it?"

"Nope. It sure as hell don't."

I twisted slightly and rolled my left shoulder before reaching up and carefully massaging the side of my neck.

"You okay?" my friend asked.

"Yeah," I replied, wincing slightly. "I think I just slept in a weird position or something. I've had this pain in my neck off and on all morning. Nothing bad, really, just kind of annoying."

"Yeah, well at least you slept."

"So, if you've been up all night then why aren't you at home in bed right now?"

"It's Sunday the twelfth, ain't it? Accordin' ta' my calendar we're s'posed to meet for breakfast, right? Must be, 'cause you're here."

"Yeah," I said, giving him a shrug. "But we started arranging these things on weekends for a reason. Since you ended up working anyway, you could have called me and begged off. I would have understood."

"Yeah, well, believe me I thought about it," he replied with a yawn and then added, "But, ya' know, I still gotta eat."

"When aren't you eating?" a female voice filled with good-natured sarcasm slid directly in behind his comment.

We both looked up to find a young blonde woman clad in blue jeans, a faded "Eat at Chuck's" sweatshirt, and a server's apron now standing next to the table. She wielded a Pyrex carafe in one hand and a ceramic mug in the other. She slid the cup in front of me, then with a quick flourish, deftly filled it with hot coffee.

"Hey, Wendy," I greeted the waitress.

"Rowan. Long time no see," she replied with a grin. "You haven't been cheating on us and going to another diner have you?"

I chuckled. "Never. You know this is my one and only. I've just been a little busy."

"I know the feeling," she said. "So, how's Felicity?"

"Doing well. Sassy as ever and twice as gorgeous."

"You wouldn't have her any other way."

I nodded and smiled. "True."

Wendy turned her gaze toward Ben. "Have I told you that you look like crap today, Storm?"

"Three times since I got here," he replied as he pushed his mug toward her. "This time makes four."

"I'm just looking out for you." She grinned as she topped off his java. "So... Are you ready or do you need a couple of minutes?"

"I've been ready," Ben told her. "I'll have the usual, with a side of aspirin."

"Headache?"

"Yeah."

She cocked her head to the side and acted as if she was inspecting him. "Yeah. Looks to me like it would hurt."

"Yeah... Funny." Ben didn't sound amused.

"Want me to just bring you the bottle?"

"Yeah, that's a good idea. Rowan could prob'ly use 'em too. He was just sayin' he's got a pain in 'is neck."

"And I'm guessing that would be you?"

"Uh-huh..." he muttered. "Still not funny."

"Okay, got it, a number twelve with chili, and the aspirin," she said.

"You forgot the extra onions," my friend reminded her.

"Actually I remembered but I was hoping you'd forget," she quipped. "I'll go ahead and bring you a roll of breath mints with that too."

"Jeez, you're a friggin' laugh a minute today, ain't ya'?"

"Aren't I always?" she said with a smile. "How about you, Rowan?"

"I don't know... Do I want a number three?" I asked.

I had learned long ago that Wendy wasn't going to let me order for myself. She always asked what I wanted at the outset, but nine times out of ten she would endeavor to talk me into something else. I still had no idea why she insisted on ordering for me because she didn't do it for everyone, only a select few. In any case, it hadn't taken long for me to simply roll with it and let her have her way.

"No... I don't think so," she returned, shaking her head. "You really look more like you want a number five today."

I didn't bother to inquire what a number five was because I already knew all of the single digit selections on the menu were varying numbers of eggs with some combination of breakfast meats and toast. Besides, she'd never steered me wrong yet. Instead I just asked, "Do I want my eggs scrambled?"

"I think you're in the mood for over hard today," she replied.

"Okay, do I want a side of biscuits and sausage gravy with that?"

"Definitely."

I grinned. "Great, I was hoping I did. Okay, sounds good to me."

Ben waved a finger at me and told her, "Oh yeah, in case he forgets to tell ya', give him the check. It's his turn ta' buy."

Wendy winked at me as she turned to go put in our orders, "Don't worry. I'll give you the cop discount."

I gave her a quick nod and smile. "Thanks."

When she was gone I turned my attention to the steaming cup of coffee she had slid in front of me. Leaning a bit to my left I snatched the saltshaker from the end of the table then tipped it up over the brew and gave it a couple of healthy jiggles. After a moment I set it aside and gave the contents of the mug a quick stir with a spoon.

Ben had been watching me the entire time, and now he grunted, "So what's your excuse, white man?"

"For what?"

"For bein' brain dead this mornin'."

I took a sip of the coffee. "What are you talking about?"

He raised an eyebrow. "Are ya' tellin' me that tastes okay to you?"

"Yeah, it's fine."

"Row, I just watched ya' put salt in it instead of sugar."

"I don't take sugar in my coffee. Except when it's really bad coffee."

"So ya' did it on purpose?"

"Yes. Besides, if you thought I was screwing up, why didn't you stop me?"

"'Cause I thought maybe when ya' tasted it, the look on your face would be funny an' I could use a laugh."

"Sorry to disappoint you."

"Jeezus," he mumbled. "Okay, I'll bite. Why'd ya' just salt your friggin' coffee?"

"It's an experiment," I replied. "I'm trying to stop the voices in my head."

"Voices in your... You mean like the *Twilight Zone* stuff?" he asked.

"Exactly."

"Why?"

"I'm retired, remember?" I offered the rhetorical question as my answer. "I'm just Rowan Gant, computer consultant now. No more consulting for the cops. I'm through talking to dead people and chasing down their killers. Finished. Done."

"Uh-huh... So then why do ya' keep dunnin' me about Devereaux every coupl'a days?"

"That's different. She's unfinished business."

"Yeah, right."

"She is." I shrugged. "But if it makes you feel better, then you can call me semi-retired for the time being."

"How 'bout I call ya' full'a shit," he grunted. "So...is it workin'?"

"You mean the salt?"

"Yeah."

"I think so."

"Prob'ly ain't all that great for your blood pressure," he commented.

"And the pot said to the kettle…" I replied, implying reference to the overabundance of salt he customarily doused on his meals.

"Yeah, whatever."

"So, since you brought her up, is there any word on Annalise yet?"

He shook his head. "I've still got some feelers out, but like I keep tellin' ya', you're askin' the impossible. Last thing I heard was she lawyered up with some kinda high-dollar dream team."

"What good will that do?" I asked. "I thought there was a ton of hard evidence against her."

"There is," he replied. "But she still gets 'er day in court, and she's got more money than God, so there ya' go… Might not get 'er off, but they might be able ta' skate on the needle if they play it right. All depends on how good they are. But what the hell, either way somebody's makin' a paycheck."

I rubbed my neck as the pain ebbed, then I let out a sigh. With a little luck, maybe things were finally starting to loosen up, and I wouldn't have to deal with the nuisance the whole day.

"Do you think you could get me some of their names?" I asked. "Maybe I could come at it that way."

"Yeah, I can get that no problem," he said with a nod. "But I doubt it's gonna do ya' any good. You're pretty much the enemy where she's concerned. Why the hell would they let ya' talk to 'er?"

"I don't know, Ben, but it's worth a try."

"Well, personally I think it's a waste of time, but then it ain't my time so whadda I care."

"Exactly."

"So lemme ask ya' somethin' anyway… Don'tcha figure you and Firehair are in the clear now? I mean it's been like what? Better'n two months now without a peep?"

"When I'm able to undo that spell, then I'll figure we're safe. Not before."

"Yeah, well I hope that works out for ya'."

"Just keep trying for me, okay?" I asked. "And if you can get me the names of her attorneys I'd really appreciate it."

"Yeah, okay. That I can do."

I switched the subject. "So, enough about that. How's Constance? We haven't talked to her in a week or so."

"Pissy," he replied. "But other than that, good…" A low trill started and began escalating in volume. Ben reached over to his wadded up jacket and rummaged around in the pocket while adding, "She's got cabin fever if ya' know what I mean. They're gonna let 'er start physical therapy next week, so I'm hopin' that oughta help 'er mood a bit."

I nodded agreement as he flipped open his phone then pressed it to his ear and said, "Yeah, Storm."

Wendy appeared at almost the same instant, carrying plates and the carafe of coffee. Settling the hot globe on the table, she shuffled one of the oblong dishes out of the crook of her arm and slid it in front of Ben then placed the other in front of me. Reaching into a pouch on her apron, she pulled out a bottle of aspirin and set it on the table as she topped off our mugs.

"I'll be right back with your biscuits and gravy," she told me quietly. "Oh, and by the way, Chuck said since you've got to put up with Storm, breakfast is on the house this morning."

"Tell him I said thanks," I whispered with a smile.

"…Okay, and you're sure?" Ben was saying. "Yeah… Uh-huh… Yeah… I'm not so sure I wanna do that…" He glanced up at me for an instant then looked away. "Yeah… I know… But, who… Uh-huh… Okay… I'll see what I can do, but I ain't makin' any guarantees… Yeah… Okay, so when is that? Yeah… Okay… No, I'm throwin' down some breakfast over at Chuck's… Yeah… Prob'ly half hour, maybe forty-five minutes… Yeah…okay, see ya' then."

"Problem?" I asked as I watched him fold the phone and tuck it away.

"No. Not really," he replied.

I wasn't convinced, but then again, I knew better than to pressure him about that sort of thing. Odds are it was work related anyway, so I definitely didn't need to hear it. Instead of pursuing the topic, I shrugged and reached for the peppershaker, but as I did, a sharp twinge erupted on the side of my neck once again. I pulled my hand back and reached up to massage it as I had done before.

"Neck again?" my friend asked.

"Yeah," I said, wincing. "I must have really seriously pinched a nerve or something."

"Maybe you should have it looked at," he said, while liberally salting the mound of food in front of him.

"I don't know. Maybe."

"Or then again, maybe it's somethin' else," he suggested, a mildly cryptic tone in his voice.

"What do you mean?" I asked, shooting him a puzzled look.

He slid the saltshaker toward me then reached for the aspirin. "Ya' might wanna salt your coffee again."

"You didn't answer my question."

"Sure you don't wanna salt your coffee?"

"Ben..."

He shrugged. "Okay, don't blame me, I tried... So I know you say you're retired and all, but lemme ask ya' somethin'. Whaddaya know about vampires?"

CHAPTER 5

"I GET IT," I REPLIED, VOICE FLAT AND CLEARLY humorless. "My neck hurts. Vampires. Witches. Very funny for a Halloween joke. Too bad it's March and not October."

Ben shrugged as he tossed back the aspirin. After taking a swig of his coffee, he picked up his fork and said, "Yeah, well tell that to the girl I watched the coroner stuff in a body bag a few hours ago."

I stared back at him without saying another word. He, however, now appeared to be ignoring me in favor of the "coronary on a plate" in front of him. Of course, what he appeared to be doing and what was actual fact weren't always the same thing, and I knew that, so I waited in silence.

After swallowing a bite, without looking up he repeated the preamble to his question, "Like I said, Kemosabe, don't blame me. I handed ya' the goddammed salt."

"So you think your homicide case is why my neck hurts?"

He shrugged. "Dunno. Maybe."

"It hurts because I slept on it wrong," I replied with heavy emphasis on each word.

Unfortunately, I had a feeling what I said was for my own benefit as much as his. There was a familiar peculiarity about the pain that I had been purposely ignoring since its onset, one that transcended the boundaries of the physical. Now, of all things, I had a gnawing bother erupting in the pit of my stomach that definitely wasn't a mere attack of hunger pangs.

"Whatever you say," he grunted, not even bothering to try hiding the fact that he didn't believe me.

"Come on, Ben... Even if I'm wrong, you aren't seriously saying that you think a vampire killed this woman, are you?" I asked.

"Didn't say that," he replied. "But you're the one holdin' your neck."

Out of reflex, I dropped my hand to my side, even though the pain had become sharper and more pronounced. "Dammit, Ben. What's that got to do with anything?"

"Just two and two, Row," he said with a shrug. "That call was a status on the prelim from the medical examiner. I got an unidentified, very dead young woman with a hole in 'er neck and most of 'er blood gone, but no blood at the scene. Now I got the king of the friggin' *Twilight Zone*—namely you—sittin' across from me holdin' onto his neck. Gimme a break... Do ya' really think I'm not gonna at least ask?"

"Fine, but that really isn't the point," I replied. "Be serious. You know as well as I do vampires don't exist. Metaphorical vampires, as in people who prey on others, yes... I'll even give you psychic vampires because I've actually dealt with a couple of them myself... But, even then it's still a metaphorical term. In the literal Count Dracula, undead, blood sucking sense of the word, they simply don't exist."

He held up his free hand and shook his index finger as he narrowed his eyes. "Yeah, but what about the wingnuts that think they're vampires?"

"That's a whole bizarre subculture in and of itself, and I really don't know what to tell you there. It's definitely not my thing."

"Okay, just wonderin'. They touched on some stuff about 'em in a seminar I was at last year. The brainiac givin' the lecture said there was a crossover with Pagans and the occult and all that jazz, so I thought ya' might know somethin'."

"Paganism in general attracts all sorts of people, and it definitely gets its share of the Goth crowd, so it wouldn't surprise me to get some of them as well. But as to the vampire types, I'm pretty sure the operative phrase there is *think they are*, Ben. Because that's all it is. They aren't really vampires."

"You don't want to say that to them," a familiar voice offered.

We both looked up to see our waitress as she was sliding a plate of biscuits smothered in gravy onto the table next to me.

I shook my head and apologized, "Sorry, Wendy. I didn't realize I was being that loud."

"You weren't. I've got really good hearing," she said then pointed to the lunch counter a few feet away. "Besides, I was just right over there."

Ben waved his fork absently. "So you actually know somethin' about these freaks?"

"A little." She shrugged. "Not a lot. I mean, it's way too weird for me, but someone a friend of mine knows is heavily into the whole scene."

"You serious?"

"Yeah," she said with a nod.

"So this person actually thinks..." he began as he settled the fork on his plate then reached over to his jacket and rummaged around for his notebook.

Reading the unspoken question in his hesitant pause, Wendy answered, "She."

"Thanks... So she thinks she's a vampire?" he finished.

"Yeah," she said with a nod. "And, she's pretty serious about it too. The first time I met her she was really offended that I thought she was joking."

"So, what, she just walked up and said, 'Hi, I'm a vampire'?"

"Not right away, or in those exact words, but yeah, it was almost something like that. She brought it up while we were chatting. She told me she was 'out of the coffin' and just went from there."

"Out of the..." Ben muttered and shook his head as he scribbled. "Jeezus, you gotta be kiddin' me."

"That's apparently what they call it," Wendy told him. "You know, like out of the closet."

"Yeah, I get it," he replied. "I just... never mind... So she just up and told you she was a vampire?"

She continued, "Yeah. She called herself a *sang vamp.*"

"So she's what," he chuckled. "A singin' vampire?"

She gave him a half shrug. "Actually, I guess so. She does sing with an all-girl industrial metal band. But the way I understood her explanation, the *sang* has something to do with blood."

"It's probably verbal shorthand for the word sanguine, then," I offered. "Bloody, or having to do with blood is one of its definitions."

Ben glanced at me and nodded then turned back to the waitress. "Hell, Wendy, sounds like you shoulda been givin' that lecture... So are ya' sure it ain't just all part of her act for the band or somethin'?"

Wendy shrugged again. "I don't know. I guess it could be. She definitely dresses the part. You know, the heavy-duty Goth chick look. But, she claimed she actually drinks blood."

He harrumphed. "Not exactly shy about this crap, is she?"

"Well, I'll admit, after she said she was a vampire, I asked," she replied. "Morbid curiosity I guess. But, I've never actually seen her do it myself, thankfully."

"Yeah, no shit... So, she happen ta' say where she gets this blood?" he pressed.

"Her girlfriend, I think."

"Is that your friend?"

"No." She shook her head. "Mary Ann just tends bar at the club where the band has a regular gig. Desiree is the singer—she's the vampire... I don't remember her girlfriend's name. She might have mentioned it, but she wasn't there, so we were never actually introduced or anything."

"Yeah, okay."

The sharp tone of a counter bell rang, and Wendy shot a quick glance over her shoulder. Turning back to us she said, "I've got an order up."

"Okay," Ben said with a nod but didn't let up. "So what's this Desiree do? Go around bitin' 'er girlfriend on the neck or somethin'?"

"I really don't know, it was all just kind of implied," she replied with a visible shudder. "And believe me, I don't want to know either. The whole thing pretty much creeps me out. I only talked to her a couple of times, and these days I try to avoid going to visit Mary Ann at the club whenever they're playing because they tend to attract a whole crowd of them if you know what I mean."

"Yeah, a bumper crop of freaks..." he answered with a nod. "Jeezus, that's some fucked up shit."

"I really need to..." she started.

"Wendy!" a gruff male voice called out from the area of the grill, cutting her off.

"...go," she finished. "Like I said, I've got orders up."

"Just a sec," Ben said, holding up his hand to delay her departure.

"Yo, Storm," the male voice barked again from behind the counter, this time much closer and louder. "Ya' think I can have my waitress back? I got customers wantin' their food ya' know."

"Just a minute, Chuck," Ben called back to him without looking. "This is cop business."

"Yeah, it's always cop business," he replied, voice not quite angry but definitely carrying an annoyed tone. "Ya' got two seconds."

"Desiree..." Ben mumbled as he pressed his pen against the page. "How's she spell that? S or a Z?"

She shrugged. "I don't really know. I'm pretty sure the band is called Lilith's Daughters though."

Ben jotted down the information then flipped his notebook shut. "Thanks, I 'preciate it, Wendy. Guess I'd better let ya' get back ta' work before Chuck has a hemorrhage or somethin'."

"No problem," she replied as she hurried off.

My friend had placed his notebook off to the side and was now resuming his full frontal assault on the dubious delicacy known as a "kitchen sink omelet." I watched him for a moment and then picked up my own fork. A handful of minutes dragged by as I pushed the food around on my plate, never actually taking a bite. It wasn't that anything was wrong with my order, but the rumble in my stomach had officially morphed into a bitter churn of nausea in the wake of all the talk about drinking blood. Given everything I had experienced and seen over the years, why the conversation did this to me I couldn't say. All I knew is that I was definitely hungry before the banter on that subject, now my appetite was beyond non-existent.

"You goin' soft on me?" Ben asked without looking up.

"Maybe I'm just returning to normal," I replied, pushing my plate to the side and cradling my mug of coffee.

"Yeah, well, you know what I have to say about that."

"I know, Ben," I said with a nod. "According to you, I 'ain't normal.'"

"So, whaddaya got planned for the rest of the day?" he asked, sharply veering the conversation onto a different course before shoveling more food into his mouth.

"Not much. I've got a potential new client who needs a quote on a custom database, but that's about it," I told him then embraced a sudden tickle of suspicion at the back of my skull and asked, "Why?"

He shrugged, swallowed, and then answered, "Just makin' conversation."

"Why don't I believe you?"

"'Cause you're paranoid, I guess."

"When it comes to you I have good reason."

"Bullshit," he huffed. "You know better'n that."

"Who's shoveling it now?"

"Truth? From what I can tell, both of us."

I contorted my face as I shook my head. "What did I do?"

"Fed me a line of crap about bein' retired."

"That wasn't crap, Ben. I'm serious."

He gave his head a quick nod in my direction. "Yeah, well the way it looks ta' me I think maybe your mouth is writin' some bad checks, Row."

Upon hearing the words I shot him another confused look, but before I could ask what he meant I noticed that my hand had returned to my neck of its own accord. How long I had been massaging the area again I didn't know, but it seemed my friend was at least partially correct—someone on the other side of the veil wanted my attention.

In all honesty, I had expected something of this sort to happen eventually and because of that had already resigned myself to dealing with it. I just hadn't been expecting the annoyance quite this soon.

This certainly wasn't the first time I had tried to renounce this curse of communicating with the dead. This go around, however, my resolve was driven by a deep fear. My unwanted ability had been bringing the horror closer and closer to home, and most recently the nastiness had literally set up shop inside my wife. While Felicity was able to find a thousand reasons why it wasn't my fault, I could only see the one that laid the blame directly on me.

I hoped that if I ignored the chatter inside my head for long enough, the disembodied voices would move on to some other unfortunate sucker. It wasn't that I really wanted to wish it on anyone else. I simply felt like my luck was running out, so I was trying to heed what I perceived to be a wakeup call and get out while I still had some shred of sanity.

"No, Ben," I said as I started shaking my head. "I can't do this. Not anymore…"

"Didn't ask ya' to," he replied. "All I did was ask if ya' knew about vampires. You don't, so no harm, no foul."

"But you had a reason for asking."

"Yeah. I already told ya' the reason. I've got a dead girl in a cold storage drawer over on Clark, and from the minute I arrived on scene this mornin', my gut's been tellin' me somethin's extra hinky about it. You and your neck just confirmed that for me."

"You aren't helping."

"Look, white man, believe me, I'm not tryin' ta' drag you into it. Hell, I'm usually the one who's tellin' ya' to stay outta the way and let us cops do our jobs, ain't I?"

"Yeah, but that's not exactly how it sounds to me at the moment," I returned.

"Maybe it's because I've been down this road with ya' before, Row. You might not know it, but right now you got that look. It's the one you get when the hocus-pocus is gonna take over and shit hits the fan. I've seen it a dozen times, and it always means you're gonna be in the middle of it no matter what."

"No. No I'm not."

He shook his head. "For your sake I hope like hell you're right. But I gotta be honest, I sure as hell wouldn't put money on it."

"Remember I just said you aren't helping?" I grumbled. "Well, you still aren't."

"Sorry, white man." He grunted. "Just callin' it like I see it, and from where I sit there's a signpost up ahead…"

CHAPTER 6

BY THE TIME I ARRIVED HOME, THE PAIN WAS SCREWING itself into my neck with a vengeance. It had gradually escalated from sharp discomfort to a tortured sting that rose and fell in intensity with each beat of my heart. Fortunately, although my stomach was still off-kilter, the acidic queasiness that plagued me earlier had subsided a bit, which was at least some small consolation. Of course, my appetite certainly hadn't made haste to return, so the still untouched breakfast was in a Styrofoam to-go box resting in the passenger seat of my truck.

I had no doubt that I was dealing with the earthly manifestations of someone else's ethereal torment. That much was a given in my mind. In fact, despite my initial objections, I was also more than willing to believe the victim in Ben's current investigation was the one assaulting me across the veil between the worlds of the living and dead. Nonetheless, I was clinging to my resolve and remained set on ignoring her no matter how much it hurt. There was just one small problem. Everything my friend had said about me earlier at the diner rang truer than I cared to admit. Whenever the dead came to me for help, I always ended up in trouble. *Always.* While I couldn't really blame him for pointing it out, just thinking about it made my mood as sour as my stomach.

After parking my vehicle in the garage next to Felicity's Jeep, I let myself in the back door of the house. As I came into the kitchen from the sunroom, both of our dogs met me and began snuffling about before finally sitting and looking at me expectantly. They immediately jumped up and followed along as I skirted around the island then pulled open the refrigerator door and started to make room on one of the shelves for the takeout container I was carrying. After a moment our English setter snorted a low sigh followed by something that wasn't quite a bark but was definitely meant to convey a message. I looked over and found both of the canines sitting a few feet away, staring at me with imploring eyes as they quivered in excited expectation.

"You ate this morning," I told them. "It isn't dinnertime yet."

The Australian cattle dog perked his ears and let out a short yip.

The English setter followed with a repeat of his non-barking dog speak. I stared back at them and sighed.

All I really wanted to do at the moment was put the carton away then down a couple of painkillers and relax for a bit. But, I knew if I was going to insist on ignoring the ethereal pokes and prods, then I was going to need to learn to function around them as well. That meant, very simply, I couldn't use unexplainable aches and pains as an excuse to eschew my responsibilities, even though I may want to do exactly that.

"Yeah, okay..." I mumbled in a tired drone, abandoning my task and swinging the refrigerator door shut.

A minute or so later I had the canine's dishes up on the island and was still in the middle of dividing the contents of the container between them when I was verbally admonished from behind. This time, however, there was no need to interpret because the scolding was spoken in perfectly understandable English.

"You're spoiling them, you know," Felicity said.

"And you don't?" I replied without looking up from my task.

"That's not my point," she returned, a smile in her voice.

"Of course it isn't," I returned, trying not to let my foul mood creep into my tone, which was no easy task since physically I seemed to be entering a steep, downward spiral. "Besides, Hon, they're getting old. They've earned a few between meal snacks."

She was next to me now and inspecting the contents of the bowls. "Snack? That looks more like a whole meal to me."

"It kind of is..." I replied. "I wasn't hungry."

"You aren't coming down with something, are you?"

"I don't think so."

"Are you feeling all right?"

"Yeah, I'm fine," I replied with a weak sigh.

The blatant lie might have worked had it not been for the fact that I winced as I said it—not to mention the fact that my free hand automatically went up to my neck.

"You sure aren't acting like it, then," she said. "What's wrong with your neck?"

"Nothing," I told her. "I think I just slept on it the wrong way or something."

"Do you want me to give you a massage?" she asked, reaching up to move my hand. Before she could pull my fingers away, however, she let out a small gasp. "Rowan, you're ice cold!"

I could feel her pressing the back of her hand against my neck and then my cheek as her maternal instincts took over and she slipped into nurturing mode.

"I just came in a few minutes ago," I told her. "I haven't warmed up yet."

"Nice try, but it's not that cold outside."

Given how truly awful I was beginning to feel, I decided not to prolong the inevitable and simply conceded. "Okay, then maybe you're right and I'm coming down with something."

"You aren't running a fever," she countered. "You're freezing."

"So maybe it's a cold," I quipped, managing to squeeze out the last drop of sarcastic humor I had left in me.

"Not funny," she replied sternly. "You're helping Ben with another murder investigation, aren't you? You're channeling someone. Damn your eyes, Rowan Linden Gant, you promised!"

At this point the dogs had grown impatient, and the English setter was doing a halting dance nearby while the Aussie was letting out a nasal whine as an accompaniment.

"No," I told her, giving my head an animated shake then picking up the food dishes from the island and stooping to set them on the floor. The canines were on them immediately, gobbling up the breakfast as if it was their one and only meal for the week.

"Don't lie to me, Rowan," she snapped.

"I'm not!" I barked in return as I stood. "I'm not helping him. But the victim apparently doesn't seem interested in hearing that, okay?"

"You aren't..."

"No," I interrupted before she could finish the question. "I'm not letting her in. I'm doing just the opposite, but it isn't working."

"Are you grounding then?" she asked, referring to the conscious connection most any Witch makes with the earth in order to avoid mishaps with magickal energies.

Even though the question annoyed me on the surface, I knew she was right to ask. Grounding was a basic skill right out of WitchCraft 101 and moreover, the first step in protecting oneself from a psychic influence. However, following the first experience with my curse a few years back, I had been left unbalanced; therefore, it was also an important ability where I had fallen woefully short for quite some time now, no matter how hard I tried.

In recent months I had been much better at maintaining my focus—or at least I thought I had.

I took hold of my wife's hand and said, "You tell me. Do I feel grounded to you?"

She twined her fingers into mine, pressing our palms tightly together. I knew she really didn't need to have the physical contact to know one way or the other if I was truly grounded, but I wanted there to be no mistake. She looked into my face, and what had been a rising flash of anger in her green eyes now turned to concern.

"*Damnú*," she mumbled. "You are grounded... That fekking *dóiteacht*, I'll kill him."

"Who?"

"Ben," she snipped. "Who else? Come on then..."

She began dragging me by the hand toward the living room, and I had no recourse but to follow.

"You can't blame him for this, Felicity," I said as I lumbered along behind her, an overwhelming weakness starting to permeate my body. "This all started before I even met up with him this morning."

"But he talked about a case, didn't he?"

"Yes. A little."

"And your channeling the victim, aren't you?"

"Yeah... That's my guess, anyway... Why?"

"Because this doesn't happen to you when it's someone else's investigation, that's why... Here, sit down."

My wife all but shoved me onto the sofa—not that it took much for her to do so given my present state. She took a moment to situate me to her liking then began covering me with an afghan after shooing one of the cats from it.

She had a point, even if it wasn't entirely on base. This sort of thing still happened to me even when it wasn't one of Ben's cases, but never to this extreme. I suppose even the tortured spirits of the dead had enough sense to know whether or not I had access to someone who would actually listen to what I had to say rather than having me hauled off for psychiatric evaluation.

"You stay right there," she told me after she finished more or less tucking me in. "I'm going to go make you some sage tea."

"Okay," I told her.

There was really little else I could do. Even if I wanted to bring up the fact that I'd been using salt and try to argue the point with her I wasn't feeling up to it. Oddly enough, however, my lack of fight wasn't because I was in any major pain. In fact, I no longer felt a single ache. The pervasive weakness had actually transformed into a sense of absolute comfort and the earlier cold that had started to seep into my bones was now replaced by welcome warmth.

I allowed my eyelids to droop as the pleasantness washed over me. I couldn't remember the last time I had felt so completely relaxed. I was on the verge of giving myself over to the darkness of sleep when I felt a quick flutter in my chest. It was followed by a second, and then a tickle started somewhere deep inside my brain.

I tried to ignore it, but it was on a mission. It persisted in the same way a nagging question would turn into a mindless obsession that kept you awake at night. As if giving in to just such a need to go check and make sure a light is turned off, I allowed the relentless itch to force me to move my arm. Had I been in any other state of mind I don't know if I would have considered the unnatural degree of effort it took to accomplish that task to be worthwhile. But since the growing nag was going to continue pecking at me until I satisfied the curiosity it had awakened, I complied.

After what seemed an endless stretch of time, I managed to bring my hand against my neck. However, the action did little to quell the tickle in my grey matter because I discovered in that instant my fingers were now completely numb. Unable to feel anything at all, I gave up and allowed my hand to fall away as I offered myself to the comfort of the encroaching darkness.

At that same instant, I could have sworn I heard Felicity's near panicked voice screaming my name.

CHAPTER 7

I DIDN'T RECALL MUCH OF ANYTHING BETWEEN HEARING the echo of my wife's voice and coming to once again. Of course, whether or not I had actually lost consciousness in the first place was a minor point of contention. I thought I had, but according to Felicity, she didn't think so; or if I had, it was for no more than a split second. Since the whole event was all really just a blank spot in my head, I had to take her word for it.

The only thing I could say for certain was that I had suddenly found her concerned face hovering over me while she pressed her hand hard against my neck—hard enough to hurt, in fact. Prior to that, about the only thing I could remember was the sensation of floating in a dark, silent void. Of course, that was nothing new. Unfathomable darkness and general disorientation were all just part of the scenery when the dead were demanding my attention. It seemed to be their way of trying to gain the upper hand, and much to my chagrin, it usually worked.

What it came down to in the final analysis was that Felicity was probably dead on with her estimate about how much time I had spent unconscious—even if that fraction of a second had felt much longer to me. But, that was to be expected. Time had an odd way of becoming an unreliable reference point on the dark side of the veil, especially when you didn't belong there.

It didn't really matter now anyway. Fifteen minutes had noticeably ticked away since then, and in the world of the living, time still retained its illusion of being a dependable benchmark. Of course, while one-quarter hour wasn't exactly the distant past, it still made a difference; for now there was no longer darkness and peaceful quiet wrapped around me—just harsh light and the sound of running water.

"Really, honey, I'm fine," I said aloud, my voice a tired drone. The words themselves were inherently positive, but my timbre painted them with a gloomy hue, which effectively defeated my purpose for making the comment in the first place.

I leaned forward with a heavy sigh, resting my hands on top of the bathroom vanity, and looked into the mirror as I struggled to actually believe the untruth that had just tumbled out of my mouth. Given what

I saw staring back at me, I was going to be hard pressed to do so. On top of that, I wasn't even taking into account that the all too familiar dull thud in the back of my head had finally arrived, which definitely wasn't going to make things easy. The symptom list of signature aches associated with my curse was sounding off one by one. But the truth is, as residual effects go, the headache was probably the lesser of my worries at the moment.

Shifting my eyes slightly, I could see Felicity's face reflected in the pane of silvered glass as well. Judging from her thin-lipped frown, she wasn't buying into my empty reassurances at all, so it was really a waste of time for me to even continue pretending.

After a thick pause, she replied flatly, giving me a verbal confirmation of her disbelief while she finished wringing out a washcloth in the basin. "No, Rowan, you aren't. Look at yourself…"

I certainly couldn't blame her for being disagreeable. After all, I was lying and not very well at that. Under the circumstances, she obviously wasn't interested in wasting time with the game of verbal hide and seek. I had to admit that I didn't really feel up to playing either. I suppose I was just doing it out of habit.

I moved my gaze back to my own reflection and took in the not so pretty picture once again. Smears of red still glistened in haphazard swaths along my jaw line and down my neck. A rusting crinkled pattern ran across my shoulder and upper chest where my now discarded shirt had recently been plastered to my body by the sticky wetness. I was an absolute mess by most any standards. In my own eyes at least, I pretty much looked like an extra from the set of a low budget slasher movie.

I continued watching in the mirror as my wife reached up and carefully wiped away more of the blood with the wet cloth then folded it over and made a second gentle swipe. Since it had already started coagulating, there were thick, crusty trails left behind on my skin that were going to take quite a bit more coercion to remove.

"This is insane, Row," she muttered. "Just insane…"

"Yeah," I agreed. "Tell me about it."

"And this was how the victim died then?"

"Uh-huh," I answered. "At least that's what I was told. Apparently, the way Ben outlined it, she appeared to have been purposely bled to death, which would kind of explain this…" I gestured at the blood with my free hand. "Except there was no blood at the scene, which obviously doesn't explain this."

"I see," she returned. "I guess I should be grateful it wasn't something a bit more immediate or you might not be standing here right now."

"I don't know about that."

"I guess that last bit is why he asked you about vampires, then" she announced, ignoring my objection.

"Yeah, I think so. I guess I can't blame him too much for thinking something like that," I said. "I mean after everything we've asked him to accept on blind faith over the years, why not? To someone like him, I don't think he sees it as that much of a stretch. Witch, vampire…"

"Maybe so, but what next? Zombies?"

I couldn't help but snort out a half chuckle. "I really doubt it. In his defense he was talking about the people in a particular subset of the Goth subculture who claim to be vampires."

"I still say it's insane," she replied then made a point of displaying the bloody washcloth to me and adding, "Especially this."

"I guess that's about as good a word as any."

Even with the grumbling, I was amazed at how we both seemed to be taking this all in stride. Of course, there had been several extremely tense minutes at the beginning, especially in light of Felicity's initial panic upon seeing what she described as me bleeding to death. Our alarm probably would have continued unchecked had it not been for my wife's hand inadvertently slipping from my neck as she struggled to reach for the phone in order to call 9-1-1. Instead of the feared spray of blood, however, there was nothing. Not even a wound. It suddenly became obvious to us both that this was an ethereal tap on my shoulder and that someone wanted my attention in the worst way.

Since realizing that, neither of us had really treated this event as much more than a severe aggravation. In a way it seemed as though we were both under the influence of a psychic anesthetic. I suppose that was a good thing, but I couldn't help wondering when it was going to wear off or if it was simply going to keep us numbed forever. I couldn't really say which option frightened me the most. I did know, however, that neither of them was particularly appealing as far as I was concerned. But as worrisome as that could be, it was actually one of the least important thoughts assaulting my grey matter at the moment.

What truly puzzled me was my earlier queasiness over the thought of blood when placed in juxtaposition to the apparent nonchalance I felt about it now. Normally I walked a line somewhere in between the two reactions—affected by the sight of it, yes, but not repulsed. This sudden shift to one extreme and then the other had me perplexed. The more I rolled it around inside my skull the more it gnawed at me, and that wasn't good. After chasing the thought around in a circle for several minutes, I finally told myself that I needed to leave it alone, especially since it was most certainly some kind of cryptic message from the spirit who was doing this to me in the first place. Dwelling on it was just going to give her reason to press the issue to the next level. After what she'd already done, that was something I definitely didn't want happening.

I turned my head to glance directly at Felicity as she continued moving the washcloth down my bare arm. In its wake were diluted streaks of the sticky fluid forming mottled trails across my skin.

"I think it would probably be easier if I just jumped in the shower," I said, looking down at how much blood was still left to remove.

"You're right," she replied. "But I wanted to see if I could find that wound. I guess I just got carried away."

"You didn't and you won't," I told her. "You've already looked at my neck, and if it was still there you would have found it by now."

"I just want to be sure."

"I understand, Felicity, but if it was there I'd be bleeding all over you," I countered. "And, obviously I'm not. It disappeared, so that should tell you something right there."

"Oh? And what should it tell me?"

"That it wasn't real in the first place."

She cocked her head to the side and raised an eyebrow. "So I suppose all of this blood is just a figment of my imagination then?"

"You know what I meant," I replied. "It was real but it wasn't. It was just there to get my attention. Nothing more."

"Well, by the Gods, it got mine," she replied.

"Yeah, I noticed," I said as I fidgeted.

"Be still, I want to have another look," she ordered then gave the washcloth a quick rinse. After a moment she let out a sigh and added, "Maybe I should have just gone ahead and called nine-one-one so they could check you out."

I shook my head in quick response and started to speak.

"I said be still," she admonished in a distant tone as she pressed the fingers of her free hand upward beneath my jaw to expose my neck.

I cocked my head to the side so as to allow her better access then said, "It was already over the minute it started, Felicity. Calling nine-one-one would have just raised questions we can't answer. Like, why I'm covered in blood but don't have any injuries for one thing."

"You should probably still see a doctor."

"And what do I say? I'm a pint low but I don't know where it went?"

"There's still a spot here that looks irritated," she said, apparently ignoring me again. "I'm pretty sure that's where it was."

"Was," I repeated. "Like I just told you… It's not there anymore. Besides, I've been rubbing my neck all morning because of the pain. I'm not surprised it looks irritated."

"Does it still hurt?"

"Not really."

"Not really? What's that mean?"

"It means it isn't hurting like it was earlier," I explained. "It just burns a little I guess. But like you said, it's irritated."

"Well…" she murmured, gingerly pressing her fingers around the spot on my neck as if she expected it to erupt once again. "I don't see anything else, and you aren't cold anymore."

"See… It's over… So, can I just go ahead and take a shower?"

"I suppose… But I'm none too happy about this."

"Trust me, honey, I'm not falling all over myself about it either, but what's done is done."

"What if it happens again?"

"We deal with it, I guess."

"And what if I'm not there to stop it?"

"You mean the bleeding?" I shrugged. "I wouldn't worry about that."

"Oh?" she said, raising both eyebrows. "And why not then?"

"Like I said, the spirit just wanted my attention. It's not like she would let me bleed out or anything. I'm no good to her dead."

"I think you're giving her too much credit, Rowan."

"Why?"

"Because if she was that smart she'd know I'm about ready to put her arse in a shoebox with a pound of salt and bury her in the back yard."

"Very funny."

"It wasn't a joke."

I shook my head. "Do you really want to take that chance? You know what happened the last time either of us tried a binding."

"On each other, yes. What about on them?"

"You can't seriously plan on binding every spirit that tries to communicate with me."

"Watch me."

"Felicity…"

"*Damnú*, I'm serious, Rowan," she said, tossing the cloth into the sink then turning and leaning back against the vanity next to me. "What do we do about this?"

"I don't know," I offered with a sigh. "Like I said, I guess we just take it as it comes."

She snorted. "That's not much of a plan now, is it? You know you can't function like this."

"Why not?" I asked, giving her a shrug. "That's pretty much what I've been doing for several years now."

"I know," she replied, casting her gaze at the floor and letting her voice drop. "But…"

I waited for the rest of the sentence; however, she simply allowed the quiet to close in.

"But what?" I finally asked.

She audibly took in a deep breath then looked up at me. "I wonder if maybe I'm asking too much of you then."

"How so?"

"You haven't any control over this… I know that. Maybe I shouldn't be asking you to fight it. Maybe you should just let it happen."

"That's an unexpected about-face," I replied.

"Maybe that's how it has to be."

"I really don't see that as an option." I shook my head to punctuate the statement. "Besides, the way I remember it, this was a mutual decision. I don't want this happening to me any more than you do."

"Are you certain of that?"

I shrugged. "Okay, I'll admit there was a time when I thought I had no choice but to accept it as my fate, but now I just don't know." I closed my eyes and rubbed my forehead as I breathed a heavy sigh of my own. "Right now, all I can say is I'm tired, sweetheart. I'm just…tired."

"I know… But when you don't fight it… When you let them in it isn't as bad. Not like this…"

"I'm not so sure that's true."

"I am…" she replied, nodding. "I'm not saying it's good when you let them in. It isn't… I've grown to hate it… But now it seems to be worse when you fight them, and I'm afraid it won't get any better."

"Maybe it will, in time. Let's just give it awhile," I said, trying to soothe her. "If I ignore her long enough maybe she'll finally get the message and leave me alone for good."

"And what about the next one? And the next?"

"If this works then maybe there won't be anymore."

"Do you really believe that then?"

"I have to hope it will work out that way," I answered, avoiding any commitment that might come back to haunt me.

"But you know it won't, don't you?"

I wanted to say no, but I had a sick feeling that she was correct. Besides, it didn't matter any longer. Even if I gave in to the urge and lied, my hesitation had already told her the real answer.

"That's what I thought," she whispered. "Go on, take a shower then. I'll heat up that tea."

WITH THE EXCEPTION OF A LINGERING FATIGUE, THE REST of my day was uneventful. Felicity made it a point to never allow me out of her line of sight, but I could definitely think of worse things to endure. In fact, it was nice to actually spend some time together instead of being cloistered away in our separate home offices. Of course, it would have been more enjoyable if it hadn't been obvious that she was expecting me to once again start bleeding profusely at any moment.

However, by evening, she had relaxed considerably and so had I. The irritated spot on my neck remained sore, and the ethereal thump in the back of my head was still making itself known, but provided they didn't get any worse, those were both things with which I could easily cope.

Under the circumstances, everything was fine.

The only thing I couldn't explain is why, when I went to sleep that night, I dreamt of a moonlit lake, the bank of which was blemished with the corpse of a single black swan.

CHAPTER 8

"GANT CONSULTING," I SAID INTO THE HANDSET AS I leaned back in my chair. "This is Rowan speaking."

I had grabbed the phone on the first ring. Customarily I didn't get to it before the second at least, and usually not even before the third. But business wasn't exactly booming right now, so when the bell began to peal I hadn't been deeply involved in anything that needed my undivided attention.

Truth be told, the lack of work was a good thing at the moment. I'd awakened this morning with the haunting vision of the dead swan still flashing in my head, and it hadn't yet faded. If anything, it had intensified. That was bad enough in itself, but the imagery was also coupled with an odd, jittery sensation that had only grown worse as the day wore on. Dealing with those aggravations was keeping me more than a little preoccupied, so concentration definitely wasn't one of my strengths right now. In fact, I'd been having enough trouble staying focused on the game of solitaire that was now sitting idle on my screen. If real work had been involved, I would be worthless.

"Yo, white man," Ben's voice buzzed from the earpiece in response to my businesslike greeting.

I pulled off my glasses and laid them on the desk before allowing the chair to rock all the way back on its springs. I reached up and began massaging the bridge of my nose with my free hand as a quiet sigh escaped. On top of the nervous agitation, yesterday's dull headache was still living somewhere around the base of my skull, and it had been randomly sending out raiding parties to the front of my brain all morning. I seriously doubted it was a coincidence that one of those infiltrators had just now managed to dig in and set up a forward base camp right behind my eyes.

To be honest, I couldn't say I was all that surprised to hear my friend on the other end of the line. In fact, more than once this morning I had almost been the one to dial the phone. I kept telling myself it would just be to see if he had the name of Annalise's attorney for me yet; but deep down I knew better than that, which is why I never followed through. I couldn't help but harbor a conscious fear that there was an underlying motive for me to make the call and that if I did so, I would fall into the trap of talking to him about his current homicide investigation. In my mind it was a tossup as to which one of us would be first to broach the subject, but I definitely didn't want it to be me. If I did it, then that just meant I had caved, and the spirit world would have gained yet another foothold in my life.

Of course, it really didn't matter who started it. The end result would be the same either way and could easily invoke a repeat performance of yesterday's events, which was exactly what I was trying to avoid. While I wasn't willing to place all the blame on Ben, Felicity had made a valid point—he and his case just might be a corporeal trigger. Unfortunately, the fresh stabs of pain inside my skull at this particular moment went a long way toward being a smoking gun where that theory was concerned.

"You still there?" my friend asked.

His tone told me I had paused far longer than I thought. I rocked forward in my chair and managed to spit out, "Hey, Ben… Yeah, I'm here."

"This a bad time?" he asked, trying to interpret the verbal cue. "You busy?"

"No, not really," I replied. "It's just… Nothing… Don't worry about it. So, how are you this morning?"

"Not bad I guess. Better'n yesterday. I actually got some sleep last night. How 'bout you?"

"Fine," I told him. "I'm doing fine."

I could feel my body tense as a fresh wave of foreboding swept over me. If he didn't pursue the previous day's events any further everything should be okay. But I knew it wasn't very likely he'd stop now. He had a motive for the contact, he always did, and exchanging simple pleasantries was never it. I tried pretending that maybe this call was for the express purpose of giving me the information on the attorney and nothing more, but unfortunately, I wasn't having much success where suspension of disbelief was concerned.

As expected, his next question made it a moot point to even continue trying.

"So how's your neck?" he asked.

"Fine."

"Any *Twilight Zone* or other weird shit to report?" he asked.

"No," I lied again and then added a bit of truth to reinforce the statement, "Not that I'd be reporting it if there was."

"Why not?"

"You know why, Ben. I'm pretty sure we've already beaten this conversation to death."

"Yeah, okay, but really? Nothin' happened?"

"Yeah, really."

He paused for a moment then said, "You're lyin'. I can tell."

"Okay, *Columbo*. So what if I am?" I asked.

He chuckled. "I ain't that short and I dress better."

"But you smoke cigars and drive a piece of junk," I offered, hoping to divert the subject.

"Okay, enough with the comedy routine. So seriously, how's your neck?"

"Like I already said, just fine."

"Bullshit. You're still lyin'."

"You know, for someone who always tells me to stay out of things and let you do your job, you sure sound like you're trying to drag me into the middle of this one. Just like yesterday."

"Nope, I ain't. Just concerned about ya' is all."

"Well, I'm fine, so don't worry so much."

"Ya' don't sound fine."

"Well, I am."

"Says you... Did ya' at least let Firehair know? I mean about your neck hurtin' yesterday."

"Oh yeah," I replied. The words came out on the heels of a low snort that I couldn't manage to contain. "She knows all about it."

"Uh-huh, see, I knew you were lyin'." His voice actually sounded like it held a note of concern. "What happened, Row?

"I'd really rather not discuss it, Ben."

"Why not?"

"Because I don't."

"You sure?"

"Yeah, I'm sure. Look, it was no big deal and it's over. But since we're on the subject, I guess I should tell you this much—Felicity doesn't think we should be playing in the same sandbox for a while. She's decided you're a negative influence."

"What? How'd I get ta' be the friggin' bad kid all of a sudden?"

"She seems to think you're a trigger for the latest ethereal crap raining down on my head."

"Me?"

"Yeah, I'm afraid so. What's worse, I'm inclined to agree with her."

"Why me?"

"Short version is you're a cop who's willing to listen to me and the spirits know that, so they're more likely to screw with me when they think I have your ear. That's our theory anyway."

"That's fucked."

"Yeah, but like I said, right now I have to agree with her."

"Great... So this means what?"

"Basically, until I get a handle on controlling this, you and I need to keep some distance between us while you're working a case."

"You seen the violent crime and homicide stats for Saint Louis, Row? I'm always workin' a case. Usually more'n one at a time."

"Yeah, well it's not like we're married or anything, you know. I think we'll survive."

"Uh-huh, yeah," he grunted. "But you know what I'm sayin'. I ain't so keen on ghosts screwin' over our friendship... So how do we fix this?"

"*We* don't." I shrugged out of reflex. "It's something I have to deal with. Of course, if it doesn't work out then I guess the theory is wrong."

"What then?"

"Honestly? I really wish I knew. But I guess then we'll be able to have a beer at the same bar."

"Yeah, friggin' wunnerful. Damned if ya' do, damned if ya' don't."

"Yeah, story of my life. And, it's not exactly turning out to be my week so far, if you know what I mean."

"Uh-huh... Well since I'm gettin' the blame, don'tcha think you should tell me what happened ta' make you two come up with this landmark theory?"

"No."

"Dammit, Rowan..."

"I said I don't want to talk about it."

"Fine. Suit yourself," he grumbled. "Just tell me this, are ya' sure you're okay?"

"Yeah, Ben, I'm okay."

"You know I'm just askin' 'cause I've seen this shit go south with you before."

"Who's lying now?" I blurted the question without thinking.

"I'm fuckin' serious as a heart attack, Row," he replied. "You think I'm not worried about ya'?"

The tone of his voice was sincere, but I could read something else beneath the words. Ben was nothing if not a loyal friend, and while he didn't usually pull punches and could occasionally be hard to read, he always had our best interests at heart, even if it didn't necessarily seem like it at the time. However, none of that stopped him from being a cop with a murder to solve, and I knew it.

"I don't doubt that you are," I told him. "But I also think you have an ulterior motive."

"Jeezus, Row..."

"Am I wrong?"

"What? Are ya' some kinda lie detector now?"

"Depends. Are you lying?"

"Okay... Fine... Yeah... I admit I'm curious what you might've come up with on this case if ya' went all la-la land, which it sure looked like you were gonna do yesterday. I've been through this kinda crap with ya' a few too many times. I guess I've gotten used to gettin' your opinion when the weird shit pops up. So sue me."

"At the risk of repeating myself, aren't you the one who always tells me the cops were catching the bad guys long before I showed up?"

"Yeah, I am," he replied. "And we'll keep doin' it too. But I'm also the guy who told you a good cop'll use whatever legal and reasonable means he has at his disposal to catch those bad guys."

"So now I'm 'Rowan Gant the investigative tool', am I? Nothing more than a means to an end?" I offered the questions in a rhetorical tone.

I suppose I should have been hurt by what he'd said, but deep down I really wasn't. Given everything the two of us had been through together, of all people I could easily see the logic in what he was saying. Still, my reaction was knee-jerk, and I knew I didn't sound terribly pleased.

"Yeah, well you're bein' a tool," he grunted then his tone turned serious. "But yeah, in a way you're definitely an investigative resource. But you can leave out the 'nothing more than' bullshit. First and foremost you're my friend, Row, and this ain't all about the case. I really am worried about you'n Firehair bein' *safe*."

His sentiment was obviously unfeigned, and the emphasis he placed on the word safe was so clear that I truly felt bad for having put him on the spot.

"Sorry," I apologized, a bit of embarrassment creeping into my voice. "I'm just a little touchy about all this right now."

"No shit," he returned, an obvious gloss of sarcasm on the words. "I couldn't tell."

"Well, in my defense this isn't exactly easy. Just because I'm quitting doesn't mean they are."

"Pretty rough, huh?"

"It's kind of hard to explain, Ben. But, remember how you felt when you quit smoking cigarettes?"

"Yeah. Hell, I had the shakes and everything. It sucked big time. That what this is like?"

"Kind of. But multiply it by about ten, and then imagine someone constantly trying to force you to smoke, and you really want to, but can't. That's pretty much how I'm feeling right now."

"So the *Twilight Zone* is really fuckin' with ya' big time, eh?"

"Yeah. A bit of an understatement, but yeah, that's about the best way I can explain it."

"So you're goin' through all that, and you're still sittin' there tellin' me you're okay," he admonished.

"I am," I replied. "It's just something I have to deal with. Sure, it would probably be easier to just let it happen and be done with it, but I can't do that."

"Yeah, I guess Firehair would have your ass, wouldn't she?"

"Surprisingly, no. She actually suggested I go ahead and give in."

"Do what? Felicity? Are we talkin' about the same person?"

"Yeah, Ben, I know. After yesterday she thinks maybe it's worse on me when I fight it."

"Worse? Jeezus H. Christ, Row… You sure you don't wanna just tell me what happened?"

"Maybe some other time, Ben."

"Okay, so then tell me this: If Firehair is okay with you goin' to the *Twilight Zone*, why are ya' puttin' yourself through the bullshit?"

"The way I feel right now, I'm starting to wonder that myself. If I figure it out, I'll let you know."

"Yeah, okay. Well, I guess if ya' ain't gonna give me details then I'm gonna hafta take your word for it."

"Pretty much," I agreed.

"Is there anything I can do?"

"No. Just sit tight and we'll see what happens."

"You realize I'm not so good at that, right? The just sittin' by part, I mean."

"Yeah, I know, but that's about all we can do right now. So

anyway, can we maybe change the subject? Constantly talking about it really isn't helping, you know. It's kind of like offering me a cigarette."

"Yeah…yeah, no problem… Actually, I did have another reason for callin'. I got that info you wanted on Devereaux's attorney."

"Great. I was afraid you might have forgotten about that."

"Didn't forget, but it wasn't exactly high on the priority list until about half an hour ago."

"Half an hour ago? Why?"

"'Cause that's about when a process server showed up downstairs with a subpoena for me from Devereaux's mouthpiece. Kinda brought it back around, ya'know."

"Subpoena? For what?"

"Deposition," he grunted. "They wanna grill me for a while. The bottom-feeders do this crap all the time. Tryin' ta' find somethin' they can twist and use to get their client off. Technicality, or whatever… It ain't unusual. But, I should warn ya'…they're prob'ly gonna ask me about Firehair and the whole thing at that motel with Lewis."

"Great."

"Just thought you should know. But I wouldn't worry about it."

"It's kind of hard not to."

"Yeah, I know, but I'm tellin' ya' don't. It'll be fine."

"Okay, but I'm still sorry you're getting sucked into it."

"Like I said, I'm used to this shit," he replied with an audible shrug in his voice. "Besides, I worked the case. I was gonna get subpoenaed anyway. I'm just surprised it came today."

"Why's that?"

"It ain't my day off."

"What's that got to do with it?"

"It's a cop thing, don't worry about it."

Obviously there was a hidden meaning in the comment, but I didn't press him for an explanation. His call actually wasn't the first I'd received this morning, and a quick glance at the clock in the corner of my computer screen reminded me that I had someplace to be in less than an hour. I simply jotted down the information he had for me then rushed off the phone.

Whether I felt up to it or not, I really needed to make it to this particular meeting. However, it had become apparent over the course of the past several minutes that I was going to need a handful of aspirin deposited into my system before I did anything else.

CHAPTER 9

"THANKS FOR MEETING ME HERE, MAGGIE," I SAID TO THE woman on the opposite side of the café table. "I know it's been a pain trying to get our schedules to jive, so I really appreciate you calling this morning."

"It's no trouble, Rowan," my mother-in-law replied as she glanced at her watch. "I'm sorry I can only spare a few minutes. I do need to be home soon."

Maggie O'Brien was petite in stature, just like her daughter. Of course, as was to be expected, there were also several other resemblances between them; therefore, even with a cursory glance there was definitely no denying their familial connection—it was just that obvious. The ever-present Celtic lilt in her voice simply cemented that observation on the audible level. However, within a scant few minutes of conversation, it was easy to see that my wife's penchant for Gaelic curses must have come from her father's side and not her mother's.

These days Maggie's shag of hair was more along the line of grey highlighted with chestnut, rather than the other way around, as it had been when I first met her quite some time ago. But other than that, she still maintained a far more youthful appearance than her actual years, and almost anyone would be hard pressed to pinpoint her true age simply by looking at her.

"I understand," I said with a nod. "But I promise this shouldn't take long."

"I must admit, you've sounded rather urgent on the phone when we've been trying to schedule this, so my curiosity has been piqued."

"I suppose I do owe you an apology for that. I didn't mean to give you the wrong impression."

She shook her head. "You didn't. Obviously it is something important. But I *am* wondering about why you insisted on speaking with me privately."

I glanced around. We were sitting in the back corner of a coffee house, and while they weren't terribly busy at the moment, that could easily change. For now, however, there were only a few patrons besides us. If I had to guess I would say they were all most likely students from the nearby university. Of course, that assumption was a no-brainer given the proximity of the college. That, and the book bags and notebook computers propped on their tables. Complimentary wi-fi internet access was one of the advertised features of this particular shop, and from the looks of things it was definitely being used.

But, the truth is they didn't really matter. They were strangers. The people I didn't want hearing this conversation weren't. They were family.

"Well, I wouldn't say private, exactly," I returned with a shrug. "Maybe just somewhat confidential."

Even though I had been trying to set up this face-to-face with her for better than two months, I was finding it hard to get the ball rolling. Now that the opportunity was finally here, I had to take advantage of it and I knew that—even though my head still hadn't stopped pounding and a phantom pain was once again setting up shop in my neck.

"In other words, you wanted to speak to me without Shamus around," she replied.

"Well, I think we both know I'm not his favorite person," I said, struggling not to wince as a fresh sting made itself known. Unfortunately, I failed miserably and felt myself physically twitch.

"Are you okay, then?" Maggie asked, furrowing her brow as she looked at me.

I nodded slightly then picked up my overpriced cup of coffee and took a sip, for no other reason than to stall while the stab faded. "I'm fine," I told her. "Just a headache is all. Tension probably."

"Did you take anything for it?"

"Yeah. I took some aspirin before I left the house. Hopefully they'll kick in soon."

I knew full well the handful of analgesics weren't going to get rid of the pain, they never did. But if I was lucky, they just might dull it enough for me to function, at least until I was back home and didn't have to do anything other than stare at a wall.

"You aren't coming down with something, are you?" she asked.

"Maybe," I agreed to appease her, just as I'd done when I'd heard the same thing from my wife the day before. As common as the simple question was, the way she asked it gave me the distinct impression Felicity had picked up a few verbal traits from her mother as well.

Before Maggie could push any further, I continued my earlier thought. "So, like I was saying, since I'm sure Shamus would just as soon not have any more contact with me than he has to, I thought we should meet someplace other than your house."

"He would just have to get over it then," she replied. "But I certainly understand your not wanting to deal with him right now. We all know Shamus can be very vocal about his opinions, not to mention totally unreasonable as well."

"Thanks for seeing my side of things," I said with a slight nod.

There was a time when I would have been shocked to hear her say that about her husband. I had long been under the impression I was merely tolerated by the majority of my wife's family, especially her parents. I couldn't be sure of all the factors surrounding the negative sentiment, but I knew the primary reason was because of my religious beliefs since I had been told as much. In fact, I had even been accused more than once of corrupting Felicity, which was laughable given that she had been a practicing Witch long before I ever met her.

However, very recently, some of the dynamic had radically changed due to an O'Brien clan secret that had been brought into the light. With it had come a personal revelation that, while minor in comparison to the secret itself, was monumental to me: it was the fact that Shamus was really the only one who truly had the issues.

Unfortunately, his self-righteous attitude where I was concerned hadn't dulled in the wake of the shakeup, even though he was actually the one harboring the dirty deeds. It didn't seem to matter to him that the family skeleton revealed was the fact that he had carried on an extramarital affair with his sister-in-law, Caitlin, and had even fathered a child with her. Granted, something like that certainly wasn't the end of the world, but it wasn't exactly nothing either. However, Maggie had apparently forgiven him since she had found out about it early on, and they had still stayed together all these years. So, in that sense, it was all water under the bridge. The real problem was that his lapse of fidelity went far deeper than simple betrayal. The child the union had produced was instantly given up for adoption under pressure from the family. Again, not a truly big deal until you considered the fact that she had eventually grown up to become a twisted serial killer named Annalise Devereaux.

While Shamus couldn't necessarily be blamed for her sociopathic tendencies, I would have thought such an outcome would at least give him pause. Especially given that a partial DNA match had prompted murder charges being brought against his daughter with Maggie— namely, Felicity.

But, it hadn't. And, since he still tried to twist everything that had happened to somehow be my fault, I was firmly convinced I would never be able to understand his particular level of arrogance.

"Are you certain you're okay, Rowan?" Maggie finally asked.

"What?"

"I asked if you're certain you are okay," she repeated. "You seem a bit disconnected."

I sighed. "I suppose I am. I have quite a bit on my mind. Sorry."

"No need to apologize."

"Thanks."

"So here we are. I understand why you want to avoid Shamus, but what about Felicity, then?" she asked, cocking her head to the side and giving me an odd glance. "Are you keeping secrets from her now?"

Her question was honest and direct, so I answered in kind, "Only when I don't want her to worry."

"What is it you aren't wanting her to worry about?"

My inability to broach the subject I had come here to discuss was now moot. Thankfully, Maggie was providing the opening, even if she didn't realize it.

I dug in my jacket pocket then extracted a small jar that had originally held some herb or spice. At first glance, the capped glass cylinder appeared to be filled with nothing more that tiny white granules. However, I gave it several rapid shakes, and the crystals shifted to reveal a delicate chain, at the end of which was a pendant. I continued carefully tapping the jar against the edge of the table until I had successfully uncovered the small half coin ornament, bringing its face fully into view.

Holding the container at an angle, I showed it to Maggie. "I need for you to tell me whatever you can about this necklace."

My mother-in-law looked through the glass at the piece of jewelry. Her face had bordered on being expressionless as she leaned forward, but I caught a quick smile that was immediately followed by a frown tugging hard at the corners of her mouth. With a quiet sigh she sat back and looked up to my face then shrugged while shaking her head as if there was nothing to tell.

"I'm used to seeing Felicity wear that. Does she know you are carrying it about in a bottle?"

"As a matter of fact, she does."

"What is in there with it?" she asked. "It looks like salt...or maybe sugar."

"You were correct on the first guess. Salt."

"Do you mind if I ask why?"

"It's complicated, but trust me, I have my reasons."

She glanced back at the bottle for a moment as if her eyes were drawn there, then looked up and stared over my shoulder. "Honestly, I try not to think too much about that necklace. Of course, that's hard when I see it around my daughter's neck."

"Why?"

"Like you, I have my reasons."

"I see. Felicity said you gave it to her," I offered.

"Yes, years ago. When she was a teenager."

"So, it's a family heirloom then?"

She finally brought her gaze back to meet mine. "Yes and no. I'm sure that it was for someone," she mused. "But, not my family. Shamus gave it to me for my birthday a long time ago."

I nodded. "So then it didn't belong to his mother or someone else on his side either?"

"No," she replied, shaking her head again. "It's definitely an antique, but he bought it while he was away on business in New Orleans."

The reference to the Crescent City alone was enough to make me catch my breath. Less than three months ago I had been there in search of Annalise, and more importantly, Miranda. It was starting to look like my suspicion may be closer to the mark than I originally imagined.

"If you don't mind my asking," I began, "if this was a birthday gift…"

She interrupted and finished the question "…why did I give it away?"

I shrugged. "Well…yes."

"Unpleasant memories," she replied, a coldness in her tone. "You see, I later found out my sister was with him on that trip. I think you know the rest of that story."

"Which would be your reason for not thinking about the necklace," I stated the obvious as my brain did the math.

"Yes."

"I'm sorry. I didn't realize I'd be dredging that up again."

She gave me a thin smile. "It isn't your fault, Rowan. It had been dredged up anyway. Don't worry about it." She bobbed her head toward the necklace. "In retrospect I really should have taken it to a jeweler or pawnbroker years ago, then I would actually have been rid of it. But I didn't and that is my fault. Felicity found it in my jewelry case when she was borrowing something." She shrugged then added, "She was just so taken with it that I gave it to her. I regret the decision every time I see her wearing it."

I nodded. "I can understand that."

"My turn for a question then. Why do you have a sudden interest in this particular necklace?"

I glanced at the bottle as I turned it in my hands, then stuffed it back into my pocket and cleared my throat. "It's hard to explain, Maggie. And I don't mean to sound secretive. Really. Let's just say I'm trying to get something straight in my head is all, and the necklace is a part of it."

"I see," she replied. "And this something would in some way make Felicity worry?"

"Yes, I'm certain it would."

"But she isn't already concerned that you are carrying the necklace around in a bottle of salt?"

I sighed. "Like I said, it's hard to explain."

She let out a flat chuckle. "Actually, I understand... Your motivation at least... I know it hurt Felicity to find out what her father had done. If she knew the story behind that necklace..."

"I won't tell her," I said as her voice trailed off. "I promise."

"I won't press you about your reasons then," she said. "I may not believe the same things you and my daughter apparently do, Rowan, but I know that you love her just as she loves you. And I believe that you are convinced that you are doing what is best for her."

"Thanks, Maggie," I said with a smile. "I appreciate that. And, you're right. On all counts." I paused for a second then continued. "So, I only have a couple more questions, I promise. Since the necklace was an antique, do you know if Shamus received any sort of paperwork with it? Something that might have given a history or identified the original owner?"

"None that I am aware," she replied, shaking her head. "If he did I never saw it."

I frowned. I hadn't expected a yes, but there was always that little glimmer of hope. Until now, that is. "Okay, last question. I know this is a long shot, but since the pendant is a half coin, do you remember if he mentioned the jeweler happening to have a mate to it?"

She nodded. "Actually, yes. There was definitely a mate. Shamus bought both of them. He gave the one in your pocket to me, and we gave the other to my sister. He thought it a fitting birthday gift since we were twins. It was after that when their story began to unravel, and I found out the truth."

My heart skipped and I swallowed hard. "Do you by any chance know what might have happened to the other necklace?"

"No, I'm afraid not," she said. "I don't recall seeing it after Caitlin died, but that was so long ago. I simply assumed that she had either lost it, or maybe even sold it. I suspect her memories of the whole incident were as tainted as mine. Maybe more so given what happened with her daughter."

I was fairly certain I had an idea where the necklace had ended up, and it wasn't either of the options she mentioned. The fact that Maggie hadn't come across it in her sister's personal belongings all but confirmed it for me. The police investigation into Annalise's background had turned up the fact that Caitlin had made multiple attempts at recovering her from the orphanage only to be stopped at every turn. She had then fallen into deep despair and eventually took her own life. Something told me one of Caitlin's final acts of defiance against her family and the system had been to somehow get that necklace to her infant daughter. When I included the fact that the night Annalise was taken into custody, she had ripped Felicity's necklace from her neck, claiming that it was hers, the final pieces of that puzzle slipped together with no effort.

Maggie glanced at her watch then back to me. "I hate to rush off, but if you don't have any more questions I should really get home before Shamus decides to get in the kitchen and make himself a snack or something. Otherwise, I'll be cleaning up forever."

I couldn't help but chuckle at the candid observation. "I understand. And, Maggie... Thanks. Believe me, you've helped more than you realize."

I WALKED MY MOTHER-IN-LAW OUT TO HER VEHICLE AND bid her goodbye, then watched as she pulled from the parking lot. With what she had just told me, my working theory had not only been confirmed but expanded as well. While I had suspected the existence of the other necklace ever since the incident the night Annalise had been taken into custody, I hadn't dreamed it would have as deep a connection, and on as many levels, as it obviously did. Because of that, my resolve to find the hardware behind the spell and put an end to it was re-doubled.

I started to head toward my truck but stopped after only a few steps. The dull pounding in my head seemed to be getting worse. In fact, it was now moving beyond hard to ignore and right into semi-blinding. I knew I had some aspirin in my vehicle, and with a little luck a quick dose might take the edge off, at least until I could get home. But it was going to take awhile to get into my system. At the rate the ethereal ache was ramping up, I felt I might need something to help it along. Since caffeine always helped speed up the analgesic effects for me, I did an about face and headed back into the coffee house.

After a short wait in line, I placed my order for a large specialty latte, peeled off a five to pay for it, then dumped the resulting change into the tip jar on the counter. While I was waiting, it occurred to me that I would be facing some traffic between here and home and the possibility that it might take longer than I expected to arrive at my destination. I'd already downed one large coffee and was about to start on another. A pre-emptive pit stop suddenly made an enormous amount of sense.

"Excuse me," I called to the young lady preparing my drink. I pointed in the direction of the restrooms and said, "I'll be right back."

She smiled and nodded that she understood my gesture.

Fortunately, the facilities weren't occupied so I was able to take care of business fairly quickly. As I was washing my hands, however, the migraine suddenly elected to ramp up several notches at once, sending a sharp lance of pain through the back of my head. Semi-blinding became near total, as light bloomed throughout my field of vision and I squeezed my eyes shut. I stumbled then caught myself and leaned against the basin for support as I gasped in response to a sudden repeat of the attack.

The side of my neck had been stinging, and it now erupted into an agonizing burn. Dizziness started creeping in, and a wave of nausea undulated through my gut. I reopened my eyes in hopes that focusing on something would help. Unfortunately, the first thing I saw were the stark splatters of bright red on the edge of the sink, trickling across pristine white porcelain as they formed spidery rivulets. I watched as the blood languidly intermixed with the still running water, tingeing it with overblown color before spiraling down the drain.

The sound of the faucet roared as if amplified down a long tunnel. It was punctuated by the chaotic thump of my heart as it pounded out an erratic cadence against my eardrums.

A familiar weakness started to overwhelm me, and I could feel myself begin to crumple where I stood. A moment later the floor came up and slammed painfully against my knees. I gripped tighter on the edge of the sink with my right hand then brought the left up to my neck. As I expected, I didn't feel any sort of wound, but I also wasn't surprised that when I pulled my hand away, bright red blood was smeared across my palm and fingers.

I heard my own echoing voice as I muttered, "Dammit. Not again... Why can't you just leave me alone?"

Another sharp wave of nausea washed over me, and I squeezed my eyes tightly shut a second time. But, instead of darkness, I found myself staring at the moonlit lake I had seen in my nightmare. As before, the water was smooth and still, without even the faintest ripple. There was, however, a pronounced change to the landscape as I remembered it. No longer was there the corpse of a black swan on the shore.

Now, there were two.

"*Help us...*" a young woman's plaintive voice begged deep inside my ears.

The image slowly faded, and with it the nausea began to subside. I opened my eyes and stared at the water rushing from the tap in front of me. The bloom of light collapsed in upon itself, and the appearance of my surroundings slowly returned to normal. A half second later, sound lost its unnatural tone as the auditory spectrum fell back into sync with reality as well.

My mind flashed on the fresh avian corpse alongside the lake. I let out a heavy sigh and rested my forehead against the cool surface of the basin.

I couldn't say that I was particularly surprised by the event. For me, hearing voices was obviously nothing new. But I had to admit that there was something about this one that went beyond many of the others. It was a kind of insistence that carried with it a cold sharpness. And it had that keen edge that cut straight to my core then slowly and deliberately began to twist.

When added up, I knew all too well what everything meant. In that instant, the nausea returned in force. Only this time, it was born of the earthly realization that I had no choice but to surrender.

With a tired groan, I pulled myself back to my feet then slowly started ratcheting the towel dispenser at my right. After a few cranks I tore off the length of rough brown paper and stuffed it beneath the spigot to soak up some water while I carefully slipped out of my jacket.

It took several minutes for me to clean up, during which time my luck held out and no one else needed the restroom. After finally gathering myself, a quick look in the mirror told me that I still wasn't anywhere near presentable. My shirt was wet where I had attempted to wash it out, and my light jacket still had enough blood on it to raise eyebrows at the very least. Fortunately, the restroom itself didn't look any worse for wear, unless you went rummaging through the waste can and found the bloody paper towels, of course. I didn't have to do a double take to decide it would be best to simply forego picking up my coffee order and just head for the exit, which is exactly what I did.

When I reached my truck, I went ahead and downed some aspirin dry and hoped that I already had enough caffeine in my system to do the trick. My head was throbbing more than I could ever remember, and it was a struggle just to see straight. Reaching to my belt, I pulled out my cell phone and stabbed at the keys. After three tries I managed to get the number in and press the send button. My call was answered on the second ring, and I started talking before Ben even finished his greeting.

"Black swans, Ben," I said, holding my forehead in my palm as I leaned forward. "Does that mean anything to you?"

"Yeah, actually it does," he replied without missing a beat, his voice even and tone matter-of-fact. "Our Jane Doe had a tattoo of one. Why?"

"There's more to it than that," I replied. "It has some kind of significance. I just don't know what."

"Well, maybe I do. We found some shit on the computer about 'em. Some crap about a swan society or somethin' like that. Apparently they're a group of wingnuts who let the other wingnuts drink their blood. Pretty fucked up, huh? Anyhow, we're already chasin' down some leads in the local freak community. No offense, Row, but you're a little late to the party on this one."

I let out a heavy groan.

"You okay, white man?" my friend asked, concern edging his voice. "You don't sound so good."

"Tell me about it," I sighed. "Listen, Ben, I may be late, but this party is just getting started."

"Whaddaya..." he began, then his voice lowered to a mumble. "Jeezus, Row... *Twilight Zone?*"

"Yeah."

After a pause he asked, "So are you sayin' what I think you're sayin'?"

"Yeah, Ben," I replied. "There's another victim. The body just hasn't been found yet."

"Fuck me... Okay, so since you're callin' and tellin' me this, should I assume you've officially fallen off the hocus-pocus wagon?"

"Yeah, I'm afraid so," I told him. "And right now it seems there's no point in even trying to get back on."

"So, what now?"

"I don't know. I guess you wait for someone to report a body. I'm going to hope this aspirin kicks in soon, so I can try to get home before this headache gets any worse, if that's even possible."

"Home? Where the hell are ya' right now?"

"Not far away. I had a meeting. I'll be fine."

"Ya' sure? You need me to come and pick you up?"

"Really, Ben, I just need a few minutes and I'll be fine. But, I do have a bad feeling I'm going to need a bigger bottle of aspirin before this is all over."

CHAPTER 10

THE DOGS WERE YIPPING AS THE GARBLED NOTES OF THE front doorbell echoed through the house in a rapid staccato. I tried not to think about it, but the racket definitely had a different idea in mind. A vague memory flitted through my brain, and I remembered hearing a very similar combination of raucous noises a bit earlier. At least I think it was earlier. I couldn't be sure about the actual passage of time, not that it really mattered much.

At any rate, I was fairly certain the original clamor was only a dream, so I had ignored it. Just like I had ignored the telephone—both my cell and the landline—when they intruded on my slumber as well. Eventually, the earlier cacophony had faded into nothingness and simply went away, which seemed to prove out my theory that it was all in my head.

Or so I thought.

Now, the ignoring didn't seem to work as well. Instead of a few evenly spaced tones and a handful of random barks, the obnoxious chime was assaulting me as a neverending non-rhythm of dings, dongs, and pings—not necessarily in any recognizable order. And based on the yelping, the dogs weren't exactly pleased by this development at all.

I dragged the pillow up and clamped it over my head with one arm. My new theory was that if I couldn't hear it then it wasn't real.

"Go...the fuck...away," I groaned out of frustration.

The insane din finally stopped and I let out a sigh. However, before I even finished expelling the air from my lungs, I heard the phone in my office begin to ring. The muffled bell pealed four or five times before eventually falling silent. A moment later the *William Tell Overture* began to warble through the bedroom. I tossed the pillow to the side and opened one eye. My cell phone was dancing in a vibrating semicircle atop the nightstand as the tune spewing from it rose through the scale, starting at mildly audible and arriving somewhere near flat out blaring.

With a heavy grunt I gave in and rolled myself up into a sitting position and reached for the device. Before I could wrap my hand around it, however, it stopped jittering and fell silent. I allowed my chin to fall against my chest then reached up and rubbed my face. Twisting around, I squinted at the digital clock and saw that it was pushing 4:30 in the afternoon.

Rocking forward, I stood up, then stumbled around the bedroom. As I found my bearings in the semi-darkness, I began moving on some sort of automatic pilot. Somewhere along the line I must have snatched up a shirt, though I didn't remember doing so. All I knew was that I noticed it in my hand sometime after my haze-filled brain figured out how to open the door. Lumbering forward on pure instinct, I decided maybe I should put it on and managed to slide one arm into the wrong sleeve after three tries.

My head still felt like it was going to explode. I didn't think it was any worse than it had been earlier, but it definitely wasn't any better. Of course, I hadn't really noticed the pain until a few moments ago when the person at the door found it necessary to roust me from the relative comfort of sleep. For that very reason, I was already displeased.

By the time I staggered up the hall and through the living room to the front door, the insane rattle of the bell had been replaced by the sound of someone pounding on the wooden barrier. I started to yell but quickly decided against it because I had a sneaking suspicion doing so would only add to my agony.

Out of reflex I squinted and put my eye up to the peephole as the door vibrated under the hammering fist. I wasn't surprised to find Ben on the other side. After all, my cell had been chirping the ring tone I had assigned to his numbers, and it was pretty unmistakable. The phantom memories I had been trying to pass off to my subconscious as mere dreams were now solidifying somewhere in the back of my head, so even in my foggy state I was able to make the obvious connections between the back-to-back calls coupled with the frantic knocking.

I took a couple of steps away from the door and shot a quick glance at the pendulum clock hanging in our dining room, just to double check myself. It read closer to quarter past four, which meant I'd forgotten to account for the intentional fifteen-minute time warp on Felicity's alarm clock. In any case, if my addition was correct, only a little more than four hours had gone by since I had last talked to my friend. Of course, it had been my experience that a lot could happen in four hours, most of it not necessarily good.

I sighed heavily, slipped my arm out of the now upside down shirt, then managed to twist it around and drag it partially back on before unlocking the door and swinging it open.

"Dammit, Ben, just stop, will you?" I said as I squinted at him. "Even the dead can't sleep."

The look on his face might have been amusing under different circumstances, but right now I didn't care.

"Jeezus fuck, Row," he exclaimed. "I've been out here for fifteen minutes. You okay?"

"Do I look okay?" I grunted, a highly detectable bristle in my voice.

"Not really."

"Well then I guess that's your answer."

I finished wrestling my way into the shirt and began fumbling with the buttons as I stepped aside to allow him entry. A moment later I looked up to see that he was still standing in the doorway. Near as I could tell, he hadn't budged.

"Well, are you coming in or what?" I asked.

My friend looked me over with a half-curious, half-embarrassed expression and said, "Ya'know, you're actin' pretty pissy. I didn't interrupt you and Firehair or somethin' did I?"

"Hell no, she's not even here right now," I replied. "Besides, if you had, she would probably be the one you'd have to worry about, not me."

"Okay, so then you're half undressed and actin' like an asshole why?"

"I was in bed trying to sleep off this damned headache," I told him. "By the way, I'm half dressed, not undressed."

He shrugged. "Half full, half empty. Same friggin' difference in my book..."

"Give me a break and just come in, will you?" I huffed.

He came through the opening, and I elbowed the door shut behind him.

"I can't remember the last time I saw you like this, white man. Do I need ta' get ya' to a hospital or somethin'?"

"No."

"You sure?"

"You know it's not that kind of headache, Ben. Why do you even ask?"

"Dunno. Maybe 'cause one of these days I figure you'll say yes or somethin'."

I let out a frustrated sigh. "What the hell are you doing here, anyway?"

"Calm down, will ya'? After that phone call ya' had me worried. That, and I need ya' to tell me what's goin' on."

"Nothing as lascivious as you obviously seemed to think. Like I said, I was trying to sleep off this headache until I was rudely interrupted by someone at my front door."

"Get over it, Row. I meant what's up in la-la land. You called me, remember?"

"I thought that was pretty self-explanatory."

"Uh-huh, I got the *Twilight Zone* part. What I wanna know is what you weren't willin' ta' tell me earlier this mornin'. I'm goin' out on a limb here and guessin' it had somethin' ta' do with swans."

"Yeah, kind of. Last night I had a nightmare. I saw a moonlit lake with one dead swan on the bank. You've got a murder victim. If I had to guess, one swan, one victim. Today, I had a repeat but instead I saw two dead swans. You do the math."

"Is that it?"

"What? That isn't enough?"

"From you, yeah, it's prob'ly more than enough, but I got a feelin' there's somethin' more."

"Nothing that's going to help," I replied. "Besides, shouldn't you be out looking for another body or something?"

"Don't have to. About an hour and a half ago I got a call that County has one, and she's wearin' a swan tatt just like the first victim. Looks like your math is pretty solid."

Unfortunately, I wasn't in the least bit shocked by the announcement. I had told him there was another victim out there waiting to be found. Of course, whenever I did something like this, I always harbored a sliver of hope that I would be wrong. Unfortunately, it seemed like I never was.

"Another Jane Doe?" I asked, reaching up to massage my forehead and temples.

"Actually no. This one's a college student by the name of Emily Foster. That ain't been officially confirmed yet, but that's just a formality at this point. They're ninety-nine percent sure on the ID. By the way, keep that under your hat for the time bein'. We aren't releasin' 'er name to the circus until the family is notified."

Circus was the nicest euphemism Ben had for the media. Some of the others he used were much more derogatory, and still others were downright profane.

"Who am I going to tell?" I replied.

BLOOD MOON | **81**

"You know what I mean."

"Yeah, okay. Look, you're going to have to give me a break. My head is still trying to reconcile the fact that it's in here talking to you instead of making a dent in my pillow." I replied.

"Yeah, no shit. So are you awake enough for that name ta' ring a bell or no?"

"Foster… Foster… Emily Foster…" I muttered. "Sounds familiar. Was she the student who went missing awhile back?"

"Ding ding, give the man a cigar. She disappeared around the end of August last year, no trace, no nothin'. We know exactly where she is now though."

"Damn. I really hate being right about this sort of thing, you know," I grumbled. "So, where was she found?"

"Dumpster, just like the JD. Only difference is it was in a light industrial park off Page, here in the county instead of in the city limits. She was half ass wrapped in a clear plastic sheet and just tossed in. An employee of the company that rents the dumpster was takin' out the trash around eleven forty-five this mornin' and just happened ta' see 'er arm stickin' out from underneath some other crap."

"Great way to screw up a lunch break I guess."

"Uh-huh. So anyway, it's been all over the news. Since she was found in a dumpster like the first vic, I kinda figured you'd be puttin' two and two together and gettin' in touch. I mean, what with that call earlier and everything…"

I started to shake my head then stopped and grimaced as my temples throbbed harder. My only consolation, as far as I could see, was the fact that my neck felt fine for a change.

"For the past few hours, if it wasn't the inside of my eyelids, I haven't seen it," I said. "Sorry."

"Yeah, well, doesn't really matter I don't guess. Right now the vultures only know what county's tellin' 'em, and that ain't much."

I was still struggling to wrap my aching grey matter around everything he'd said thus far. It wasn't that it was particularly complicated by any means, but clarity wasn't one of my strong suits just yet, so mentally I was probably a good half step behind. Unfortunately, the more I thought about it, the more I felt like I had missed something.

"So, wait a minute…" I said, gesturing with one hand as I scrunched up my forehead. "Let's back up a second. If she disappeared over six months ago, how did they manage to identify her remains so quickly? There couldn't have been much left to work with for a visual ID, could there?"

"That's just it, Row. She may have vanished last year, but accordin' to the estimate from the county coroner, she's probably only been dead between something like twenty-four and thirty-six hours."

"And she died the same way as your Jane Doe?"

"Some strings got pulled, and they took 'er to the city morgue, so there hasn't been time for an autopsy. But she's got a hole in 'er neck. So I can't say for sure, but yeah, it looks real possible."

"You know that could mean the killer is keeping the victims alive for a while."

"That's one of the possiblities."

"Gods..." I mumbled. This was a turn I hadn't seen coming. "I take it Major Case will be stepping in?"

"Yeah, already have. And the Feebs too, of course."

"So... I guess that means you're here to recruit me?"

"I dunno. The way you look right now I'm not sure I want ya'."

"Thanks."

"Hey, just returnin' the favor."

"Yeah, I figured as much."

"So now that you're not retired anymore, you wanna fill me in? Whether you think it's important or not, I'd like ta' know what happened that you're not sayin'."

"Why do I feel like we've had this conversation before?" I asked.

"Prob'ly because we have. Every time you decide you're gonna quit. Jeezus, you really are out of it, ain't ya'?"

"Actually, I was being facetious."

"Yeah, well don't," he grunted. "It's kinda hard ta' tell with you right now. So what gives? What is it you didn't wanna tell me?"

I looked down and noticed that my shirt was buttoned off kilter. In my stupor I hadn't really paid much attention to what I was doing, so I started about the process of straightening out the mess.

"Okay," I said as I redid a button while watching my fingers this go around. "Remember the problem I had with my neck?"

"Yeah."

"To make a long story short, when I got home I started bleeding from the general area of the pain even though I had no visible wound."

"Bleedin' from your neck? Jeezus, Row... That's fucked up."

"I'll agree with you there, but you've seen how aggressive the dead can be when they want my attention. It's not the first time there's been a physical manifestation."

"Yeah, but still… Bleedin'? That can't be good."

"I know. But, fortunately, it didn't last long, and like I said, there was no wound. All in all it really just looked worse than it was. It had Felicity a little on edge though."

"Ya'think?" he spat.

I ignored the sarcasm and continued. "Either way, the only residual effect was one of my signature headaches and the nightmare about the swan, so I thought I'd be fine."

"Why do I hear a *but* coming?"

"Because there is one," I returned. "Cutting to the chase, the same thing happened again today. Right before I had the vision of the second swan."

"Today? How bad? How much blood did you lose?"

I shrugged. "I have no idea. But it was messy enough that I needed to take a shower to get cleaned up before I hit the sack."

"Great. So are ya' sure you're okay? "

"People keep asking me that."

"Yeah, well I wonder why?" he said, the sarcasm creeping into his voice again. "You shoulda seen a doctor after the first time, Row."

I shook my head and answered, "Now you sound like my wife."

"Great…that just tells me that if you didn't listen to Firehair, you sure as hell ain't gonna listen to me."

"It would be a waste of time. At the moment, other than the headache, I think I'm fine."

"You think?"

"Yeah."

"Seems to me that was what ya' just said about when it happened the first time?"

"Yeah, I guess I did." I shrugged. "Well, if I start bleeding again I guess we'll know I'm wrong."

"Fuck me… You ain't gonna up and die on me or somethin' are ya'?"

"I hadn't planned on it."

"Yeah, well we both know all about how your plans work out, white man."

"I'm still here, aren't I?"

Ben shook his head then reached up to massage his neck. "Jeezus… Have you told Felicity about this yet?"

"You mean the incident today? No, not yet." I glanced at the clock and squinted. I hadn't realized until now that I'd forgotten to put on my glasses, which probably explained why the world was still so blurry to me even though the fog around my brain was lifting. I turned back to my friend and said, "Unless she ran long she should be home any minute. I figure I'll tell her then."

"Damn..." he muttered. "You know she ain't gonna be happy."

"Yeah, especially when she finds you here."

"Hey, you're the one who broke the playground ban when you called me."

"You're right," I agreed. "But I'm still going to blame it on you."

"Why the hell would ya' do that?"

"Because you woke me up, that's why."

CHAPTER 11

"OKAY, SO WHERE TO FROM HERE?" I ASKED. "ARE YOU wanting me to go look at a crime scene or something? If so I need to make myself presentable."

"So I take it that means you actually wanna help?"

"Yeah, I guess so," I grumbled. "I don't think I'm being left with much choice, am I?"

He gave his head a vigorous shake. "Hey, I'm not pressurin' ya'... It's your decision."

"Yeah, right. Do you really expect me to believe that part of why you're here isn't to try talking me into helping with these cases?"

"Well, no... Not exactly... But yeah... Jeezus H. Christ..." he stammered.

"Okay, Ben, I've had enough," I said, throwing my hands up. "You've been acting strange ever since yesterday. You ask questions like you want my help, but then you keep dancing around the subject like you aren't sure what to do. One minute it seems like you're pushing me, the next it seems like you're backpedaling or trying to protect me from something. Why don't you make this easy on both of us and tell me what the hell is really going on?"

My friend reached up, smoothed back his hair, and then let his hand fall to his neck. After a moment he sighed and said, "Look, Row, I was tryin' not ta' say this, but I'm tired of it too, so here it is... Whether the brass likes to acknowledge it or not, they know damn well you've got a major track record when it comes to this sorta shit."

"Are you trying to say it's not just you doing the asking? It's the higher ups?"

"Well..." He nodded. "Yeah. It is."

"When?"

"When what?"

"When did they first ask?"

"Remember that call I got when we were havin' breakfast yesterday. Well, it wasn't just a prelim report from the coroner. Apparently, I wasn't the only one ta' get a hinky feelin' about that Jane Doe. I don't know for sure who made the decision, but my lieutenant strongly suggested that I try ta' get ya' involved if I could. I didn't bother ta' tell 'im you were sittin' right across from me."

"Now it makes sense," I replied. "No wonder you've been so squirrelly."

"I'm pretty sure Helen calls it conflicted," he said.

"Yeah, that sounds about like her. So, why didn't you just tell me you were getting pressure from the top?"

"What would ya' have done if I had?"

I shrugged. "I don't know, but…"

"But what? That's bullshit and you know it, white man. I got your number, even if ya' don't think I do. You woulda said yes because you feel like you owe me."

"Well, yeah… You're probably right. And yes, I do owe you."

"Which is exactly why I didn't tell ya'. You've been tellin' me ya wanted out. Shit, you'd just finished sayin' it again when they called, and I wanted ta' respect that. I figured I'd just toss out a few feelers and see if you'd bite. I thought if I kept it all between us and if ya' came up with somethin' I could use, maybe I could keep everything from goin' overboard."

I shook my head slightly, even though it hurt to do so. "Hell, Ben, even I can't do that. It does that of its own accord and nobody can stop it."

"Yeah, so I've noticed," he grunted then fell silent for a moment. When he spoke up again he asked, "So how bad did I fuck up, Row? You pissed at me now?"

"I never said you did."

"Yeah, but I feel like I did."

"What is it you told me? Get over it? Besides, I think it's pretty obvious I was going to get dragged into this no matter what I wanted. Your victims are seeing to that."

"I'm sorry 'bout that. I didn't want this ta' happen."

"Don't worry about it. It's done and we can't change it."

"So what now?"

"We go back to my first question. Do you need me to go look at a crime scene or something?"

"Actually, as far as goin' anywhere, ta' be honest all we really have is a couple of dump sites," he explained. "So unless you got some kinda major *Twilight Zone* inspiration at the moment or you think lookin' at a dumpster is gonna help, you can prob'ly just relax."

"Did you hear that, ladies?" I announced, looking up toward the ceiling. "The man said I should relax. You should too. I'm going to need your help with that."

"Who are ya'…" he started then caught himself. "Oh, yeah, never mind."

"Doesn't matter. I really doubt they're going to listen," I replied then motioned with my hand. "Come on…"

Ben followed along as I trudged through the dining room and into the kitchen. If I was going to keep from turning into a blithering idiot, I needed more aspirin and a giant cup of coffee to wash them down. I knew I could find both of them there.

A quick glance at the time on the microwave reminded me I had yet to give any thought to what I was going to fix for the evening meal. I was already late with getting it started, considering that Felicity would probably be home at any moment, so I didn't have many options unless we wanted to eat later than usual.

"I need to do something about dinner," I told Ben absently. "Are you staying?"

"Depends. What're ya' havin'?"

"I don't know yet. But the way my head feels, I'm suddenly seeing carry-out high on the list of possibilities." I pointed to the stack of menus held to the side of the refrigerator with a large magnet. "Want to see if anything there strikes you? I'm buying."

"Ta' be honest, I appreciate the offer, but I can't stay," he returned. "I actually got plans with Constance."

"Uh-huh," I grunted. "You just don't want to be here when Felicity gets home."

"Well, normally I'd say you're right, but the way you look and after what ya' told me, I ain't leavin' ya' alone. So I'll be here until she gets in."

"I'll be fine."

"Nope. Ain't arguin'."

"Okay, fine. If you're just going to stand around then make yourself useful," I said as I reached into the pantry and grabbed a bag of coffee beans. I turned and tossed them to him then pointed. "The grinder is in the cabinet above the coffeemaker."

"How much?" he asked, waving the bag.

"Better make it extra strong," I replied.

I was already turning my back to him as I embarked on a personal mission. The ever-so-brief encounter with the pantry had managed to spark an idea. I didn't know that it was necessarily a good one, but I hurt bad enough that my tortured brain was blindly following along anyway. I swung the door wider, tugged on the swing-out rack, and then started fumbling around the liquor shelf in the far back.

"I don't use all this fancy ass shit like you, Kemosabe. How much do ya' put in for extra strong?"

"Just fill the grinder up to the rim," I called over my shoulder. "Then put the cap on and hold the button down for ten or fifteen seconds until it looks like what you would normally get out of a can. Sound doable?"

"Y'okay. Full, cap, button, can. Got it."

By the time Ben set about the task, I already had my head partially buried in the opening of the deep cabinet, inspecting bottles as I shuffled them around in the dark interior. Even so, behind me I could hear an initial hesitant clinking, eventually followed by an all out dull rattle as he poured the roasted beans into the device. I continued working on the task at hand, and when I finally hit upon what I was after, I wrapped my hand around the neck of the bottle and pulled it out. It was at just about that same moment when I was closing up the pantry that my friend finished replacing the cap and leaned on the grind switch.

The screaming whirr of the blades was joined by the sharp clatter of the java beans being violently crushed. The blended clamor instantly bit into my ears and ricocheted around the inside of my skull. Unfortunately, as the coffee was ground, the blades began to move faster, and as they did, their pitch increased. In direct proportion, so did my agony. When he finally released the button, even though I could barely see straight, the relief of the relative silence was almost overwhelming.

I let out a heavy sigh then hooked around the island as he emptied the fresh grind into the filter basket and swung it shut. While he was filling the reservoir on the coffeemaker with water, I was in the process of rummaging through a nearby cabinet for a tumbler. Finding one in short order, I pulled it out then uncorked the bottle of bourbon I currently had death-gripped in my other hand. After pouring roughly the equivalent of a shot and giving it a quick glance, I turned the bottle up once again and didn't stop until I'd counted to five.

I set the still open bottle to the side and glanced over at Ben while pointing past him at a basket on the counter. "Do me a favor. Could you hand me that bottle of aspirin?"

He pulled the bottle out and gave it to me. I popped the cap and shook five or so into my palm while he watched.

"Think maybe you oughta take it easy with those?" he asked.

I tossed them into my mouth without answering and twisted the cap back onto the bottle. Settling it on the counter, I picked up the tumbler of bourbon.

"You ain't really gonna wash those down with booze, are ya'?"

I didn't bother to answer that question either. I simply placed the glass against my lips then tilted my head back. When the tumbler touched the surface of the counter again, it was drained.

"You're fuckin' nuts," my friend grunted.

"Want one?" I asked.

He glanced at his watch. "Thanks, but I'll wait for the coffee. I still got some time yet before I hafta go."

I could already feel the first twinge of the alcohol rushing into my system. It seemed a bit quick for that to be happening already, but by the same token I also knew I was downing it on an empty stomach. At any rate, I wasn't worried. In fact, I began to wonder if maybe bourbon was a better catalyst for the aspirin than java.

I turned the bottle up and began filling my glass once again.

"You sure you wanna do that?" Ben asked.

I ignored him again and kept pouring. When it was at about the same level as before, I lifted the tumbler, but this time a large hand slipped in and clamped onto my wrist. I shot an annoyed glance at my friend but didn't fight him.

"I don't know what you're worried about," I said. "I'm not the one planning on driving anywhere."

"Yeah, maybe so, but have you asked your liver how it feels about what you're doin' to it?"

I half chuckled. "So when did you become the health police?"

He shook his head. "I keep tellin' ya' that I'm just bein' concerned about ya', Row. If what I just saw is any indication, you're eatin' aspirin like breath mints, and ya' know damn well you ended up poisoned and in the hospital last time ya' did that. An' if that ain't enough, I haven't seen ya' drink like this in forever... Not since Eldon Porter was on the loose at the very least."

"That's because I'm pretty sure I haven't hurt this bad since then. Hell, to be honest I'm pretty sure I've never hurt this bad at all."

"Well ain't there somethin' else you can do ta' help with that? Some kinda hocus-pocus or somethin'?"

"That's what I was doing until you grabbed my arm."

"Yeah, right. I meant Witch stuff... you know..."

"I've been down that road already..." I shrugged. "I guess I could go out on a limb and try Voodoo."

"Okay. So how do ya' do that? There some way I can help?"

"Sure. You can put the bourbon away and get me the rum instead."

"Dammit, Row, get serious. You know what I mean."

"Yes, I do, but I've exhausted all those other options, Ben."

"Well crawlin' into a bottle ain't gonna help."

"How do you know?"

"Because you've said yourself that booze doesn't fix it."

"Yeah, right. When did I say that?"

Before he could answer, a higher pitched and softly accented voice interrupted. "Several times that I can remember, then."

There was certainly no mistaking to whom the Celtic lilt belonged. I looked past my friend as he was turning toward the source himself and found Felicity standing in the doorway between the kitchen and dining room. Obviously she'd been there long enough to hear at least the most recent exchange in our conversation. Her eyes were fixed on me, and she definitely didn't look happy.

"Why didn'ju come in the back?" I asked, as much out of curiosity as to divert the conversation.

"Someone's van is blocking the driveway, so I couldn't drive around," she replied then looked over to Ben. "How much has he had to drink?"

Obviously it didn't escape her notice that my tongue was no longer in complete synch with my brain. I couldn't honestly say that I was oblivious to that fact either, but given the analgesic effect the bourbon seemed to be having on my migraine, I didn't really care.

Ben held his hands up in front of himself as if surrendering. "Listen, Firehair, before this get ugly, he called me. I'm innocent here..."

"Thangs a lot, Sheef," I mumbled.

"You're just pissed 'cause I said somethin' first," he replied.

"Yeah, well whad I actually thing is pritty funny that you're 'fraid of 'er."

"*Cac capaill*," my wife almost snarled the words. "Will you two just stop? You're both acting like a couple of little boys caught stealing from the liquor cabinet."

"Like I said, it was his idea," Ben quipped.

"*Damnú*, don't even go there," she replied with a roll of her eyes.

"I'm just sayin' he's the one who's snockered, not me…"

"Obviously. So stop worrying about passing blame around. I don't doubt that he called you, but that doesn't make you innocent either, and it definitely doesn't explain what's going on then."

"I'm self medicaning," I slurred.

"I see that," my wife snipped. "Why? What happened?"

"Headaig," I said.

"Is that all?"

"An' the swans…"

"Swans?"

"Yeah, the den swans."

As fast as I had thought the alcohol was working a few moments ago, it seemed to have shifted into high gear now. My face was actually beginning to feel numb, and for the first time since this all started, my head didn't hurt in the least. Of course, the apparent tradeoff was the fact I was no longer able to focus my eyes or successfully convey a complete thought to anyone but myself, and even that was suspect.

Out of reflex I raised the fresh tumbler of bourbon, but before I could get it anywhere near my lips I heard Felicity yelp "stop!" followed by something else.

My brain didn't really register the rest of the sentence, but it seemed as though Ben understood without question because he quickly snatched the glass from my hand and upended it over the sink.

I simply watched him pour the liquor down the drain, then looked at my hand, then back to the drain. For some reason I flashed on the fact that Ben had referred to me as snockered. He was correct. I was flat out drunk and I knew it. However, for some reason the word he had chosen to describe my state of inebriation now struck me as hilarious. I started to giggle and soon found that I couldn't stop.

"Gods," Felicity spat. "How much has he had, Ben?"

"Just one," my friend replied, taking my arm and leading me over to the breakfast nook where he guided me into a seat. "It was stiff, yeah, but still just the one, and I've seen him drink a hell of a lot more without gettin' like this."

Even though I was almost completely unable to communicate with them, I still seemed to be able to understand what they were saying, but only if I made it a point to pay close attention, which was getting harder and harder by the second. I doubted I would remember any of this in the morning, but for now, I was convinced that I was at least following along, be it a half step or so behind.

"Something else is wrong then…" my wife muttered.

"Listen," Ben said. "Since he's obviously in no shape to tell ya' I guess I'd better. He told me he did the bleedin' thing again today."

"Again?" she barked. "Like last night?"

"Yeah, that's what he said."

"And you let him drink alcohol?"

"What am I, his goddamn babysitter? How is this my fault all of a sudden?"

She ignored the question and aimed her gaze back in my direction. "Gods, Rowan! Why didn't you call me?"

I heard the question clearly, but even if I had been able to make my mouth work, I couldn't answer because I was too busy passing out.

CHAPTER 12

I HELD MY HEAD BETWEEN MY HANDS AND IMAGINED that if I stayed that way, maybe, just maybe, my brain wouldn't burst through my temples and try to escape. The one semi-comforting thought that kept going through my head was that I had a very good imagination. Now, I just needed to remember where I put it.

I was squeezing my eyes tightly shut in a bid to keep out the unnatural glare from the overhead track lighting of the kitchen, but it still shone through with a vengeance. In truth, the level of brightness was nowhere near what my retinas seemed to believe it was, but it wouldn't have mattered if I were sitting in a pitch-black room. I would still be overwhelmed. That was just part of the price one paid for stupidity.

"Rowan?" my wife's voice blasted into my ears.

The last time I had chanced opening my eyes, she was sitting across the table from me at the breakfast nook, and judging from the relative direction of the sound she hadn't moved. I was fairly certain she wasn't speaking any louder than normal, but once again my warped perceptions were starkly contrasting with reality. To me it sounded like she was yelling directly into my ear from no more than six inches away.

"What," I grunted, wincing at the movement necessary to form the word.

"I'm just checking," she replied. "You seemed to be drifting off again... Why don't you drink some more coffee? It might help."

She had already forced me to drink her family recipe hangover remedy followed by what seemed like a gallon of water before placing the cup of java on the table and demanding I down that as well. I had taken a sip, but that was about it. I wasn't exactly thirsty at the moment.

I carefully moved my left hand around and pressed my index finger against the center of my forehead, right between my eyes. I spoke slowly and deliberately. "Bullet. Right here. Maybe. Coffee, I really don't know..."

"Try it anyway," she instructed. "I'm saving the bullet for when you really screw up."

I wasn't really in the mood for sarcasm, even if it was a joke, but I was also in no shape to argue. Of course, there was also the fact that as far as any sort of defense was concerned, I didn't have a leg to stand on. So, rather than complain, I simply tried to respond in kind.

"Shoot me anyway," I said. "You have my permission."

"Aye, don't believe for a minute I didn't think about it," my wife quipped. "But then I decided it would be better if you suffered for a while. Now drink some coffee then."

Obviously I wasn't going to be able to match wits with her in my present condition, so I figured I should just do as I was told before she decided to physically help me with the task like she had done with the family remedy. I opened one eye just long enough to wrap my hand around the mug she had placed before me several minutes earlier then carefully lifted it to my mouth. The coffee had cooled enough not to burn my tongue, but it was still to the high side of warm, which was a good thing in my book. I took a gulp and swallowed hard then took a second before settling the cup back onto the table.

"You absolutely sure we don't need ta' take 'im to the hospital?" Ben asked from across the room.

"He'll be fine," Felicity replied.

"You sure about that?"

"Aye. He's just hung over."

"Well I gotta say it's the worst hangover I've ever seen on one drink."

"Have you ever given blood?"

"Yeah, why?"

"Remember how they tell you not to drink alcohol for at least twenty-four hours afterwards?"

"Yeah," he replied. A second later when he spoke up, the spark of realization was instantly apparent in his voice. "Crap. I didn't even think about that."

"Obviously, he didn't either," she said then gave my leg a none too gentle nudge beneath the table with the toe of her shoe.

"I had other things on my mind," I grumbled.

"I had a friend in college who would sell plasma, then take the money and go to the bar," Felicity continued for Ben's edification. "Cheaper, quicker drunk. But she would get so dehydrated that she'd have these massive hangovers. In this case, I'm sure the aspirin didn't help much either." Just to punctuate the statement she kicked me under the table again.

"You can stop that anytime you want," I told her as I shuffled my legs back.

"I'll let you know when I'm finished," she quipped.

"And, for your information," I added, "The aspirin helped my headache."

"Really? I didn't notice. I mean, since you're sitting there holding your head and all."

"It helped then. Not now."

"That was only about an hour and a half ago, Rowan."

"Okay, so they didn't last."

"Apparently," she snipped, the sardonic bite still sharp in her voice. "I wonder if the bourbon had anything to do with that?"

"Give me a break, will you?" I appealed.

"You think I'm not?"

"Actually, now that you mention it, I did notice that you're being pretty calm about all this. You haven't screamed any Gaelic at me yet."

"Don't worry," she replied. "I'll gladly do that while I'm beating you later. I'm just waiting until you can feel it, so I don't feel like I'm wasting my time."

"Yeah, that sounds more like you. Thanks for the reality check."

"You're welcome."

"Okay, if you two are through with the pissin' match, or foreplay, or whatever the hell," Ben interjected, "I got a question."

"What's that?" Felicity asked.

"I understand about the hangover, but what about the whole bleedin' thing? Shouldn't we take 'im to the hospital for that?"

"No," I said. "It wouldn't do any good."

"Why's that?" he asked.

"There's nothing they can do about it," I told him. "In case you've forgotten, it doesn't exactly have an earthly explanation."

"Yeah, so?"

"As much as I hate to admit it, he's right," Felicity said. "That's exactly how I felt yesterday, but then I had to face the facts... What would he tell them? He can't exactly walk in and say he's running low on blood. If he tells them he's been bleeding, they'll want to know from where, and he doesn't have a wound to show for it. Give them the real reason and he'll end up in a psych ward. Make something up and at best they would run a bunch of tests that won't give them any real answers but would surely raise a few questions, which would just mean more tests with no answers."

"Yeah, okay, I see what you're sayin'. So then what do we do?" he asked.

"Not we, me," I answered. "The bleeding is nothing more than a knock at the door. It's a way for the spirits to get my attention. I just have to stop ignoring them and it will be all good."

"I thought you already had."

"After the second incident, yes, I did," I explained. "And I haven't bled since."

"Yeah, well you'll pardon me if I don't take that as hard evidence that you won't again."

"I'll be fine, Ben."

"Jeezus, are ya' listenin' to yourself? It ain't like we haven't heard that one before, and look at ya' now."

"You know, I could do without this whole tag team beat up Rowan thing you two have going on."

"Yeah, well get used to it. It's for your own good."

"You do realize there's nothing I can do to stop all this, don't you? I think it's pretty obvious that I've tried and it didn't work, so why are you taking it out on me?"

"We're just concerned," Felicity offered, her voice actually taking on a bit of softness for a change.

"What Firehair said," Ben agreed. "I've been tellin' ya' that all along." He let out a heavy sigh before continuing. "Okay, so let me ask ya' this. What if goin' ahead and listenin' to 'em doesn't work?"

"Then I guess I keep bleeding until you stop whoever is doing this."

He sighed. "Not exactly what I wanted ta' hear."

"Trust me, Ben, I'm not very excited about it myself."

"Okay..." He harrumphed. "So the way I see it, right now we're pretty much on the same page. So far you aren't tellin' me anything we don't already know."

"Sorry... Sometimes that's how it happens, you know that."

"I ain't complainin'," he countered quickly. "I'm just thinkin' out loud. Besides, it goes both ways. I also got nothin' for ya' to look at, so it's kinda mutual. Anyway, unless I missed my guess, as far as the hocus-pocus goes, we're at a dead end unless ya' go all *Twilight Zone* again. Right?"

"Yeah, I think that pretty much sums it up. Why?"

"It's been a very long and very weird afternoon, white man. I'm just gettin' it straight in my head. So, Firehair, you got my cell number, right?"

"Aye, of course I do," Felicity answered. "Why?"

"In case Beefy the Vampire Snack over there starts bleedin' again.

Because, if we ain't takin' 'im to the hospital or somethin', then I'm gonna get outta here. I promised Constance I'd take 'er ta' dinner and I'm already forty-five minutes late."

"Just blame it on me," I said.

"Oh, I plan to, Kemosabe," he returned. "I definitely plan to."

WHEN THE PHONE STARTED RINGING THIS TIME, I WAS awake. In fact, I had been out of bed for almost two hours, already showered, and was working on a fresh cup of coffee when the obnoxious peal of the bell rattled through the house.

Fortunately, this time I didn't feel the need to plug my ears or hide under a pillow. A good eight hours of uninterrupted sleep had turned out to be far better medicine than the aspirin with a bourbon chaser. While pain free wasn't an accurate description by any means, I was once again dealing only with the familiar dull thud hanging out in the back of my head. As annoying as that could be, it was at least bearable—and even something I could ignore if need be.

On the flip side of that coin, however, just prior to the initial ring of the phone, I had felt an icy chill run the length of my spine. While I certainly wasn't one for believing that anything and everything was some type of sign, I had definitely learned to recognize when something was truly meant to get my attention. The way the hair stood up on the back of my neck following the sensation, I was certain this was one of those times.

I stepped over to the kitchen phone and glanced at the caller ID box. Under the circumstances I fully expected to see Ben's name and cell number displayed, but instead the digits were completely unfamiliar. I furrowed my brow as I scanned the LCD and saw that the call appeared to be coming from the federal government. With a hard frown I snatched up the handset, cutting it off mid-peal, and then placed it against my ear.

"Hello?" I said.

The voice of a slightly cheerful but still businesslike woman answered. "Good morning… Is Miz Felicity O'Brien available?"

"I'll have to check. May I tell her who's calling?"

"Yes. This is Doctor Jante with the FBI," she replied.

My outlook on the day took a sudden turn, and it definitely wasn't a good one.

Tuesday, March 14
10:04 A.M.
FBI Field Office
Saint Louis, Missouri

CHAPTER 13

FELICITY AND I WERE CLOISTERED AWAY IN THE conference room to which we had been ushered shortly after arriving downstairs. I looked at my watch as I continued about my self-assigned task of wearing a ten-foot long stripe in the carpet. Fifteen minutes had elapsed since the door closed behind our escort on her way out, leaving us alone to inspect the four walls of the windowless room.

I shot a second look at the timepiece just to be sure I'd read it properly because to me it felt more like an entire hour had gone by. Of course, given that I'd already spent over two months waiting for this meeting and had for all intents and purposes given up on it ever happening, a few more minutes shouldn't be an issue. Unfortunately, I was having an enormous amount of trouble convincing myself of that fact.

"Rowan, that's the tenth time you've looked at your watch in the past five minutes," my wife voiced her observation. "We're actually here early as it is. Just relax."

She was parked in a chair on the opposite side of the conference table from me, watching quietly as I ambled back and forth. While my personal display of nervous energy was far more overt than hers, she wasn't exactly at ease herself. It hadn't escaped my notice that she had removed her visitor's badge and was absently twisting it between her fingers as she fidgeted.

"I'll relax when this is all over," I told her. "And, I hate to burst your bubble, but we're only early by Felicity time. They're actually four minutes late."

"Four minutes isn't really late."

"Like I said, Felicity time. In real time if you arrive on schedule you're already fifteen minutes late," I said, reminding her of my personal philosophy where such was concerned.

"You could have stayed home, you know," she told me.

I stopped mid step and looked at her as if she'd lost her mind. "You're kidding, right?"

I resumed pacing and covered the last few steps before pivoting to head back to the opposite end of the table. I glanced in her direction again and added, "Actually, I think I would have been a lot more comfortable if *you* had stayed home."

"I'm sure," she replied. "But if you remember correctly I'm the one they asked to come down here. Not you."

"Yeah," I spat. "I'm still not clear on that one myself. I asked Ben to get *me* access to Annalise. Not you. Not us. Just me."

"Well, I'm not really sure what this is about. They just said they wanted to talk to me about her and that they were only going to be in town today. It seems a bit weird to me."

"Yeah, me too. And, Ben still hasn't called me back yet, so I don't know if he had anything to do with this or not."

Silence filled the space behind my comment for several heartbeats. I made my steady back-and-forth trek two more times and started on a third before the quiet was once again disturbed by my wife.

"Maybe it's because I'm prettier than you," she quipped.

"What?"

She grinned. "Maybe they asked for me because I'm prettier than you."

"Uh-huh, very funny."

She feigned a pout. "Well, I am."

"While I'm inclined to agree with you, I'm also reasonably sure that's not one of the qualifying criteria... Besides, this is no time for joking, Felicity."

"Who says I'm joking?"

I held up my hand and thumbed my wedding ring. "Me, because I've known you for a long time. Besides, that comment was so far out in left field it had to be a joke."

She nodded agreement, adopting a slightly more serious tone. "True... But I'm just trying to get you to lighten up. You're starting to make me nervous."

"Sorry, but there's not much I can do about that right now."

"Actually, yes there is. You could stop pacing and sit down. That would be a start."

I ignored the comment and continued my twenty-mile hike in a ten-foot space.

Her voice suddenly took on the quality of soft concern. "So, how is your head doing, then?"

"Same old ache," I replied with a shrug. "Much better than last night though."

"And your neck?"

I reached up and absently touched the spot that had been the source of the bleeding, and it felt perfectly normal. "Not even a twinge," I told her then added, "Thankfully. I really don't need the distraction at the moment."

"What's gotten into you then?" she asked. "Something definitely has you wound up."

"I don't honestly know," I replied with a sigh, and I was telling the truth. "Just having all this with Annalise come back to the forefront maybe."

"It's been there all along, Row."

"I know, I know. But we've been able to put it behind us a bit... Or, pretend we have, at least."

"*Cac capaill.* Don't lie."

"What makes you think I'm lying?"

"Because you've never put it behind you and you know it," she said. "So do I."

"You're imagining things."

"I am? Well then why have you been obsessing over my necklace ever since that night?"

I feigned innocence with a forced chuckle and said, "I haven't."

"*Thug tú d'éitheach.*"

"Seriously, honey," I appealed. "I have no idea what you're talking about."

"Really?" she replied then clucked her tongue. "Why don't you show me what's in your jacket pocket that has your hand so occupied then?"

I stopped pacing again and looked at her. She caught me flat-footed with the comment, and denying her observation wasn't going to do me any good. My right hand was stuffed into the pocket, and I had been fidgeting with the small jar ever since we arrived. It had been completely subconscious on my part, but she had certainly noticed it. Still, I wondered how she knew what it was.

"So, you've been going through my jacket?" I asked, trying to turn the table.

She shook her head. "No. I was right behind you going through the metal detectors downstairs when you had to empty your pockets, remember? I'm not blind, you know."

I hung my head and sighed at my attack of stupidity then looked back at my wife and muttered, "Duh."

"That's what I was thinking, but I wasn't going to say it."

I pulled the jar out and looked at it. "I'm kind of surprised they let me bring it in, actually."

"I guess you were convincing enough not to make them suspicious."

"Yeah, I guess," I replied as I stuffed it back into my pocket. "So, you pretty much just played me just now to see what I'd say?"

She shrugged and said, "Yes."

"Any conclusions?"

"That you're predictable."

"Great…" I huffed then said, "Okay, so what makes you think I didn't bring it along just because of the meeting?"

She didn't say a word. Instead, she mimicked my earlier action by holding up her hand and thumbing her wedding ring as she smiled.

"Touché," I said. "Guess I should have known."

"Yes, you should have…" she agreed. "So would you like to tell me why you're still so fixated on that?"

"I already told you. I'm sure it has something to do with Miranda and her connection to you."

"I know. But you still haven't told me exactly why you think that."

"Well, actually, I can't. Not yet, anyway."

"Can't or won't?"

"A little of both I guess."

"Well, if it's because you're worrying about me you can stop. I'm fine."

"If it's just the same to you I think I'll worry anyway."

"Why? I said I'm fine."

"I know you are," I said, pausing for a moment then adding, "Now…" I spoke the word with emphasis, not to belittle, but to remind her that I knew all too well what it had taken for her to be able to say that and actually believe it. I followed the punctuated acknowledgement by saying, "And, whatever it takes, I plan for you to stay that way."

"You're being overprotective again," she grumbled.

"That's a matter of opinion."

"No. It's a matter of fact."

"So sue me."

"If I do I'll win," she jibed, playfulness once again edging out her annoyance.

She apparently wasn't going to give up trying to lighten the mood, so I caved and tried to play along. "If you win then I guess I'll just be at your mercy."

She shot me a disarming grin and said, "Aren't you always?"

While I was a far cry from being at ease, I couldn't help but chuckle lightly and return the smile. "Yeah, you have a point, I usually am."

"Okay then... So, since you agree, what do you say when we get home we put that to the test?"

"Just so I'm sure I'm not misunderstanding, was that a proposition?" I asked.

"Is that a problem?"

"No, not at all." I shook my head. "It's been awhile, you know... What with everything that happened... And... Well, I guess I just wasn't expecting it. Especially here..."

"I know," she replied and shot me a sheepish grin. "But the mood just came on me a little while ago..."

"Don't get mad at me for asking this, but since this seems a little sudden I just need to know... You aren't experiencing any kind of identity crisis right now, are you?"

She chuckled and shook her head. "No. I'm still me. You don't have to worry."

"Okay, that's good to know. So, what sort of test did you have in mind?"

There was a familiar fire in her eyes that told me she was already getting herself worked up the more she thought about it. "Well, I was just thinking that I already cleared my schedule, so if this meeting only takes a couple of hours we'll have plenty of time to explore a few things."

"Okay, so by *things* you mean..." I let my voice trail off.

"Yes, by *things* I mean we could..."

Before she could even start into what was certain to be a far more detailed description of her ideas for the afternoon activities, she was interrupted by the sound of the conference room door swinging open. I already had a good inkling of where she was headed since we had discussed it before. Under the circumstances, I didn't know whether to be slightly relieved or greatly disappointed by the untimely intrusion. But, given that our carnal activities had been nonexistent since Miranda's interference, I had to admit I was leaning toward the latter. Besides, making her happy was my prime concern, so in effect I was already well on my way to the role she wanted me to play.

Oddly enough, whatever had triggered her amorous mood must have been contagious. Because, the more I thought about it, the more I wanted to forget about this meeting and make a beeline for home, immediately if not sooner.

CHAPTER 14

ABANDONING THE LIBIDINOUS THOUGHTS THAT WERE forming in my head, I turned to see a man and a woman following the door in as it pivoted along its arc. They were roughly in their early fifties although the man might have been younger or even older, I couldn't be sure. His features were just nondescript enough to leave you wondering. They were both dressed business casual, carrying briefcases and, not surprisingly, sporting FBI ID's.

While there was nothing in particular about either one of them that I could readily identify as setting me off, I felt my body tense of its own accord. All I could say for sure is that the moment they entered, the exact same sharp chill I had felt earlier once again ran along my spine, and my ethereal defenses came up automatically.

"Sorry we're running a bit behind," the woman greeted me, extending her hand as she spoke. "You must be Mister Gant. I'm Doctor Ellie Jante."

"Nice to meet you, Doctor Jante," I said, taking her hand.

"And this is Agent Douglas Hanley," she offered, nodding toward her partner.

While I was almost certain I didn't need to worry about any sort of paranormal threat from the pair, taking notice of the briefcases, I wondered for a moment if I might need to put in a quick call to our attorney just in case the danger was something mundane. However, I had learned better than to second-guess my intuition. What I felt wasn't a corporeal kind of chill. There was something far more ethereal and sinister connected to my sense of alarm, and it was a good bet her name was Miranda.

"Are you okay, Mister Gant," Agent Hanley asked, apparently noticing my distant introspection as he shook my hand.

"Fine," I said, nodding as I quickly formulated a lie. "I'm just preoccupied with something from work is all."

"Oh yeah, I know how that goes," he replied with a grin. Whether or not he actually believed me I wasn't sure.

I shot a quick glance over to Felicity who had already stood up and was making her way around the end of the table. I could tell by the look on her face that she was sensing the same thing I was and that her own defenses were up in force. Simply knowing that allowed me to relax somewhat, but I still wasn't about to drop my guard where she was concerned. And, while she was usually much better at masking her expressions than me, I had the distinct feeling she was suddenly very relieved that I was here with her rather than letting her go it alone as she had earlier suggested.

"And obviously you would be Miz O'Brien. It's nice to meet you," Doctor Jante said, making a half turn toward my wife and reaching to shake her hand. "I spoke with you on the phone this morning. Thank you very much for taking the time to talk with us on such short notice."

"It's no problem," my wife answered. "Although I'll admit I'm at a bit of a loss about why you would want to speak to me."

"We're just doing some information gathering," Hanley explained. "Doctor Jante and I are with the BAU out of Quantico. That's the Behavioral..."

"...Analysis Unit," I finished for him.

"Exactly," he replied with a slight grimace creasing his face. "So you've heard of us."

"It's hard not to."

"Yes, these days I suppose you're correct. But please, don't buy into the fiction you see on that television show."

"What television show?" I asked.

He gave me a sideways glance, raised an eyebrow as if he was trying to determine whether or not I was yanking his chain, then smiled and said, "Well, any of them actually, but I was specifically referring to..." His voice trailed off as he cut the explanation short and shook his head while muttering, "Never mind..." Then he reached past me to shake Felicity's hand. "Miz O'Brien."

"Now that the introductions are over, is there anything you need before we get started? Restroom break? Something to drink? Coffee? Bottled water?" Doctor Jante asked.

"I'm fine," Felicity replied.

"Nothing for me," I added.

"Excellent. Then why don't we all have a seat, and we can get down to business," she suggested.

"So, we're it? Just us four?" I asked, shooting her a puzzled look.

"I'm sorry, were you expecting someone else?" she asked, wearing her own confused expression.

"I just..." I started, paused, then furrowed my brow and asked, "I mean... Aren't we going to talk to Annalise Devereaux?"

"No," she replied, shaking her head.

"But, isn't that what you told Felicity this is about?" I asked, glancing over at my wife. "Annalise?"

"Yes," she nodded. "This is certainly about Devereaux, but we won't be talking directly to her. She isn't even being held in Saint Louis. What made you think that?"

Out of frustration I found myself preparing to ask if they had received a call from Ben but stopped before the first syllable was spoken. Obviously they hadn't, and they were here for something other than what I originally hoped. Besides, they had never actually told Felicity that we would be speaking to Annalise, just *about* her. Now, the reason they hadn't asked for me was becoming clearer, but what they wanted with my wife remained a deepening mystery. In that instant I decided it would be prudent not to show my hand just yet—especially if my friend was still trying to pull strings for me. Because, as slim as my chances of getting that meeting with Annalise already were, running off at the mouth now could possibly erase even that.

I wasn't sure if my moment of indecision made me pause too long or not, but by way of answer I splayed my hands out in front of me and said, "Sorry. I guess I must have just misunderstood."

"That's all right," Doctor Jante replied, cocking one eyebrow upward as she spoke.

I could tell by her expression that she had just mentally logged an observation about me. Without a doubt I was being profiled, and she wasn't being the least bit secretive about it. I wasn't so sure I liked being under the microscope all of a sudden, but then given the situation and my verbal misstep, I suppose I knew it was to be expected.

"Actually," Agent Hanley began, directing himself at Felicity, "The reason we asked you here is that we've been conducting an ongoing criminal investigative analysis of Devereaux in order to compile information for our serial offenders database. It's simply part of the standard procedure to interview relatives, victims, friends, co-workers, and so on whenever possible. It allows for a much broader and more detailed picture."

"So you're just getting all that out of the way before sitting down with Annalise herself," I said, nodding to indicate I now understood where this was going—or so I thought.

"Actually, we've already been conducting one-on-one interviews with Devereaux for over a week now," he replied.

I screwed up my face with a puzzled expression and asked, "How `are you able to get away with that? She hasn't even been convicted yet. Isn't her attorney objecting to that?"

"Oh, he objects all right," he replied. "But she requested the meetings with us herself."

"She did?"

He shrugged. "I know, it doesn't seem to make sense, and we're sure she has a hidden agenda. But it's an opportunity we simply cannot afford to pass up."

"Yeah, I guess so…"

"So, I guess you're killing two birds with me then," Felicity offered. "Victim and relative all rolled into one."

"You are definitely a somewhat unique case," Doctor Jante agreed, giving her head a slight nod. "What with being her half sister, and…" She allowed her voice to trail off and left the second observation unspoken.

"*Unique* is one way to describe it," my wife replied. "But I prefer thinking of it as DNA being a *fekking saigh*."

"I'm sorry, a what?" Jante said.

"It's Gaelic," I offered. "Just think copulating female dog and you've pretty much got it."

"Copul… Ahh, okay, I see."

"Yes… Well, obviously we have copies of the case files and are very familiar with the situation," Special Agent Hanley interjected. "Your arrest for the homicides was unfortunate."

Felicity snorted and rolled her eyes. "Unique… Unfortunate… Unintended… No offense, Agent Hanley, but I think I've heard all of the UN words from the bureaucratic handbook already. You might want to try a different page."

Her voice tone was cold, and it was obvious to everyone in the room that a nerve had been struck.

"Miz O'Brien, I really didn't mean to offend you…"

She held up her hands and shook her head. "I'm sorry… Really…" She took in a deep breath and sighed heavily before she continued. "I know it isn't your fault. My apologies. It just isn't a very pleasant memory."

"We certainly understand," Hanley replied.

Felicity looked over at me, and I knew from the quick flash in her eyes that what she really wanted to tell him was that he had just fed her yet another of the overused UN words. Instead, she simply nodded and said, "Thank you."

Doctor Jante looked my way and said, "Mister Gant, we're mainly interested in speaking with your wife at this point, so if you have something else you need to do…"

I gave her a curt nod. "No offense, Doctor Jante, but is that just a polite way of asking me to leave?"

Before she could answer, Felicity interjected, "I'd really rather he stayed, then."

"That's fine. It's really no problem, either way," she reassured us both then motioned to the conference table. "Shall we?"

After some shuffling of the chairs, the doctor took a position at the end of the table. Felicity was already seated diagonally next to her at the corner with me on her left, and Special Agent Hanley took a place directly across from us. Given that they waited for us to choose places first, I had a feeling it was a strategically calculated move on their part.

Doctor Jante extracted a notebook computer from her briefcase and placed it on the table. Pivoting the screen upward, she pressed the power button and started it into its boot process as she spoke. "In all honesty, while we regularly conduct interviews with serial offenders, the primary reason we are so interested in Devereaux is her classification."

"You don't mind if we record this, do you?" Hanley interjected, waving a digital voice recorder as he spoke.

"That's fine," Felicity replied with a nod, then looked over at the Doctor and quipped, "So the FBI actually has a classification for serial bitch?"

Jante gave her a thin smile. "Actually, Miz O'Brien, we use something called the Kelleher Typology nine-point categorization in order to divide serial killers into different groups. Devereaux herself falls into the classification of sexual predator, and while that is not at all unusual for male offenders, for women it is incredibly rare. In fact, until now there has been only one other."

"Aileen Wuornos," I offered.

"Correct," she replied. "Do you have an interest in serial killers, Mister Gant?"

"They aren't a morbid hobby or anything," I returned. "But circumstances seem to dictate that I end up dealing with them on a regular basis, so I've done a little homework to stay ahead of the curve."

"Of course," she replied. "We are certainly familiar with your work helping local law enforcement."

"I pretty much assumed you would be."

"Yes, I don't doubt that." Her tone was guarded, and it was obvious that I was still being sized up. She flashed a quick smile then continued, "It might interest you to know, however, that there are some who reject that classification for Wuornos, as the evidence suggests she had motivations for the murders other than sexual gratification. It really depends on how strict one interprets the typology."

I nodded. "Actually, I've heard this before from one of your own. Right about the time Annalise's second Saint Louis victim was discovered, in fact."

"So exactly what is it you're wanting from me then?" Felicity asked, interrupting before we could diverge any further.

Hanley replied, "Well, Miz O'Brien, as I was telling you earlier, it's standard procedure to interview most anyone the offender has ever had contact with in order that we form a comprehensive model of the psychopathology relating to the crimes."

"That sounds reasonable, but my contact was extremely limited and very recent," my wife objected. "I didn't even know she existed until a few months ago, much less that we were related. I don't really see how I can help."

"Well, that's what we are hoping to find out today," Doctor Jante replied. "For some reason Devereaux is extremely fixated on you."

"No offense, but that isn't exactly a news flash," Felicity said with a shrug and an animated shake of her head. "She wanted me dead. One of your agents saved my life and almost lost hers in the process."

"Special Agent Mandalay, yes, of course," Jante replied. "We've seen the report. However, the issue at hand isn't merely her fixation, which, to be honest, is actually somewhat of a mystery. And that is why we wanted to speak to you about it. You see, on the surface Devereaux appears to be suffering from Dissociative Identity Disorder. In lay terminology, you've probably heard it referred to as multiple personalities.

"In her case she seems to have two very similar but, at the same time, very distinct personalities. However, neither of these identities is childlike, which is disturbing because one of the hallmarks of a true dissociative disorder is the child persona. Still, both of her apparent personalities are unnaturally preoccupied with you, Miz O'Brien. The interesting thing about them, however, is that their obsessions run to diametrically opposed extremes."

"Miz O'Brien," Hanley spoke up. "As I said, we've reviewed the case reports and are familiar with the various, shall we say, incidents, which in part led to your implications in the crimes."

"You mean my trip to the bondage club and motel," my wife said in a flat voice.

He glanced at me then back to her. "I was trying to be tactful, but yes."

She shook her head. "I prefer a straightforward approach. But either way, if you've seen the case reports, then obviously you also know I was cleared, so where exactly are you going with this?"

"Please don't misunderstand, Miz O'Brien," Doctor Jante rushed to clear up the perceived implication. "You aren't being accused of anything. However, there are some pressing questions that do raise a few concerns in that regard. Specifically the fact that Devereaux's secondary personality appears to have an extensive and very intimate familiarity with you and your husband, even though she herself has only a cursory knowledge. Such disparities certainly aren't uncommon with identity disorders, but under the circumstances we feel it bears investigation."

"Why is that?"

"The apparent connection," Hanley answered. "According to the case files, the name used by her alternate personality is mentioned prominently in conjunction with you as well, Miz O'Brien. So given that she seems to know so much about you, we were hoping you could help shed some light on Miranda?"

CHAPTER 15

MIRANDA.

Hanley spoke the three syllables with clinical sterility, as if they formed nothing more than a mere appellation. I suppose to him, and most everyone else for that matter, that is exactly what it was. But for Felicity and me, the name held a very different meaning. Because of the memories it conjured, I had been making a point of not saying it aloud whenever my wife was around. I seriously doubt my personal moratorium on the noun kept her from thinking about all that had happened to tear our lives apart in recent months, but I liked to believe that it helped, even if only a little.

Hearing it spoken by the federal agent now, however, the rolling syllables that would most likely sound pleasant to anyone else's ear were no less than a dull knife twisting in my gut. Unfortunately, for us Miranda wasn't a pretty name at all. Instead of "someone to be admired" as its Latin root suggested, it was just the opposite. Even worse, it had become a garish pseudonym for evil incarnate.

I took a deep breath and heard Felicity do the same. If nothing else, the direction this interview was taking served as a confirmation of the reason behind the persistent chill running the length of my spine. Not that such verification was needed, or even wanted. It simply was what it was.

"Miz O'Brien?" Doctor Jante prodded.

Felicity sighed then looked away and fixed her distant gaze on the opposite wall. After a moment she finally muttered an answer to the question. "*Grodag... Uathbheist... Fekking Ban-àibhistear.*"

The doctor wrinkled her forehead. "Gaelic again, I assume?"

My wife pursed her lips and looked over at her. Then with a frigid voice, she translated the string of foreign words into a simple summation, "You wanted to know about Miranda... There it is. She's a monster... If Satan exists, she's the fekking manifestation."

"I take it you mean Devereaux's secondary personality? Agent Hanley asked. "Or are you saying there is an actual Miranda?"

"Her personality if that's what you want to call it then," she spat. "You've been talking to her. She seems real enough, don't you think?"

"Can you tell us about her?"

"I don't know what I can possibly tell you that you don't already know. Like I just said, you've been talking to her, not me."

"Obviously you know something about Miranda, or you wouldn't be having this type of reaction."

Felicity's voice turned hard. "Of course I do. I know what she did. I know I was accused of it. And, I know she made my life a living hell. Isn't that enough to warrant my reaction?"

"In this case, I don't think so," he replied.

"Maybe you should think a bit harder then."

"Allow me to explain my reasoning, Miz O'Brien," he continued calmly. "I think you know more than you are saying because according to the early police reports, you actually identified yourself as Miranda on at least one occasion."

I straightened in my chair at the comment but remained closed-mouthed for the moment. However, I couldn't say how long that would last. The earlier mistrust I had apparently been too quick to rule out was rearing its head once again. I felt the prickle of gooseflesh as the hair on the back of my neck stood at attention. In concert with the sensation, my brain sorted through the various directions this could go. Unfortunately, none of them seemed particularly appealing.

"That's a different story," Felicity told him.

"Different how?"

She shrugged. "Just...different."

"Well, even you have to admit that it seems a bit coincidental," he pressed.

"You said it yourself," she replied. "Coincidence."

"As I said, Miz O'Brien, we've read the case files."

To my knowledge, with the exception of the handful of detectives and federal officers with whom I had closely worked, the name Miranda had been nothing more than an alias used by Annalise. Now, however, the harsh light of the BAU appeared as if it was being trained on a ghost, even if they didn't realize it, and my wife was being caught in that beam as well.

In response to my wife's silence, Agent Hanley made a capitulatory gesture with his hands as he raised his eyebrows. "Honestly, I think you're hiding something. Why can't you at least tell us why you chose to refer to yourself by that particular name?"

My comfort zone was already being severely stressed, and his latest comment served only to push it to the limit. Instead of allowing its walls to be breached I interrupted. "I think maybe we're finished here."

My tone carried a sharp edge that, judging from the looks I received, definitely appeared to annoy or at the very least surprise the two FBI agents. At this point, however, I really didn't care. I wasn't going to let Felicity be railroaded again, especially not like this.

"I was speaking to your wife, Mister Gant," Hanley replied.

"I caught that, Agent Hanley," I shot back coolly. "But, just so we avoid any misunderstanding, I was speaking to *both* of you."

"I agree with Rowan, then," Felicity announced. "This suddenly seems more like an interrogation than an interview."

Doctor Jante spoke up. "Miz O'Brien, I understand how you must feel about this after everything you've been through, but you have nothing to worry about. No one is accusing you of anything."

"That certainly isn't the impression you're giving me," Felicity replied.

"I apologize for that," Doctor Jante said, offering a smile. "To the both of you. That isn't our intention at all. We're simply trying to gather as much information as we can, and with our time limited as it is, sometimes the stress can creep through, even for us." She glanced at her partner. "I'm afraid Agent Hanley was just a little overzealous."

Hanley gave her a shallow nod of agreement then muttered a quick and blatantly insincere apology in our direction. Other than that he remained quiet, with a somewhat stoic expression on his face as he stared across the table at us.

In that moment the two of them had officially established their roles as good cop and bad cop. Any other time I probably would have pointed out to them that I was onto their game, but the obvious posturing seemed just exactly that—*obvious*. Their less than subtle attempt at manipulation bothered me enough that I had to wonder why they had been so transparent. I knew I should be listening to my instincts to cut and run, but there was just one small problem. My curiosity was taking over.

"We'd like to continue if you're agreeable to that," Jante said, directing herself to Felicity, although she did cast a quick glance in my direction as well.

Personally, I wasn't excited about the situation, but the nagging wonder in the back of my head was getting the better of me. I wanted to know just exactly what they were after and why. I turned toward my wife and wrestled with the momentary indecision.

After a heartbeat or two I abandoned the struggle and chose a different path. I would allow Felicity to be the barometer. As curious as I was, I knew she would be pragmatic. She always was. If she wanted to leave now, we would. If she wanted to hear them out, then I would just be sure to pay even closer attention to my gut. If my inklings grew any stronger, I figured I could just pull the plug then and there. At least, that's what I hoped.

I shrugged. "I'll leave it up to you unless you want me to decide. Just say the word."

She looked at me and gave a shallow nod then absently chewed at her lower lip. A thick quiet filled the room, underscored by the low whirr of the cooling fan on Doctor Jante's notebook computer as it kicked on for a moment.

"Maybe I can help with your decision," the doctor finally said, breaking the silence and taking advantage of the fact that my wife had not yet said no. "May I show you something, Miz O'Brien?"

"What?" Felicity asked.

"It's a short clip from a video recording of an interview with Devereaux."

"Why do you want me to see it?"

"I think that after you do, you'll have a better understanding of why we are so interested in your apparent connection with Miranda."

Felicity looked over at me again then back to Doctor Jante. She closed her eyes and sighed, then gave a quick nod to the affirmative as her eyelids fluttered open. "Okay. I'll watch it."

Jante skillfully fingered the computer keyboard then twisted the whole unit so that it was aimed in our direction.

"This particular clip is from an interview conducted last week," she told us as a simple introduction then reached around and tapped the touch pad to start it playing.

As the image opened on the screen, I experienced an excruciating moment of déjà vu. Annalise Devereaux was almost a dead ringer for Felicity. There were differences to be sure, but they were subtle enough that even I had to do a double take. What made this worse for me, though, was the fact that the woman in the video was clad in a prison issue orange jumpsuit and wearing handcuffs. When my wife had been arrested and accused of the murders, I had visited her at the Justice Center where she had been held. The image before me now was almost like a snapshot taken directly from my memory, and it brought a phantom wave of the emotional pain flooding back without warning.

I watched as the video doppelganger settled back in her chair, regarding the person seated across the table from her with a curious expression. While the camera was primarily focused on Annalise, I could make out enough of the interviewer's profile to reasonably assume that it was Doctor Jante herself. As the clip moved forward, audio began to stream from the computer.

"Actually, she reminds me of how Annalise was in the beginning," Devereaux said, her voice a sweet Southern drawl even through the tinniness of the small speakers. "But, better. Much better."

Judging from the third person reference, it was apparent that Miranda was in control.

"Miz O'Brien, you mean?" the half image of Doctor Jante on the screen asked.

"Felicity, yes," Miranda replied.

"How is it that you know her?"

"Serendipity."

"Would you like to explain?"

"No."

"I see. So, what is it that makes her better than Annalise?"

"Her spirit, of course," she said, shaking her head and smiling. The tone of her voice made her reply sound as if the answer was so obvious that the question itself was wholly unnecessary. "She fights her desires, and that just makes them all the sweeter when they are realized. For the both of us."

"And those desires would be?"

"To accept their love completely and without hesitation."

"Love?"

"Yes."

"By 'accept their love' exactly what and who do you mean?"

"Accepting their love by giving them what they want."

"'They' being men?"

"Of course."

"So what you really mean is torturing and killing men for your own sexual gratification?"

"No." Miranda shook her head. "I mean exactly what I said. Loving them."

"I'm not sure I comprehend how what you do to them equates to love."

Miranda flashed her wicked smile. "Of course you don't. You don't have the capacity to understand."

"Perhaps if you explained it to me."

"That would be like trying to explain algebra to a flea, now wouldn't it?"

"I don't know. I'm a little smarter than your average flea. Why don't you give it a try and we'll see?"

Miranda leaned forward and adopted a serious visage. "Do you have children, Ellie?"

"Do you?" the doctor countered without missing a beat.

Miranda smiled and leaned back. "Of course you don't. You're far too wrapped up in yourself to have had time for a partner, much less children."

"That's an interesting observation."

"No it isn't." She shook her head. "I'm merely stating the obvious."

"I see."

Miranda looked her over then leaned back in the chair once again. "Or maybe you're a lesbian. Is that it? Do you prefer the company of women, Ellie?"

"I really expected better from you," the onscreen Doctor Jante replied, her voice even and unfazed. "That's exactly what Virgil Leroy Belton asked when I interviewed him. I even wrote about it, so I would have to assume you've read my book."

"Actually, that isn't exactly what he said. Belton asked if you were a 'pussy licking dyke.' I'm not that crude."

"Yes, you are correct. So obviously you did read it."

"No, but Annalise did."

"I see. What did she think?"

"She thought it was sophomoric and speculated that your PhD came from a box of caramel corn."

"Still trying insults? Isn't that ploy a bit common?"

"No more common than the questions you've been asking me, Ellie. I'm merely slumming. As distasteful as it is, I'm bringing myself down to your level to help you understand what you couldn't otherwise. You should really show some appreciation for the sacrifice I am making on your behalf."

Video Jante remained silent. Eventually Miranda cocked her head to the side and grinned.

"Do you know why I wanted to know if you have children?" she asked.

"I have my own theory, but I'm fairly certain you would say I'm wrong if I were to tell you."

"That's because you are. I don't even have to hear it to know that." Miranda sighed. "I suppose I should just tell you. I asked you about children because it might help you better understand. You see, Ellie, the bond between a mother and child is unlike anything else. No love runs as deep, even the love I feel for them, and they for me. And, I imagine that when a mother sees her child take its first step, she must feel just exactly like I did that night."

"Which night would that be?"

"The night in the motel with Felicity," she replied. "That's what you *really* want to know about, now isn't it?"

"Motel?"

"Don't pretend to be any more stupid than you already are, Ellie. It's unbecoming. Obviously you don't have breeding, so at least try to live up to your supposed education."

"Humor me."

Miranda sighed. "You bore me."

"Then let me speak to Annalise."

"You bore her as well."

"Really." Jante said the word more as a statement than a question.

Miranda answered it anyway. "Yes, of course you do. Unfortunately, Annalise is too damaged to know better."

"And why is she damaged?"

"Because she's weak, of course."

"So you damaged her?"

"No, she damaged herself."

"How?"

The two of them sat staring at one another in silence as the progress bar on the video player crept along and seconds ticked off on the digital counter.

"That isn't what you are here to talk about, Ellie. You know that."

"Are you certain of that?"

"Don't play games."

"I'm not. You know exactly why I'm here. You've been directly linked to seven brutal murders, maybe even several more. I'm here to find out why."

"That answer is so simple you should have seen it by now, which simply proves my point."

"The answer is rarely simple in cases such as these."

"This one is. I did it for Felicity."

"Are you saying that Miz O'Brien told you to kill those men?"

Miranda cocked her eyebrow. "See. I give you the answer and you still miss it entirely. Try thinking before you open your mouth. What makes you think anyone could tell me to do anything?"

"I never said anyone could. I merely asked if someone did."

"You still want to know about the motel, don't you?"

"I think you want to tell me about it, or you wouldn't keep bringing it up."

An almost wistful look seemed to pass across Miranda's features. The struggle for control between the two women had been gently teetering like a carefully balanced see-saw on a still summer day. But now the imaginary wind picked up, and the nudge it provided seemed to dip matters in Jante's favor.

"I'm talking about the motel where Felicity took the man Annalise used for revenge," Miranda finally said.

"Brad Lewis? Your last victim?"

"I suppose that was his name. What they call themselves isn't important. All that matters is that they love and are loved." Miranda shook her head again. "But, as usual, you're wrong. He wasn't my victim. None of them are my victims."

"You murdered him. That makes him a victim in my book."

"I never said he wasn't a victim. I simply explained he was not *my* victim. Annalise murdered him, not me. She did it out of spite because she is jealous of Felicity. I, on the other hand, would have loved him."

"Semantics. He's still dead."

"See. I told you that you were too stupid to understand."

"All right, since I'm so stupid, educate me. What is it about that night you want me to know?"

Miranda let out a contented sigh and stared into the distance with a pleased smile on her lips. The yearning look remained on her face as she began to talk. "It was a very special night. It was when Felicity first started to understand her true capacity to love."

"How do you mean?"

"We both loved him. Together. And, when I left she was still loving him."

"You mean torturing."

"Loving. She was giving him what he wanted and needed. And, in return, she was accepting his love."

"I see. What do you mean, 'when you left'? Were you there with her?"

Miranda continued to stare off into space. "I should have stayed longer to make sure she didn't stumble, but Annalise was being needy and I had to leave. I should have ignored the bitch and stayed where I belonged. I blame myself for not being there for Felicity. If I had I wouldn't be sitting here talking to you."

"Where would you be?"

"Where I belong, of course. And where I will be soon enough. With her."

The video clip ended, and the player automatically paused on the last frame. Staring back at us, frozen in two-dimensional space, was the image of Annalise wearing Miranda's almost frightening smile twisted across her lips.

The flesh and blood Doctor Jante reached over and carefully spun the notebook computer back around before leveling her gaze on my wife. "Miz O'Brien," she said, her voice even. "I think perhaps now you can see our situation a bit more clearly."

Felicity sighed and gave her a shallow nod.

Jante continued. "I'm afraid I need to ask you a somewhat disturbing question. Was Annalise Devereaux in the motel room with you that night before the police arrived?"

CHAPTER 16

FROM THE SOUND OF DOCTOR JANTE'S QUESTION, IT appeared that I should have stuck to my guns about drawing this interview-turned-witch hunt to an immediate close. Hindsight being what it was, my earlier curiosity-induced myopia had me feeling incredibly stupid for allowing it to continue even though I'd left the decision up to my wife. Unfortunately, there didn't seem to be anything I could do about it now without making Felicity look just as guilty as Annalise. Of course, it seemed they had already come to that conclusion without my help.

"Not that I recall," Felicity replied.

Cliché though they were, I knew she had chosen the words carefully. Even if Annalise had been at the motel with her, she wouldn't have known because, for all intents and purposes, Felicity had been there in body only. Her consciousness had been elsewhere, and her memory of that night had a several hour gap. But Annalise wasn't the real issue here anyway, Miranda was, and she had most definitely been present. Just not the way they meant.

"Are you absolutely certain?" Hanley pressed.

"Exactly what are you implying?" I asked, issuing the demand before my wife could respond to his question. "What happened to the part where no one is accusing her of anything?"

"We aren't implying anything," Doctor Jante interjected. "And we certainly aren't making accusations. We're merely trying to find the truth and establish how Devereaux came to know these facts."

Even though I knew the real answer, unbelievable as it was, I objected in the only way I could, waving my hand at the computer as I spoke. "What facts? That was just vague rambling. If anything she got lucky telling you what you wanted to hear. Not to mention the fact that I'm sure her attorneys have subpoenaed the same police reports you've been reading. They could have told her everything she just said."

"Agreed," she replied. "I think maybe you are misunderstanding our intent."

"From where I sit it sounds to me like you're trying to paint my wife as her accomplice. Is that the intent you're talking about?"

"Actually, it's just the opposite," Agent Hanley offered. "We're working to rule out Miz O'Brien completely."

"Oh please." I let out an abbreviated harrumph. "Do you really think I'm going to believe you aren't lying through your teeth right now? Ten minutes ago you hit us with a purposely transparent good cop-bad cop routine. Why, I haven't quite figured out, but it's obvious you're trying to run a game down on us. I sincerely doubt we can believe anything you've said since you walked through the door. You probably aren't even with the BAU at all."

"I can assure you we are with the BAU," he replied. "And what you choose to believe is up to you, but you do need to calm down. The simple truth is we're on your side, whether you realize it or not."

Doctor Jante directed herself toward me. "We're gathering information for a criminal analysis, Mister Gant. The supposed Miranda personality has recited various other facts about Miz O'Brien, all of which we have been able to corroborate."

"Corroborate how?"

"Primarily through public records."

"Since you're the FBI I suppose I shouldn't bother to ask if it occurred to you that she, or again her attorneys, did a bit of research via those same public records?"

"Of course it did," she replied, shaking her head. "In fact, it's our working theory."

"You keep saying 'supposed Miranda personality'," Felicity interrupted. "What do you mean by that?"

"We aren't exactly sure what to call it," she answered. "To put it simply, it all comes back to what I mentioned before. In cases of Dissociative Identity Disorder, the psyche splits as a defense mechanism. It compartmentalizes the effects of severe psychological trauma but will then act out when subjected to triggering stressors. Since the origin of the disorder can usually be traced back to a recurring trauma such as extreme abuse or sexual molestation, generally the fracture focuses on a childlike personality where the individual can create what they perceive as a safe space. There may be other identities, yes, but the childlike aspect is a dominant and driving force. As I told you before, Annalise has no such fracture. She simply has Annalise and Miranda. Both of who are wholly aware of one another and appear to have some type of symbiotic relationship, although that seems to be disintegrating rapidly. I'll admit that initially I believed her to be faking the disorder, however, if that is the case she is very adept. If she is for real, then she is a very unique case indeed."

Felicity and I looked at one another briefly but remained tight-lipped. Puzzle pieces were starting to fall into place, and the picture they made was less than pretty. However, it wasn't the image I'd been conjuring in my mind's eye over the past half hour. Instead, it was an updated version of the one I'd feared all along.

I don't suppose any of this should have come as a surprise to me. After all, I had always been of the belief that Miranda would continue to use Annalise until she could find a way to reconnect with Felicity, and she was obviously doing just that. She knew full well my wife wouldn't come to her willingly, so she needed a way to make it happen, and establishing complicity seemed to be her plan.

"So why am I really here then?" Felicity asked with a quick shake of her head. "What is it you want from me?"

"For exactly the reason we told you in the beginning," Hanley said. "So we can gather information."

"But it's not just for your database, is it?" I asked.

"Admittedly, there is another need for the information, yes," Jante answered. "Everything we gather will be provided to the prosecution. But, at this point, we don't know what her attorney might try, and we have to be absolutely certain of our facts where this case is concerned. Given what we have learned so far, it is a near certainty that you'll be brought into court to testify, Miz O'Brien."

"About what?"

"The connection between the two of you."

"That's exactly what Miranda wants," I replied.

"Why is that?"

"Long story."

Felicity jumped in. "Do you think her attorney might try to shift blame to me?"

"We don't know for sure what his plan of attack will be. Right now we're just speculating," Agent Hanley answered. "Insanity defenses are a long shot at best, and he most certainly knows that, but that is the most likely starting point given her current state. Still, he would be a fool not to use you in some way. If the insanity ploy fails, then he will be pulling out all the stops, if for no other reason than to lessen the severity of her sentence."

"You sound like a prosecuting attorney yourself instead of a profiler," I observed.

"Case investigator is what we prefer," he replied. "At the BAU we *create profiles*, but the title Profiler is actually a term coined by the media and hyped by Hollywood. However, you're somewhat correct. I worked as a prosecutor before joining the bureau."

"Hmmph," I grunted. "Well, that's what I get for assuming. I figured you'd need to have a background in psychology not law."

"I have both, actually. A Masters in Law and a BS in psych."

"I guess it's good to keep your options open," I replied, for lack of anything better to say. "What about you, Doctor Jante? You actually sound like a psychologist."

"I am," she replied.

"Well, at least there are no surprises there."

"Let's get back to your original question," Hanley said. "Our data will be a part of the prosecution's case, as is customary whenever a serial offender goes to trial. But it's usually just a profile for comparison. In Devereaux's case, she'll no doubt be facing a court-ordered psych evaluation given the nature of her crimes—also not unusual. But by having unfettered access to her now, we may well end up with invaluable data at our disposal that wouldn't come out in a standard psych eval. However, whatever we come up with needs to be accurate. We can't afford a misstep with this."

"Okay, but what about the evidence?" I asked. "The way I understood it, there was more than enough to convict her."

"In theory there is, but did you ever hear of a little media circus called the O. J. Simpson trial?" he asked.

"Point taken," I said with a nod. "But still…"

"Believe me, we're right there with you. But, we also have a job to do, and believe me, her 'dream team' isn't made up of underpaid public defenders. She has some serious hired guns."

"So why didn't you just tell us what this was really about in the first place?" Felicity asked.

Doctor Jante shook her head. "To be honest, it's easier to tell if a subject is lying if you catch them off guard. And we had to be sure."

"Great," I muttered. "So this was all one big lie detector test."

"In part, yes," she replied.

"But did I pass then?" Felicity asked.

Jante shook her head. "Not really."

CHAPTER 17

"AND THAT MEANS WHAT?" FELICITY PRESSED. "YOU'RE going to arrest me again?"

"No," the doctor replied. "But you're still holding something back and that concerns us."

"Trust me, I'm not keeping anything secret that would help you."

"So then you admit that you are withholding information?" Hanley asked.

"This is turning into an interrogation again," I objected.

"I'm sorry to tell you this, Mister Gant, but it's the two of you who are turning it into an interrogation by not cooperating," he replied, voice stern and even.

"We'd be a lot more cooperative if you were being honest with us."

"We are."

"Only when it's convenient for you," I replied. "Or did you forget the big reveal just a minute ago?"

"Mister Gant, believe it or not we are trying to help you."

"You've got a hell of a way of showing it."

"Mister Gant," Doctor Jante interrupted. "We need you to calm down. Devereaux and her attorneys are trying to drag your wife into this, and so far they are doing a damn good job. Essentially, Devereaux is placing herself at the scene of your wife's extramarital tryst with Lewis…"

"That's not what it was," Felicity objected.

"Be that as it may, that is exactly how it will be portrayed in court," Hanley replied with a dismissive gesture.

Jante continued. "Either way, she appears to be trying to make a mutual connection between the two of you that goes beyond her simply having an obsession."

"So why doesn't she just come out and accuse Felicity of being her accomplice then?" I asked. "Wouldn't that be easier?"

"She's far too intelligent for that," Jante replied. "It might sound easier, but it would be less effective. She knows making an accusation like that would be far too obvious under the circumstances. Instead, she's painting Miz O'Brien into the picture. Remember, all it takes is reasonable doubt."

"She's not after reasonable doubt," I blurted, forgetting to hold my tongue. "She's after complicity."

"Why do you think that?"

"Have either of you wondered why she wanted to talk to you pre-trial?" I asked.

"Of course," she replied. "It's obvious she is up to something, and it would appear that somehow implicating Miz O'Brien in the crimes is it."

"Like I said, complicity."

"But complicity gets her nothing."

"Actually, it gets her access to my wife, which is what she really wants."

"Why?"

I knew I was getting carried away, so I slammed on the brakes and tried to recover by saying, "Just call it a hunch."

Felicity recognized that I had talked myself into a corner and jumped in to divert the conversation. "So what do we do now?"

Jante looked over to her. "Unfortunately, we can't simply assume that she is fabricating everything she says. The real sticking points are the mentions of Miranda in your arrest record, so we need to be clear on why exactly that is."

"It sounds like you consider that some sort of damning evidence," I observed.

"It is. It indicates a connection."

"Then let me ask another question and hope like hell I don't regret it later. Why does the federal government care whether or not my wife is implicated in this?"

"Contrary to what you might believe, Mister Gant, the government does actually care whether or not an innocent person is wrongly accused or convicted of a crime."

"No offense, but you'll have to forgive me if I take that with a shaker full of salt."

"I'm merely answering your question. We aren't here to change your opinions."

I didn't press any further. I felt certain there was something going on behind the scenes here, but I wasn't quite sure what it was. However, what I did know for a fact was that some unnamed benefactor within the FBI had pulled my fat out of the fire when I had been arrested in New Orleans while unofficially investigating this case on my own. Something told me that same mystery person was behind this as well. I suppose I should have been thankful, and in many ways I was, but in the back of my head I couldn't help but wonder what price I was going to pay and exactly when the bill was going to come due.

"We are simply trying to find the truth," Doctor Jante said. "We need to determine if anything Devereaux has said is both accurate and at the same time inaccessible without her first having direct contact with Miz O'Brien." She shifted her gaze to Felicity and added, "If you had such contact with her, we need to know about it, and why."

"And if there is something she knows that she shouldn't?" my wife asked.

"Then we could potentially have a problem," Hanley said.

"I think we have one then," she replied.

"How so? Did you have direct contact with Devereaux?"

"No, not until the night at the zoo when she was captured. And when she called to threaten me. But you already know about all that."

"Then what is the problem?"

"I'm sure Miranda knows quite a bit about me," she sighed. "Much more than she reasonably should."

"It would help if you could be a bit more specific about that," Doctor Jante pressed.

"Believe me," I spoke up. "That's just about as specific as you want her to get."

"And why is that, Mister Gant?" she asked.

I had already slipped twice and managed to duck and run. I didn't know if I could get away with it a third time. But, since this conversation was rushing headlong toward parts unknown, I elected to give them my standard answer anyway. "Because if either of us tell you who Miranda really is, and how we came to know her, you won't believe us."

"How can you be so sure?" Hanley asked.

"Got the t-shirt," I told him with a matter-of-fact shrug.

"May I ask if this has anything to do with your personal contention that Miranda is actually some sort of Voodoo spirit and that Devereaux, as well as your wife, have both been possessed by said entity?" Doctor Jante asked.

The question caught me cold, and I simply didn't have an immediate response for it. In fact, I wasn't entirely certain I had a response at all. The one thing that kept going through my mind, however, was Ben Storm's voice saying, "Yeah, tell it to a judge."

After a moment I let out a chuckle and shook my head. "You two are good. I walked right into that, didn't I?"

"We're simply after the truth, Mister Gant."

The question in my mind at this point was how they knew. Obviously they were in possession of the case files; they had said as much right at the outset. But, I wasn't aware that any of the less tangible information had ended up in those official records. In fact, I was somewhat flabbergasted that it apparently had.

Both Ben and Constance were fanatically meticulous about premeditated omission of the paranormal details when it came to their reports. There were simply some events that had no logical explanation—certain happenings that, when committed to paper, came off as too bizarre for belief, especially to the uninitiated and devoutly skeptical. If either of them actually tried including some of the things they'd personally witnessed, they would most likely find their careers becoming stagnant or even non-existent.

Of course, how they found out really didn't matter in the grand scheme of things. What it now boiled down to was the fact that I was correct. My third attempt at ducking the radar was a bust. So were the first and second apparently. I no longer had "you wouldn't believe me if I told you" to hide behind, and that left me suddenly feeling very naked.

"Okay..." I finally said. "Since you are all about the truth, are you hiding anything else up your collective sleeves, or are we all really on the same page now?"

Special Agent Hanley spoke first. "This is nothing we were hiding. Obviously we're familiar with both your backgrounds. I mean it's really no secret to anyone, especially given the high profile cases on which you've consulted for the local police in the past."

"The official reports don't include the paranormal aspects of the investigations," I countered. "You and I both know that."

"Official reports, no. But neither of you are particularly shy about your beliefs, and trust me, what you do when consulting on a case makes its way through the grapevine even if it doesn't go into a report."

"Obviously... Well, I guess I really shouldn't be surprised by that. Or by the fact that you did your homework. Actually, I suppose I should be shocked if you hadn't, especially since you've been playing us from the word go. But, like you said, since we don't hide our beliefs, that's really a moot point." I shifted in my seat then tossed my glance back and forth between them before adding, "I am a bit curious about where this is going, however. So, let's continue our trend of honesty here. I'm guessing you're both more than just a little skeptical about our take on Miranda, which is no surprise either."

"Well, we certainly don't subscribe to a belief that the immortal soul of a dead woman is taking possession of living bodies in order to commit crimes," Doctor Jante replied. "Quite honestly, Mister Gant, that's ludicrous."

"Okay, so obviously 'skeptical' wasn't a strong enough word," I remarked as I shrugged. "You pretty much think we're nuts. Fine. Once again, no big surprise there. I've got a few of those t-shirts too."

"Neither of us said we think you're insane," she countered.

"No, but you didn't have to," I replied. "I've seen the look before. So, let's quit dancing around and get to the real issue here. The way I figure it, either you're actually afraid that Devereaux's attorney is going to use this to somehow discredit the prosecution, or you have a different agenda."

"No agenda, as you put it, Mister Gant," she replied. "We're simply doing a criminal investigative analysis to support the federal prosecutor, like we just explained. All of our cards are on the table at this point."

"Yeah...until the next one appears," I huffed. "So, unless I missed my guess, you have a different theory about who Miranda is?"

Doctor Jante shook her head and tossed her gaze back and forth between Felicity and me. "Actually, I wish I could say that you're correct, but right now we're just working on the basis that there must be something latent that is shared between Devereaux and you, Miz O'Brien. Something we've missed that could explain her intimate knowledge of you."

"The only thing we share is some DNA, and I'm none too excited about that," my wife spat. "Like I already told you, I didn't even know Annalise existed until a few months ago when this all started."

"Devereaux says the same thing. In fact, it would appear her base personality is even more in the dark than you. She isn't aware of your familial ties at all."

"Good. I'd like to keep it that way if you don't mind."

"I have no intention of telling her, but I'm certain her attorney knows. And, you must understand that it will come out at some point during the trial, if not before. That much is a given."

"*Fek...*" my wife muttered.

"The concern, however, is the alleged personality called Miranda. She knows far too much about you, as you already heard. Any way you slice it, Miranda or Annalise, she is creating a tangible connection that can be used to implicate you in the crimes."

"That connection is exactly why Annalise wanted to kill me," Felicity returned, exasperation in her voice. "Just like Miranda said. Believe me, none of it was my choice."

"None of what?"

"None of what you refuse to believe."

"Miz O'Brien, even if we chose to believe such a thing could happen, there's no possible way to prove it in a court of law," Agent Hanley insisted.

"Which is just another reason I wasn't saying anything about it in the first place," my wife spat as she looked over at him then returned her gaze to Doctor Jante. "So, do I pass your test now?"

"At this point we aren't doubting that you sincerely believe what you are saying," she replied.

"Do you believe in God, Doctor Jante?" I asked, attempting to shunt the conversation toward our favor.

Hanley interjected. "I know where you are going with that Mister Gant, and it won't work. I can assure you the court will gladly agree that you are free to believe anything you want, but belief in something does not make it a tangible fact."

"Okay, different avenue then. If I've been following you correctly, Miranda is the problem. Annalise is simply oblivious. So if all you are dealing with is Annalise, no problem."

"Yes, that's correct, more or less."

"Then I guess that's our option," I replied.

"What do you mean?" Jante asked.

I took a deep breath then let the sentence fly before I could talk myself out of it. "I need to make Miranda go away for good."

Hanley shot a skewed look at Jante then back to me. When he spoke again there was a note of warning in his voice. "Mister Gant, you should know that..."

"Please don't misunderstand..." I said, cutting him off. "I'm not implying anything sinister or illegal. Like I said, Miranda, not Annalise."

"All right, I'll play along. Let's assume for a moment Miranda really is what you say she is. How do you propose to make her go away?"

"I haven't quite figured that out yet," I said. "But I know it has to start with me talking directly to Annalise myself."

CHAPTER 18

"ROW, WOULD YOU MIND IF WE POSTPONED THIS afternoon's plans," Felicity asked as we exited the lobby of the FBI field office on Market Street, downtown.

"Not in the mood anymore?" I returned.

"Yes and no," she said. "I mean, I am in some ways, but all that talk about Miranda has me a bit squeamish. It kind of put a damper on the idea if you know what I mean. It's just that… Well we could… But, you know I'm afraid I might…"

I slipped my arm around her shoulder and gave her a squeeze then kissed her on the forehead. "You don't need to explain, hon, I know exactly what you mean. Don't worry about it. Why don't we just grab some lunch and maybe catch a matinee or something instead."

I could tell the whole encounter still had her rattled just by the way her voice was slipping into a heavier brogue. Just like exhaustion, intense emotions had a way of doing that to her. Her anxiety definitely wasn't uncalled for. She had every right to it, and even more.

"Aye, sounds like a plan," she agreed.

"How about the Metro Diner?"

"What? Not Charlie's? I mean, anywhere is fine with me, but we're already downtown after all, and Metro is back toward the suburbs."

I shook my head. "Yeah, I know. But Chuck doesn't serve liver and onions. Metro does."

"Liver and onions… Having a craving are we then?"

"Yeah, actually… I think maybe I am."

"I'll pass on that," she added. "I think maybe I'd be happy with a BLT or something of that sort myself."

"I'm pretty sure Metro has them on the menu."

We stopped at the curb and waited for a car to cross in front of us. The sun was shining between a light scattering of clouds, and there was a soft breeze blowing. We were at the tail end of the unusual warm spell, so the temperature had only crept up near fifty and probably wasn't going to climb much farther. Closer to typical for a Midwestern March, but then, this was Saint Louis. Weather always seemed to be a roll of the dice here, no matter how hard the meteorologists tried to nail it down. Even so, to me it seemed almost springlike.

As we waited for a second vehicle to roll by, I shrugged out of my jacket and slung it over my shoulder then slipped my arm back around Felicity. Once the lane was clear, we stepped off the curb and aimed ourselves toward her Jeep.

After a moment she spoke up again. "Do you think they'll actually go for it?"

"Who go for what?"

"Letting you speak to Annalise."

"Oh, that," I replied. "I guess we'll have to wait and see. They definitely didn't seem sold on the idea, did they?"

She shook her head and pursed her lips as she frowned. "Even if they change their minds and will arrange it, I can't imagine her attorney would be too happy about letting you then."

"True story," I agreed. "But, if she decides she's willing to talk to me, and it's her choice, then maybe there's a chance. If the people with the badges will go for it."

She fell quiet until we split apart, and I ushered her in front of me between a pair of parked vehicles.

"And what you need to talk to her about is the necklace," she said over her shoulder, offering the words as a statement rather than a question.

"Yes."

She slowed then stopped and turned to face me. "So do you maybe want to explain that to me *now*, or is it still a big secret?"

"Want, yes," I replied, shaking my head. "But like I said, I can't...not just yet."

"Why not?"

"I made someone a promise."

"Who?"

"Honey, I can't really say..."

She studied my face for a moment then let out what sounded to be an abbreviated version of an exasperated sigh. "It's a good damn thing I trust you, Rowan Linden Gant."

"Yeah, believe me, I know."

I felt a tickle on my side, somewhere even with my beltline. The soft vibration was quickly followed by a short chirp and a muffled feminine voice. I reached down and pulled my cell phone from its holder then glanced at the display. As I suspected it was notifying me that I had several new voicemails. I flipped the device open and scrolled through the missed calls. Every single one came from the same familiar number.

"Ben," I said aloud, turning the display toward Felicity and holding it up for her to see.

"Aye, no surprise that." She nodded, glancing at the LCD. "Better call him back before he works himself into a snit."

I half chuckled. "This is Ben you're talking about. I'm sure he already has…"

She turned and continued walking the dozen or so steps to her Jeep. As I followed along, I thumbed the button so the cell would dial the most recently missed call then placed it against my ear.

"It's about time," Ben's voice issued from the speaker following the first half of the third ring. "I been tryin' ta' call ya' back for two hours, but all I got was your friggin' voicemail."

"Whatever happened to just plain hello?" I asked.

"Simple. Our fast-paced lives and caller ID made it obsolete."

"Listen to you…" I jibed. "Mister high tech social commentator."

"Not a chance… I just heard some asshole say that on the news the other day. I think he was talkin' about manners or somethin', but it sounded like it would fit."

"Yeah, I should have figured as much," I grunted. "Well, I'm sorry for the delay in calling, but apparently I wasn't getting a signal for the past couple of hours, so I just now got the voicemail notifications."

In that moment anything resembling lightheartedness fled from his voice. "So listen, Row, did I understand your message right? You'n Firehair actually had a meetin' with the Feebs this mornin'?"

"Unfortunately, yeah. We just got out of it as a matter of fact."

"Unfortunately? That doesn't sound good… So what's the deal?"

"Long story short, Miranda is still trying to get to Felicity."

"Yeah, you've been sayin' that'd happen. But what've the Feebs got ta' do with it?"

"Well, it seems that at the moment her plan of attack is to implicate Felicity in the murders."

"Fuck me… We've already been down this road…"

"Tell me about it."

"So they ain't buyin' into 'er story, are they?"

"I don't think so. At least, they say they aren't, but I really don't know for sure. We were talking to a pair from the BAU, and they weren't exactly forthcoming with the whole story in the beginning. It took a bit to drag it out of them, and I'm still not convinced they aren't leaving something out."

"Not surprisin'. So, that just a hunch or did ya' get a hinky feelin'?"

"A little of both, I think. Something weird is definitely going on. I just don't know what it is. I'm not freaking out just yet, but I'm definitely just this side of worried."

"Great... So, weird how?"

"Weird like maybe someone behind the scenes is calling the shots."

"Could it just be chain of command?"

"Maybe, but I don't really think so. It seems more like a *pay no attention to the man behind the curtain* sort of thing. You know, like the whole episode with the cops in NOLA suddenly dropping the charges against me because someone at the FBI requested it."

"Okay, yeah. I get it. See why I hate the Feebs? You can't trust 'em."

"Yeah, so what about Constance?"

"She's the exception, not the rule. Speakin' of Constance, you want me ta' have 'er make some calls and check some shit out?"

"Well, I'll admit I'd sure like to know who it is I'm indebted to before he or she suddenly decides to collect," I replied. "So, if you think she'd be willing I'd really appreciate it."

"Yeah, well you know how she is. All I gotta do is mention it and she'll start snoopin'. She may still be on medical leave but that sorta shit's never stopped 'er before. B'sides, it'll give her somethin' to do. She's climbin' the walls right now, and she's still got two weeks left before they'll even think about lettin' 'er back on the job."

"I know, but please tell her not to get herself into any trouble over this. It's mine and Felicity's problem, not hers."

"Yeah, like she's gonna listen ta' me. Get real."

"I know, I know... It's just that we owe her so much as it is. I don't want her screwing up her career any more."

"You ain't gonna be able ta' stop 'er, Row. She's kinda attached ta' you two in case you ain't figured that out yet."

"Well, the feeling is mutual."

"Yeah...okay... So let's change the subject before this turns all fuckin' sappy and shit," he urged. "Listen, you doin' all right today?"

I shrugged out of reflex. "As well as can be expected under the circumstances, I guess. I mean, I'm annoyed, but..."

He cut me off. "No, Kemosabe, I mean with the *Twilight Zone* and all."

"Yeah, pretty much I suppose, why?"

"So, no bleedin' or anything?"

"No, Ben, just a bit of a headache."

"Aspirin kinda headache or…"

This time I interrupted him instead. "Yeah, Ben, it's a la-la land headache, but it's not a bad one. Just your average, everyday 'Rowan's talking to dead people again' headache. Is that what you're wanting to know?"

"Well yeah, actually…"

"Okay, so what's up?"

"You still downtown?" he asked.

"Yeah."

"Both of ya', right?"

"Uh-huh," I grunted. We had arrived at the Jeep several minutes ago, and Felicity was already belted in behind the wheel. Out of habit I was still standing next to the passenger side with the door hanging open. "In fact, I'm looking at Felicity right now. She says hi."

"Yeah, whatever. So where are ya' exactly?"

"On the FBI's parking lot, why?"

"Good, then you ain't far away," he said.

"Ben, are you going to tell me what you are going on about, or do I have to guess?"

He huffed out a sigh. "R'member that freak job with the metal band Wendy was tellin' us about the other day?"

"Yeah… What was her name… Desiree or something like that, right? Don't tell me she was murdered."

"No, she's not dead. Turns out 'er real name is Margaret Lucas, but that ain't the point. What is the point, however, is that she reported 'er girlfriend missin' last night."

"Missing as in…"

"We don't know. But, it looks suspicious, and she's apparently been missin' better'n forty-eight hours."

"Are you certain?"

"No," he replied, oozing sarcasm. "We're runnin' around with our thumbs up our asses and throwin' darts at a board. Any more stupid questions?"

"Sorry…" I said. "I'm still in that suspicious mindset."

"Yeah, me too," he apologized. "I shouldn't have snapped like that. It's just been a long day already."

"I can imagine. So how did homicide get involved?"

"Goddamn computer did somethin' right for a change. Listed under identifyin' marks is a tattoo of a black swan just over 'er heart. When they were enterin' the info, it raised a flag and got kicked over to Major Case."

"Dammit," I muttered.

"Yeah, that's kinda what I said," he agreed. "Looks like our bad guy got 'imself a fresh victim."

"The question is, how long before this one turns up in a dumpster somewhere..."

"E'zactly," he replied. "So listen, had our own meetin' with the Feebs about forty-five minutes ago and things are startin' ta' get busy if ya' know what I mean. On top of that I got my brass buggin' me about you. I told 'em you were on board, so now they're kinda wantin' ya' to weigh in on this. If ya' could put in a little face time down here it'd be a good thing."

"You know, I still don't get that. When the hell did I become their golden boy?" I asked. "It hasn't been too long since I was a pariah. And before that I had Albright on my ass at every turn."

He hesitated for a moment then replied with what seemed to be a cautious note in his voice. "Yeah... You got me, Row... I know what you're sayin'... But like I said last night, they know you get results..."

"Is something wrong?" I pressed.

"No, why?"

"You sound a bit strange all of a sudden."

"Sorry... Just a bit preoccupied with some shit... So anyway, if it's any consolation, the word from on high is that they definitely don't want ya' talkin' ta' anybody but me about this...'specially not the media clowns."

"Keeping it compartmentalized, eh? More or less a help us, but don't embarrass us scenario..."

"Yeah, that's about it."

"You sure there's nothing wrong?" I pressed again.

"Yeah. It's all good. Just a lot of shit goin' down right now, and I'm swimmin' in it."

I didn't have to see him to know he was probably sitting at his desk, massaging his neck with his free hand as he ruminated over that very fact himself. I couldn't help but wonder if the invisible puppeteer that seemed to be controlling my destiny where the FBI was concerned also had a few strings attached to local law enforcement as well. Of course, the more I thought about it the more I wondered if I was finally losing my ability to entertain rational thoughts in favor of conspiracy theories. I hoped I hadn't, but I figured if I started seeing black helicopters from the corner of my eye, it would be time to check myself into a padded cell under Helen Storm's care.

"Hold on a sec…" I told Ben.

I covered the mouthpiece on the phone and looked in through the open door of the Jeep at Felicity. I started to speak, but before I could form the first word she nodded and said, "Aye, I'll take a rain check on the movie, but let him know he's buying lunch and fast food doesn't qualify."

CHAPTER 19

WHEN WE ARRIVED AT CITY POLICE HEADQUARTERS, WE were lucky enough to grab one of the parking spaces directly in front on Clark Avenue. Felicity nosed her Jeep in at an angle to the curb then set the parking brake and switched off the engine before looking over at me. We hadn't really talked much on the way other than me giving her a quick rundown of the conversation with Ben; of course even with traffic, the drive had taken less than five minutes, so there hadn't been much time for anything more in-depth.

"What now?" she asked.

"He said if we don't see him to just stay where we are and give him a call on his cell," I replied.

I glanced around but didn't see the towering Native American anywhere. In fact, pedestrian traffic was so light that I noticed only a single pair of uniformed officers walking across the street. Judging from their direction, they appeared to be heading for a cop hangout diner called 40 that was located diagonally across from where we were now parked. I twisted in my seat to scan the area but saw no one else.

Turning my eyes back front, I followed Ben's instructions, dug out my cell phone and gave him a call. I wasn't sure if this was all some clandestine part of keeping me away from the press or what. I certainly hadn't noticed any news vans nearby when I was looking around, but at this point I was just speculating anyway.

When my friend picked up, he seemed rushed, and therefore, our conversation was clipped. In fact, it really didn't qualify as a conversation as much as a quick interrogation.

"Where are you?" Ben asked immediately, again bypassing any form of salutation.

"We're parked right out front," I replied.

"Stay put, I'll be right down."

Then, as quickly as he had answered, he was gone without even a goodbye.

"Well, what did he say?" Felicity asked as I folded the phone and tucked it away.

"He said he's coming down. I don't know why," I replied.

Twisting slightly in my seat, I gazed past her at the diner on the other side of the street. I wasn't overly hungry, but for some odd reason I was feeling inexplicably drawn to food at the moment.

I had eaten at 40 with Ben on a few occasions. It had actually started out as a coffee shop and had enjoyed a steady, if not exactly brisk, business for what seemed like ages. But in the past few years, it had flourished under new management after adding actual food to the menu.

After a quick mental inventory of what I remembered about their selections, I sighed then mused aloud, "Hmmm… I'm pretty sure Forty just does sandwiches… I don't think they serve collard greens, so that won't work either."

"Collard greens? Where did that come from?" Felicity asked, shooting me a confused look. "What happened to liver and onions?"

"I'm pretty sure they don't serve that either," I muttered absently.

"So now you want both?"

"Yeah, actually… I do."

My wife shook her head. "If you were a woman, I'd wonder if you were pregnant."

"If that was the case wouldn't I be craving pickles and ice cream?"

"That's a…"

"I was kidding," I said, cutting her off as I half chuckled. "Just kidding."

"All right then, I'll let it go this time," she replied, then chewed at her lower lip for a moment before musing, "Well, obviously this must be because of the stress—just look at everything you've been through. But I wonder if it's connected to the bleeding somehow…"

"What, you mean the cravings?" I asked.

She nodded. "Aye. You seem to be obsessing over foods rich in iron. Liver, collard greens… How would you feel about broccoli then?"

"Actually, it sounds pretty good at the moment," I said, nodding agreement. "I'll take all three."

"That must be it then because you do seem a bit preoccupied with food and that's not like you."

"Makes sense to me. Like you said, stress, bleeding, iron… But yeah, the funny thing is I'm not even all that hungry at the moment."

During the conversation, I had been keeping an eye on the front entrance of police headquarters, waiting for Ben to show. I gave my watch a quick glance then huffed out a sigh.

"I say we give him another five minutes," I grumbled. "Then if he hasn't shown I call again."

"Irritability is a sign of an iron deficiency too," my wife announced.

"Should I start calling you Doctor O'Brien?" I asked, humor in my tone.

"Not right now," she replied, cocking her eyebrow. "But maybe we could still play doctor later."

"Hmph… What happened to the damper on your mood?"

"I guess it went away."

I shook my head and snorted. "Aren't we a pair? I'm obsessing about food, you're obsessing about sex, and neither of them is what we need to be worrying about at the moment. "

She chuckled lightly. "Aye. You're right. I think maybe we both need a break."

"Tell me about it."

"All right then, what do you think about taking a vacation?" she asked.

"I think it sounds good in theory…" I returned.

"Well? Why don't we?" she pressed, peering back at me with brows raised and the question swimming in her green eyes. "We haven't been on a real vacation in years."

"Yeah, okay, sounds like a hell of an idea," I replied with a mocking note. "Where are we going and when do we leave?"

"I'm serious, Rowan." She sounded a bit hurt.

I quickly backpedaled. "I'm sorry, honey. That came out wrong. Actually, I'm serious too, sort of. Unfortunately, we need to wait until this is over."

"And until Miranda is gone for good too, I suppose?" she said with an almost accusatory note in her voice.

"Yeah… That's pretty much a given."

"So, what you're really saying is don't make any plans."

I had obviously misinterpreted how serious she was about this, and her sudden change in demeanor was a wake-up call. Reaching over, I carefully began to massage her shoulder through the leather of her jacket. "No, that isn't what I'm saying. We just can't leave right this minute. You know that as well as I do."

"Aye, I do. But when?"

"I don't know," I replied and gave her a half-hearted shrug. "Think about it. I tried backing away from all this, and we saw where that got me. I mean, even you wanted me to stop fighting it. So, now… Well, I'm kind of stuck until this is over."

"I know," she murmured. "But remember? We promised ourselves…"

Her point was valid. We were more than due for a break, and we really had promised ourselves we would get away from things for a while once Annalise was in custody. Unfortunately, life got in the way, as usual, and now the dead were once again taking their turn playing roadblock.

It wasn't as if we couldn't afford a vacation financially. Money was the least of our problems. All we really needed to do was clear our schedules, get someone to housesit, and just go. It was the whole schedule-clearing thing that had become our ubiquitous sticking point.

I drew in a deep breath then let it out slowly. "Tell you what," I said after a thoughtful moment. "I'll make you a deal. As soon as this case is over we're outta here."

"And what about Miranda then?"

"If she's taken care of, fine. If not, well, I'll just carry the jar around in my suitcase, I guess."

"Are you certain?"

"Yeah... We need the time away."

"I'm fairly sure that's what I was just saying."

"I know, and I was listening even if it didn't seem like it. There's just one caveat... We can go anywhere you want except New Orleans. I don't want you that close to that bitch ever again. Besides, I don't even know if I'm exactly welcome there anymore."

"Actually, I was thinking more along the line of home."

"Home, eh? Well, I guess that will save us the trouble of packing."

"Rowan..."

"I know, I know... Just joking again... I get it... You want to go to Ireland."

"Aye. It's been too long."

"Can't I just blindfold you and take you to one of the local pubs and pretend?"

"Joking again?"

"Trying to."

"Well stop. You aren't funny." She underscored the comment with a grin.

I laughed and nodded. "Ireland it is."

A hard rap sounded on the windshield to my right, making me start at the noise. I turned to see Ben peering in at us from the passenger side of the Jeep. Apparently both of us had been so preoccupied with our conversation that we hadn't noticed him standing there. I popped the latch on the door and pushed it open, so he reached out and took hold of the upper edge of the frame and swung it wider. Bending down, he looked through the now open gap.

"Am I interruptin' you two?" he asked.

"Well, yeah, sort of," I returned.

"Too bad."

"Wow, Ben, thanks for understanding," I retorted.

"Yeah, well I been standin' here forever."

I glanced at my watch then back at him. "Maybe a minute or two at the most."

"Uh-huh, like I said, forever."

I climbed out of the Jeep, and he moved back as I swung the door shut. Felicity was already coming around the front of the vehicle and stepping up on the sidewalk.

Ben glanced over at her then waved a finger at the Jeep and said "Yo, Firehair... Make sure ya' lock it up."

"We're in front of the police station," she replied.

"Yeah, and your point?"

Felicity replied by cocking her head to the side and giving him a nonplussed stare as she slid her hand into her jacket pocket. Almost instantly the clunk of the locks sounded next to me.

"There. Better?" she asked.

"Hey, it's your shit, not mine," Ben returned then stepped back up onto the sidewalk. "By the way, you got any salt?"

Felicity gave him a puzzled look then quipped, "Not with me. Why, are you out or something?"

"Here," he said as he reached into his jacket pocket. When he withdrew it, small, white paper packets were protruding from between his fingers. He held them out to her, and she instinctively cupped her hands beneath his as he let them fall into her palms.

"I didn't bother sortin' it, so there's prob'ly some pepper in there too, sorry 'bout that," he told her. Then jerking his head to the side, he motioned up the street and grunted, "C'mon, let's get movin'."

"What's all this for?" Felicity asked, stuffing the unsought bounty into her pockets.

He pointed at me as he started turning to head up the sidewalk. "Ta' keep his sorry ass safe. Got a bottle'a aspirin too if ya' need it."

"We're going straight to the morgue, aren't we?" I asked, my voice coming out in a flat drone because I already knew his answer.

"Yeah," he replied. "We're goin' straight to the morgue."

I'D MADE FAR TOO MANY SUCH VISITS TO THE SAINT Louis City Medical Examiner's office over the years, and even though I had become prematurely jaded to the sight of corpses and the cold feeling of death, I still never could get used to the place.

Every time I walked through the door of the innocuous building situated next to police headquarters, it was like being the unexpected celebrity guest at a morbid party. It almost always began with a stunned silence that went unnoticed by everyone but me—simply because the ethereal hush was falling over the ghostly voices of the dead that only I could hear in the first place. Of course, the stillness never lasted long. Within moments the screams, the cries, and the pleading voices from the other side of the veil would fill my ears in a deafening cacophony.

And then above it all, there was always the one clear voice of the soul I was supposed to help. That one always shared with me the most pain, anguish, and even physical torture. I suppose it needed something to set it apart from the crowd, although I would have gladly settled for a gentler way of capturing my attention.

As expected, today was no different. And just as I had done on each and every occasion, I fought to ignore the screams in favor of the here and now that was unfolding in front of me.

"Where's Ceece?" Ben asked the woman behind the desk in the lobby. We were barely through the door, and she hadn't even been afforded the chance to greet us.

"I'm sorry?" she replied.

"You know, the lady who's s'posed ta' be sittin' where you're sittin' right now," he explained.

She nodded as a look of understanding tweaked her features. "Oh, you mean Cecelia. She just ran out to pick up lunch. May I help you?"

Ben flashed his badge. "Yeah, I'm Detective Storm. We're here ta' see Doc Sanders."

"I'm sorry, Detective, I'm afraid she's also at lunch."

"She should be expectin' us."

The woman shook her head. "I'm certain she's at lunch."

"She go out too, or is she in 'er office like usual?" he asked.

"I believe she's in her office, but as I said, she's taking a break for lunch. She should be…"

Ben held up his hands to stop her and began shaking his head. "Ceece knew we were comin', so did Doc Sanders."

"I'm sorry, but neither of them said anything about it to me," she returned.

"Well, they musta forgot."

"Let me check..." she said as she carefully glanced over a schedule sheet while running her pen along the side and then gave it a second pass. She began shaking her head slowly as she looked up and said, "I'm very sorry, Detective Storm, but you don't have an appointment listed here and Doctor Sanders is..."

"...at lunch, yeah, I know. Look... I'm serious. Ceece knew we were comin'. If that ain't enough for ya', try this on. *My* boss sent us over here to talk to *your* boss. Now I really don't wanna have my boss jumpin' on my ass and then callin' your boss' boss, 'cause in the end the shit's just gonna roll downhill on top of both of us. Know what I mean? So just do me a favor... Pick up the phone and let the doc know we're here." He shook his head again. "She says no, all good. We let her explain it. Okay?"

The woman looked at him with a sideways glance. "Are you always this intense?"

"Yes, he is," another voice came from the doorway to our right, and a definite tone of exasperation surrounded the words.

We looked over to find Cecelia coming into the lobby from the back, door slowly swinging shut behind her. Her purse was slung over her shoulder, and she was juggling a pair of large carryout bags in her arms.

"Ceece," Ben crooned with an air of relief.

"Don't *Ceece* me, Storm. You aren't supposed to be here yet," she snipped as she walked across the lobby and deposited the bags on the desk. "I told you Doctor Sanders would be available after lunch."

"Yeah, well shit happens, ya'know."

"Especially with you," she sighed. "Is there really some pressing reason why you have to see the doctor now?"

"Yes," he replied.

She stood staring at him expectantly. After a moment she said, "I take it I'm not going to get an explanation?"

"I can't get into it," he said. "Let's just say the doc owes me."

"Owes you? Are you sure you don't have that backwards?"

"Nope."

Cecelia shook her head. "I'm not even going to ask."

"Yeah, that's prob'ly a good idea. B'sides, couldn't tell ya' anyway."

"You're incorrigible," she mumbled.

Ben nodded. "Yeah, I've heard that."

Cecelia directed herself to the woman at the reception desk. "Go ahead and buzz Doctor Sanders, Caroline. He really is supposed to be here." She paused for a heartbeat then added with emphasis, "After lunch."

CHAPTER 20

"I THINK IT'S WARMER OUTSIDE THAN IT IS IN HERE," BEN mused aloud as he shuffled in place. I was fairly certain his dance was more out of impatience than an attempt to keep warm, even though his observation was certainly dead on the mark.

Shortly after the receptionist had buzzed Doctor Sanders, we were signed in then escorted to the cold storage area and autopsy suites at the back of the medical examiner's building. Unfortunately, we had already been standing here for several minutes, and it was beginning to look like the M.E. was going to make us wait indefinitely.

"Yeah," I agreed with my friend then looked over at my wife. "You okay, honey?"

She merely nodded in response. She tended to be a bit more sensitive to the cold than me, so she had already zipped up her leather jacket and was now pulling on her gloves. I was almost regretting having left my own coat back at the Jeep even though I knew there was more to the gelid atmosphere than simply the physical temperature.

I gave Felicity's shoulder a quick squeeze then glanced around at the tiled room. It had been awhile since I'd ventured this far into the bowels of the building, but little had changed since then. Stainless steel rectangles still formed an evenly spaced checkerboard on the far wall, each one a doorway into a cubicle where earthly remains awaited their turn under the knife. At the back end of the room were doors leading into the garage where an overt but acceptable form of segregation occurred on an almost daily basis. Living people entered and exited in the front, corpses there in the back. The only thing missing was a sign reading "Dead Persons Only."

"I guess Doctor Sanders decided to finish her lunch first," I finally said after completing my visual inspection for a third time.

"Yeah," Ben grunted. "Sure seems like it. You'd think they'd at least have us wait someplace warm."

"Aye, if you hadn't been so pushy, maybe they would have," Felicity offered.

"Just doin' my job," he returned.

He was still shuffling about, allowing his gaze to wander just as mine had, but with one overt difference—he was avoiding eye contact with me, and Felicity as well. Impatience, I could understand, but this was more than that. I'd seen him play the stone-faced cop more than once, so I knew for a fact something was bothering him that he simply couldn't mask.

"What are you so nervous about, Ben?" I asked.

"I ain't nervous." He shook his head.

"I don't believe you."

"Well then maybe you got trust issues."

"These days, you're probably right, but I'm pretty sure that's not it. Why don't you tell me what this is all about. What's really going on?"

"Whaddaya mean?" He shrugged and waved his hand toward the far wall as he added, "What's it always about when we come here, white man? You, a pissed off stiff, and la-la land."

He finally stopped avoiding eye contact and looked at me expectantly as his words dissipated on the cloud of steam that was his breath. I stared back and frowned.

Pissed off stiff. My friend's less than eloquent way of referring to the body of a murder victim was just another hallmark that told me something was amiss. Granted, any corpse I came here to see during an investigation had some form of brutality responsible for its date with one of the stainless steel tables. And, yes, the spirits once housed by the now lifeless bodies were less than happy about it. But Ben customarily showed at least some amount of reverence.

Still, I knew exactly what he was trying to say. I was here, for all intents and purposes, to translate. To tell the living what the dead had to say, all in hopes that it would shed light on why they were here in the first place.

But that was obvious. Moreover, it wasn't what I was asking, and he knew it.

"No kidding, Ben. I pretty much figured that out when you herded us up here," I said. "But you know it doesn't work that way."

"Yeah? So when have ya' ever *not* gone *Twilight Zone* when you were here?"

"That's not my point, and you know it."

"Maybe not, but it's mine."

"Okay, so what if I do? You know how convoluted this can get. There's never a straight answer from the dead. I'm not going to be able to just hand you a name or anything."

"Yeah, I know that," he nodded. "Just do what ya' do, and we'll go from there. That's all I'm askin'.."

"Dammit," I grumbled. "I let you sidetrack me again."

"Me? Whaddid I do?"

"You avoided my question. You know that's not what I was asking."

He splayed out his hands in mock surrender. "Sounded like it ta' me. You asked what…"

"Stop it," I said, cutting him off and holding my own hands up, palms toward him as a sign that I'd had enough. "No double talk. Just answer the question."

He shot me a concerned look. "You feelin' okay, Kemosabe? You're actin' a little freaked."

"Don't turn this back on me," I demanded. "Something's up or you wouldn't have been in such a rush to get us in here."

"What rush?" he asked with a shrug.

"Give me a break. You met us at the Jeep, hurried us up here, and then bullied your way in."

"I was just savin' ya' some time. 'Scuse me."

"Bullshit."

"Look, Row, I don't know what's eatin' ya', but you need to calm down. Okay?"

"What's eating me is that you're lying about something, Ben. I can tell by the way you're acting."

"Jeezus, didn't we already go through this shit last night?" he replied.

"Yes," I snapped. "Which is why I'm not overly pleased about going through it again."

"Then don't."

"I wouldn't have to if you weren't acting all squirrelly again."

"You're imaginin' things. Listen, it's simple… Just like I told ya' on the phone, we got a missin' woman who fits the victim profile of the two stiffs that just checked in here. But based on the pattern, she's prob'ly still alive." He pointed over to the storage drawers to punctuate his next statement. "Brass wants your input so maybe she doesn't end up movin' in over there next to the first two."

"Okay, I can understand that."

"Wunnerful. See? There ya' have it. So if it seems like I'm in a rush, maybe I am… And for a damn good reason, don'tcha think?"

"I wish I could believe it's that simple, Ben. But I can't. Something else is going on here."

"Well I said it once and I'll say it again, you're imaginin' shit. Just chill out, okay? It's all good."

I shook my head. "No it isn't. I still don't get why your brass suddenly wants my advice on this."

"I already told ya'. Prob'ly because of your track record," he replied. "You've been instrumental in solving every case you ever consulted on. They know that. Some of 'em definitely don't like it, but they know it. Enough said."

"Even if I buy that, there's got to be more to the story…"

"Why?"

"Remember asking me if I had a hinky feeling earlier? Well, guess what? I've definitely got one now."

"Maybe you're wrong."

"You know I'm not."

He let out a heavy sigh and threw his hands up. "Look, just drop it. It ain't important."

"So there is something," I replied, my tone sharp.

"Yeah, okay. There is, but I'm tellin' ya' it ain't important," he replied, waving his hand in a dismissive gesture. "And right now you're just blowin' shit outta proportion."

"You aren't helping with the double talk."

"Maybe not, but I'm kinda stuck in the middle here."

"Unstick yourself. Just tell me what's going on."

"Listen, a wise man once said, what ya' don't know won't hurt ya'. I highly suggest you listen to the wise man."

"Uh-huh, well it just so happens another one said, when in doubt, do nothing," I shot back. "And I'm having more than my share of doubts right now."

"Well do us all a favor and get over 'em is all I got ta' say."

"I will when you tell me what's really going on."

"Trust me, you wouldn't believe me if I told ya'."

"Very funny." I wasn't laughing when I made the comment. "This isn't the time to beat me over the head with irony. I'm not in the mood."

"Irony? What… Oh, yeah, I did kinda sound just like you right then, didn't I?" he harrumphed and then gave me a sidelong glance. "Frustratin' as fuck, ain't it?"

"Yes it is, but you also know exactly why I say that."

"Yeah, and I know 'zactly why I'm sayin' it too," he countered. "Just leave it alone, Row. Seriously. It ain't important."

"Is the FBI involved in this?"

"Well hell, sure they are. I already told ya' that."

"No, Ben, I mean me being here now." I wasn't yelling, but my voice had definitely risen in concert with my darkening mood.

"Calm down. The Feebs got nothin' to do with you bein' here."

"Who then?"

"Me, who else," he spat. "Now like I said, just calm down."

"And your brass?"

"Yeah, some of them too. Jeezus, you oughta be happy you got a few friends in high places for a change."

Felicity, who had remained conspicuously silent as the discussion turned to an argument, now spoke up. "Aye, Ben, I have to agree with Rowan. Something doesn't feel right about this. We've had our fill of hidden agenda's today. What aren't you telling us?"

"Dammit, where the hell's the doc?" he muttered as a response.

"Okay, if you aren't going to tell me what's going on, then I'm done," I announced. "Come on, Felicity, I think we can probably still catch that movie."

"Jeezus, Row, give it a rest. Nobody's out ta' get ya'."

I took my wife's arm, and we headed toward the exit. We made it to the door before my friend gave in.

"Okay, stop! Just stop right there," he barked, struggling to keep his voice at a reasonable volume. "Sonofabitch... I told 'em somethin' like this would happen."

"Are you going to quit jerking us around?" I asked as I glanced back toward him.

He huffed out a heavy sigh then reached up and smoothed back his hair. He closed his eyes and hung his head for a moment as his hand slid down to his neck and came to a rest.

"Goddammit..." he muttered before bringing his gaze to meet mine. "Fine... Okay... You win... Ya' happy?"

"I will be when I know what's really going on here," I appealed.

"Maybe... Maybe not," he said. "But it doesn't matter. Truth is I know it won't make any difference as far as you helpin' goes."

"So someone thought it would?" I asked, confusion wrinkling my face.

"Yeah." He nodded. "Which is exactly why I'm under orders not to tell ya'."

"What the hell is it?" Now I was thoroughly perplexed.

Finally, he simply blurted out, "The missin' woman's name is, Judith Albright."

"Albright," I repeated the name back to him. "As in…"

"Yeah," he said, cutting me off. "Albright as in she's Bible Barb's niece."

The revelation definitely gave me pause.

I stared back at my friend and he at me, neither of us uttering a word. Even Felicity remained silent, which was a shock because I was fairly certain she despised the woman even more than me. Still, Ben was correct. I wasn't about to withhold my help on this case because of a grudge against a victim's relative, although I was fairly certain the same would not be true if the tables were turned.

To say Captain Barbara Albright and I had a turbulent history was the understatement of the century. I was a Witch and she was a fundamentalist Christian with a badge—obviously not a good mix. Still, it shouldn't have been an issue, and to be honest it wasn't, at least not for me. However, she decided otherwise before we'd even met, and the rest was downhill from there.

Live and let live simply wasn't a part of her credo. If you didn't share her beliefs you were damned to hell. To that end, she was more than happy to use her position within the department to cram Christianity down your throat and then find a way to legally harass you if you dared to gag and spit it back out.

Behind her back the majority of the police force simply called her Bible Barb, or BeeBee for short. She definitely had her share of lackeys and supporters interspersed throughout the ranks, but among the cops on the street they were few and far between. Still, you had to watch what you said if you weren't sure where someone else's loyalties might lay because it would definitely make its way back to her ears.

If ever I'd had a nemesis who just happened to be on the correct side of the law, she was it. Our first run in had come when she was a lieutenant and had unceremoniously taken charge of an investigation with which I was involved. From that point forward she'd been on a mission to sever my ties with local law enforcement as a consultant. While she had eventually been promoted out of any direct contact where I was concerned, I never felt as though I was fully out of her sights. Even as recently as the debacle with Felicity's false arrest, Albright's fingerprints were all over some of the harassment and bureaucratic stumbling blocks we had faced.

And now, here she was again.

"So that's what you were all nervous about?" I finally asked.

"I told ya' I wasn't nervous. What I was, was pissed off about havin' ta' lie to you."

"That seems to have become a theme lately," I agreed. "The lying thing I mean."

"Tell me about it," he huffed. "It's been givin' me a friggin' ulcer. But, like I said, you're the one who blew this all out of proportion."

"You're right," I said with a nod. "Sorry... It's been a bad couple of days. And then the whole thing with the FBI... I know that's not much of an excuse, but it's all I've got."

"Yeah, well I probably shoulda just blown off the orders and told ya' anyway."

I pondered the situation for a moment then let out a bemused snort. "So your brass actually thought I was so shallow that I'd refuse to help because of Albright?"

"Actually, no. She's the one who thought you would say no."

"She *knows* I'm helping?" I could hear the incredulity woven through my own voice.

"Yeah, she knows all right," Ben told me as if he was having trouble believing his own words. "Believe it or not, as soon as her niece went missin' she started demandin' you be brought in to consult, even if Major Case had to arrest you ta' make it happen."

"Not exactly subtle, is she?"

"Listen, Row," Ben continued. "You won't have to deal with 'er. After she threw that fit, the chief put 'er on administrative leave."

"Like that's going to stop her?" I replied.

"Yeah, I know, but I'm tellin' ya' you won't have to deal with 'er. I'll make sure of it."

I waved him off. "It doesn't matter. You can tell your higher ups I'm not a complete ass. I'm not going to walk away from this just because of my history with Albright."

"Yeah, I told 'em that already, but they wanted to play it safe."

"Well be sure to let them know that playing it safe almost did cause me to walk out."

"Oh yeah. Believe me, that's right at the top of the list."

"And, do me another favor, okay?"

"What's that?"

"Can we try remembering that we're friends and stop with the tiptoeing around the truth? I think we've established that it's not helping either of us."

He nodded. "Yeah, definitely. I don't need the stomach problems."

"Good. Now that we have that settled why don't we see if we can find out what's keeping Doctor Sanders. I'm ready to get this over with..."

CHAPTER 21

"HOW WAS LUNCH?" BEN ASKED THE MEDICAL EXAMINER when she finally arrived in the autopsy suite. The acerbic aura surrounding his words was anything but subtle.

"A little rushed," she replied, no less caustic in her tone.

"Yeah, don't ya' just hate that?" my friend quipped.

"How was *your* wait?" she returned her own verbal stab.

"Long. And a bit chilly."

She nodded and shot him a wry grin. "Really? Don't you just hate that?"

"Havin' a bad day, Doc?"

"I wasn't until about twenty minutes ago."

"Well then you're already doin' better'n me because mine started yesterday."

She ignored him and gave me a quick nod. "Mister Gant, Miz...ummm...O'Brien, isn't it?"

"Yes," Felicity replied.

"Doctor Sanders," I said, returning the nod. "Sorry we interrupted your lunch."

"No need for you to apologize," she replied with a quick smile. "Detective Storm, however, is a different story." Making a half turn, she peered over the top of her glasses at Ben. "You know, we're still waiting on the labs. Neither of the postmortems is finished yet, so I don't know exactly what it is you want from me. I already gave you the preliminary findings."

"Yeah, I know," he told her. "I was thinkin' maybe you could just fill us in on the high points so far to get Row here up ta' speed, and we'll take it from there."

"Which victim would you like to start with?"

"Either one is fine. You pick."

She shook her head then repositioned her glasses while shuffling a pair of file folders. Flipping open the first one, she turned and started walking toward the far wall. As we followed her across the room she began to recite, "Foster, Emily. Caucasian female, approximately twenty-three years of age. Height one hundred sixty-five centimeters, weight fifty-nine kilograms. As you already know, the apparent mode of death was desanguination. In layman's terms, she bled to death."

The doctor stopped at the bank of stainless steel doors and quietly perused the file in silence, lifting a page, then another, with her free hand. After a moment she closed the folder and tucked it under her arm before quickly donning a pair of latex gloves and inspecting the tags on the doors. Finding the one she sought, she reached out and yanked the shiny rectangle open.

Before continuing, Doctor Sanders turned to me with a questioning look. "Since you are here, Mister Gant, I assume you intend to do whatever it is you do by way of…"

As her voice trailed off uncertainly, Ben offered, "Just call it *Twilight Zone*, Doc."

"I was thinking more along the line of unconventional forensics," she replied.

I gave her a nod. "I think that's pretty much why they asked me here."

Doctor Sanders was no stranger to my facility. She had witnessed me channeling victims on more than one occasion—in this very autopsy suite, in fact. While she was far more inclined to stick with tangible scientific data as opposed to the supernatural riddles that often came of such episodes, she also wasn't one to completely dismiss me out of hand.

"Will you need to touch the body?" she asked.

"That's hard to say," I shrugged. "But, yes, it could happen."

She reached into the pocket of her lab coat and withdrew another set of gloves. "Then you'd better put these on."

"I might need skin to skin contact for what I do."

"Even so, I'm going to have to insist that you put them on."

Rather than argue the point, I accepted the gloves and complied, stretching the latex over my chilled skin with much less expert dexterity than she had earlier displayed.

We stood to the side in a loose semicircle as Doctor Sanders took hold of the handle that was formed into the end of the metal drawer. Before she could start to pull, however, Felicity spoke up.

"Aye, just a second." Without offering a single word of explanation, my wife reached into her jacket then withdrew a handful of the salt packets Ben had given her, which she then stuffed into my pocket. Once she was finished with that task, she took my left hand into hers and stripped off the latex glove. "I'll watch after this one, then," she told the doctor as she interlaced her fingers with mine and tightly locked her grasp. Then she nodded and said, "Go ahead."

"Whoa..." Ben interrupted. "Just a sec... That's just the salt. Don'tcha need to dance around and say a poem or something?"

My wife shook her head. "No."

"Why not?" he pressed. "Isn't that what ya' did last time? I know it's been a few years but, remember? Didn't you do that thing where..."

My wife cut him off with her sharp appeal. "Let me worry about the WitchCraft, then. Okay?"

"Jeez, yeah, okay," he surrendered. "I'm just makin' sure."

"And your concern is appreciated," I told him.

"Aye, it is," Felicity added, her tone somewhat softer. "But this situation is different. Trust me."

"Yeah, okay. You're the Witches," he said with a shrug. "Go ahead, Doc."

A few seconds later, the full suspension drawer came outward with a metallic rattle as the doctor held tight and slowly stepped backward. Underscoring the louder noise was the soft ball-bearing hiss of the rollers beneath. The combination of the sharp and dull sounds joined together in a disharmonious clatter that tried its best to glance from the tile walls but was quickly swallowed by the chilled air as if it had never existed.

Emily Foster's corpse lay naked and prone in the shallow, tray-like drawer before us. Her skin was pallid in a way I had never recalled seeing in the past. The hooked loops of the sutures that stitched her torso shut formed stark dotted lines along the oversized Y incision. Subcutaneous ink outlined a stylized black swan tattoo on her upper arm that stood out like a surreal cartoon against the ashen color of her cold flesh. Dark hair framed her expressionless face, supplying yet another harsh contrast for the overall comparison.

Corpses were always pale. I'd seen more than my share of them, so I knew that. Still, there was something peculiar about Emily Foster's ghostly complexion. After a long moment of staring, it dawned on me that she was missing the normal markings of lividity I had grown accustomed to seeing on dead bodies—the dark postmortem "stains" left where blood would begin to pool in response to gravity soon after the heart stopped beating. Of course, since she was all but devoid of blood, it only stood to reason they wouldn't be prevalent.

"You okay, Row?" Ben asked.

"Yeah…" I replied. "Yeah, I'm fine."

Felicity gripped my hand tighter, and I gave her a quick glance. Whether or not I succeeded in reassuring her I couldn't really tell.

"Okay, Doc. Give us the rundown," Ben instructed.

Doctor Sanders stepped around to the far side of the drawer then drew her index finger along an impression in the dead woman's ultra-pale flesh. "As you can see there are obvious ligature marks around her ankles." The medical examiner traced her finger farther down the top of the foot, continuing her recitation. "They bear across the lower ankle and upper foot at an inward slant, continuing into the arch. The depth and angle of the indentations would seem to indicate significant additional stress being applied to whatever was used as a binding. There are also both antemortem and postmortem abrasions as you would expect."

An eerie sort of calm had settled over me immediately after the body had been rolled into view. While I still had the makings of a headache taking random shots at the back of my skull, they were nowhere near the intensity to which I had become used to coping with at times like this. Over the years, excruciating pain and deafening screams had become the norms associated with my curse, especially whenever in close proximity to a victim. But, for some reason, such was not the case today.

I certainly didn't want for either of those plagues to befall me again. However, the fact that they were strangely AWOL had me more than just a bit unsettled. I actually began to wonder if I had finally been granted my wish to be rid of this bane. But, if that was the case, even I had to admit the universe had certainly picked an inopportune time to smile upon me.

Doctor Sanders continued, moving up along the body as she spoke. "Examination showed no evidence of vaginal or anal tearing, and the rape kit came back negative. In fact there was no evidence whatsoever of sexual activity either consensual or non-consensual."

"That's because this wasn't about sex," I blurted.

"You gettin' somethin'?" Ben asked, perking up at my sudden pronouncement.

"I'm not really sure."

"Whaddaya mean you're not sure? Either ya' are or ya' aren't."

"You know better than that," I explained. "Things don't seem to be happening for me like they usually do, but I just know this wasn't about sex."

"Do ya' know, like hinky hocus-pocus *know*, or are ya' just speculatin'?"

"All I can say is that my gut feeling is the killer had no sexual interest in the victims."

"Well, for the record the Feebs disagree with ya' on that." Ben pulled out his small notebook and thumbed through the pages. "They think our bad guy has...yeah, here it is... Haematophilia, which means blood gets him off."

"Well, I think they're wrong," I said.

"Ya'know, just because there's no evidence of rape doesn't mean the guy didn't...you know..."

"Masturbate?" Doctor Sanders offered to fill in the expanding void where Ben had gone quiet.

"Yeah, that," he returned.

"Why are you always so squeamish about sexual acts?" she asked.

"I'm not... It just ain't polite ta' talk about it in mixed company."

"I'm a doctor."

"Yeah, you're female too. Like I said, mixed company."

"Come on, Storm... You can be just plain crass at times. Even when women are around you'll toss the word 'fuck' out there like it's from a grade school vocabulary test, but you're getting antsy when it comes to talking about sex?"

"That's different."

She shook her head. "You're an enigma."

"What can I say?"

"Well, I still say the FBI is wrong," I announced, trying to bring the conversation back on track. "This wasn't about sex, including autoeroticism."

Ben looked over at me and said, "Okay." Unfortunately, he didn't sound as if he was convinced.

I cast a sideways glance in his direction. "Why do I get the feeling you're just humoring me?"

"Sorry, Row." He shrugged again then shook his head. "Don't mean it that way... I guess I'm just used to a bit more of a dramatic presentation from ya'."

"Sorry to disappoint you."

"Well, since I got ya' both here how 'bout a second opinion?" my friend asked, aiming his gaze at my wife. "Whadda you think, Firehair? The killer sexually motivated or no?"

"I'm concentrating on something else at the moment," she replied, her voice flat and distant.

"What?"

"In your words, keeping my sorry ass safe," I answered for her. "She's grounding me."

"Well see there?" Ben made a sweeping gesture at the two of us. "Maybe that's the problem with your ghost radar or whatever. She's doin' too good a job and shortin' you out or somethin'."

"I didn't know there was a problem."

"Well, ya'know... You don't seem to be goin' ta' la-la land and all..."

"So you're saying that unless I go into a trance or try to swallow my own tongue I'm not credible?"

"I'm not sayin' that," he grumbled. "It's just... Well, you know what I'm talkin' about..."

"Unfortunately, yes, I do," I replied. "Would it help if I told you I have a headache?"

"Maybe. Do ya'?"

"Yes."

"But is it..."

"The *Twilight Zone* kind? Yes."

"See... Yeah... That does help a bit."

"Good, I'm glad." I tried hard to keep the sarcasm out of my voice, but I knew some of it had to have leaked through.

"If the two of you are finished, shall I continue?" Doctor Sanders asked.

"Yes, I'm sorry," I replied.

"Superficial ligature marks on the wrists indicate her hands were bound at some point prior to death," she began her recitation anew. "There are several healed scars on both arms that appear to have been inflicted by something small and sharp, such as a razor blade, but the most recent of them is at least several months old. There is, however, a more recent needle puncture in the left arm. From the level of bruising, it occurred probably one to two days before her death. We're testing the surrounding adipose tissue for any trace of drugs which may have been injected."

Taking a pair of steps toward the end of the drawer, she rolled Emily Foster's head to the side and held it in place while she used the index finger of her other hand to point out a ragged trauma on her neck. "Now, as I said earlier, the mode of death was desanguination.

Everything points to her having bled out from this wound on her neck." She moved her finger around to indicate an anomaly straddling the gash. "Notice the indentations here and here. We were able to take an impression, and even though it is only partial, what we have is definitely a bite wound. The profile appears to be human, although due to the degree of tearing, we weren't able to get much more than the upper incisors and the right cuspid. However, the depth of the impression showed that the cuspid is markedly elongated."

"You mean long like a vampire fang?" Ben asked.

"Yes, like a fang," she replied. "But I really wouldn't say 'vampire' since there is no such thing."

"Yeah, I know, Doc," he said. "What I mean is like the fruitloops who think they're vampires."

"Well, I suppose," she assented with a nod. "Since the bite is in fact human, it's possible the subject might have a removable prosthesis, or even a cosmetic dental veneer. But, I'm afraid that unless you find someone we can match up with a dental record it may be moot. Unfortunately, no saliva was detected, even deep into the wound itself, so we aren't getting any DNA to run against the database.

"Also of note, the lack of bruising would seem to indicate that the bite was made postmortem. We're checking for free histamine levels in the surrounding tissues to verify that." Doctor Sanders looked up and pointed across the room with her free hand. "Storm, do me a favor. There's a magnifying glass on the table over there, I need it."

Ben strode over to the table and searched for a moment before returning with the instrument.

Doctor Sanders paused and adjusted the woman's head to bring more light onto the wound then carefully held a flap of sagging flesh in place with her finger. Holding the lens over the area, she began speaking again, "We've actually excised a sample here, but if you look closely you can see that the bite rips through the external jugular vein, which is the point where she bled out."

I leaned in to look through the magnifier, but not being versed in vascular anatomy, all I really saw was a jagged gash in a dead woman's neck. I kept staring, but apparently the angle at which I was leaning was starting to affect my balance because a nasty wave of vertigo was causing my head to swim. That being the case, I decided I should just step back and rely on Doctor Sanders to explain.

"Okay, just a sec…" Ben interjected. "She bled ta' death so that would make all kinds of sense, but you also just said you think the bite came after she was already dead. So how does that work?"

"I'm coming to that," Doctor Sanders replied. "The sample and vein section we excised bore indications of a large gauge needle puncture."

"So the killer drained 'er with a needle?"

"Most likely a catheter and IV tubing, but yes."

"Sonofabitch," Ben muttered then let out a thoughtful sigh.

Doctor Sanders voice floated into my ears with a questioning note firmly attached. "Mister Gant?"

A handful of seconds later Ben's echoing words followed. "Hey, Row... You're pretty quiet over there. You gettin' somethin'?"

Unfortunately, I wasn't able to answer him. He was, however, about to get his earlier wish for the dramatic.

CHAPTER 22

THE ONSET OF THE VERTIGO SHOULD HAVE BEEN MY first clue that something wasn't right. Unfortunately, I had allowed myself to be lulled into a false sense of security by the almost complete lack of usual warning signs leading up to it. Therefore, by the time I had actually backed away from Emily Foster's corpse, it was too late. Of course, since I knew this moment was really just another step in an already runaway supernatural process, I was also painfully aware that it shouldn't have come as a surprise. Truth be told it was already too late the day I awoke with the inexplicable pain in the side of my neck.

"Rowan?" Ben's voice hurtled past me once again, pausing in its flight just long enough to send a distorted echo down my ear canal before continuing along its random trajectory through the room.

I don't know how long it actually took me to figure out that the ricocheting noise was my name being called, but it really wasn't important. Whether minutes or only fractions of a second passed, the point was moot. For me, time was no longer a constant.

For a third time, he called my name, adding even more insistence as if I simply wasn't listening. I still didn't answer. It wasn't that I didn't want to. I simply couldn't form the words, either physically or mentally. In fact, all I could manage to do was stare downward at the edge of the slide out drawer but, more specifically, at my hand resting upon it. Of course, it wasn't so much that my hand was resting on the metal as much as the fact that it was also in full contact with Emily Foster's arm.

I couldn't help but stare in wonderment. My right hand was still sheathed in the surgical glove Doctor Sanders had insisted I wear. Heretofore, even such a thin layer of latex had seemed to be an insurmountable barrier whenever I was purposely attempting to connect with the dead. But now, that had obviously changed. With a single accidental touch I was now spiraling into an encounter with this dead woman's horrors, and there was little I could do to stop it from happening.

The dizziness was taking over now, swirling around behind my eyes as my stomach churned out of synch, making a strong bid to work itself into a frenzy of nausea. I could feel my heart thumping just behind my face instead of in my chest where it belonged, and an odd pressure forced outward from inside my skull. The headache that had been knocking on the back of my head let itself in and fell into a wildly syncopated rhythm with the frantic beat.

Ben's voice corkscrewed its way through the rush of blood in my ears. "Somethin's wrong... Felicity? You with us?"

Hearing him call my wife's name sent a wave of panic ripping through my intestines. In the past few moments, I had all but forgotten that she was fighting to anchor me in the realm of the living. I now feared that the solid connection she had formed to protect me was now placing her in jeopardy.

I tried to alleviate the threat by releasing my grip on her hand but immediately found that the signals from my brain were being stopped well before they made it to my fingers. Realizing that there was nothing I could do, the terror now shot upward through the pit of my stomach and settled into my chest. As it began spreading out into a cold fear, a second voice slammed headlong against my eardrums.

"*Caorthann*," my wife said, calling my name in Gaelic.

What I managed to glean from the sound was not that she was in distress but that she was concerned. While that fact didn't completely quell the panic, it at least put a damper on the fear that she was in any danger. If she was talking to me, then she was obviously in much better shape than I was at the moment.

The influx of relief forced my guard down just enough that the incorporeal Emily Foster gained an even more solid foothold in my psyche. In a flash she slipped through and demanded to be heard. I had no other choice but to listen.

I felt myself falling, but it wasn't the dreamlike sensation of endless descent to which I was accustomed. This was the real thing. My knees buckled. Soon, what followed was my body pitching to the side and then back. The fall came slowly at first, then with an ever-increasing rate as I crumpled in place.

I heard Felicity yelp. "Rowan!"

As I hastened toward the floor, I felt a quick tug on my hand. I thought I heard my wife let out another sharp cry, and then I experienced the sensation of cold tile slamming against my back and shoulder. Not to be outdone, my head cracked against the floor, sending a fresh and very intense pain to join forces with the migraine as everything shuddered. As it morphed into a dull ache, I could feel the coolness of the floor seeping into my cheek. A split second later the air was unexpectedly forced from my lungs by a squirming weight landing hard on top of me. I realized, as the object continued moving and then scrambled to the side, that it was Felicity. My hand was still locked tight with hers, and I had apparently dragged her down with me.

"Are you all right?" Ben's voice bounced through the room, but I knew he wasn't speaking to me.

"Aye," Felicity answered him in slow motion. "Rowan? Rowan?!"

I could feel something prying at my fingers. I was struggling to stay planted in this plane, but a tortured spirit had a much different idea about where I needed to be. Emily Foster had something to show me, and she was pulling me backward into darkness in an insane tug of war across the veil.

And as I expected she was already starting to win.

"Just a little sting..." an androgynous and wholly unfamiliar voice echoed. But it wasn't in my ears; it was inside my head.

I can't see anything.

The world is completely black for me.

I feel pressure against my neck.

"Don't worry," the voice says again. *"It will all be over soon...very soon... I envy you. To be chosen like this. It's such an honor... I wish it were me..."*

I still can't move. I'm facing the tiled wall lined with stainless steel doors, and I see shadows moving across it. There is a hard pressure against my neck now. Although I can barely make it out over the din of blood rushing in my ears, I can hear what sounds to be a flurry of activity just out of my line of sight.

My ankles are burning... The rope is biting into them hard.

I can no longer feel my feet. They've gone completely numb.

Dizziness...

Headache...

I wish I could see.

I won't be afraid... I won't be afraid...

I am chosen...

It is an honor...

I have been prepared...

I can hear the chanting now...
The time must be near...
It is an honor to be chosen...
It is an honor to be chosen...
I won't be afraid...

The last thing I heard before blacking out was Doctor Sanders voice puncturing the drone in my ears with a sharp note of controlled alarm threaded through her words. "I can't stop the bleeding. Get the paramedics now!"

CHAPTER 23

I SLOWLY OPENED ONE EYE AND LET IT ROAM. THERE was no mistaking where I was based simply on the institutional colors now bleeding into my limited field of vision. But, even if the drab hues didn't give it away, there was a failsafe to back them up, that being the antiseptic smell that was now tingling my nostrils. I closed the eye once again and tried to remember what was going on prior to this particular moment in my life.

Unfortunately, my head was throbbing too much to allow for anything resembling deep thought. I remembered being at the morgue, accidentally touching Emily Foster's corpse, then becoming acquainted with the floor of the autopsy suite. All of that pretty much consumed the space I had left in my grey matter that wasn't being taken up with pain. However, there was still enough room in between the cycling aches for me to wonder where my wife happened to be.

"Felicity?" I barely croaked in a dry, wispy voice.

I didn't get an answer, but since I could barely hear myself, maybe she couldn't hear me at all. I cleared my throat then opened both of my eyes this time and lifted my head slightly as I sent them searching. To my disappointment, there wasn't a single petite redhead in sight. In fact, I appeared to be the only one present here in hospital hell.

I laid my head back against the pillow as the throbbing started to increase. I took a moment to slowly adjust my position when I felt the sore spot on the right side of my scalp. That triggered a vague memory of my head hitting the floor, which I suppose would explain the whole lapse of memory. At least, as far as my addled senses were concerned it did.

I ran down a mental list just for the sake of my sanity. I knew who I was, I knew where I was, and I was fairly certain I knew what day it was, although I didn't have anything or anyone handy to confirm those facts. I even remembered the incident that had most likely landed me here. I just couldn't remember the time between then and now.

That annoyed me. But, what truly had me concerned was the fact that I didn't know where Felicity was or, more importantly, her condition. I was relatively certain she was uninjured. After all, she had been speaking to me, and I even recalled Ben asking her if she was okay. Unfortunately, my brain was in no hurry to remember any of the other pertinent details, no matter how much I willed it to do so.

After a minute or two passed, I started pondering the idea of getting out of the bed and going to find my wife or, at the very least, someone who could tell me where she was. As I started to reach for the side railing I felt a tug on my finger, which led me to realize something was attached to it. Feeling around with my other hand I felt a tug on it as well. I held them both up for a bleary-eyed inspection that ended with a heavy sigh. Getting out of the bed now became a bit more complicated between the IV and the monitor hookups.

Of course, if I couldn't go to them I figured I might as well bring them to me. Taking hold of the pulse oximeter probe that was firmly clamped to my finger, I popped it off, laid back, closed my eyes, and waited.

As expected, a shrill tone immediately bit into my ears. Even though I knew it was coming, I groaned in response to the noise anyway. I didn't bother to open my eyes, I simply laid there, unmoving all except for the handful of muscles that were necessary to twist my face into an annoyed grimace.

Soft but slightly hurried footfalls sounded a few moments later. I felt someone fumbling with my finger, and then the mild pressure clamped down upon it once again. There was a chirp, and then relative quiet fell again.

"Where's my wife?" I asked, still holding my eyes tightly shut.

"Mister Gant, you're awake I see," a woman's voice said.

"Very astute observation, but I'm afraid that doesn't answer my question," I grumbled.

"I believe she just went to the lounge down the hall to get herself a soft drink," the voice told me. "She should be back any minute."

"So, she's okay?"

"Of course. And you will be too if you just rest."

I could hear her punching buttons on the monitor. It would occasionally chirp, give an abbreviated alarm tone, and then fall quiet again.

"Can't you just shut that damn thing off?" I asked.

"I'm resetting it. Don't worry. The sensor just slipped off your finger."

"No, actually I pulled it off," I replied.

"Why?"

"Because I needed someone to answer my question."

"We have call buttons for that."

"I know. I've had the displeasure of visiting several such accommodations in the past."

"Then why didn't you use it?"

"My way was faster."

"Well, you can't just take the probe off your finger, Mister Gant."

"Seems to me I just did. Want to see me do it again?"

"Aye, is he giving you trouble then?" Felicity's voice entered the conversation from what sounded to be several feet away. Hearing her prompted me to open my eyes, but of course the first person I saw was the nurse, who was sporting an unnaturally black, shoulder-length pageboy and scrubs patterned with a stylized avian print.

"He was asking for you," the nurse said. "He's grouchy but we're used to that around here."

"Just standing up for my rights," I mumbled.

"More like being a curmudgeon, I would say," my wife replied. "Let Amanda do her job and stop giving her such a hard time. She's been taking very good care of you all afternoon."

While she was talking, the nurse adjusted the angle of the bed so that I was inclined enough to see her without straining. Felicity was now standing near the footboard with a thin smile on her lips.

"How is that?" the nurse asked. "Comfortable?"

"Close enough," I muttered.

"You're a horrible patient, do you know that?" my wife asked.

"I happen to know you aren't any better," I returned.

"Aye, but we're talking about you."

"The doctor should be coming by to check on you shortly," the nurse interjected. "If you need anything, please use the call button."

"Okay," I told her. "Sorry to be a pain."

"You're forgiven," she replied with a smile. "Besides, shift changes in less than an hour. You can grumble at someone else."

"Can I ask you something?" I said to her as she turned to go.

She twisted back around to face me. "Sure."

"That design on your scrubs. Is it supposed to be geese or ducks?"

"Swans, actually."

"Really..." I mumbled.

"Anything else?" she asked.

"No... ummm... Thanks." After the nurse left the room I rested my gaze on Felicity. "Swans, go figure."

"Do you think it's some kind of sign?" she asked, but I could tell she wasn't all that serious.

"Hell, I don't know..." I grumbled.

"I'm sure it's just a bizarre coincidence. Don't you think?"

"Yeah... You're probably right."

She pulled a chair alongside the bed and took a seat then carefully slipped her fingers around mine. When I looked down I took notice of the fact that her right sleeve was rolled up and an elastic bandage was woven around her hand and wrist.

I furrowed my brow and asked, "Are you okay?"

"Of course," she replied, shaking her head. "Why?"

"Your hand," I said, motioning half-heartedly with my free appendage.

"Just a sprain," she said with a quick shrug. "I twisted it when you went down, and then I fell on top of you."

"Sorry about that."

"It wasn't your fault."

"I'm still sorry."

"You can make amends later," she said with a small grin. "How are you feeling?"

"My head is killing me," I said. "Other than that, I'm just really tired."

"Well I'm not surprised. You're body has been through quite a shock," she told me. "They estimated you lost just under two pints of blood before arriving here, and you were already running low as it was."

"I bled again?" I reached up with my free hand to feel my neck even though I didn't expect to find anything of consequence. However, to my surprise there was a heavy bandage taped firmly in place.

Felicity nodded. "Yes, this time there's actually a wound." She paused then added, "And the bleeding was much worse too. It didn't seem to want to stop."

"Wonderful," I groaned. "So I'm still alive why?"

"Because I told her it was mine," Felicity said.

"Told who what?"

"Emily Foster. You don't remember any of that?"

I shook my head slightly then grimaced. "No. I don't. I vaguely recall somebody saying something about bleeding, but I actually assumed I was here because I hit my head. I definitely remember that part."

"That really wasn't that bad," she replied. "Just a bit of a bump. The doctor says you don't even have a concussion."

"Well, at least there's that. So, are you saying you were actually able to communicate with Emily Foster's spirit?"

She chuckled. "Of course I was. You aren't the only Witch here, you know. So do you remember anything else?"

"Not much really," I replied. "Not after hitting the floor anyway. I do feel like there's something rolling around in there, but I just can't nail it down."

Felicity gathered herself up from the chair then lowered the railing on the side of the bed and perched herself next to me. As she softly brushed my hair away from my face she said, "Maybe if you just relax it will come to you."

"You could be right," I agreed then took a deep breath and let it out slowly. Relaxing wasn't one of my more proficient skills, but I knew I desperately needed to remember what I had seen if I was going to help stop this killer and, more importantly, save Judith Albright's life if at all possible.

Unfortunately, something new was cropping up in my brain that had me preoccupied. I puzzled over it for a long moment, concentrating between stabs of pain, then gave up and asked my wife, "What did you mean when you said you told Emily Foster's spirit 'it was yours'?"

"Oh, that. I can show you," she replied.

I scrunched my forehead in confusion. "Show me?"

She shot me a broad, toothy smile, but by the time I realized what I was seeing it was too late. She had already buried her fangs into my neck, and I was trying to scream.

I FELT MYSELF GASP AS THE SCREAM CAUGHT IN MY throat and formed a hard lump. Light bloomed in my eyes and slowly settled to a contrasty blur that eventually became the tile wall of the autopsy suite filling my vision once again. I was still seeing it sideways and from floor level, but I didn't care. It definitely beat what I had been seeing a split second before.

I heard Doctor Sanders calling out to someone. Her voice was calm but held a strong sense of urgency. "I can't stop the bleeding. Get the paramedics now!"

A quickly moving wave of panic washed over me upon hearing the string of syllables, and a solid sense of déjà vu informed me that I had been here before. This time, however, no darkness encroached upon my corner of the world. No hospital room, no Goth nurse wearing swan print clothing, and most especially, no vampire wife.

I still couldn't move, or even speak. My heart hadn't stopped thumping inside my head and neither had the noise of the blood rushing in my ears, but unlike before, I could hear everything going on around me as clear as crystal.

Ben's businesslike but very dire voice was sounding nearby. "Yeah, this is Detective Benjamin Storm. We need paramedics at City Medical Examiner's office on Clark. We have a male in his early forties hemorrhaging from his neck. Uh-huh... Yeah... Yeah, Doc Sanders is already on that..."

"Tell them to come in the back entrance," Doctor Sanders instructed. "It will save time."

"Yeah, the back entrance..." my friend repeated. "It's closer."

From somewhere behind and very near to my head I heard Felicity blurt, "The drawer!" Her voice was a rapid burst and just to the low side of a shout.

"What?" Ben barked in return.

My wife didn't take time to answer. I could hear the soles of her tennis shoes squeak against the tile floor as she scrambled up and skirted around my prone body. Even though I couldn't actually see it happening, I knew it was she who was attached to the noise.

A heartbeat later I heard her normally singsong voice now brimming with unbridled rage as she recited aloud, "Emily, it's time to go, I want you gone as you well know. Goodbye now, and stay away, unless I call another day."

As my wife's words were still tumbling from her mouth, I heard the sound of the rollers on the drawer hissing and clattering as before, beginning with a slow ka-chunk then ramping up to a fast chatter. A heavy thump came a second later, and the clacking rollers stopped in the same instant. The dull noise was followed by the hollow clank of the insulated stainless steel door slamming shut.

Thick silence filled the room as the oddly final sound dissipated into the cold air. After a tense moment I heard Felicity growl with bitter calm, "And don't make me stuff your eternal arse into a shoebox, *saigh*."

CHAPTER 24

"DO ME A FAVOR AND SMILE REALLY BIG," I SAID TO MY wife.

I had just finished glancing at the IV tube running into the back of my left hand and the pulse oximeter probe attached to a finger on my right, so I was once again feeling an overwhelming and terribly unpleasant sense of déjà vu. At least we weren't in a hospital room; however, we were at a hospital, sitting in a treatment room in the emergency ward. Well, actually, she was sitting; I was laying on the table, albeit at an incline.

I knew the instant I opened my mouth and asked her to smile that I was letting irrational paranoia guide the odd request. But under the circumstances and at this particular moment, I wasn't entirely certain I could reasonably distinguish reality from lifelike ethereal visions, and I needed to be sure.

Felicity's brow pinched up as she cocked her head to the side and stared at me. "Why?"

"Just humor me," I said, the tone of my voice adding an obvious if unspoken *please*.

She shook her head as if she thought I had lost my mind, but still curled her lips into a quick smile.

"Bigger," I urged. "So I can see your teeth."

"Is this about that vision?" she asked.

"Kind of…"

She sighed then repeated the smile, this time baring her clenched teeth and rolling her eyes. After turning her head side to side, she relaxed her mouth and asked, "There. Was that good enough for you?"

"Yeah, thanks. By the way, how is your arm?"

"It's fine."

"You're sure you didn't twist it or anything when we fell?"

"No. I already told you I'm not that fragile."

"Okay, as long as you're sure."

She didn't even try to mask the bother in her voice as she responded. "It was just an errant vision produced by your imagination, Rowan. That's all. It was something put together by your subconscious because of everything that was happening on top of everything else that has happened in the last few days. You've been through this sort of thing before. You know that's what it was."

I reached up and felt my neck for what was probably the sixth time. There was still nothing there that shouldn't be.

She watched me then shook her head and asked, "What do I have to do to convince you?"

"Don't suddenly sprout fangs would be a good start."

"I'm serious."

"So am I."

In a sharp huff she let out an exasperated breath. "I think the blood loss must have affected your brain."

"Maybe so, but the whole thing felt pretty real, so I have to figure there's something to it."

"What, you actually think I'm a vampire?" she quipped. "Now I know something's wrong with your head."

"No, that's not what I mean. I just think there's some significance to the vision that I'm missing," I explained then tilted my head back and stared at the ceiling. After a minute or so of silence, I looked over at Felicity again and said, "By the way, I think I probably forgot to say thank you. That was some pretty quick thinking you did back there at the morgue."

"What? You mean salting a dead woman's corpse into submission?"

"Hmmph. Well, I couldn't really see what was happening, so I didn't know about the salt. But I could definitely hear you rattling off the banishing spell. How long have you been carrying that one around in your pocket, cocked and ready?"

"I haven't." She shook her head. "I made it up on the spot."

"See there… Like I said, quick thinking."

"Aye, it was a lucky rhyme. I was angry, and anger trumps everything. I could have recited a recipe for crab dip as long as the intent was there. Miz Foster's spirit should actually be glad I didn't pluck a hair out of her dead little head and do some real damage."

"Yeah, I caught your addendum as well."

"Apparently she did too, because she left," she spat.

"So… You sound like you're still a little on the angry side."

"I suppose I am," she admitted.

"At me?" I asked.

"No." She punctuated the reply with an animated shake of her head. "Not at you… At the situation. To be honest, I think it's really frustration more than anything else. I mean, you were perfectly grounded, and on top of that you had me anchoring you as well." She shrugged and threw her hands up in exasperation. "But look what happened anyway… There was just no way to control it."

"I know," I told her. "But for the whole process to work I have to let them in, and once the door is open… Well… You've been there… You know…"

She nodded. "Aye. They're like houseguests from hell who refuse to leave."

We both heard a sharp knock then the door to the treatment room slowly swung open and Ben poked his head through the gap.

"Hey, white man," he greeted me as he continued pushing the door open wider and stepped inward then allowed it to pivot shut in his wake. "How ya' doin'?"

"As well as can be expected, I guess," I replied, glancing up at the IV bag and pointing to it. "They're topping me off or something."

"Heya, Firehair," he said, glancing over at Felicity.

She nodded.

"So listen," he began as he looked back over to me. "The description of your *Twilight Zone* nurse pretty much fits with our Jane Doe. As much as you were able to give us anyway. So just ta' be safe, they're gonna run the name Amanda against missing persons."

"Well, that's a good thing, right?" I asked.

"Maybe. We'll hafta see. Woulda helped ta' have a last name."

"Sorry about that."

He shrugged. "No need to apologize, it was la-la land stuff. I get that even if they don't. But the big problem is the name could be an alias or something, so we could get false hits. And if she was never reported missin' in the first place, then we aren't gonna get any hits at all. If that happens then we still have a Jane Doe… Or an Amanda Doe… However you wanna look at it."

"But, what you aren't saying is that no matter what you get, it still doesn't bring us any closer to figuring out who is doing this or to finding Judith Albright," I offered as I laid my head back and closed my eyes.

"Yeah, well, I wasn't gonna point that out. Not just yet, anyway," my friend told me. "But don't count it out. Something as simple as a name can still produce a lead."

I let out a long sigh then spoke aloud to myself as much as them. "Emily kept saying, *It is an honor to be chosen, I won't be afraid.*"

"Yeah, you already told me that," he grunted. "No offense, white man, but that ain't a whole lotta help either. Now, *help, I'm being held at xyz house on whatever street* would be a definite step in the right direction."

"I know," I replied. "And you also know it doesn't work like that."

"Yeah. Trust me, I've been tryin' to explain that to the brass."

"If I can figure out what she meant about it being an honor to be chosen, maybe it will set us on the right path."

"Well, based on the amount of time between when she disappeared and when her body turned up, maybe it's some form of brainwashing, then," Felicity suggested. "Like a Stockholm Syndrome type of thing."

"Yeah, they tossed that idea out there when I called all this in a little while ago," Ben replied. "Then when I mentioned you said she heard chanting, they started in with the whole Satanic ritual murder angle."

"They just love that one, don't they?" I replied.

"Yeah, well some things just ain't gonna change, Row."

"I guess I can't blame them," I offered. "Even with what I know, I have to admit that some kind of ritual murder scenario crossed my mind too."

"So you think maybe there's some kinda cult operatin' in the area?"

I shook my head. "I really don't know, Ben. Unfortunately I'm just as confused by all this as the rest of you. But I have trouble believing there is a whole mob involved in the killing. Two killers, I can wrap my head around. But several killers working in conjunction, I just don't see it."

"Or maybe you just don't wanna..."

"You know, Ben, as much as I hate to admit it, you may be right about that."

"Yeah, I was afra..."

Another knock sounded at the treatment room door, and this time the ER doctor who had been assigned to my case entered. When he saw Ben standing there, a look of annoyance screwed itself onto his face.

"We don't really allow..." he began.

Ben slipped his badge case from an inner jacket pocket then quickly flashed his shield and ID inches from the doctor's nose. "You were saying?"

"Is there a problem, Officer?" the doctor asked, taking a step back.

"Not really," Ben replied as he tucked the case back into his pocket. "And, by the way, that's Detective."

"My apologies."

"That's okay. I thought you were a nurse," Ben replied then continued speaking before the doctor could say anything. "So, here's the deal. Rowan is one of our civilian consultants, and he happens ta' be helpin' us with a fairly important case right now. I just needed to talk to 'im."

"I see," the doctor said with a curt nod. "You know the sarcasm was completely unnecessary."

"Go have yourself half the day I've already had, then come tell me that," my friend returned without missing a beat.

Rather than argue, the doctor turned his attention to me. "How are you feeling, Mister Gant?"

"Confused, hungry, and a little tired, pretty much in that order," I replied. "How about you?"

"Confused?" he asked.

"No need to write it down, Doc, it's not a symptom," I told him. "It's just something we were discussing about the case is all."

He nodded and said, "I see," again. He didn't sound particularly happy about anything at the moment, but I couldn't really tell if that was his natural demeanor or if Ben had set him off by sticking a badge in his face and generally being an ass.

"So, what's the prognosis?" I asked.

"At the moment your vitals are stable," he replied while looking through a file. "Your blood work appears normal... I am however, a bit concerned that we haven't yet been able to pinpoint the actual source of your blood loss."

"You won't," I told him.

"Why do you say that?"

"It's a long story you wouldn't believe even if I told you."

He repeated his pat phrase. "I see. Well, I'd like to admit you for some tests anyway."

I shook my head. "I'm afraid I'm not going to be able to do that."

"Mister Gant, it's important that you realize the risk this could pose. If you are bleeding internally..."

"I'm not," I said, cutting him off and waving at my neck. "Remember? All the blood was on the outside."

He sighed hard. "What is it going to take to convince you to stay overnight for some tests?"

"Nothing you have, I'm afraid," I told him. "Seriously, you aren't going to find anything."

The doctor turned and looked past Ben at Felicity. "Miz Gant... Can you talk to your husband?"

She didn't correct him on the *faux pas* with her name. She simply shook her head and shrugged. "What makes you think he'll listen to me then?"

The doctor closed his eyes and hung his head for a moment before giving it a shake and letting out another sigh. "Fine. I can't make you stay against your will," he said then checked the nearly depleted IV bag hanging above me. "But, I do want you to stay until we get the rest of this fluid into you. That will take maybe fifteen or twenty minutes. Can you spare that much time?"

"Okay," I agreed with a nod.

"I'll get your paperwork taken care of and then you can go. I'd like to suggest that you get some rest and stay hydrated. Avoid alcohol, coffee, soda, and caffeinated beverages. Drink water and apple juice instead. I would also like for you to take an iron supplement. An over-the-counter one will do."

I nodded again. "Okay."

He continued. "If you experience any extreme fatigue, headaches, heart palpitations, or especially any more bleeding, get yourself into an emergency room right away."

"I can do that," I replied.

He scribbled something on the chart then stepped around Ben and exited the treatment room without another word. It was obvious he wasn't happy with the way the conversation had gone, but I was convinced he'd get over it quickly enough. There was bound to be someone coming through the doors at some point who needed his attention far worse than me.

While we were waiting for the IV bag to run out, Ben looked over at Felicity and said, "I s'pose now wouldn't be a good time ta' say I told ya' so, huh?"

"I told you so about what?" she asked.

"Ya'know, the sayin' a poem thing with the salt before Row did the *Twilight Zone* thing."

"Aye, you're right." She nodded thoughtfully.

"Yeah, I thought you might've wanted ta'..."

She cut him off mid sentence. "I mean you're right that it isn't a good time."

"Yeah, okay, but I did tell you so."

"Ben..." she warned. "I'd hate to have to turn you into a cockroach and step on you."

He snorted and gave her a bemused look. "Yeah right, gimme a break. Remember who you're talkin' to here. I've been around long enough to know the hocus-pocus shit doesn't work like that." He glanced over at me. "Right, Kemosabe?"

I shook my head. "You know, Ben, you might want to be careful. After what she managed to pull off back at the morgue, I wouldn't put anything past her."

"You ain't serious, right?"

"About which part?" I asked.

He let out a nervous chuckle then mumbled, "Yeah, great... Okay..." After a long pause, he cleared his throat while reaching up to give the back of his neck a quick massage. "So, listen... I know you're just fuckin' with me, but at the risk of endin' up on the bottom of Firehair's shoe anyway, I need to ask ya' somethin'... The powers that be wanted ta' know if you'd take another run at this."

"What?!" Felicity almost yelped. "Are they *fekking* insane?"

"Don't worry," he said, holding up his hand to stave her off. "I told 'em I'd ask, but I also told 'em not ta' count on it. So, no pressure from me here at all. Believe me."

As soon as a lull fell between them I spoke up. "Yeah. Tell them no guarantees, but I'll give it a try."

"Rowan..." Felicity admonished.

"Hey... Row..." Ben chimed in, shaking his head. "Like I said, I told 'em to expect a no."

"So they'll be pleasantly surprised, and maybe you'll score some brownie points."

"That ain't what this is about," he insisted.

"I know that," I replied. "But I also know—and both of you do too—that until we solve this, Emily Foster's spirit isn't going to leave me alone. I can bleed there with a doctor on hand, or I can bleed at home without one. Either way, it's pretty obvious that it's going to happen whether I like it or not."

"Aye, maybe not. I think she got the point earlier," Felicity objected.

"Maybe you're right," I said with a nod. "Who knows? But where does that leave Judith Albright?"

"Damn your eyes," Felicity conceded.

"Sorry."

"Okay, you're right," she offered. "But before you try this again, we take more precautions."

"Agreed. What did you have in mind?"

"Maybe you oughta go ahead and say a poem first this time," Ben interjected.

My wife shot him a death glare but didn't take the bait. "I haven't figured that out yet," she said as she looked back to me.

"Well, we have a little time to think about that," I told her. "Because before we do anything I need to eat."

"Yeah, I could definitely eat," Ben said with a nod. "You wanna grab somethin' at Forty's, or would ya' rather keep your distance from the morgue until you're ready?"

"I don't really care as long as it's someplace that serves liver and onions," I replied.

"Liver? Jeez... I dunno how you eat that shit."

"With a knife and fork," I quipped.

"Yeah, real funny, Row," he returned. "I mean it tastes like crap."

"Well, that's a matter of opinion, but I admit I don't usually crave it like I am today."

"You're cravin' the stuff? Hmmph. Well maybe it's leftover *Twilight Zone* screwin' up your taste buds."

"Why do you say that?"

He shrugged and gave me a thoughtful nod. "Oh yeah, I don't guess I told you about that yet. Doc Sanders is still waitin' on the labs, but she did get a read back on Emily Foster's stomach contents. Looks like her last meal was beef liver."

AS I'D PREDICTED EARLIER, WE FOUND OURSELVES AT the Metro Diner because it was the closest establishment in the downtown area that could accommodate my sought after menu selection. Ben's recently shared revelation had actually taken the edge off my craving, most likely because he was correct in his assumption that there was an ethereal element to it, and Emily Foster's last meal was the culprit at the root.

Still, even with my desire for the dish having been substantially dampened, I had worked up a taste for it. Besides, the doctor wanted me to take an iron supplement, and liver was loaded with the stuff.

As it turned out, I wasn't disappointed. The liver was fork tender and swimming in gravy with a generous helping of caramelized onions sitting on top. The mashed potatoes were lumpy just like homemade, and the pile of buttered green peas next to them was a culinary imperative.

Something was finally going my way for a change, which was a good thing because deep down I knew this sudden stroke of luck wasn't going to last.

CHAPTER 25

"YOU GET ENOUGH?" BEN ASKED, GIVING ME A QUICK nod.

"Yeah," I replied. "I couldn't eat another bite."

He shook his head. "I still dunno how you can eat that crap ta' begin with."

"To each their own," I said with a shrug. "I like it."

"Yeah, well we already knew there was somethin' wrong with ya'. That's just more proof."

We were still sitting in a booth at the Metro, Felicity and I on one side, Ben on the other. We had arrived well after the lunch rush, and the dinner rush was still around an hour away yet, so the diner was only around half full. Still, given that our conversations tended to take unexpected turns, my friend had asked them to seat us back in the corner away from the rest of the patrons.

"What about you, Firehair?" He glanced over at Felicity.

Half her Reuben was already stuffed into a Styrofoam carton and was sitting on the table in front of her.

"Aye," she returned, nodding toward the container. "And lunch tomorrow."

"So I guess I'm the only one thinkin' about those pies behind the counter?" he asked.

"You're on your own," she told him.

"What she said," I echoed.

He glanced at his watch and from the look on his face did some mental calculating. Finally he mumbled, "Aww hell, why not…"

A second later he flagged down our waitress and ordered a slice of the coconut cream.

"So, other than you trying to backfill that bottomless pit you call a stomach, what's the grand plan?" I asked.

"Whaddaya mean?"

"Well, I know I'm the one who insisted we eat first, but we seem to be ignoring the gorilla, if you know what I mean."

"Hey, you tell me," he grunted then wagged his finger between us. "You two were s'posed ta' be figurin' out your precautions. I'm just along for the ride."

I turned to look at Felicity. "I don't know that we really need any. You seemed to handle things just fine earlier."

"Yes I did," she replied. "But that doesn't mean I'm comfortable with not having something to back me up."

"Backup's a good thing," Ben agreed.

"Of course it is," I said. "But, I'm not sure what it would be in this case. I definitely don't want to drag anyone else into this."

Felicity nodded vigorously. "Aye, I agree with you there."

"Not ta' change the subject, but how you feelin' anyway, Row?" Ben asked.

I turned back to my friend. "Fine, why?"

He shrugged with his eyebrows. "Just wonderin'. I couldn't help but notice that ever since the hospital, you haven't had your face all pinched up like normal."

"My face what?" I asked.

He waved his hands and shook his head. "Not normal normal... I mean like the normal when you're havin' a la-la land headache... Ya' don't have that crease in your face that usually comes along with 'em."

"Oh... Well... You know, I hadn't thought about it," I replied. "Actually, my head feels fine for a change."

"That could be another problem then," Felicity chimed in.

I glanced her direction once again. "What do you mean?"

"I banished Emily Foster," she said. "She might be gone for good."

"You left that spell open ended enough to summon her back though."

"True, but you know as well as I do there's still no guarantee she'll come."

"As pissed as you sounded?" Ben interjected. "I wouldn't if I was her, ghost or not."

"Really?" Felicity scoffed. "It's never seemed to stop you before."

"Yeah, I know," he replied. "Me, cockroach, squish. I get it. Honestly I think you just take a perverse pleasure in givin' me a hard time."

"Yes, I do," she said with a grin.

"Coconut cream," the waitress said as she appeared and slid a generous slice of pie in front of Ben. "Would anyone like more coffee?"

Felicity passed on the java, but Ben and I both opted for a fresh cup even though the doctor had warned me off. Once the waitress was gone, I tried to steer the conversation back into the proper lane. "Look, right now Judith Albright needs to be our concern. Maybe we should skip the morgue and go straight to the crime scene."

"We don't really have one," Ben explained. "The last place she was seen was the house where she lived with the vampire whacko. Already been over that with a microscope. No sign of struggle, no nothin'. Her purse, keys, and car were gone, and that's it. The geeks are goin' over 'er computer but nothin' yet... So there's not much ta' see. All we know is..."

Before he could complete the thought, he was interrupted by the sound of a cell phone, which was warbling deep inside his pocket. He settled his pie-mounded fork onto the plate and then fished around until he retrieved the screaming device. Giving a quick glance at the display, he raised an eyebrow then flipped the phone open and put it against his ear.

"This is Storm," he said, his voice taking on a somewhat more official tone than usual. "Yes... What time? Okay. Actually, we were just discussin' a different approach ourselves. No, I don't think that'll be a problem. Just a second, let me get somethin' to write with."

He switched the phone to his other hand but continued holding it against the same ear as he sent his newly freed appendage searching for a pen. A moment later he had a notebook out on the table and a ballpoint in his fingers.

"Go ahead," he told the person at the other end. "Yeah... Yeah... Okay, got it. CSU there yet? Good. Who's runnin' the scene? Yeah, got it. Uh-huh, we're on our way."

He folded the phone and tucked it back into his pocket then re-inspected what he had written before doing the same maneuver with the notebook.

"I take it we're going somewhere?" I asked.

"Looks like you kinda got your wish," he replied. "Seems we all of a sudden officially have a crime scene. State trooper just found Judith Albright's car at a rest area on Highway Seventy just outside Wright City."

"That's an hour from here," Felicity said.

"Yeah, just about," Ben agreed then shoveled in the forkful of pie, which he quickly followed with a second much larger portion. After swallowing he added, "So, we better get movin'. It's already gonna be dark by the time we get there."

My wife pulled out her cell phone and stabbed a speed dial number then tucked it up to her ear as she said, "Let's hope RJ can run by the house and let the dogs out, or we'll be having a mess to clean up."

In his typical fashion, he managed to down the rest of the pie before Felicity and I were fully out of our seats.

JUST LIKE MY WIFE HAD SAID, THE ROADSIDE REST AREA was something on the order of an hour from where we were when the call originally came in. However, with Ben behind the wheel the trip was instantly reduced to 45 minutes. If he had elected to use his emergency light and siren, that probably would have shaved it back to 30 or even less. Having white-knuckled a few rides with him in the past, I was perfectly content with taking the extra time.

For the better part of the trip we had engaged in idle chitchat, both about the case and about nothing at all. However, for the last 10 minutes or so, things had fallen relatively quiet. I didn't really mind since I was still dealing with the aftereffects of my earlier episode at the morgue, so I had laid my head back and closed my eyes under the guise of resting for a bit.

Unfortunately, the physical drain that was pulling me down was the least of my worries. While there was a lull in the conversation between the three of us in this plane of existence, inside my skull it was a completely different story. The ethereal chatter was almost deafening. I couldn't make out the words just yet, but I knew that would be changing.

Like always, it was starting with the pain boring its way into the back of my grey matter. I couldn't say that this time was really any more intense than usual, but perspective changes everything. The simple fact that I had been devoid of the torture for the last few hours made it seem even worse now that it returned.

Still, it was the routine ache of someone from across the veil pounding on my inner door, a thing I had grown to know and hate, but ultimately accept. However, something about this caller was inexplicably disturbing. Although still clouded in a curious fog, there was something intensely intimate about the feeling—different, but all too familiar in a way I simply couldn't pin down.

I felt certain it wasn't Emily Foster calling upon me again. I could tell that simply by the way the pain was touching me. Unfortunately, I had no idea who it was demanding my attention even though something told me I should. Given the circumstances and the sickening churn in the pit of my stomach, unchecked speculation made me fear it might be Judith Albright.

Right or wrong I decided to keep this fresh round of torment to myself. I didn't feel much like fielding any questions just yet nor was I in the mood to fend off concerns. I already knew there would be enough of that to deal with once we arrived.

I could feel the van swaying to the right and starting to slow, so I opened my eyes. I saw immediately that Ben was veering from the highway and onto the shoulder to avoid a line of brightly burning road flares that had been set out to block the entrance to the rest area. Hooking around them, he aimed the Chevy along the ramp and began to slow even more. Ahead of us, framed in the swath of the vehicle's headlamps, was a highway patrol cruiser, light bar flickering and parked diagonally across the access road. We rolled to a stop several feet away as the officer inside the car slowly climbed out and held up his hand. After a moment he cautiously made his way toward us with the butt of a large flashlight resting on his shoulder while he aimed the beam at us. His other hand was hanging conspicuously close to his sidearm.

Ben pulled out his badge case then rolled down his window and waited as the trooper approached on a wide arc.

"I'm sorry, but this rest area is temporarily closed," the officer stated, still standing several feet back and to the side with his hand now resting on the butt of his pistol.

"Detective Storm," my friend announced, offering his badge and ID. "Major Case Squad."

Angling the light on my friend's hand, the trooper relaxed, but only slightly, before stepping forward and taking it from him.

Even though it was well away from Saint Louis proper, the rest area was located in Warren County. Since the Major Case Squad was handling this investigation and both the Warren County Sheriff's office and Missouri State Highway Patrol were participating agencies with the MCS, Ben was still operating within his jurisdiction.

The uniformed man inspected the ID then handed it back to him with a nod. "Thanks. They've been expecting you," he said then beamed his flashlight along the road. "Veer right to the car park area and head straight back. It's on the other side of the lot behind the facilities building. Can't miss it. You'll sign in up there."

"Thanks," Ben told him.

We waited as the trooper returned to his vehicle then backed it up a few feet to allow us room to pass.

"Whatever ya' do, stick close to me. Both of ya'," my friend told us as he rolled up his window and started nudging the van forward. "I don't feel like gettin' into a yellin' match right now."

"Why would that happen?" Felicity asked from the rear seat. "Didn't he just say we were expected?"

"Yeah... And we are," he replied. "But since the hubcap chasers found the car, they're gonna wanna take the lead on this. We just gotta let 'em think they're in charge while we do what we're here to do. So that means hang close, let me talk, and you two just do the *Twilight Zone* thing."

"In other words, we're dealing with inter agency politics," I offered, my voice flat and emotionless as I was still intent on keeping my inner turmoil under wraps.

"Yeah, the big, nasty P word... that's about the size of it. And as usual everybody's gonna want the credit on their resume."

I wasn't surprised by his commentary. Jurisdiction alone didn't mean cooperation was going to come easy, and I had first hand experience with that. I'd actually witnessed the backbiting he'd just described on more than one occasion.

"What about you?" I asked out of idle curiosity. "Don't you want to bolster yours a bit?"

"Yeah, right, and risk a fuckin' promotion? Hell no. I already sit behind a desk long enough as it is," he replied. "I move up too much farther I'll be stuck in a goddamn office with no windows, spendin' all day lookin' at crime stats on a friggin' computer screen and gettin' a chronic case of numb ass."

I forced myself to chuckle lightly. "You've said yourself that we're both getting too old for this stuff. I thought maybe you'd be ready for a desk job."

"No," he huffed, shaking his head. "Old's one thing, but I ain't dead yet."

We cruised through the empty expanse of parking spaces then rounded the backside of the rest area, heading for the far end of the lot as we had been directed. The moment we reached the beginning of the bend and just before the turn toward the left, a chaotic dance of luminance blossomed across the windshield. The cluster of flashing emergency lights had not been visible from the highway as we approached, but from this vantage point they lit up the night.

Several squad cars, both from the state patrol and the sheriff's office were stationed on either side of the vehicle in question. Crime scene tape ran between trees, lampposts, and bumpers in order to cordon off the area. A second flashlight-wielding officer waved us toward a parking space beneath one of the light standards and began walking in our direction while Ben pulled the van in and shut off the engine.

I unlatched my seatbelt then climbed out of the passenger side and jerked open the sliding door for Felicity. The cold night air was a crisp shock against the bare skin of my face after sitting in the warm interior of the vehicle for the past hour. In that moment I was very glad we had stopped by my wife's Jeep to retrieve my jacket before heading out.

Dusk had fallen hard, and even though we had recently been through an abnormally warm stretch, a cold front was encroaching, and the temperatures dipped quickly as soon as the sun went into hiding below the horizon. Since the day had been clear and no cloud cover had yet to roll through, there was no insulation to keep in what little heat the ground had accumulated over the past few days. Therefore, the outside temperature was making my memories of the earlier chill in the morgue seem almost warm by comparison.

My wife levered the van door shut then turned to me with a concerned look on her face. "Rowan… You've seemed a bit out of it for the past few minutes. Are you feeling okay then?"

I sighed as I reached up to rub my temples. My short reprieve was over, and lying to her wasn't going to do any good, so I gave in. "The headache is back… But, it isn't Emily… I'm not sure who it is… It feels familiar…too familiar…but foreign as well… Does that make sense?"

"You don't think it's…" She allowed her voice to trail off.

I could tell by her words that she was thinking the same thing I had been. I shook my head and muttered, "I'm trying not to."

Ben was already talking to the state trooper by the time we hooked around the back end of the van and joined him. They both looked over at us, and my friend gave a nod in my direction.

"I was beginnin' ta' think we were gonna hafta send a search party lookin' for ya'," he quipped.

"Just getting situated," I replied.

"Here," he said as he held a clipboard out to me. Then he directed his words to the trooper. "They'll need ta' sign in too. They're special consultants for Major Case."

"No problem," the man replied with a nod.

I stepped forward and took the proffered crime scene log, signed my name, and then under the heading for title entered exactly what Ben had just called us, "special consultant." When I was finished entering the "time in" I handed it to Felicity so she could do the same. When she gave the clipboard back to the officer, he glanced at the signatures then looked us both up and down.

"The crime scene guys are already here," he stated. "What kind of consultants are you two?"

Without missing a beat I replied, "Reluctant."

Once again he gave the clipboard a one-eyed stare for a second then mumbled something not quite intelligible.

"Wait a minute," he finally said. "Gant... Yeah, I knew I'd heard that name before. You're the psychic."

I wasn't surprised at what he said. Between media coverage and word of mouth, I didn't meet too many cops in the state who hadn't at least heard of me—in one sense or another. Unfortunately, the rumors weren't always true or particularly flattering either.

"Yeah, something like that," I half agreed rather than launch into an involved explanation.

In truth, his assessment was probably closer to the mark than I really wanted to admit. Witch or not, my facility was at least as much psychic as it was magick, probably even more so. The big difference was that I didn't make a career of bilking grieving families out of money to tell them vague and ambiguous stories about their departed loved ones with whom I was supposedly conversing. Instead, I worked for free to offer the police vague and ambiguous clues in order to stop the voices inside my head. Unfortunately, my payoff never lasted long.

"I thought so," he replied then snorted out a small laugh. "Yeah, my sister is all about the psychic stuff. She watches the shows on TV and everything."

"As long as she's entertained," I said with a slight nod and no enthusiasm whatsoever in my voice. "But, do her a big favor and tell her not to spend money on telephone and TV psychics."

"Yeah, I've told her that. The way I see it they're just a bunch of crooks, right?"

I shrugged. "Probably not all, but most of them, yeah, that would be my guess. All I can say for sure is that no amount of money is worth having dead people bounce around inside your head on purpose, so that should tell you something right there."

"What about you?" he asked, giving me a stoic nod. "What makes you different from them?"

"I only do this because I haven't got a choice," I replied.

My headache had been ramping up ever since we'd arrived, but for the most part I was once again becoming acquainted with the pain and, more importantly, treating it as nothing more than the usual chronic nuisance. Or so I thought.

I had scarcely finished speaking when a violent stab of agony drilled its way through my brain with enough force to make me grimace and stumble forward before catching myself. I reached up with both hands and cradled my head between them as if it was going to explode.

"Something wrong?" the officer asked.

"Shining…example…of what…I…just said," I groaned the sentence in a halting rhythm.

Nausea was beginning to churn in the pit of my stomach, and my ears were ringing as the parking lot seemed to undulate beneath my feet. I stumbled in place once again, nearly pitching face first onto the asphalt.

Felicity instantly took hold of my shoulder in an attempt to steady me. Ben was only a half step behind her as he came forward and grabbed me beneath the arms then propped me back against the van and held me up.

"You gonna be okay, Kemosabe?" my friend asked.

"Do I look like it?" I answered between clenched teeth.

Felicity spoke up, directing herself to the state trooper with an air of calm authority. "Officer, the next town isn't far from here, aye?"

"Yes ma'am, Wright City. Do we need to get him to the hospital?"

"No," she replied, urgency seeping into her voice. "But we need salt, and a lot of it."

CHAPTER 26

"BEEN ALMOST FIFTEEN MINUTES," BEN STATED IN A matter-of-fact tone. "He should be getting back here any time now."

We were all sitting in the van once again, but the vehicle was stationary, parked where Ben had originally nosed it in upon our arrival. We were waiting for everybody's favorite seasoning to be delivered to us, which was something I hadn't been expecting. All I knew was that Felicity had made the urgent comment, and then Ben had picked it up and run with it. How he managed to convince a Warren County Sheriff's deputy to make a lights and siren run for as much salt as two twenty-dollar bills could buy, I had no idea. I wasn't entirely sure I wanted to know either.

I had my eyes closed, but I could hear movement up front. Judging from the sound, I assumed my friend was twisting around in his seat to check on me since I was sitting in the back. Both Felicity and he had been doing that quite a bit.

My blind assumption was proven out when he spoke again, and his voice came at me from a more direct angle. "How you doin', Row? Hangin' in there?"

"It isn't as bad as you two are making it out to be," I mumbled. "It's just one of the headaches. You should be used to them by now. I am."

Of course, the believability of my comment was rendered null and void by the obvious strain in my voice. The truth is, I wasn't even managing to convince myself.

"Yeah, right," he countered. "And it was just another one of *those headaches* earlier too, and then ya' started bleedin' all over the place. What if that happens again?"

"It won't."

"Oh yeah, and how do ya' know that?"

"Because this isn't Emily Foster trying to communicate with me."

"You're sure about that?"

"Yes. I can tell by the way it feels."

"Bullshit. Pain is pain, Row."

"Trust me, it isn't."

"Uh-huh, well big deal. So maybe it's not Foster. What if it's the

Jane Doe?" He pressed. "Do I need ta' remind you she died the same way? She might just decide ta' make ya' bleed too, and she might not be as nice about it."

Before I could object again, Felicity spoke up. "I have to agree with him, Row. You don't really know who it is trying to talk to you, and you told me yourself that it feels odd. It's not worth the chance. You can't afford to lose any more blood. Your body can't take it."

"I still say you two are being paranoid," I groaned. My voice still wasn't convincing, especially to me.

Ben turned his attention toward my wife. "So, Firehair, lemme ask ya' somethin'. The salt didn't work at the morgue, so what makes ya' think it'll work here?"

"Actually, it did work at the morgue," she replied. "Just not the way I intended."

"Coulda fooled me. You wanna explain that one?"

"Simple. It made Emily Foster leave. It just didn't keep her from wreaking a little havoc first."

"You call the white man bleedin' all over the floor a *little* havoc?"

"Okay, a lot of havoc. It's just an expression, Ben."

"Uh-huh... So what you're sayin' is that it was s'posed ta' keep all that from happenin' in the first place?"

"Yes."

"Yeah, okay..." he grunted. "So 'splain that one. Why didn't it work right?"

"There were extenuating circumstances. It's complicated. Better you just trust me and not worry about it."

A lull fell between them for a few heartbeats.

"Wait..." he finally said, distress welling in his voice. "Was it my fault? It wasn't 'cause there was pepper in there with the salt too, was it? Dammit, I knew I shoulda picked those out!"

"No," she replied, her own voice a mix of forced reassurance and mild irritation. "That wasn't it. The pepper didn't matter."

"You sure?"

"Aye, Ben, I'm sure. It wasn't your fault."

"Good. So, why didn't it work right then?"

"Like I said, it's complicated."

"Uh-huh... Complicated as in you think I won't understand, or complicated as in you're hidin' somethin'?"

"It's WitchCraft, Ben, it isn't your forte. Isn't that what you always tell us?"

"Yeah, but it's my *for-tay*," he stressed, "to know bullshit when I smell it. I'm thinkin' maybe it didn't work right 'cause you didn't say a poem."

"I really think you need to stop dwelling on that," she told him coolly.

"Of course you do. Because I'm right, ain't I?"

"Keep it up and I *will* hurt you," she told him, a frost in her voice that chilled the words in such a way as to add harsh punctuation to the threat.

"Do you think you two could play nice?" I asked. "Your bickering really isn't helping my head at all."

"I am playing nice," my wife returned. "For the moment." She paused then added, "That could change very quickly though."

"Looks like he might be back," Ben announced. "I'll go check." The absent tone in his voice told me he had already taken a left turn away from the previous conversation and was now re-focused on the original issue at hand, namely the salt.

I heard his door latch clunk, and the dome light popped on, making the previously dark world behind my tightly closed eyes illuminate with a dull, reddish glow. A second or two later, the same noise sounded on the other side of the vehicle. The out of synch stereo of both doors opening told me that Felicity was climbing out as well.

A blast of cold air blew through the interior of the van, swirling into the back and brushing its unseen fingers across my face. It actually lent some momentary relief to the throb in my skull, but momentary was the key word. I knew there wasn't enough cold out there to act as an analgesic for what was going on inside my head—not without literally freezing me to death that is.

"Rowan, stay here," Felicity instructed. "I'll be right back."

"Yes ma'am," I muttered in return.

Seconds later the out-of-phase stereo of the doors thudding closed dropped my world back into cold darkness, with the small exception of the nearly imperceptible flicker of the emergency lights through the back windows. I let out a slow breath and continued rubbing my temples even though the massage wasn't proving to give me any relief from the pain. What I really wanted was a handful of aspirin. At least I knew those would take the edge off before this became any worse.

Outside the van I could hear muffled voices. Just as was the case with the murmurings inside my head, I couldn't make out any of the actual words, but I could pick out Ben and Felicity as two members of the conversation. The third person sounded angry, female, and a little familiar, but I couldn't attach a name to it.

As I sat there listening to what seemed to be escalating into an argument, I tried to focus on it, but the pain in my head caused my concentration to abandon me, leaving my mind to wander off wherever it so desired. My recent thought of wanting aspirin seemed to be its favored destination, and it made a beeline to it. Self-preservation was trumping everything else.

As I dwelled on the desire to be pain free, I vaguely remembered Ben mentioning earlier that he had a bottle of the over-the-counter painkiller on hand if I needed it. Soon I found myself wondering if it was possibly stashed somewhere in the van. Logically, I knew it was one of the last things I should be putting into my body at the moment, but the growing migraine had pushed me to the point of no longer caring about doctor's instructions. I needed something to at least dull the ache because it was now well past the point of being ignored.

I remained motionless for a moment, now ruminating over whether or not the mere act of moving would only serve to make the pain worse. If it did and I managed to find the aspirin, no big deal, but if I couldn't locate the meds, then I was going to be royally screwed. I weighed the two options as carefully as my throbbing brain would let me then decided to take the chance. Unfortunately, my decision to do something other than just sit here and suffer came too late to do any good. The second I opened my eyes and started leaning forward to begin my quest turned out to be the exact same second the side door of the van flew open with an unceremonious grind and thump.

Angry words instantly blasted through the interior, centered directly on me. "What in the name of God do you think you're doing, Gant?"

I looked over to see Captain Barbara Albright glaring at me, her gaze a mixture of anger and insistence. The identity behind the mystery voice now became painfully apparent.

"I told you to back off!" Felicity shouted from behind her. "Leave him alone!"

Peering past the angry cop who was now blocking the opening, I saw Ben latch onto my wife just as she started forward. Then he pulled her back before she could literally assault the woman.

"Storm," Albright spat the words without tearing her eyes away from me. "Cuff that bitch and get her out of the way right now."

If I hadn't been hurting so much I think I would have been

surprised by her blatant use of profanity, mild as it was. It was definitely out of character for the holier-than-thou Albright. Of course, what I heard next was no shock at all considering that it came spewing from the livid redhead behind her.

"*Fekking saigh!*" Felicity growled. "*Póg mo thóin! Damnú*, Ben, let go of me!"

"Look, Captain, I'm not gonna cuff 'er..." Ben insisted. "There's no reason for it." Then he quipped, "I'll try ta' keep 'er from kickin' your ass, but I'm not makin' any guarantees."

"I gave you an order," she told him.

"Yeah, but I'm not takin' it."

"Fine, I'll do it myself." Albright wheeled around and reached beneath her coat.

My friend snorted and twisted so that he was between Felicity and her. "Not happenin'... There's no reason for this ta' get ridiculous. Listen, you need ta' just calm down and give the man some room like she said."

Of course, with all of this commotion confined to a small space that just happened to be more or less surrounded by cops, the altercation had attracted more than a little attention. Without even trying I counted three state troopers and two sheriff's deputies descending on us already and wouldn't be surprised if more showed up at any minute.

"What's the problem here," one of the uniformed officers asked.

Albright waved her badge in the air and announced, "I'm Captain Albright... I have it under control. I'm just asking Mister Gant a few questions."

"You know you aren't even s'posed ta' be here, Captain," Ben said, loud enough for everyone to hear. "You're on administrative leave."

She disregarded his comment and ignored the growing turmoil. Instead, she wheeled back around to face me and demanded, "Answer me, Gant."

Felicity suddenly let out a banshee screech, there was a heavy thump, Ben yelped, then I heard him snarl, "Goddammit, Felicity, don't fuckin' kick me again! And stop squirmin' or I *will* cuff ya'!"

One of the deputies leapt forward and grabbed my wife by the arm and wrenched it back then immediately began slipping his own handcuffs from his belt. My wife let out a pained scream as he continued twisting her arm in an attempt to subdue her. I could also see that one of the troopers had unholstered his taser and was holding it at the ready.

"Goddammit! Just back off for a minute!" my friend barked as he muscled the deputy away while keeping an arm hooked around Felicity. "And, you, put that damn thing away! There's no reason for this to get stupid."

The whole situation was heading south in a hurry, and none of it was helping my head in the least. My already foul mood was souring even further, and it definitely wasn't going to be a good mixer for the volatility forming right before my eyes. Unfortunately, my head was hurting too badly to allow me to give Albright anything other than an honest, gut response. I simply stared at her and said, "I was looking for some aspirin. Got any?"

"Get out here!" she demanded, motioning for me to exit the van.

"Captain, I'm tellin' ya'," Ben insisted. "Ya' need ta' just back off. You don't understand what's goin' on here."

"I can still have you suspended, Storm," she shot back.

"That's a two-way street," he countered. "You know you aren't supposed ta' be here. All it'd take would be a phone call, and you'd be in more hot water than you could stand. You know I'm right."

She didn't reply but turned to look at him. I could only imagine the glare he was receiving.

He held fast and said, "Whaddaya say we just call a truce before this gets any uglier."

The standoff had multiplied by several more uniformed officers, and I knew my friend wasn't going to back down. Something told me Albright wasn't going to budge either.

"Let me handle this," I called out to the serious detriment of my headache. Slowly, I twisted in the seat, so I could face Albright. She turned back to face me, wearing a look of disdain. I carefully leaned forward, resting my elbows on my knees and held my head between my hands as I muttered, "What is it you want from me, Barbara?"

I knew from past experience that she hated it when I called her by her first name, but I wasn't in the mood for honorifics at the moment. Especially those I felt were undeserved. If she wanted a one-on-one with me, then that was what she was going to get—raw, unabashed, and as close to being on my terms as I could get.

"I want to know what you're doing just sitting there?" she snapped. "You're supposed to be helping find my niece."

"What makes you think I'm not?" I asked, my voice a pain-wracked mumble.

"You're just sitting there," she insisted. "And you sound like you're intoxicated."

"I wish I was, but I'm not. I'm just in a lot of pain."

"Well don't expect me to feel sorry for you."

I snorted then said, "I wouldn't dream of it."

"I can't believe you're just sitting there," she repeated.

"And exactly what is it you do when you pray?" I asked.

"Don't you dare compare my religion to your Godless heathenry."

I let out a heavy sigh. "You know, I'm not even going to waste my breath explaining to you everything that's wrong with that statement. However, I am going to say this: We both know you hate me, but we also both know that you're the one who insisted on my being here. My guess is that your love for your niece outweighs your contempt for me. In any case, here I am. Now do Judith a favor, back off like my wife asked and just let me do what I do."

"You're pushing your luck, Gant," she snipped.

"No, Barbara. You are. If this killer really has your niece, then right now you're screwing with her life by wasting my time. Like I said, do her a favor. Let me do my job. If you really want to help then go home and pray."

I hadn't bothered to look up at her for the entire span of the conversation, relying instead only on auditory cues. I didn't move to do so now. I simply continued holding my head between my hands, kept my breathing as even as I could manage, and listened to the relative silence in the wake of her non-response.

Finally, I raised my voice slightly and called out, "Did the salt get here?"

"Aye," Felicity returned, bitterness still in her voice, though I knew it wasn't directed at me. "It's here."

"How about the forensics? Are the crime scene techs finished?"

"Yeah," Ben answered. "They were already done when we sent for the salt."

"Last question. Do they have any problems with me touching the car?"

"I'll check again, but it's already been okayed," he assured me.

"Good," I grunted, shifting forward and starting to climb out of the van. "Then let's do this thing before my fucking head explodes."

198 | M. R. SELLARS

CHAPTER 27

"YA'KNOW, I BET I'M GONNA HAVE A BRUISE ON MY SHIN," Ben complained aloud as we walked.

"Aye, you'll get over it," Felicity replied, no sympathy in her voice whatsoever as she glanced over at him for a second and watched his stride. "It's not like you're limping or anything, then."

"Yeah, but I could be."

"Quit being such a crybaby. You don't hear me whining about my arm."

"I didn't do that to ya'," he reminded her.

"Doesn't matter, it still hurts and I haven't complained," she replied. "Unlike you, the big, tough cop."

I tried to ignore their verbal sparring because as long as they were at it like this I knew everything was okay between them. If either of them were truly angry with the other, they would be sulking in silence and that would be cause to worry.

We rounded the end of a highway patrol cruiser and aimed ourselves to the right. A small clutch of officers next to it parted without a word to allow us through. We paused when we reached the crime scene tape. Ben reached out and lifted the yellow plastic ribbon so that Felicity and I could slip beneath it a little more easily, then he ducked under the barrier himself and followed us into the no man's land of the cordoned off zone.

From the looks of the asphalt landscape, it appeared as if the crime scene had now become akin to a small arena, and the surrounding cars and sidewalk were the stands filled with uniformed spectators. Cops and crime scene technicians alike stood next to or leaning against their vehicles, chatting quietly among themselves as they watched us make our way across the empty expanse. There was even a paramedic propped against a life support vehicle that had been called out to the scene at Ben's request, just in case things didn't go as we planned. Of course, they rarely ever did, so that was probably a smart move on his part.

I noticed one of the troopers point in our direction then make a comment to a nearby colleague who chuckled and nodded vigorously before passing it along to the cop next to him. I could only speculate about what they were actually saying. Thus far they were making it a point to keep their voices low, so the occasional staticky blip of a radio combined with the constant drone of the traffic on the nearby highway prevented me from actually hearing them. Even so, it wasn't hard to make an educated guess each time I saw their lips moving. I'd been down this road too many times before, although I had to admit that this time around I felt much less like a part of the team and more like I was a curiosity on display.

I gave the small crowd a second cursory glance and noticed Captain Albright hadn't bothered to take my advice, not that I even began to imagine she would. She was standing front and center among the other officers; however, she didn't appear to find anything they were saying to her amusement. She simply watched us with a stoic expression creasing her face; although, even at a distance I could see the inner worry in her eyes.

"Why do I suddenly feel like the new kid who's about to get the crap beat out of him on the playground?" I mumbled as the three of us continued on toward Judith Albright's abandoned Hyundai sedan.

"Prob'ly 'cause ya' pretty much kinda are if ya' don't come up with somethin'," Ben replied.

"That's not very encouraging," I told him. "You of all people know how this works. There are never any guarantees."

"Yeah, I know." He nodded. "But you're the one who said it. I'm just agreein' with ya'."

"Ignore them," Felicity interjected.

"Yeah… That was pretty much my plan," I returned. "Let's hope it actually works."

I was still fighting the hammering inside my skull and doing so without the benefit of aspirin or anything else for that matter. Once the escalating altercation at the van had been dialed back to a manageable level, everything else had started moving fairly quickly, so I hadn't had a chance to ask Ben where they were hidden or even if he actually had any to offer. Almost immediately following my insistence that we get started, two plastic grocery bags, both filled with unmistakable cylindrical containers, had been unloaded from the passenger seat of a deputy's patrol car. Then, everyone backed off and waited for something to happen. I suppose it was a good thing their tickets to this show were free because special effects-wise I was fairly certain they were going to be disappointed.

The three of us came to a halt a few steps away from the sedan and simply stood there. Staring at my faint reflection in the driver's side window, I struggled not to think too hard about the dog and pony show this had now become. I was used to letting the psychic events occur of their own accord, which never seemed to be an issue. Now, however, there was an enormous amount of pressure for me to make it all happen on cue, complete with a skeptical audience. While I had forced such to occur before, doing so was a rarity, so I had to hope that whoever was murmuring inside my head would listen and seize the opportunity to speak up instead of just endeavoring to make me miserable.

After a substantial pause where I had scarcely moved, Ben asked, "You goin' all *Twilight Zone?*"

"No," I replied, sighing as I reached up to massage my forehead from sheer force of habit. "I was just thinking that a double extra huge bottle of aspirin would be good right about now."

"Why didn't ya' say somethin' earlier?"

"Things got a little crazy, if you recall."

A few seconds later I heard a soft rattle, and his large hand appeared in front of me, holding a generic brand bottle of the pain reliever that had apparently been stashed in his jacket pocket all along.

"Thank the Gods," I mumbled as I took it from him and immediately twisted off the cap.

"Rowan, you really shouldn't…" Felicity began to object.

Before she could complete the sentence I had already swallowed something on the order of a half dozen of the white pills, dry. After choking them down and gagging on the bitterness at the back of my throat, I held the bottle back out to Ben and said to her, "You can yell at me later."

"You know those aren't going to help matters if you start bleeding again," she admonished. "Aspirin is a blood thinner."

"So I've heard," I replied. The recollection of having chronically overdosed on the analgesic some months back for a very similar reason was still fresh in my mind, so I knew the risks all too well. I sighed then added, "I know it's dangerous, honey. But, right now I need to be able to see straight, or we aren't going to get anywhere with this."

"I understand," she replied softly. "No bleeding then, okay?"

"Okay. No bleeding." We both knew there was no way I could guarantee such a thing, but if it made her feel better to hear it, then I was good with making the empty promise.

"So, whadda we do now?" Ben asked. "Just stand here like the stooges or somethin'?"

"Aye, give me the salt and stand over here next to me," Felicity said, motioning to him.

"Since you're givin' orders I take it you're Moe," he replied with a small laugh in his voice.

"Just give me the damn salt and quit being a comedian," she countered.

"Hey, chill out. It's been one of those days, ya'know," Ben said as he hefted the bags toward her. "It's just a little humor. It's how I cope with this shit."

Felicity took the weighty bags from him with much less ease than he had displayed when he held them out to her. As she settled them to the ground she muttered, "*Úmpaidh*."

Fortunately, Ben didn't appear to catch the Gaelic insult, not that he would have understood it if he had. At any rate, while over the years I had personally come to understand his use of humor at somewhat inappropriate moments as a safety valve for the stress, we really did need to get on with things. And, in this particular case another round of bickering between the two of them, no matter how good-natured, simply wasn't on the short list.

My wife fished out two containers of salt and handed one of them to him as she said, "Just open them and keep them coming when I tell you."

"Do you want me to help?" I asked.

"No, I want you to concentrate on staying grounded," she instructed me in no uncertain terms. "We can handle this part."

Then, breaking the seal with her fingernail, Felicity flipped up the metal spout on the top of the carton, then knelt and began to draw a thick line on the asphalt with the contents. As soon as the container was empty, she handed it to Ben and took the fresh replacement from him. After a minute or so, she had scribed almost two-thirds of a wide circle around the three of us.

Just as she was taking a newly opened carton from Ben, one of the cops on the perimeter called out, "You want some pepper to go with that?"

Even with the road noise, there was no missing the burst of chuckles that skipped through the group. Felicity paused for a second, shook her head slightly as she muttered something unintelligible, and then continued on with her task.

"I'll be right back," Ben grunted.

"Don't worry about it," I told him. "They just don't understand."

"I ain't worried," he replied. "And, I'm gonna make 'em understand." With that he turned and strode away in the direction of the cop who'd made the comment.

"Just ignore them, Ben," my wife instructed, but she was too late. With his long stride he was already a quarter of the way to the boundary tape and didn't hear her. Of course, even if he had he wouldn't have listened. I could tell he was on a mission; I'd seen the look before.

I watched on as he gestured in our direction and engaged the officer in what appeared to be a deeply earnest conversation. At one point he held his right hand over his heart for a second then held it up palm outward as if taking an oath. A minute or two later he was purposefully striding back toward us. Looking past him I could see that the cop he had just spoken to was staring at my wife with a quizzical and maybe even slightly fearful expression in his eyes.

"Sorry 'bout that," Ben said as he reached down into one of the bags then withdrew a container of salt and broke the seal. "You ready for another one yet?"

"What did you just say to him?" Felicity looked up and asked.

"I just gave 'im some friendly advice."

"Did you threaten him?"

"Not exactly."

"What then?" she pressed.

"Don't worry, nothin' bad... Well, not too bad I don't guess... I just told 'im that one time I saw you do some kinda evil eye thing on a copper I worked with who was givin' ya' shit. Then the next day all his hair fell out real sudden like," he replied in a low voice. "And, I made sure he understood I meant *all of it* fell out."

"You didn't..." she replied.

He gave her a half shrug. "Yeah, well, actually I did. I mean, I didn't figure he'd believe the turnin' 'im into a cockroach bullshit ya' threatened me with, so I hadda tell him something."

My wife shook her head as she gave him an empty carton then took the new one out of his hand. "You're incorrigible."

"Yeah, I know," he grunted. "But I'm bettin' that copper would piss himself if you leaned over and gave 'im *the look*."

"The look?"

"Ya' know... The one ya' always use when you're pissed at me."

"Oh. That look," she said in a flat tone. "Maybe some other time. I'm almost finished and we have more important things to do. How much salt do we have left?"

"Another whole bag," he replied. "Looks like ten... maybe twelve containers."

"Good, that's more than enough," she announced as she bent back down and continued scribing the salt circle on the parking lot. "This should be the last one I need for the moment."

"Then what?" Ben asked.

"Then you get your wish," she told him.

"What wish?"

"As you put it, I say a poem."

"Yeah," he replied, starting to nod. "See, I knew I was..."

Felicity cut him off quickly, "Don't push me, Ben. I'll still hurt you."

"Yeah, I keep forgettin' that's your thing."

She stood up and handed him the empty salt container. "Yes, but since we've seen that you don't take pain all that well, it probably wouldn't be much fun for me."

He snorted out a light chuckle. "So that'd mean I'm safe."

"Oh no," she told him. "I'll do it just for spite."

"Jeez... You're a friggin' piece of work." He shook his head then diverted the topic by glancing around at the circle. "Wait a sec, I think ya' missed a spot. Don'tcha need to fill this in over here?" he asked as he pointed toward a void in the salt that measured almost three feet in width on the side nearest the car.

"No," Felicity replied as she turned slowly in place while surveying the circle herself. "That would be the door."

"The door?"

"Aye."

"Okay... Whatever you say," he muttered.

"Stand over here," my wife told him as she took his arm and led him into the center with me.

"Don't you want me ta' go over there or somethin' while ya' do the hocus-pocus?" he asked, pointing toward the tape line.

"No," she replied with a shake of her head. "I want you to stand right here so you can help."

"Whaddaya mean help? I ain't a *Twilight Zone* freakazoid like you two. What am I gonna be able ta' do?"

"If I'm following her logic, I think you just became an honorary signpost," I groaned out between waves of pain.

"Pretty much," she acknowledged.

"What's that s'posed ta' mean?"

"It means that you're now Rowan's anchor," she replied. "Obviously you have more physical strength than I do, so if this starts to go bad, I'll tell you to pull him into the circle. Once you do that I'll handle closing the door."

He made a sweeping motion toward the salt with one of his hands. "So I just grab 'im and pull 'im in here?"

"More or less."

"Uh-huh, so what's the more part, or do I not wanna know?"

"Well, if you have to pull him in, he's likely to start grounding through you as soon as you touch him. Initially, anyway, until I can take over."

"Yeah, okay, but now you're talkin' la-la land stuff and I don't know what that means."

"It's kind of like having electricity pass through you," she explained. "But different."

"Yeah, wunnerful, now I understand perfectly," he said with a heavy dose of sarcasm. "So how's the *Twilight Zone* shit gonna affect me since I ain't like you?"

"It probably won't."

"Whaddaya mean prob'ly?"

She shrugged. "I can't be sure. I've never actually done it this way before."

"But you've done it this way with other Witches before, and it worked okay, right?"

"Actually, no," she said. "If you must know, I'm making this up as I go along."

"Fuck me..." he grumbled as he shook his head.

"Don't worry, then," she told him. "I know what I'm doing. It shouldn't hurt too much. Besides, he'd do the same for you."

"Yeah, I know," he replied. "That's the only reason why I'm still standin' here."

"It's okay, Ben," I grunted through a hard grimace. "It's a basic principle. Just trust her and let's get on with this."

"Yeah, well if my hair falls out or somethin', I ain't gonna be real friggin' happy, ya'know," he replied sternly.

"Don't worry," Felicity quipped. "I'll make sure only part of it falls out."

"Who's bein' a fuckin' comedian now?" he grumbled.

"Aye, Row, are you ready?" my wife asked, ignoring his complaint.

"Yeah…" I told her. "I've been ready."

"Just another minute or so," she said. "This is down and dirty. Nothing fancy."

"Felicity…" I started.

"What is it?"

I pulled her close and whispered in hopes that Ben wouldn't overhear. "Are you sure you're okay with this? You've had your own grounding troubles since… Well, you know…"

"Miranda?" she replied, speaking the name I'd chosen not to utter. "Don't worry. I'll be fine."

She gave my arm a squeeze for reassurance then moved around behind us. I didn't turn to watch her, but I knew she was most likely standing at the edge of the circle, facing toward the east. After a short pause I heard her make a shuffling turn and take a step as she began walking slowly along the inner arc. In that same moment her singsong voice floated on the air as she began to rhyme aloud.

"In this space I do create, a haven safe where we await. A gate I leave now open wide, but through it comes who I decide."

Her voice rose and fell in volume as she carefully skirted counterclockwise along the inside edge of the salt, passing by first on my right, then in front of me, and finally to my left. The last word of the verse was fading on the night air as she reached her original starting point once again.

"Judith is who we now seek, she must soon be allowed to speak. As Rowan travels through the veil, in search of her he will prevail."

For a second time, my wife stepped lightly around the full circumference of the somewhat unfinished circle, chanting out another verse of her off-the-cuff spell and uttering the ending syllable at the east, just as before.

"Harm to him it will not come, nor to fear will he succumb. He will return through the gate, to a haven safe where we await."

On her third and what turned out to be her final pass, she glanced up when she crossed in front of me. I caught her eye and would have smiled were it not for the preoccupying thump in the back of my head. When she finally came to rest behind us once again, she paused, and from the lack of sound I assumed she simply stood in place.

Apparently, Ben's story about the sudden hair shedding effects of the redhead with the evil eye had been passed around, as no jeering or offhanded remarks came from the watchers on. Except for the swish of the slight, but cold, breeze and the hum of the highway traffic, everything was quiet.

After a handful of heartbeats had tapped out time in my chest, I heard Felicity shuffle and walk toward the center of the circle.

"Ben," she said. "If I say the word *now*, you grab Rowan and bring him right here to this spot, no matter what. Okay?"

"Got it."

"*No matter what*," she stressed again.

"Yeah," he repeated with a nod. "I got it."

I heard the rustle of a plastic bag then the unmistakable squeak of metal against pasteboard as my wife opened a fresh container of salt. A few seconds later, she was at my side.

"Okay, Rowan…" she said softly. "We're ready. Go ahead then."

I stepped forward through the opening in the salt circle then slowly and deliberately placed my hand on the Hyundai's driver's side door handle.

CHAPTER 28

AT FIRST, WHEN MY FINGERS MADE CONTACT WITH THE door handle, nothing at all seemed to happen. Psychometry was fickle like that sometimes. Given that reading the psychic residue from inanimate objects through physical touch lent itself to all manner of interference, there were even a good number of occasions when it didn't work at all.

Latent impressions of past events weren't always present. And if they were, for the most part they didn't just automatically form an immediate picture in my mind. Instead they would come to me like water soaking into a too dry sponge. Seeping slowly in around the edges at first then suddenly becoming a thirsty swell to fill the void between then and now.

I certainly hadn't expected a shower of sparks or a choir of disembodied heads bellowing out an off key chorus. I knew better than that. However, I had hoped that maybe the ethereal voice in my brain would have become a bit clearer. Instead, all I heard was the murmuring gibberish that had been rolling around inside my head for the past two hours or so. If anything changed at all it was the series of stabbing pains at the base of my skull. Unfortunately, it was a change I could have done without since they seemed to become worse, not better.

While I was fairly certain I wasn't displaying it outwardly, I had a feeling that I was just as disappointed by the beginning of this process as were the spectators. I shifted my grip on the handle and held tight, trying to increase the area of object-to-skin contact for maximum effect.

I remained unmoving for one of the longest minutes I could remember, hoping for at least a hint of something. A tingle…some sensation other than the ramping undulation of pain inside my skull. But there was still nothing. All I felt was cold metal leaching the warmth from the palm of my hand, and the sensation was definitely a product of elementary science on this side of the veil.

"I've got nothing so far," I said, forcing my voice to be loud enough for Ben and Felicity to hear me. "I'm going to open the door."

"Just open it, that's all," my wife ordered. "Don't get in."

I was beginning to feel like I was on a bomb squad detail, slowly picking my way toward a ticking explosive with Felicity as my guide. I suppose in a way that was as good an analogy as any. The primary difference was that I wasn't trying to avoid an explosion. I fully intended to set off this ethereal booby-trap so that I could see what it had to say.

I had just popped the latch and was starting to pull the door toward me when Felicity called out again, "Aye, did you hear me, Rowan? Don't get in the car. That might be too much for you to handle right now."

"I'm not," I answered verbally, which I hadn't bothered to do earlier, but it was apparently what she wanted. However, I didn't voice the addendum to the reply that flitted through my head, which was "not yet."

The interior of the car smelled like a familiar perfume—cloyingly sweet but with a hint of earthiness and a peculiar sharp note hidden somewhere in the center. It was intermixed with the fresh odor of tobacco smoke. It took me a moment to identify the olfactory mélange as all coming from the same source, clove cigarettes. Whether or not any importance resided in the scent, I had no idea just yet, but it was prominent.

I pulled the door open wide then stepped forward, bending down so that I could inspect the interior more closely. Residue of fingerprint dusting powders coated the passenger side dash and steering wheel, just as they had the door handle. Other than that, however, the automobile appeared to have been all but cleaned out by the crime scene technicians who had bagged and tagged everything in sight.

A sharp auger of pain drilled into my skull to join the continuous jackhammer-like ache that was trying to break through from the inside. I let out a heavy groan as I tensed and then dropped my face into my hands. Although I'd tried to stifle the noise, it was loud enough to be heard. Combined with the fact that since I felt myself double forward, I knew it had to be noticeable. I wasn't surprised to hear my wife's voice from only a few short feet behind me.

"Rowan? Are you all right?" she asked, concern underlining each word with a bold stroke.

I didn't answer right away for the simple reason that I couldn't get my mouth to form the words since my jaw was clenched in a tight grimace.

She waited only a few seconds before calling to me again, the distress in her voice moving several notches up the scale within a pair of syllables, "Rowan?!"

"Okay." I managed to blurt out the muffled reply on the tail end of a heavy breath. Sighing for a second time as the latest addition to the orchestra of agonies began to subside, I lifted my face out of my palms but kept my eyes squeezed shut as I added, "I'm okay."

I knew full well that I didn't sound okay. The truth is, I didn't actually feel okay either. I just didn't want Felicity slamming the door on this before it was even fully open. Of course, it was two against one at this point, in this plane of existence at any rate. Counting the other side of the veil and what it was doing to me, I was even more outnumbered than that. So if my wife decided to pull the plug on this endeavor, there was nothing I would be able to do. I was barely up to keeping myself upright, much less fending off a six and a half foot tall cop on a mission to rescue me from myself.

I opened my eyes and focused on the interior of the car once more. The voice in my head was still unintelligible, but it was getting louder by the second. I was beginning to wonder if it was actually a lone voice or merely the background chatter of an entire chorus of tortured spirits clamoring for my attention. It certainly wouldn't be the first time that had happened. The only thing that kept me believing this was singular was the uncanny familiarity of its pitch and tone along with the lack of any other ethereal noise to dull it.

Several seconds had ticked by, and my wife had yet to send in the cavalry. However, the recent and painfully overt stress in her voice told me she was only inches from doing so. All it would take is another stumble, and I had a feeling I was going to be flying backwards by my belt. If that happened, and Felicity closed the circle, there was a good chance I would lose connection with the other side. It certainly wasn't a given, but it was a chance I didn't want to take. Not yet.

I looked at my palm and then back at the interior of the car. I knew it was possible I might glean something by reaching in and touching the steering wheel. Another option would be to touch the headrest on the seat. Both of them may well hold what I was seeking, but by the same token, one could be a crystal clear connection and the other like a frayed speaker wire cutting in and out.

I continued to stare into the dark passenger cabin of the sedan. My eyes kept being drawn back to the fingerprint powder on the passenger side dash. I was certain that it was merely standard procedure to check for prints throughout the entire car, but there was something gnawing at my gut where that was concerned.

After a lengthy pause, I straightened back up and made a quarter turn back toward the circle but remained standing next to the opening. I was about to make good on my earlier omission, but I had to make sure my timing was at least in the ballpark if this was going to work.

"Rowan?" Felicity called my name, a quizzical note in her voice replacing at least part of the concern.

"I'm fine," I told her, looking over my shoulder and forcing the comment out in a tired drone.

I cast my glance toward the crowd of cops, and my gaze fell on Captain Albright. She was still wearing a stoic frown, but her eyes broadcast a far different message. I didn't have any way of knowing what her exact relationship was with her niece, but the anguish flowing from her was akin to what I would expect from a parent.

This woman had caused me nothing but grief since the day I had met her. While I could rightfully be accused of having turned the other cheek more than once in my lifetime, where she was concerned I had long ago grown tired of her slapping me each time I did. I owed her nothing. I knew it, and so did she.

Judith Albright, however, was someone I had never met. But, like all of the other victims I had never met but helped anyway, I owed her nothing either. Still, between the two of them and my own conscience, I felt somehow compelled to pay whatever price was asked.

I hung my head and sighed before casting my glance toward Ben. "Hey, Tonto," I said, trying to keep my voice even. "Do you have a Slim Jim in your van?"

He gave me a puzzled look as he said, "Yeah, wh..." Before he could manage to get the "why" fully out of his mouth, his eyes widened and he started forward as he barked, "Goddammit! Don't do it, white man!"

Before the last word had finished passing his lips, I ducked into the driver's seat of the sedan, slammed the door and hit the lock.

Felicity instantly screamed a severely pissed off "damn your eyes" that was still perfectly audible to me even through the tempered glass of the car.

I knew that neither Ben nor she could possibly be surprised that I had pulled this particular stunt. After all, we'd been doing this sort of thing long enough that they had to know I would do something they considered stupid but that I felt absolutely necessary. I had merely managed to catch them off guard. But regarding that particular coup, I still wasn't quite sure if I should consider myself lucky or not.

My wife was at the door, yanking hard on the handle, and glaring at me with the same emotion she had just voiced, but her eyes were glistening with a healthy dose of fear as well. Unfortunately, I didn't have time to offer her any reassurances, verbal or otherwise. With as many state troopers as there were standing around the perimeter, I knew a Slim Jim or other tool for unlocking the door was likely to be produced at any moment, whether from Ben's van or one of their trunks. The way I had it figured, I probably had somewhere around thirty seconds before I was wrestled out of this seat by someone. What they probably didn't realize was the fact that I was actually counting on them to do just that in case this turned out to be a worse idea than I already thought it was.

Through the windshield I could see uniformed bodies moving in every direction as trunk lids began flying open. The tableau outside seemed almost like a surreal picture as my contact with the seat began to melt into an ethereal connection to things past. The murmuring voice inside my head stepped upward as if someone had just twisted the volume knob to full. I still couldn't make out what was being said, but it was becoming clearer with each sound it uttered.

I wasn't able to keep literal track of the seconds as they ticked by, but I knew my hesitation over my own doubts had already cost me part of the already short span of time. I now began to wonder if thirty seconds would be enough to accomplish what I needed to do.

I took another glance out the driver's side window and saw Felicity. Though I could no longer hear her, or anything other than the preternatural noise inside my skull, I saw her lips moving in slow motion and could make out the words, *"Damnú! Rowan, open the door!"*

A few feet behind her I saw Ben snatching a Slim Jim from a state trooper and turning toward the car. My hoped for thirty seconds was about to become something closer to fifteen or twenty at the most.

I realized then I couldn't wait for the connection to take its normal course. Unfortunately, the only way I knew to speed it up added yet another layer of peril to the unbridled risk I was already taking. Given that fact, I might well be glad to be pulled out of here in twenty seconds instead of thirty.

Ben was already nearing the car, sprinting in an extruded slow motion through my distorted view of the here and now. If I wasted any more time, this whole undertaking would be for naught.

I grasped the steering wheel with my left hand, slapped my right palm onto the passenger side seatback, and then leaned back against the headrest as I purposely stopped grounding and allowed all of my psychic defenses to fall by the wayside.

There was a bloom of color then a bright flash of blinding white. After that, my world was no longer my own. In that instant, I was no longer who I was, I was no longer where I was, and I was no longer what I was.

I simply *wasn't*.

CHAPTER 29

ANGER...
>*Sadness...*
>*Betrayal...*
>*And back to anger yet again.*
>*The emotions are shifting through me like a storm... Random, but always beginning with anger and ending with the same, as the semi-jumbled cycle repeats once again.*
>*Memories flood around me, none of them familiar because none of them are my own. They don't stop to acquaint themselves with the stranger grasping at them. Instead they flit past, as if in a hurry to escape something yet unseen.*
>*I catch only the barest glimpse of what they might be but nowhere near enough to grasp what they truly are.*
>*I see nothing but their flickering trails as they fade into the distant void to remain a private mystery.*
>*I feel nothing but the circular list of painful emotions.*
>*Then I feel nothing at all...*

>*Thirst...*
>*Want...*
>*Need...*
>*Thirst...*
>*A new flight of feelings penetrates my soul. Something is different about them—something beyond the obvious.*
>*They are darker...*
>*More ordered...*
>*More frightening.*
>*I try to embrace them anyway, but they recede at my touch. They have as much fear of me as I have of them.*
>*Falling...*
>*Falling...*
>*Falling...*
>*I feel as though the brass ring has been ripped from my grasp. The answers I seek are now nothing more than Doppler-shifted pinpoints in the distance.*

I am left only with questions.
And, frustration...
I try to scream, but no sound can penetrate the emptiness.

Falling...
Floating...
Falling...
Absolute darkness surrounds me.
There is no longer anything in the void.
No emotion.
No memories.
Nothing...
Only me, and I am nothing.

A chorus of screams echoes in my ears as light blooms in my eyes. They come to an abrupt end as once again silence falls swiftly like a sharp guillotine blade.

There is a complete end to all sound.

The light dulls to blue-black night. Muted colors bleed into a grainy landscape before me as my eyes try to adjust. Sound fades in once again, but all I hear is the beating of my own heart and the rhythmic rush of blood in my ears.

I am standing on an empty street. A lone streetlamp casts a dim sodium vapor glow around me, sending my own oblique shadow across the cracked asphalt to meld with the darkness.

I stare at the shadow where it falls across the curb. There is a storm drain to my right. The street is dry, but a narrow river is flowing along the gutter and into the gaping mouth of the sewer.

But it isn't water.

It is red...

And thick...

It is blood.

I look up and away from the horrid sight. In front of me is a boarded up house. I try to focus on it. It is old, and the brick facing is streaked black where smoke and fire once billowed out. Fallen leaves choke the stands of browned weeds that cover the yard.

A short flight of concrete stairs leads up to the front door. They are in a state of extreme disrepair, pocked with holes where chunks have been broken off through years of abuse and neglect. The vinyl soffit is scorched, now hanging in drip-like slags where it eventually cooled, frozen in time. Warped and greying plywood covers the windows. Graffiti marks the boards with names and crude drawings, but the weather has faded them beyond recognition.

It appears that even the vandals have abandoned this place.

I stare at the unlit porch light to the left of the door. It is really nothing more than a metal protrusion jutting from the outer wall. The glass globe is long missing, and a dead yellow bulb sags beneath as the detached socket in which it is set dangles from the frayed electrical wires. The motion draws my attention to the area below where reflective numbers step downward across the brick at a shallow angle.

2 – 3 – 0 – 2.

The last 2 in the sequence is canted to the right, apparently missing the top fastener that held it to the brick. The curve at its back rests against what remains of a frame for a now missing storm door.

Something soft brushes against my palm then gently clasps around my fingers. I don't start with surprise, as I would expect. I simply accept it and look down to see what appears to be a woman's hand holding mine. I bring my eyes up to a face that isn't there. I find only darkness where it should be.

She feels familiar. I am certain I should know her, but without a face I can't attach a name. I stare into the darkness where it should be but still find nothing.

I don't feel fear, only curiosity. I sense secrecy. I feel that she is hiding from me. As if she does not want me to know her identity.

As I watch, she lifts her other arm, bringing a pale hand into the air before me, index finger stiffly extended as the others curl against her palm. As she stretches out, I follow her finger with my eyes, turning my head slowly to gaze upon where she is pointing. Sitting atop a metal post, directly in my line of sight, I find a rectangular sign that reads South Millston Street.

The faceless woman tugs on my hand, and I turn to see that she has already stepped onto the curb. She starts up the leaf-strewn walkway, and I follow her without question.

As we silently make our way up the crumbling stairs, time shifts, leaping forward, then back, then forward again. There is no warning, yet there is no surprise.

It simply is.

I am standing in an empty room. The walls bear soot marks from the fire. There is water damage to the sheetrock, causing it to warp *and crumble, leaving holes that reveal the bare wooden studs beneath. Trash litters the floor, and a heavy coat of grime and dust seems to coat every surface. I know that I am in the house.*

I glance around and see that the woman is now gone.

I understand that she has brought me here for a reason but has left it unspoken. I am beginning to feel like I am acting out a scene from a twisted parody of a Dickens novel. As if the ghost of murders past, present, and future has brought me to witness my own fate.

I wonder at the feeling.

Curiosity at my lucid state creeps in and tries to usurp the vision before me. The grainy tableau shifts and flickers.

A sharp odor assaults my nostrils—metallic, harsh, and unique as it overwhelms me. It is liver being cooked. I feel a thin wave of nausea tickle the back of my throat. I can tell by the stench that it isn't being properly prepared.

The softness touches my hand again.

The faceless woman is pulling on me now. She seems impatient, as if dealing with a small child who won't listen.

I realize that I am the reason for her irascible state.

I follow her as she tugs, leading me through the trash-scattered room and deeper into the house. We stop before a door. It is partially burned. A pattern of thin cracks spreads out along the edge of the charred wood in a scaly pattern, like those on a burnt out shard of blackened log from a fireplace.

I look at the woman and she merely points.

I turn back to the door then reach out and touch the surface. The fire-ravaged wood is stone-like to the touch. I grasp the handle and pull it toward me. The barrier opens, and I see a long flight of stairs descending into blackness.

I look to my guide, but once again she is no longer there, so I bring my gaze back to the stairs. As I stand there, for the first time since crossing the veil, I hear something besides the sound of my own heart.

Wafting up from the darkness comes an androgynous voice. "Just a little sting... Don't worry it will all be over soon...very soon... I envy you. To be chosen like this. It's such an honor... I wish it were me..."

I feel a slight pressure on my back.

I turn around and find the faceless woman standing there. Without a word she thrusts her palms outward against my chest, and I fall backward into the darkness.

A barrage of words assaulted my ears with an unmistakable Celtic accent wrapped firmly around them. "Damn your eyes, Rowan Linden Gant!"

Behind the crystal clear exclamation, a flood of other voices were chattering, yelling, and generally creating an unintelligible cacophony. Some sounded authoritative, while others came across as excited, and still others seemed almost conversational. In any event, they blended together to create a boisterous hum in the cold air that only served to add to my disorientation.

My head was pounding again, my too brief respite from the migraine now over with a vengeance. However, that wasn't the only pain with which I was forced to contend. My shoulders were arched up into the sides of my neck, and it seemed that someone was manhandling me. I could feel knuckles digging into my chest as a pair of arms hugged beneath my own. It took me a second to realize I was still moving backwards, but instead of a sensation of falling as before, I could tell I was now being dragged.

"Is he bleedin'?" Ben Storm's gruff voice penetrated the overbearing murmur.

"I can't see," Felicity said. "His shoulder is in the way…"

"Get that paramedic over here!" my friend shouted.

My wife's soft hand slipped into the fold between my neck and shoulder then pulled away.

"No blood," she announced. "Thank the Gods."

We had stopped moving, but Ben was still holding me up in a bear hug from behind. Disorientation was now giving way to a thin thread of lucidity, and I seemed to be remembering where I was. Of course, knowing my location didn't keep me from being completely out of synch with my surroundings. After such an intense trip through the veil between the worlds, my mind was still trying to sort out what was real here, what was real there, and the in between where it all overlapped. This was far from a new experience for me, but old hat or not, it was never an easy process.

It crossed my mind that it would probably be a good idea to let them know that I was okay, instead of letting them run amok as they seemed to be doing at the moment. I tried to say something but couldn't seem to get the words out. It was then I realized that Ben was holding so tightly around my chest that breathing, in and of itself, was more than enough effort on its own. Talking was simply out of the question. However, before I could attempt to wave my hand or try to grab their attention some other way, a fresh voice entered the mix.

"We need to get his jacket off," the paramedic ordered.

The pressure released on my chest as Ben let go and supported me with a single arm while the paramedic quickly stripped off my coat. I immediately wheezed in a deep breath then exhaled heavily. After drawing in another, I started to speak, but apparently I still wasn't able to form actual words, and all that came out was a moan. By then, they were already lowering me onto the asphalt. A shadow immediately came over me as I felt a pair of hands groping around my neck and another pushing up my sleeve.

I sputtered as I tried to demand that they stop, but for my trouble I was treated to a flashlight in my face and a pair of gloved fingers in my mouth as my head was tilted back.

"Labored respirations, but there's no obstruction," the paramedic barked. "Get the oxygen."

A soft hand pressed against my forehead as my wife brought her face in close to mine. "Rowan, can you hear me?"

"Ma'am," the paramedic said, trying to push her away. "You need to step back so we can work."

As he pushed her, I was already moving my arms to fend him off before he hurt her or could continued gagging me. I slapped his hand from Felicity then grabbed his wrist and wrestled his other hand away from my mouth. I was still out of breath from the bear hug, but I managed to suck in a fresh lungful of air and finally form words that made some kind of sense as I groaned, "Better watch it. She'll make your hair fall out."

"Rowan?" Felicity was up in my face again.

"Yeah…"

Her concern made a quick metamorphosis into anger, "What the hell were you thinking?"

I gulped air again and said, "That you were going to be really pissed."

"Aye," she replied. "You're right about that."

"We still need to check you out, Mister Gant," the paramedic told me.

I tried to shake my head as I objected, "I'm fine."

"Best see if you can do something about his thick skull while you're at it then," my wife snipped as she pulled herself up to her feet and stalked off.

I was going to have to worry about patching things up with her later. Right now, I needed to talk to Ben.

"Get off me, dammit," I exclaimed as I pushed the paramedic away and levered myself up into a sitting position. "Ben? Where's Ben?"

My friend's voice hit my ears. "I'm right here, Kemosabe. You really better let 'em check you out."

"There's no time for that," I said, as I started struggling to my feet.

With a quizzical look on his face, Ben reached out and gave me a hand up. "What's up, you see another dead swan or somethin' over in la-la land?"

"No," I said as I focused on the grainy memory looping through my mind and rushed to get the words out in a frantic declaration. "I saw the killer's address."

CHAPTER 30

"IS JUDITH ALL RIGHT?" CAPTAIN ALBRIGHT DEMANDED.

I had barely finished blurting out the revelation about the address to Ben when her words came at me from behind. I turned to find her staring at me with the same look of concern she had been wearing earlier, but there was no mistaking the thread of hopefulness in her voice.

"I don't know," I replied, shaking my head. "I didn't see her."

"What do you mean you didn't see her?" she insisted.

"I mean I didn't see her," I replied before swinging back around to face Ben and fire off, "Twenty-three oh two South Millston Street. The killer is there. Right now."

"You sure?" Ben asked.

"Yes, I'm sure," I said.

Albright stepped around and grabbed me by the collar. With urgent panic in her tone, she shouted, "Damn you, Gant! Where is my daughter?"

I reached up and grasped her wrists as I started to respond, but the moment the question sank in I hesitated. Instead of struggling, I simply stood there motionless and stared back into her contorted face. Her outburst brought an instantaneous halt to all conversation around me, or so it seemed.

After a few seconds that felt as if they dragged on for minutes, Ben cleared his throat and said, "Um, Captain... Don't ya' mean niece?"

Albright didn't even bother to look at him. A dim flicker of realization over her slip showed in her eyes, but rather than respond to my friend's question, she let out a small shriek then pushed me. I stumbled back but maintained my footing.

"Is Judith with the killer?" she spat.

"Maybe..." I replied, shaking my head. "I don't know. All I can say is that I think he had someone..."

She cut me off. "You think?"

"Barbara, I told you I didn't see her. I just heard the killer talking to someone."

"Are you certain it wasn't Judith?"

"Whoever it was didn't say anything," I replied. "But, you're missing the point here. I saw the killer's address and yes, he has someone with him. Don't you think you should send someone to at least check out what I'm telling you?"

She huffed out a heavy breath and glared at me. After a moment she looked over to my friend and said, "He's your devil worshipper, Storm. Do you think he's telling the truth?"

I sighed and dropped my forehead into my hand. I couldn't win with this woman no matter what I did. I had to bite my tongue, but I knew getting into another altercation with her would just be wasting valuable time.

"Listen, Row… This address you gave me. Is it around here?" Ben asked, gesturing with a sweep of his arm.

"I don't know," I told him.

"But you're sure about the number and the street?"

"Yes." I nodded vigorously. "Absolutely."

"Okay, what I can do is call it in and have dispatch run a search on Millston Streets," he offered. "But here's the problem—we either need a warrant or some serious probable cause to kick down a door. Like I've told ya' before, you and the *Twilight Zone* don't qualify on either count."

"Hey, if I remember correctly, it was the police who insisted on my involvement in this," I countered. "Especially you, Barbara."

"I know," my friend replied. "I'm just sayin' this is a sticky situation. And if you're wrong and what we end up with is a grandma sittin' there readin' 'er Bible…"

"I'm not wrong, Ben," I appealed before he could finish. "Besides, it's an old, boarded up house. It looked like it had been burned at one time, so you aren't going to find a grandma with a Bible there. Just a killer and a potential victim, unless you keep screwing around and let her become a statistic."

"Chill out… Now, you're sure about all this?"

"Goddammit, will you stop asking me that?" I shot back. "Why the hell are you doubting me all of a sudden?"

He reached up and smoothed back his hair then rested his hand on the side of his neck while gesturing with the other. "No offense, white man, but this ain't how you usually work. Normally, ya' don't just hand us an address and say go get the bad guy. Ya' tell me somethin' like ya' saw a bunch of blood and a flash of light, or a spirit makes ya' write bad poems and ya' have nightmares about flyin' monkeys or some shit." He shrugged. "Somethin' off the wall like that... Ya'know... *Twilight Zone...*"

"So maybe I'm getting better at this," I snapped. "Are you going to completely discount what I'm saying just because I'm being specific this time?"

"Okay... Okay... Calm down."

"How can I calm down? I just told you where to find the killer and that he has someone with him. But instead of doing something about it, you're just standing here giving me the third degree."

He glanced over at Albright who was remaining completely silent.

"Look, Row, I told ya', we'll check it out," he replied, turning back to me and pulling out his notebook. "Gimme that exact address again."

"Twenty-three oh two South Millston Street," I repeated.

"Twenty-three oh two..." he mumbled back to me. "You're..."

My frustrated retort was already poised on the end of my tongue, but fortunately he stopped himself before completing the question.

"Yeah, I know," he muttered as he scribbled. "You're sure." He turned and looked toward some of the other cops a few feet away. "Hey... Yeah, you. Is there a South Millston Street around here anywhere?"

"No," the deputy replied, shaking his head. "Don't know of one in the immediate area. Maybe in Saint Charles."

"Okay, thanks." Ben pulled out his phone and directed himself back to me. "I'm gonna call in and have dispatch run a search for me. Just so ya' know, this is prob'ly gonna take a coupl'a minutes, so ya' need ta' just get a grip and calm down."

I stooped and snatched up my jacket from the asphalt where it had been dropped during the earlier havoc. I slipped into it while he started punching a number into the keypad of his cell. I wasn't excited about the delay, but there was nothing else I could do. At least he was starting the ball rolling instead of interrogating me further.

I let out a heavy sigh then glanced around and spotted Felicity leaning against a light standard in the distance, well on the opposite side of the crime scene tape. If there was going to be a wait, then now was as good a time as any for me to start my own ball down the lane.

"Well let me know what you find out," I said to my friend, my voice unintentionally sharp. I nodded my head in the direction of my sulking wife then added, "I'll be over there finding out how long I'm going to be sleeping on the couch."

"WHY DO YOU HAVE TO BE SO RECKLESS, THEN?" FELICITY asked, her voice calm but still betraying a definite subtext of annoyance.

I had taken it as a good sign that she didn't simply walk away when I approached. She was still leaning back against the light standard, and I was next to her doing the same, more or less sitting on the edge of the large concrete base and pressing the back of my head against the cold post. At first it seemed to afford a little relief from the pain in my skull, but as expected it didn't last long.

We had been standing in silence for a long measure. I was keeping an eye on Ben as he talked on the phone while at the same time trying to focus my aching brain on a suitable apology I could offer my wife. I certainly wasn't going to say something empty just to get myself out of hot water. I wanted to honestly attempt to make amends to her. I just wasn't sure where to start except to simply say I was sorry, which seemed a bit lame under any circumstances.

Since I was finding myself at a loss for the appropriate verbiage, she beat me to the punch with her straightforward question being the first thing either of us had uttered. I was actually a bit surprised that she was talking to me in such an even tone. Had she snarled a string of acerbic Gaelic at me, it would have been much closer to what I was expecting.

I paused then grunted in response, "That's a good question."

"I'm serious, Row."

"I know you are," I offered with a heavy sigh. "I just don't have a good answer."

Quiet fell between us again for several heartbeats, and I waited for her reply, watching my breath condense in a frosty cloud in front of me before dissipating into nothingness.

Finally, I heard Felicity sigh and shuffle as she repositioned herself against the post. "You know I think what bothers me the most is that I know I would probably have done the same thing."

"Yeah, you've had your share of moments too," I replied.

"You needn't remind me," she said.

"Sorry."

"Aye, now *that*, you definitely needed to say."

"I thought I might," I said. "Sorry about the whole thing with the car too. I just felt I needed the strength of the physical connection if I was going to get anything tangible."

She responded without pause. "I know."

"It worked..." I offered sheepishly.

"I heard," she replied. "I think everyone did. You were your usual vociferous self where that was concerned."

"They weren't listening."

"I know."

I glanced toward Ben for a visual check on his progress. He still had his cell phone pressed to his ear, and he seemed to be waiting. I was at least heartened by the fact that he appeared to be edging toward impatience himself.

I sighed. "Now if it just pans out."

"It will," she murmured.

After a brief pause I shifted slightly and glanced over in her direction. "So... Still mad at me?"

She didn't turn, but she held her hand up over her shoulder with her index finger and thumb around a half inch apart. "Just a little."

"Could be worse I suppose."

"Aye."

"Am I sleeping on the couch?"

She shook her head out of reflex as she spoke. "No. I'm sure I can think of a suitable punishment for you though."

I felt my brow furrow automatically at the way she almost purred the comment. "Umm, honey... Are you in one of those moods again? Because, you know, this really isn't the time or place..."

"I know, I know..." she replied, rushing to explain. Her voice sounded almost as if she were ashamed of what she had just said. "I wasn't and then suddenly I was. It just came over me. I know this isn't the time, believe me. But...the feeling is more than just a little overwhelming."

"Like with Miranda?" I nearly whispered the question.

"Almost," she replied, giving her head a shallow nod. "Not exactly, but almost."

She definitely hadn't given me the answer I had hoped for, but it was better she was honest rather than lie about something like this.

"That's not good," I said, unable to find any other words that fit.

"I was thinking the same thing, trust me."

On a whim I reached into my jacket pocket and checked for the bottle containing the necklace. I breathed a small sigh of relief when I felt my fingers wrap around it. Even if I had lost it I couldn't think of any way for it to end up back in Annalise's hands. But I also wasn't sure what effect it might have if it was released from its salt-filled coffin.

Although I knew by feel that the bottle was still in my pocket, just to be safe I pulled it out and inspected it closely. I even gave the glass vessel a light tap against my palm in order to uncover the piece of jewelry just enough to make sure it was still entombed in the salt. Once satisfied, I shook it again and stuffed it back into my jacket.

I pondered what to say for a moment before finally venturing, "I hate to ask this, but I feel like I have to. Are you certain you are in control of yourself?"

"Aye," she replied. "It isn't like that. I'm still me."

"Sorry again... I just needed to know."

"I understand..." She paused for a moment then continued with, "I'm fine, Rowan. Really, I am. Don't worry. I have to admit that I'm embarrassed by the situation though...if you know what I mean. I really shouldn't be getting aroused right now. It seems rather sick, don't you think?"

"If things were different, I would probably say it was odd, yes," I admitted. "But, right now, I'd have to say it's sick only if it's for the wrong reasons."

"I don't know if there are any right reasons for it to come on me now," she replied. "But, it certainly isn't because of all this. At least, I don't..."

"Hey Rowan!" Ben called out, interrupting the balance of her explanation.

We both looked up to see him half jogging across the parking lot then ducking beneath the crime scene tape a few feet from us.

"Did you find it?" I asked hopefully.

"Probably," he told us. "There're seven Millston's in a fifty mile radius—three in Illinois, two in Saint Charles, and two in the county."

"Are all of them being checked?"

"Yeah, but you said the house looked like it had been through a fire, right?"

"Yeah," I replied, nodding quickly. "It was boarded up and you could see where the fire had scorched the brick above the windows. And, it was near a corner intersection, but I didn't get the other street name."

"Well, one of the addresses in the county fits that description," he said. "It's in Overmoor. Got torched by an arsonist about four years ago and been vacant ever since. The local coppers are doing a drive-by right now, and SWAT is on standby if they find anything."

"Overmoor? That's thirty-five or forty miles back the other direction," I said.

"Yeah," he said with a nod. "That'd be about right."

"Then why is Judith Albright's car abandoned all the way out here?"

"Who knows how these wingnuts think," he said with a shrug. "More'n likely ta' send us lookin' in the wrong direction. Besides, even you said ya' didn't know if she was with the SOB."

"I know," I replied. "I know... But it doesn't make sense."

"None of it does, Row. I thought you'd be used ta' that by now."

"I don't think I want to get used to it."

"Yeah, I know what you're sayin'. So listen, we prob'ly need ta' head out. Dependin' on how this shit goes down, it could be over before we even get there, which ain't such a bad thing in my opinion. I don't need you goin' off half cocked like usual."

"What did Albright say?" I asked.

He shook his head. "I haven't talked to 'er yet. Figured I'd go ahead and fill 'er in before we hit the road ourselves." He looked around and huffed, "Just gotta find 'er first."

A state trooper was walking past us just as Ben made the comment. He paused then doubled back and interrupted, "Are you talking about Captain Albright? She's gone."

"Whaddaya mean gone?" Ben asked, turning toward him. "She was here just a couple of minutes ago."

The trooper glanced at his watch then back to Ben. "More like five or six."

"Yeah, okay," my friend retorted. "She say where she was goin'?"

"No," the officer replied. "But she crossed the median and was heading east with her dash light going."

"Goddammit, Beebee..." Ben sighed then spoke up. "Get on the radio and give your guys a description. Have 'em pull 'er over."

"Isn't she responding to..."

"Yeah, she is. That's the problem. Just pull 'er over and detain 'er." With that said, Ben pulled out his cell phone and started stabbing numbers as he mumbled, "Jeezus fuckin' Christ..."

CHAPTER 31

I REACHED DOWN AND CHECKED THE CLASP ON MY safety belt, giving it a tug to make sure it was tight. I had lost count of how many times I had made the inspection by feel since we left the rest area, but I was betting this wouldn't be the last time by a long shot. I knew I shouldn't be so nervous. After all, I had been on countless insane rides with Ben and his infamous "move it or lose it" attitude behind the wheel, but for some reason this one seemed worse than all the others combined.

My friend's own magnetic bubble light was strobing atop the van, casting a flickering glow down onto the dash as we sped along the highway. A slice of cold air was whistling in through an ultra thin gap along the edge of the driver's side window caused by the emergency beacon's coiled wire, which was threaded through to the accessory plug powering it.

Thus far, I hadn't been brave enough to glance in the direction of the dimly lit speedometer. It was bad enough that we were whipping by cars so fast that they appeared as little more than blurred lights rocketing past us in reverse. I feared that knowing where the needle was actually hovering would just be too much for me to take right now.

The siren Ben had mounted behind the grill of the vehicle was warbling, burping, and vomiting a string of randomized alert tones to help clear the way, but it soon became obvious that some people simply didn't listen. Every now and then the van would sway violently as he would be forced to steer around a car whose driver wasn't paying attention and therefore hadn't bothered to move to the right. As usual, each time it happened the blaring siren was joined by an angry string of verbiage from my friend, aimed squarely at the receding headlights reflected in the rear view mirror.

I turned in the seat as best I could and glanced back over my shoulder at Felicity. She was braced in her own seat with one hand gripping the armrest, while the other was hooked tightly to the shoulder harness across her chest in a white knuckled hold. She was known to have a heavy foot herself, but this was obviously excessive, even by her standards. She stared back at me, eyes wide, and all I could do was shake my head.

When I turned back around, I saw that we were topping a low hill, and the brightly lit casino on the Saint Charles riverfront was looming in front of us on the left. The aircraft anti-collision lights ringing the roof of the tall structure winked on then off in a rapid cadence, but we were moving so fast that the top of the building disappeared from view before I could see more than two cycles of the warning flash.

The Fifth Street exit had been coming up when I turned around to face forward but was now already long behind us as we rushed along the outer lane of Highway 70 toward the Blanchette Bridge. I shot a quick glance at my watch. In a little over twenty minutes, we had already covered a distance that at normal speeds would have taken better than a half hour.

With Ben's attention focused on keeping the van on all four wheels—although I wasn't convinced we had stayed that way the entire time—conversation between the three of us had been non-existent. I wasn't about to distract him with chatter, idle or otherwise. Unless it was earth shattering and I felt he desperately needed to know, I was keeping my mouth shut. Felicity's silence told me that she had either adopted the same attitude or was simply too frightened to speak.

We had just blown beneath the first overhead girder of the eastbound bridge when Ben's cell phone began to ring. My heart jumped into my throat as he swerved around yet another oblivious driver, while at the same time fumbling for the warbling device. After barking an angry slur at the vehicular obstacle, he flipped open the cell and pressed it against his ear.

"Storm… Yeah… Yeah… *Dammit!* Any sign of 'er yet? Jeezus… No, nothin' here… Yeah, but she had a good ten minutes on us, so she could show up at any minute. Better keep an eye out… Yeah… Good deal… What? Yeah, we're just crossin' the river now. If the idiots'll stay the fuck outta my way, we should be there in ten, fifteen tops. Yeah… See ya'."

Folding the phone shut with a flick of his thumb, he shoved it back into his pocket then grabbed the steering wheel. I felt better now that he was guiding the van with both hands instead of just one—but, only slightly better.

"Hubcap chasers didn't find Beebee," he said, casting a quick glance at me before returning his attention to the road.

"I pretty much gathered that from your reaction," I replied, breaking my self-imposed reticence with more than a little internal trepidation.

He huffed out a heavy breath. "Shit... Guess I can't really blame 'er. I'd prob'ly do the same if it was my kid. Know what I mean?"

"Knowing you, probably," I agreed. Obviously he expected an answer, so I had little choice but to talk. Since we were still traveling in a straight line, I went ahead and asked, "By the way, did you know about that little secret?"

"Hell no." He gave his head a slight shake to punctuate the response even more. "I was told she was a niece. But, lemme tell ya', I'm bettin' somebody up on high knew about it."

"It kind of explains something I was wondering about," I offered. "I wasn't quite sure how she reconciled her particular set of strict values with a niece who was involved in the whole vampire scene— and apparently bisexual at the very least. That didn't really seem to fit with her holier-than-thou attitude."

"Yeah," he grunted. "Extended family is one thing. But your own kid is somethin' completely different. Ya' love 'em no matter how much you think they're fuckin' up."

"Yeah..." I replied. "I suppose that might explain why she claimed she was her niece, too. Some part of her still had to spare herself the perceived embarrassment."

After a brief pause Ben shot another quick glance my way and asked, "So, you two doin' okay? Both of ya' been pretty quiet."

"As well as can be expected."

"What about you, Firehair?"

"The same," she replied, her voice pitched slightly higher than usual.

"You havin' a *Twilight Zone* moment or somethin'?"

"No. Just a fear of low altitude flight."

"Of what? Oh... you mean... Jeez, c'mon, my drivin' ain't that bad. I don't hear Firehair complainin'." On the heels of the comment, he jerked the van to the right then quickly back to the left while growling, "Fuckin' assholes."

Felicity yelped in time with the maneuver then a few seconds later sighed and said, "Yes, Ben, it is that bad."

He shot a look over his shoulder. "Yeah, well, that's just how it is sometimes."

"Please keep your eyes on the road then," she appealed. "I'm not ready to die just yet."

"Gimme a break."

"Just keep your eyes on the road, please?" she appealed.

"Relax. I know what I'm doin'."

I heard my wife quietly mutter, "Gods, I hope so."

"So anyway," Ben reverted back to his original train of thought without ceremony. "No Albright yet, but you can bet that's where she's headed. As far as the house itself goes, the Overmoor coppers are pretty sure they saw a light go on then back off through one of the basement windows."

"That's where the killer was in the vision," I acknowledged. "The basement."

Ben snorted. "So, were ya' plannin' ta' tell anyone about that part?"

"Sorry. But, I had enough trouble convincing you about the address as it was, don't you think?"

"So you're blamin' me?"

"The situation, mostly. But, yeah, maybe just a little."

"Yeah, whatever," he replied in a dismissive tone. "So you pick up on anything else we should know?"

"The vision was a bit disjointed, and some of the imagery was classic la-la land, as you call it. But, if I'm remembering correctly, just beyond the front door is what appeared to be a living room..."

He interrupted. "You got a floor plan?"

"Some," I answered. "Not all."

"Hold on," he snapped.

Reaching into his pocket, he pulled out his cell and flipped it open once again. With a quick stab he hit redial and then speaker. The phone beeped then trilled briefly. On the second ring it was answered.

"Sergeant Madden," a woman's voice said.

"Sergeant Madden, it's Detective Storm, you got anyone from SWAT handy?"

"Yeah, just a second..."

There was a brief pause, and we could hear a mix of voices, then someone else came on the line.

"This is Lieutenant Penczak."

"Lieutenant, Detective Storm, Major Case. I think I might have a partial floor plan on the house for ya'."

"I'll take it," the man replied.

"I'm handin' ya' over ta' Rowan Gant," Ben told him then thrust the phone at me.

I took it from him quickly out of an attack of self-preservation since he was already paying more attention to it than the road. As I grabbed the phone I stabbed my finger toward the windshield and shook it. My friend just rolled his eyes but returned his focus on the blurred white lines in front of us.

"Lieutenant," I started. "The front door opens into what appears to have been a moderate-sized living room. Maybe fifteen feet wide by fifteen deep, best guess. There's trash everywhere, but I don't recall any major obstacles. On the back wall, there's an arched doorway that leads directly into a hallway running parallel to the room. If you go to the right, it T's with another corridor coming in on the left. Down that corridor, there is a charred door that leads to the basement. It's on the right, about mid way."

"What about the back?" Penczak asked.

"Sorry, I'm afraid that's all I have."

"That's all right. It's more than we had a minute ago," he replied. "So how do you know all this? Have you been in the house?"

"Sort of."

"What do you mean, sort of?"

Ben reached over and snatched the cell phone from my hand. "Trust me, Lieutenant, you don't want 'im to explain it. Are you ready to go?"

"We've got spotters on the house. There hasn't been any activity for almost fifteen minutes now, so we're setting up to move into position soon."

"Good deal," Ben grunted. "We'll be there in five."

"We'll hold the party until you get here."

"Yeah, thanks," he replied with a definite note of sarcasm. "Captain Albright show up yet?"

"Not that..." The lieutenant's reply was cut short by a burst of static and a voice in the background. When he spoke again he simply said, "Hold on..."

There was a clatter as if the cell phone was dropped, or at least tossed onto a hard surface. Over the tinny speaker, we could hear the muffled sounds of physical activity along with several unintelligible words being barked. Even though we couldn't make them out, the brevity and tone told us they were probably a series of commands.

"What's happening?" I asked Ben.

"Dunno, but it doesn't sound good."

We exited the highway and shot through an intersection, slowing only enough to avoid a collision and make a quick right. A languid forever later, a voice came back on the line.

"Storm, you still there?"

"Yeah, Madden, what's goin' on there?"

"It's gone to hell in a hand basket," she replied. "A spotter just put eyes on a woman entering the back of the house. He's pretty sure it was Captain Albright. SWAT is already moving."

"Goddammit..." Ben moaned. "Don't you have a friggin' perimeter set up?"

"Of course we do," she replied harshly. "We have no idea how she breached it."

"What a fuckin' mess," my friend huffed.

"Yeah, tell me about it."

"We're about three minutes out," Ben told her. "Do what ya' gotta do."

He snapped the phone shut then tossed it onto the console as he slowed at another intersection then quickly accelerated the van while threading it through the cars that were still coming to a halt.

CHAPTER 32

THREE MINUTES BECAME FIVE WHEN BEN MISSED A LEFT turn from his hastily scribbled directions, and we were forced to double back up to the main thoroughfare from a narrow dead-end street. A quick flash of his badge saw us through the vehicular barricade at the end of South Millston, and thirty seconds later we had coasted down the block-long hill to a cluster of emergency vehicles scattered haphazardly around the T intersection at the bottom.

Splashes of luminance played across the fronts of the houses from active lightbars, casting an angry harshness across the entire scene. However, the strobing lights seemed to be the only things garish about the tableau. Everything—and everyone—else appeared to be almost somber.

Ben levered the van into park then switched off the engine as he watched the uniformed officers milling about in the street. On the sidewalk we could see a few members of the SWAT team who appeared to be casually chatting, their weapons pointed toward the ground in a somewhat relaxed posture.

"Yeah…" my friend breathed. "It's all over but the paperwork."

I scanned the area as I unlatched my seatbelt and allowed it to slowly recoil through my fingers. The metal buckle eventually struck the upper stop with a dull thunk as if to highlight his comment. After several seconds and multiple sweeps with my eyes, I said, "I don't see Albright anywhere."

"Yeah…me neither," Ben muttered with a slight nod. "And that ain't good. Let's just hope she's either bein' a nuisance or warmin' a seat in the back of a patrol car."

We climbed out of the vehicle and into the cold night air. There was a palpable chill that transcended the physical, for me at least. I glanced over at Felicity as she slid the door shut on the side of the van, and from the way she shivered then cast her eyes around, I could tell that she was feeling it too.

"Detective Storm?" a questioning female voice called out from several yards away.

I heard my friend respond, "Yeah. You Sergeant Madden?"

By the time Felicity and I came around the front of the vehicle to join him, Ben was facing a sprightly, uniformed woman with a shoulder length shag of medium brown hair. She was resting one forearm casually atop her high-riding sidearm with the thumb of her other hand hooked into her belt. Being of average stature like the majority of the people on this planet, she was forced to look up at the tall Native American cop in front of her.

They had dropped their voices back down to a normal level, so the ambient noise of radios and other officers kept us from making out their conversation until we drew close. We probably hadn't missed much, but when we were only a few steps away, the first intelligible thing we heard was the tail end of a sentence from Madden. "...still inside. I'll warn you, it's not pretty."

"It never is," Ben sighed.

"These two with you?" Madden asked, leveling a stone-faced gaze on us as we stopped near Ben.

He nodded. "Yeah. They're consultants for Major Case." He wagged his index finger between us. "Rowan Gant, Felicity O'Brien. This is Sergeant Madden, Overmoor Police."

"Sergeant," I said, reaching out and briefly shaking her hand. Felicity did the same.

Madden lowered her forearm back to its waist level prop then jerked her head toward the house. "I'm not sure what kind of consultants you are, but I was just telling Detective Storm it's definitely not for the squeamish in there."

"Unfortunately we've seen our share," I replied.

"Sorry to hear that."

"So, how many?" Ben asked.

"Two that they've found, and that's counting the one Captain Albright shot," she replied, focusing back on him. "Both of them are in the basement. The upstairs is pretty much empty, but they're going through it again just to be sure."

"Was it a clean shoot?"

She shook her head. "I'm not the one to ask. It was already going down when SWAT made entry. We heard two shots coming from the interior. Sergeant Gordon was first in, and from what I understand, he saw what was probably a muzzle flash light up the stairwell. But he was still in the hallway and hadn't made it to the basement door yet."

"Same weapon?"

She shrugged. "One of the vics has two holes in him, center mass. Two shots, two holes, so that's how it looks."

"He have a weapon on 'im?"

"That's being determined," she offered carefully, glancing at us then back to him. "We'll know more as soon as they talk to Captain Albright."

"Yeah," my friend muttered in response to the veiled comment. "I got ya'… So how is Albright doin' anyway?"

Madden shook her head. "I'm not really sure. Physically she looks fine, but she hasn't said much. Just surrendered her weapon, flashed her badge, and then sat down in a corner. They're working on bringing her out right now."

"Yeah, well I'm sure ya'know one of the vics is prob'ly one of 'er relatives. Her…" He gave a barely perceptible pause as he caught himself and then quickly finished the sentence with, "Niece."

"Would that be Judith?"

"Yeah."

Madden shook her head again. "Then I don't think so. That's about the only thing she *has* said so far. *Where are you, Judith?*"

"Hmmph," he grunted as he furrowed his brow. Then he asked, "So, you okay with us goin' in?"

"Let me check with the crime scene guys just to be sure," she said. "The scene is pretty straightforward as far as the physical evidence goes, so I doubt there will be a problem."

The sergeant left us and engaged in a short conversation with someone who appeared to be the technician running the scene. He glanced up in our direction as she pointed at us and then gave her a quick nod. A few seconds later she returned, pausing briefly to point us out to someone else.

"Sign in with Officer Fisk," she told us, gesturing in the direction of the uniformed man she had most recently spoken with. "He can give you shoe covers and gloves too." Then she leveled her gaze on Felicity and me. "Are you two really sure you want to go in there?"

"I never want to," I sighed through a heavy frown. "But I do my job."

"Yeah…" She nodded. "I hear you on that one."

"Ya'know, this is pretty much over," Ben said, looking over at us. "You can prob'ly skip it… I don't think anyone'll blame ya', and you've already done what the brass asked ya' to do."

"No," I replied. "I'm going to need to go in."

"TZ?" he questioned.

I didn't miss the inherent meaning behind the initials. "Yeah. Pretty much."

He shot a glance at my wife. "Firehair?"

"Aye," she said with a slight nod. "I need to be there for Rowan."

"You gonna need any salt?" he asked.

Sergeant Madden cocked an eyebrow and gave Ben an odd look.

Felicity nudged me, so I glanced at her then shook my head.

"No," she replied. "Not here."

"Yeah, okay…" Ben said with a nod. "Then let's get this over with."

I could feel Sergeant Madden's curious gaze burning into our backs all the way to the door.

THE UPSTAIRS INTERIOR OF THE HOUSE WAS JUST AS I had earlier described it. What I had seen of it in the vision, anyway. The basement itself was no more and no less than I expected. It was in large part barren. Little more than a low-ceilinged rectangular room with pock marked cement walls and peeling paint—and of course, the two slowly cooling bodies that occupied it.

I had seen worse, but that didn't make the garish scene any easier to look at. The first horror to befall us when we reached the bottom of the stairs was the nude corpse of a young woman, hanging upside down from the rafters. Her flesh was pallid and so devoid of color as to appear ghostly, just as we had seen before. Her arms were bound tightly behind her in such a way as to bend her shoulders back into what had to be a painful curve. As with the two victims resting in metal drawers downtown, a starkly defined swan tattoo stood out on her right upper arm.

The odor of the musty basement mingled with the smell of old smoke from the fire that had partially destroyed the upper level. A sharp note of urine pierced through the aged funk, most likely where one or both of the victim's bladders had evacuated upon death. As bad as it was, the intermingled malodor was an almost welcome change to the sickening stench permeating the atmosphere upstairs. It turned out that my stomach-churning ethereal brush with improperly prepared liver was nothing as compared to how it truly smelled in this plane of existence. I was beginning to think I would have to swear off the dish for some time to come.

Bright flashes from a camera strobe burst every now and then as a crime scene tech documented the sadistic tableau. I flinched upon the first then barely noticed when the second and third erupted to cast harsh shadows across the walls. Albright had already been taken out of the house by the time we entered, so it was just the corpses, him, and us down here. However, in some odd sense I felt all alone.

I stood motionless for a full minute, staring at the woman hanging from the rafter above. The crown of her head was only inches from the floor, her blue-black, stringy hair hanging down and splayed out behind her across the filthy cement like the strands of an old cotton mop tossed carelessly aside.

Still mute, I continued slowly around the suspended corpse. As I reached her left side, a plastic tube came into view. It was taped against her neck where it terminated in what appeared to be a large gauge needle piercing a vein. The opposite end was still dangling inside the mouth of a glass gallon jug, which was almost half full of red fluid. It didn't take deep thought to figure out exactly what it was.

Glistening shards of a similar vessel were shattered in an outwardly showering pattern nearby. The same red fluid was pooled around it, as well as splattered several feet in an oblique circle. A healthy measure of it was already drying to deep rust on the dead woman's face. Tented evidence markers littered the area.

"You okay, Row?" Ben asked in a low voice.

I didn't reply with words. I simply looked back over my shoulder and gave him a shallow nod.

"We in your way?" he asked, looking past me and addressing himself to the crime scene photographer.

I hadn't been paying attention, but I now noticed that the flashing from his strobe had stopped. I looked over at him and saw that he was standing off to one side of the room, observing me. He wore a flat expression, neither curiosity nor surprise evident in his features.

"No," he replied, shaking his head. "Just waiting."

"Sorry. I can move," I offered.

"You're fine," he told me. "I'm done with her."

I glanced around the basement but remained quiet. I wasn't quite sure what he was waiting for, but I didn't figure it was my place to ask.

I returned my gaze to the latest victim, wondering who she was when she was alive. I found myself in an odd quandary. My headache had subsided before we even arrived at the top of the street. I was certainly grateful for the relief, but at the same time I cursed the fact that I now seemed completely numbed to the ethereal. If this woman's spirit was trying to talk to me, I couldn't hear her. I was completely unaware.

I closed my eyes and took in an even breath. There seemed as though there should be some humor in the fact that I was mentally cursing the sudden lack of something I considered to be a curse in and of itself. Unfortunately, I couldn't find it.

I opened my eyes and turned away from the woman. Several feet across the room, against the back wall of the basement, the second body was resting. He was nondescript, though somewhat effeminate in appearance. His skin was almost as pale as that of his drained victim.

He was in a slouched sitting position, partially propped up and appearing almost as if he had simply sat down on the floor right where he had been standing and fallen back. The obvious evidence to the contrary was the dark, wet stain on his chest and the two large blood spray patterns on the wall just above his head. Their relative positions told me they would be right at chest level if the man had been standing.

I took notice of the fact that his arms lay relaxed at his sides, hands empty. Sergeant Madden's answer to Ben's query about a weapon rolled through my mind, and I now considered it in a different light. I didn't see anything nearby that would qualify. Nor were there any of the evidence markers that were prevalent in other parts of the room.

I kept my gaze leveled on the dead man for a moment, looking into eyes that were staring out of darkly rimmed sockets. A trickle of blood was running from the corner of his mouth, and I had to wonder if it was his or the woman's. Although his face was slack, there seemed to be a surprised look in his sunken eyes. But the perceived expression was all I had to work with. Even where he was concerned I could feel nothing.

No malevolence.

No insanity.

Nothing.

As we stood there I heard the sound of footsteps above us, creaking and thudding purposefully across the floor. A few seconds later they grew louder as they started down the stairs. Soon afterward, a uniformed officer stepped off at the bottom and gave Ben a nod.

"You Detective Storm?" he asked.

"Yeah," Ben answered.

The officer regarded him for a moment. "We just finished talking to Captain Albright," he said then raised an eyebrow and nodded toward Felicity and me. "Lieutenant Penczak said you'd probably want to clear your consultants out now."

Ben gave him a shallow nod in return as something secretive passed between them in the silent gesture. Turning to me he asked, "You done, white man?"

In a slow turn, I surveyed the horror one last time. There was nothing left to see, and for some reason, nothing left to feel. I came back around to face him and gave my own curt nod. "Yeah... I've seen enough."

"Thanks," Ben told the uniformed cop as we walked toward the stairs.

"All good," he replied.

We started up the rickety wooden staircase, and a quick flash caught the corner of my eye. I assumed that the tech was snapping pictures once again and that it was simply his strobe that grabbed my attention, but out of pure reflex I still paused and turned my head in that direction.

"Keep movin', Row," Ben urged, giving me a light push in the middle of my back.

I continued up the steps, but before the upper wall obscured my vision, I caught a second glint of light through the railings. The cop was now squatting next to the body of the dead man, and I was almost certain I saw what appeared to be a large butcher knife clutched in a cold, once empty hand.

As we topped the stairs, I distinctly heard the uniformed officer say, "Okay. You can take pictures over here now."

CHAPTER 33

I STOOD IN THE FRONT YARD OF THE HOUSE, LOOKING UP into the sky with a blank stare. Cops and crime scene technicians were still moving in and out of the front door behind me, but I paid them no heed. I was well out of their way, and my attentions were focused elsewhere at the moment.

Felicity was snuggled against me, one arm slipped beneath the folds of my coat to wrap around my back and the other bent upward to hold my hand where I had my own arm draped around her shoulders. I could feel her warm breath against my neck whenever she would exhale. A sharp chill would fall in behind it whenever she would turn her own face upward to stare with me.

"And the sun became black as sackcloth of hair, and the *moon became as blood...*" I whispered.

"Revelations?" Felicity whispered the question.

"Chapter six, verse twelve," I replied. "And I beheld when he had opened the sixth seal, and, lo, there was a great earthquake... And the sun became black as sackcloth of hair, and the *moon became as blood...*"

"I suppose it's ironic, isn't it then?"

"That's one word for it," I replied. "Not the one I had in mind though."

"They're just stories, Rowan," she said. "You of all people know that. You can even quote them better than most Christians. The Bible is a book of allegorical prose. It's filled with misunderstood and misinterpreted metaphors and similes from a different age."

"I know," I sighed. "But everything has an element of truth to it somewhere... And sometimes...with everything I've seen...I just... Well, I just have to wonder if some prophecies are universal... If perhaps we're driving ourselves headlong into the darkened abyss of our own insanity. Why else would so many people do the horrible things they do?"

"Don't overanalyze," she offered. "Just try to forget about it. This is over. You've earned a rest."

I gave my head a slow shake. "Something tells me it isn't."

"Why?"

I let out a heavy sigh and pulled her closer as I struggled to find the words to express what I was feeling. "This wasn't right... I mean, the way it all happened. This killer escalated far too quickly. From a victim who disappeared several months ago, to a sudden spree."

"I'm sure the serial killer experts have an explanation for that."

"You're right, they probably do. But something still feels very wrong about it to me... And, that isn't the only thing. Ben made a valid point back at the rest area. I just handed him an address for the killer, and here we are. We all know that isn't how it happens. Everything usually comes to me in cryptic messages I have to decipher. That's how communication across the veil works. It's like a language barrier."

"Maybe you're just learning the language then," she replied.

"Maybe..." I said. "But that's not how it feels. It's almost as if someone was translating for me."

"Who?"

I sighed again. "That's the problem. I have no idea. I feel like I should, but I just don't..."

"You two okay?" Ben's voice came at us from behind. "You been standin' here for damn near fifteen minutes."

"Yeah," I replied. "We're okay."

"Good," he harrumphed. "Listen, I thought ya' might like ta' know... I just got word that Judith Albright's been found..."

"She's dead, isn't she?" I said in a soft voice, commenting more than questioning.

"Yeah," he replied. "Afraid so..."

"And her body wasn't found here either," I continued my emotionless observation.

"No. Just a few miles further west of where they found 'er car, actually. Looks like she was raped and then strangled. Might've been a carjackin' or somethin' of that sort that went south. That's not confirmed yet, but it definitely looks like a separate crime. They're already workin' it on that basis. Gotta get an ID from next of kin too, but that's just a formality. They're ninety-nine percent sure it's her."

I let out a short, bemused snort. "It's a black swan."

"No," he replied. "Like I just told ya', it's unrelated. Nothin' ta' do with this whole deal as far as they can tell."

"I know," I explained. "I don't mean what you're thinking. Black swan is a label given to a theory of improbability regarding unexpected, hard to predict, high impact events that are beyond the normal expectations or assumptions.

"We assumed Judith had fallen prey to this particular killer because she fit the victim profile and because of the time frame in which she went missing. It made sense. However, we couldn't predict that she would in reality be the victim of a wholly different, but no less heinous crime... Her death is more or less a black swan."

"Yeah, well, call it whatever ya' want, it's still a friggin' homicide."

"Has anyone told Barbara?" I asked.

"Yeah," he sighed. "A coupl'a minutes ago. She ain't takin' it too well, but then, who would..."

"Nobody with a heart."

"Yeah... So about that whole swan thing... Ya' think maybe the *Twilight Zone* was tryin' ta' tell ya' about somethin' else besides our Count Dracula wannabe in there? Maybe warn ya' about Albright?"

"I wish I knew..." I mumbled. "All I can say is that this particular juxtaposition of reality and the ethereal definitely gives me something else to make my head hurt..."

"Yeah... Well... Sorry about that."

"I'll get over it... I hope."

"Well, maybe this'll help a bit," he offered. "The crime scene guys cleared up one of Doc Sanders' mysteries. Found a pair of slip joint pliers with fake vampire teeth epoxied to 'em. Pretty much explains the postmortem bite marks with no DNA."

"Yeah, I guess it does..." I muttered.

"Found a boom-box with a CD of weird-ass chanting in it too," he added. "That'd prob'ly cover what ya' thought ya' heard back at the morgue."

I sighed but didn't verbally respond.

"You sure you're okay, white man?" he asked again.

Eventually I breathed, "It's been a long day."

"Yeah, tell me about it," he replied then paused for a second. "So, what're you two starin' at?"

"The moon, Ben," my wife told him.

"Yeah, what about it? It about ta' crash into us or somethin'?"

"Take a good look at it," she answered.

He was quiet for a moment then said, "Okay, it's a full moon. That's like a big deal for you or somethin', right?"

"You don't notice anything else?"

He shrugged with the tone of his voice. "It looks kinda red and the one edge is kinda dark, so? Fuckin' air pollution and clouds."

"No," I said. "It's actually a partial lunar eclipse."

"No shit?" he mumbled.

"No shit," Felicity replied.

"That kinda rare or somethin'?"

"What rock have you been living under?" she asked. "It happens anywhere from two to five times each year."

"Hey, the moon crap is your thing, not mine. But if it's that common, what's the big effin' deal?"

Still staring upward I asked, "Would you like to know what else it's called, Ben?"

"Lemme guess, the moon?" he replied with audible sarcasm.

"A *blood* moon," I said.

He was quiet for several heartbeats before he muttered, "Fuck me..."

"Yeah. That's closer to the words I had picked out," I replied.

"What?"

"Nothing."

"Yeah, okay," he said. "So it's weird and all, but coincidences happen. You've said so yourself."

"Maybe..."

"You don't think it is?"

"I really can't say," I told him. "But the alternative isn't a pretty thought."

"You're soundin' all doom and gloom there, white man."

"Yeah... I know."

"You absolutely certain he's okay, Firehair?" he asked after a substantial pause.

"He's just tired, Ben," she answered. "Like he said, it's been a long day."

"Yeah, no shit. Speakin' of which, are you two ready to get outta here? I can get ya' a ride."

"You're staying?" Felicity asked.

"Kinda hafta," he told her. "But you two are free and clear. And if ya' wanna just head straight home, I can make a call, and I'm sure your Jeep will be fine till tomorrow mornin'."

"Aye, I think maybe that would be a good idea."

"Well c'mon," he said. "I'll get ya' hooked up."

I found it hard to tear my eyes away from the blushing disk in the sky, but after Felicity tugged at my arm for a second time, I dropped my gaze and followed her. As we crossed the yard, skirting past the county medical examiner on his way in to retrieve the bodies, our path intersected with Sergeant Madden's.

"Were you watching the eclipse?" she asked.

"Yes," Felicity answered for the both of us, glancing up at it then back to the officer.

Madden glanced upward quickly as well and then back to us. "My kid is doing a paper on it for school," she offered before clucking her tongue and regarding us with a quizzical look dressing her features. "You know, maybe it's none of my business, you being with Major Case and all, but mind if I ask exactly what kind of consultants you two are?"

"Independent," I said, giving her the first mundane word that came to mind. "I'm afraid what we do is a little hard to explain."

She cocked her head to the side and gave me a hard look. Then, like the state trooper had done back at the rest area, she stared at the ground for a second as she twice repeated my name, as much to herself as us. Looking back up at my face with recognition flashing in her eyes, she slowly shook a finger at me.

"Wait… Rowan Gant. I knew I'd heard that name before. You're the…"

Psychic… Witch… Neither of the labels really mattered to me right now. So I cut her off before either word could pass her lips, and with a lifetime's worth of weariness creeping into my voice I said, "Yeah. Whether I like it or not, apparently I am."

Friday, April 21
7:49 P.M.
Flipdoodles Restaurant
Delmar Loop
University City, Missouri

CHAPTER 34

"WHAT THE HELL KINDA NAME IS FLIPDOODLES?" BEN asked.

"Ben!" Constance quietly admonished, reaching to the side and slapping him on the shoulder.

"What?" my friend replied, raising his eyebrows and splaying out his hands in surrender. "I'm just askin' a question."

This was the first time we had been out with the petite FBI agent since the shooting in December that had left her in critical condition for a time. She was healed for the most part and back to work now. The Bureau had her on desk duty for the time being, but considering how amazingly well she seemed to be doing I seriously doubted the assignment would be permanent.

"You're really looking good, Constance," I said, picking up my drink and raising it toward her. "Here's to your continued health."

"*Slainté*," Felicity said, picking up her drink as well.

"Thank you," Mandalay said with a smile after joining us in the toast, then brushed a shock of brunette hair back from her eyes as she settled her tumbler back to the table. "I'm feeling good. I still tire a bit quicker than I used to, but I'm getting stronger. I really think getting back to work has helped."

"I was actually surprised you went back so soon," I commented.

"I had to," she replied. "I was going stir crazy."

"I heard. You know, we were pretty worried about you there for a while."

"Aye," Felicity agreed. "And I don't know how I can ever repay you for what you did for me."

Constance blushed slightly and shook her head. "You don't owe me anything, Felicity. It's my job. I'm just happy you weren't injured. And, it's good to see you back to your normal self."

"Here-here," Ben announced, lifting his glass and taking a swig. As he set it back on the table, he looked at us quizzically. "So... you gonna answer my question or just fawn over the Feeb?"

"You don't think she deserves it?" I asked.

"Dunno. She's startin' ta' get a bit demanding. Don't wanna feed the attitude, or she might start actin' too much like Firehair."

Mandalay gave him another slap and he jokingly smirked.

"It's really just a nonsense name, Ben," Felicity told him as she shrugged. "It's what Ailleagan wanted to call the place. I like it. It's fun."

"Yeah," he grunted. "Fun. And that just begs the follow-up question—what the hell kinda name is Ale-again? Sounds like someone orderin' another round at a old timey bar."

"For your information, it's Gaelic," my wife replied. "It means gem or jewel."

"Then why doesn't she just call 'erself Jewel?"

"Because her name is Ailleagan," Felicity said. "Not Jewel."

"Yeah... So I take it she's a foreigner like you?" he quipped.

"I'll have you know I was born in the United States, and I maintain dual citizenship."

"Can't make up your mind, eh?"

"Don't make me kick you."

"Ya' already did as I recall. Still got a bruise."

"*Cac capaill.* You do not. But I'll be delighted to give you one. Maybe two or three if you keep it up."

"Yeah, whatever. So, anyway, when ya' get right down to it, you're all just a bunch of foreigners, ain't ya'?" He grinned and thrust his thumbs back at himself. "I'm the only one that really belongs here."

"For someone who denies his heritage on a regular basis, you sure like to play that Native American card when it suits you," I chuckled.

"Whatever works, white man," he said with a wider grin then looked around the restaurant and gestured. "So are we ever gonna get some menus or what?"

"No," Felicity replied.

"Whaddaya mean no?"

My wife simply smiled and left him twisting in the wind, so I explained. "They don't do menus here, Ben. They plan a meal for the evening and that's what you get."

He regarded me with a confused expression. "Bullshit. Very funny."

"No, I'm serious."

"Aye, he is," Felicity added. "Look around. Doesn't it look to you like everyone is eating the same thing?"

He gave the dining room another glance then faced us again and cocked an eyebrow. "Yeah, well seems ta' be a whole lotta big groups here tonight. They prob'ly got some kinda deal or somethin'."

"Actually, they probably aren't big groups," my wife explained waving her finger around. "Normally you just sit wherever there's space and eat with everyone else. The only reason we have this smaller table is because I know how you are, and I asked Ailleagan for a favor." She sat back and regarded him with a faux smug expression. "So, the way I see it, you owe me."

"Uh-huh. Right. We coulda' just gone someplace else, ya'know," he replied.

"It wouldn't be as good."

"Yeah, back ta' that. So you're really tellin' me I don't get ta' order what I want?"

"Correct," I replied. "But, you get the pleasure of eating what they serve you."

"That's just great," he snorted. "So what if it's somethin' I don't wanna eat?"

"Then I guess you go hungry," Constance interjected.

"I've never been disappointed by a meal here, Ben," I replied. "Seriously. Ailleagan is an amazing chef."

"Don't worry," Felicity spoke up. "When I called this afternoon I asked what she was making. They're serving Spring Chicken Wellington tonight. It's her signature dish, and it's absolutely wonderful."

"Yeah, says you, but is it gonna have somethin' in it I don't like?"

Constance shook her head. "Who knows when it comes to you."

"I ain't that bad," he objected. "There's just some stuff I don't wanna eat."

"Unless it's a donut?" I asked.

"Yeah, right. Very funny."

"Or anything that isn't a hamburger or a pizza?" Mandalay quipped.

"Not true. Now you're makin' me sound finicky."

"You are."

"Yeah, so what about you, Little Miss Sprouts-and-Tofu?"

I chuckled again. "I see the two of you are getting along just as well as usual."

"Yeah, well I'm cuttin' 'er some slack, ya'know," Ben replied.

"I think I'm the one cutting someone slack here," she countered. "I suppose I should be grateful you haven't asked them if they want to see my scars." She waited a beat then added, "Yet."

Felicity looked at her with a mildly stunned expression. "He did that?"

"Just once, so far," she replied, rolling her eyes. "And he was talking to my SAC no less."

"Ben!" my wife scolded. "That's just insensitive."

"Feebs got no sense of humor," he returned.

"I didn't shoot you, did I?" Constance asked.

"Yeah, whatever," Ben chuckled.

"So, Constance," Felicity said, leaning across the table toward her. "If you don't happen to have any duct tape handy, in a pinch a washcloth and a nylon scarf make an excellent gag."

"I'll keep that in mind," she giggled.

"Yeah, you would know somethin' like that, wouldn't ya'?" my friend said.

"I can't imagine you're surprised," my wife told him.

"I'm not, but you both know I ain't inta' that kinky shit," he huffed.

"Are we embarrassing you?" Constance asked.

"Yes." He emphasized the terse answer.

"Good," she replied with a wicked grin. "If we keep it up maybe I'll be even with you by next year."

"Uh-huh," he grumbled. "So can we talk about somethin' else?"

"Okay, what would you like to talk about?" she asked.

"Well, you comedians never did tell me what was in this spring chicken thing…"

"Oatmeal, chicken livers, chicken gizzards, and suet," a woman's voice said. "All ground up with onions, a few special seasonings, and slowly steamed in a sheep's stomach."

Ailleagan was standing behind my friend and now rested her hand on his shoulder. I had seen her coming when she exited the kitchen, but as soon as she saw me looking her direction, she held her finger up to her lips, so I had kept my mouth shut. The look now twisting Ben's face made me glad I had played along.

"You're friggin' kiddin' me," he replied, turning to look up at her.

Ailleagan was a petite woman with pleasing curves and an ample bosom. Her hair was a shade or two brighter red than Felicity's, and it framed a fresh, cherubic face. The sleeves of her chef's tunic were rolled up to expose intricate and colorful tattoos on her forearms, which continued up to disappear beneath the white folds of the jacket's fabric.

She looked back at him through her stylish, dark rimmed glasses and without cracking a smile said, "Why would I do that?"

My friend shook his head and held up his hand. "No offense, but that just ain't my thing. Don'tcha have a coupl'a burgers back there or somethin'?"

"You must be the infamous Benjamin Storm," she said, holding her hand out toward him.

He took it but maintained a confused expression.

"And, you must be Constance," she continued, patting Mandalay on the shoulder. "I've heard all manner of stories about you two from Rowan and Felicity."

"How are you doing tonight?" I asked, giving her a smile and a nod.

"Fine, just fine," she replied, shooting a wide grin toward us. "So I finally get to meet these two."

"Aye, finally," Felicity agreed.

"Wait just a minute," Ben interjected. "Let's get back ta' the food. You ain't really gonna feed us a bunch of chicken guts, are ya?"

"Rowan's right," she replied. "You're awfully gullible for a cop."

He looked at me. "You said that?"

"Only about certain things." I shrugged. "Not the important stuff. Mostly just when it comes to food."

"Food's important."

"You know what I mean. For example, I got you to eat ostrich."

"Yeah, I still haven't forgiven ya' for that one."

"Relax," Ailleagan told him, patting his shoulder again. "I just gave you the basic recipe for my personal variation on haggis. We aren't serving that till next week."

"What day?"

She cocked her head to the side, looked thoughtful, and then said, "Probably Wednesday."

"I won't be here," he grunted.

"Then I won't set you a place. Seriously though, Spring Chicken Wellington is just chicken," she continued. "It's baked in a pastry just like Beef Wellington. I can't tell you any more of the recipe than that or I'll have to kill you, and since you're a cop…"

"Yeah, I see you're a funny one too," Ben told her.

"I like to think so. Now let's see, where was I… Oh yes… On the side, we're serving Sicilian green beans sautéed with garlic and diced salami. And for dessert, fudge brownie sundaes."

"I heard salami and fudge sundae," Ben said with a nod. "Those I can work with. I'll let ya' know on the chicken thing. Usually I have mine fried."

"Believe me, this will be better," she said.

"So, Ailleagan, this might be too much to ask," I said. "But you wouldn't happen to have any of the sacred pie back there, would you?"

She grinned. "As a matter of fact, when Felicity called I made one just for you."

"You're a doll."

She feigned a curtsy. "I know."

"Okay," Ben grumbled. "What the hell's sacred pie?"

"Oh, you'll find out. If Rowan let's you have any, that is," she quipped then paused and gave the dining room a quick scan before adding, "Things look under control out here. Doug should be out with your dinner in just a minute. I think I'll go grab a plate for myself and join you."

"That would be wonderful," Felicity said.

"So you're gonna eat with us?" Ben asked.

"Is that a problem?" she answered with her own question.

"No…" he said. "I don't guess so. Just not used to the chef sittin' down with me."

"Welcome to Flipdoodles," she said with a disarming smile.

"Yeah, thanks," he grunted. "So lemme ask ya' somethin'. If you're gonna eat with us, can I just call ya' Jewel?"

Without missing a beat she replied, "Can I just call you Geronimo?"

It was obvious from the look on his face and the length of his pause that Ben hadn't been expecting the quick retort. Before he could answer, she nodded her head and winked. "Ailleagan will do just fine, Benjamin."

He shook his head and cast his gaze back and forth between Felicity and her. "Ya'know, if ya' had an accent I'd swear you two were sisters."

"Oh, you have no idea," she said with a grin. "I'll be back in just a minute. Doug might be needing some help, and I still need a plate for myself."

As soon as she scurried off, Ben looked across the table at my wife and said, "You're enjoyin' this, aren't ya'?"

"Why shouldn't she?" Constance interjected. "I am."

"This is gonna be a long friggin' night," he muttered.

"I wouldn't worry," I told him. "If Ailleagan didn't like you, she wouldn't…"My sentence was interrupted by the trilling of my cell phone as it started to vibrate on my belt. I reached for it while finishing the thought. "…she wouldn't screw with you. Relax. You're all good."

I pulled the device up and glanced at the LCD. The caller ID was displaying an unfamiliar number with an out-of-state area code. I pursed my lips thoughtfully for a second and then slid the warbling phone back into the belt holder without answering.

"Screenin' your calls?" Ben asked.

"Sort of, I guess. I don't recognize the number, and it's from out of state. I'll just check my voicemail later. If it's a client or something, they'll leave a message."

After a few seconds, my cell fell silent and stopped tickling my side.

"Okay, so since according to you your friend apparently thinks I'm okay, is she gonna be pickin' at me for the rest of the evenin'?" Ben asked.

"No more than Constance or me," Felicity replied.

"Great. Like I said, long friggin' night."

"What are you complaining about?" I asked. "All this attention from three beautiful ladies… I'm a bit jealous, myself."

"Yeah, right. *Ipecackle* or whatever it is Firehair always says."

"*Cac capaill*," she corrected him. "Horse shit."

He wagged his finger in her direction and said, "Yeah, that. Twice."

The conversation was again interrupted by the jangling tones of a cellular phone, but this time it wasn't mine. Felicity raised an eyebrow and then reached under the table for her purse. Pulling it up she extracted her cell and gazed at it.

"That's odd," she mumbled then held the device over in front of me. "That look familiar?"

I glanced at the number and let out a soft humph. "Actually, yeah. I think that's the same number I just ignored."

My wife pulled the cell back then flipped it open and leaned her head to the side as she slipped the earpiece beneath her bright auburn tresses.

"Hello?" she said. A look of recognition spread across her face a split second later, but it definitely wasn't accompanied by happiness. "Yes, Doctor Jante," she continued, turning to look at me as she talked. "I'm fine, and you? That's good… Yes, actually he's right here, but I am afraid we're out to dinner at the moment. Is there any way I can have him call you back?… Oh… I see… Just a second then."

254 | M. R. SELLARS

Felicity pulled the phone from her ear and held it out to me. I returned a slightly puzzled look but took it from her anyway. A solid month had passed since we had spoken with the FBI psychologist, so the fact that she was calling, especially late into a Friday evening, piqued my curiosity at the very least.

Constance was already whispering across the table, "Is that Doctor Ellie Jante with the BAU at Quantico?"

Felicity nodded and mouthed, "Yes."

"Doctor Jante," I said into the phone, my voice guarded. "This is Rowan."

"Mister Gant," she replied. "I'm sorry to bother you this evening. Your wife already explained that you are out to dinner, but I personally felt this was important enough to warrant a call."

"Is something wrong?" I asked.

"That remains to be seen," she replied. "Annalise Devereaux is asking to have a face-to-face meeting with you."

I didn't reply. I simply sat with the phone against my ear and pondered the words she had just offered. This was something I had been trying to make happen for what seemed like forever. But now, just coming off this recent case that still had me questioning myself, I wasn't so sure I wanted to be mired back in the ethereal quicksand so soon.

"Are you still there?" she asked.

"Yes, sorry," I replied. "I'm just... Just a bit surprised I guess."

"I understand," she told me. "Normally this is something I would advise against, especially with the way her attorneys were posturing in recent weeks. However, this morning she fired the entire team. And, since you seemed rather adamant about just such a meeting when we spoke last week..."

"Fired?" I asked, a bit of disbelief in my voice. "All of them?"

"Yes, Mister Gant, the entire legal team. I haven't quite figured out what her ploy is, but on a clinical level she seems to be extremely vulnerable at the moment. If we are even going to think about putting you into a face-to-face with her, now would be the time."

"By now you mean..."

"I'd like to get you on a plane as early as tomorrow morning if you are agreeable."

"Tomorrow morning?"

"Yes."

"If I say yes to this, where am I going?"

"She's currently being held in the psychiatric wing of FMC

Carswell in Fort Worth, Texas while awaiting trial. It's a federal medical center specializing in female inmates."

"Sounds lovely," I huffed then paused for a moment. "Okay... I'll come... Just let me have my dinner, then when I get home I'll look into a plane ticket and get..."

"That won't be necessary," she interrupted. "The Bureau will handle the travel arrangements. I'm going to have the Saint Louis field office assign an agent to accompany you as well."

"I said I would be there," I replied. "Do you think I'm lying?"

"No, Mister Gant. I would just be more comfortable if you had an escort."

"Okay... Can I have you hold on a second?"

"Certainly."

I clicked the phone over to mute but held it under the table with my hand covering the microphone pickup just in case.

"What's going on?" Felicity asked.

"It seems Annalise Devereaux wants a one-on-one meeting with me," I replied.

"She wants, or you want?" Ben asked.

"Yeah, I know I've been pushing for one. But now she's the one asking for it," I replied with a shake of my head.

"And you're goin'..." he returned, the words more an observation than a question.

I glanced over at Felicity's frowning face then back to him and nodded. "Yeah. This is something I really need to take care of."

"What does Doctor Jante think about this?" Constance asked.

"She seems like she might be a little on the fence," I replied. "But, apparently Annalise fired her entire legal team, and Jante thinks she's in a vulnerable state at the moment. She said if this is going to happen, the time is now."

"She's one of the best, Rowan," Constance told me. "She knows what she's doing."

"You really think so?"

She nodded. "I took several of her classes at the academy. In my opinion you can trust her. If she is sanctioning this, even reluctantly, there must be a good reason."

"Okay, then let me ask you this. How do you feel about Texas?"

"What do you mean?"

"For some reason Jante says she wants to have the local field office assign an agent to escort me."

"If I heard you correctly, you're leaving tomorrow morning?" she asked.

"That's apparently the plan."

She nodded. "I can pack tonight."

I looked over at Ben. "Mind if I borrow your girlfriend for a day or two."

"Not a problem," he replied. "At least Firehair and I will know you're not runnin' off gettin' yourself into trouble if she's with ya'."

I turned back to my wife. "Honey... I know you aren't exactly okay with this, but... Well... Are you okay with this?"

She nodded, but her expression was still sour. "Aye. It's something you have to do, I know that. And I agree with what Ben said. If Constance is with you I'll at least feel a bit better about it." She turned her gaze toward Mandalay and added, "Just don't trust him if you tell him not to do something and he agrees with you too easily. It's a good bet he's lying."

I ignored the addendum then drew in a breath and muttered, "Okay," as I noticed Ailleagan and Doug coming through the swinging door that led in and out of the kitchen. Both of them were hefting food-laden platters that looked amazing even at a distance.

I quickly thumbed the mute button then tucked the phone back up to my ear and said, "Sorry about that Doctor Jante."

"That's all right. I assumed you would want to speak to your wife."

"Uh-huh," I acknowledged. "So as far as this whole escort thing goes, do you mind if I make a request?"

"What is that?"

"Agent Mandalay has returned to..."

Before I could finish the sentence, she replied, "And you would like for her to be assigned as your escort."

"Well, yes. Since we've worked together and she's familiar with..."

She interrupted me again. "Understandable. Consider it done."

Saturday, April 22
4:56 A.M.
Saint Louis, Missouri

CHAPTER 35

"I SHOULD BE BACK SOMETIME MONDAY AFTERNOON," I told Felicity. "At least that's what Jante said. I suppose it all depends on how this goes."

"Just don't do anything stupid," she replied.

"That's why Constance is going with me, remember?"

"Aye." She nodded. "But I've never been able to stop you from getting yourself into trouble, so why should I believe she can?"

"She has a gun?" I replied.

She sighed as she slipped her arms around me and laid her head against my shoulder. "I know you're trying to make me feel better, but I know you, *Caorthann...*"

As usual, my wife had a tendency to resort to the Gaelic pet name when she was deeply concerned. I knew she was already bothered by this trip, but her whisper drove the point deep.

"I'll be okay," I soothed. "I promise not to do anything stupid. And I'm not just agreeing with you to..."

"Don't make a promise you know you can't keep," she said, cutting me off before I could finish. "Just...be safe."

"I will."

She pulled back slightly and looked up into my face. Her jade green eyes were already glistening with dampness, and the corners of her mouth were turned slightly downward. I brushed a spiral of wayward hairs from her cheek then pulled her close once again.

"You call me when you arrive," she mumbled.

"I promise," I told her. "And that's one I can keep."

The pendulum clock in our dining room softly thunked, and then a muted whirr sounded as the spring began to wind out. A half second later a dull bong echoed through the room, followed by four more to announce the top of the hour.

"I'm loving you," Felicity said.

"I'm loving you too," I replied.

As if on cue, the doorbell chimed through the house, setting the dogs off as usual. Felicity began shushing them as I released my grip on her and turned to answer it.

"You ready?" Ben asked as soon as I had opened the door.

He was holding the outer storm door with one hand and cupping a travel mug in the other.

"Yeah," I nodded. "Give me just a second."

He glanced at his watch. "All good, we got a few minutes." Nodding toward the floor just inside the doorway, he asked, "That your bag?"

"Yeah."

"I'll put it in the van and wait for ya'," he said, holding the storm door with his leg as he reached in and grabbed the handle of the small suitcase. "Heya, Firehair," he said, nodding at Felicity as he straightened up.

"Ben," she replied.

The metal door slowly swung shut with a slight creak and hiss of the closure piston as he backed out with my luggage then turned and started down the front steps.

I bent over and scratched the dogs behind their ears while saying, "You two take care of your mother while I'm gone."

They snuffled and whimpered as if they knew something was amiss. We never could fool them.

"It's going to be okay," I said to Felicity, straightening from my stooped position. "It will all be over soon."

"I know," she said with a nod. "That still doesn't make it any easier."

Taking a deep breath, she wiped her eyes then slipped her arms around me again. Turning her face up, she pressed her lips against mine in a deep, longing kiss that was tainted slightly by the sense of sadness it also carried.

When we finally parted, I pulled back and looked at her before saying, "I'm missing you already."

"Me too."

I lingered for a moment, though I knew prolonging the inevitable was just making this harder. I took in my own deep breath then slowly let it out as I nodded. I turned to leave, but as I stepped through the door I paused again then looked back at her and said, "Why don't you see about booking that vacation while I'm gone?"

"For when?"

"For when I get back," I replied. "You pick the dates. Just leave me enough time to pack and get someone to cover any emergency support calls that might come in."

She nodded. "I will. Do you think we can go for two weeks?"

I smiled. "We can go for as long as you like."

With that, I headed down the stairs into the cold, dark morning and climbed into the back of Ben's van.

"All good?" he asked, looking at me in the rearview mirror as I buckled myself in.

"Yeah. As good as it can be, I guess," I replied.

"She'll be okay," Constance told me, turning to look back from the passenger seat.

"Yeah, white man. I'll keep an eye on 'er," Ben added.

"I know," I replied. "It's not really her I'm worried about."

"You'll be fine too," Constance reassured me.

"Yeah... Let's hope you're right," I muttered as I slipped my hand into my jacket pocket. "Ben, I need you to do me a favor."

"What's that?" he asked, now twisting in his seat and looking over his shoulder.

I pulled the glass bottle containing the salt bound jewelry from my pocket and shook it before looking at it carefully. Even in the dark interior of the van, I could still make out the shape of the necklace peaking up from beneath the snowy crystals. After a thick pause I held it forward to him.

"Hang onto this for me until I get back, and whatever you do, don't open it, and keep it the hell away from Felicity."

"What is it?" he asked as he reached back and took it.

There was no mistaking that I was deadly serious when I replied, "Evil incarnate."

AUTHOR'S NOTE:

While the city of St. Louis and its various notable landmarks are certainly real, many names have been changed and some minor liberties taken with some of the details in these stories. In an instance or two, they are fabrications, such as the existence of a coffee shop/diner across the street from the Metropolitan Saint Louis Police Headquarters. These anomalies are pieces of fiction within fiction to create an illusion of reality to be experienced and enjoyed—In short, I made them up because it helped me make the story more entertaining, or in some cases, just because I wanted to. After all, this is *my* fictional version of Saint Louis.

And since we are talking about *fiction*, please note that this book is *not intended* as a primer or guide for WitchCraft, Wicca, or *any* Pagan path. It is important to mention that the vast majority of rituals, spells, and explanations of these religious, spiritual, and "magickal" practices used in these works are, in point of fact, drawn from actual Neo-Paganism – *but they are not tied to any one specific tradition or path.* The mixture of practices engaged in by the characters in these novels is often referred to as "Eclectic Paganism" and "Eclectic WitchCraft," being that they borrow from *many different religious paths and traditions across the full gamut of spirituality* in order to create their own. Therefore, some of the explanations included herein will not work for all Pagan traditions, of which there are countless. This does not make them *wrong*, it simply makes them *different*.

If you are actually seeking in-depth information on the subject of Paganism and WitchCraft, there are numerous **Non**-Fiction, scholarly texts readily available by authors such as Margot Adler, Raymond Buckland, Scott Cunningham, and more.

Also, remember that the "magick," and of course, the psychic abilities depicted here are what some might call "over the top," because it *doesn't really work like that*, as we all know. But, like I have been saying all along, this is *fiction*. Relax and enjoy it for what it is…

Finally, if you are saying, "I'll bet he had to write this note because someone took these stories way too seriously," give yourself a cigar.

MORE FROM M. R. SELLARS

ROWAN GANT INVESTIGATIONS SERIES
(In order of release)

HARM NONE
NEVER BURN A WITCH
PERFECT TRUST
THE LAW OF THREE
CRONE'S MOON
LOVE IS THE BOND
ALL ACTS OF PLEASURE
THE END OF DESIRE
BLOOD MOON
MIRANDA
(Available in both print and e-book editions)

SPECIAL AGENT CONSTANCE MANDALAY SERIES

MERRIE AXEMAS: A KILLER HOLIDAY TALE
(e-Novella)

IN THE BLEAK MIDWINTER
(Available in both print and e-book editions)

OTHER

YOU'RE GONNA THINK I'M NUTS…
*(Novelette included in **Courting Morpheus** Horror Anthology)*

LAST CALL
*(Flash-Fiction Short included in **Slices of Flesh** Horror Anthology)*

SPECIAL E-BOOK ONLY OMNIBUS TITLES

GHOUL SQUAD
(Harm None, Never Burn A Witch, and Perfect Trust)

DEATH WEARS HIGH HEELS
(Love Is The Bond, All Acts of Pleasure, and The End Of Desire)

ABOUT THE AUTHOR

A member of the ITW (International Thriller Writers), M. R. Sellars is a relatively unassuming homebody who considers himself just a *"guy with a lot of nightmares and a word processing program."* His first full-length novel, *Harm None*, hit bookstore shelves in 2000 and he hasn't stopped writing since.

Sellars currently resides in the Midwest with his wife, daughter, and a pair of rescued male felines that he describes as, "the competition." At home, when not writing or taking care of the household, he indulges his passions for cooking and chasing his wife around the house. She promises that one day she will allow him to catch her.

M. R. Sellars can be found on the web at:
www.mrsellars.com

And on major social networking venues...

CPSIA information can be obtained
at www.ICGtesting.com
Printed in the USA
LVHW04s1543240918
591190LV00011B/1046/P